ONCE IN A WHILE

By

Linda Ellen

Jess!
Thanks for
being so patient!
Linda Ellen

This novel emerged from the poignant story of my parents' romance and of their lives during their youth, which encompassed the waning years of the Great Depression, natural disaster…and a tragic misunderstanding.

Reviews

"This story took me through a rollercoaster of emotions. I couldn't help but fall in love with the characters as they wove me through this brilliant story. It is a rich blend of history, tragedy, love, and most importantly hope. With each chapter Linda Ellen opened up the untouchable world that was 1930's Louisville, and made me feel like I was part of that nostalgic time. It is a story that I will hold dear in my heart for years to come."

~Author Venessa Vargas

"A heartfelt story about life, love, and finding your way back."

~Amazon Bestselling Author H. D'Agostino.

"I have read, 'Once In A While' and loved the book. Linda was nice enough to give me a sneak preview of her work. She is very talented. Her novel brought me to tears and made me laugh too. She captures a great sense of love, loss and struggle. Thumbs up Linda on this book, I would recommend it to anyone."

~Katheryn Ragle, author and owner of Gibson-Ragle Publishing.

Once in a While

Book 1 of The Cherished Memories Series

Written By Linda Ellen

Gibson-Ragle Publishing Co.
PO Box 21
Bronston, Kentucky 42518

Trade Paperback Release: November, 2014
Electronic Release: November, 2014
www.gibsonraglepublishing.weebly.com

ISBN: 978-0-9909044-0-3
Print Edition

Although this book is a work of fiction, the story was loosely based upon events in the lives of the author's parents. Names were changed or details altered; characters, places, and incidents are products of the author's imagination, or are used fictitiously. Brands are used respectfully. Details regarding Louisville and the Flood were taken from several sources, including Rick Bell's wonderfully illustrated book *The Great Flood of 1937*.

The following story contains themes of real life, but is suitable for all ages, as it contains no gratuitous sex or profanity.

Cover design by Kari March at K23Designs
Cover photography by Bill Klein of Bill Klein Photography
Formatting by BB eBooks

Table of Contents

ꕤ

PROLOGUE

Present day, Louisville, Kentucky

"HERE, MOM, SIT down. We'll take care of it," I said as I tried for the fourth time to get my eighty-nine year old, still feisty mother to rest. My brothers and I were moving her belongings from a house she'd lived in since 1966, and there was a ton of things to do. Nervous energy kept her fretting and trying to help.

"I want to make sure my blue dishes don't get broken," she fussed regarding her beloved collection of Liberty Blue, even as she acquiesced and slowly lowered herself onto a kitchen chair.

"Jim took care of it. He packed them tight, and put the boxes in the back seat of his car. Don't worry," I reassured her once more. But, of course she would worry, that's just her nature. And in truth, moving all of one's worldly possessions halfway across town would worry anyone. What's that saying… 'Count on it, at least one thing will get broken in a move'?

I managed a smile out of her and she nodded, satisfied for the moment. Then, her mind as sharp as always, she thought of yet another detail.

"Oh, did we get the important papers from the closet under the stairs?"

"Yes, Mom. Remember? They're in the back seat of my car," I replied, glancing over and seeing my oldest son, Will, bringing in one of the boxes just then. "See? Here they come."

"Oh good," she intoned. "Honey, bring that here for me, will you?" she called to him and he turned on his heel and switched directions, placing it on the table at her elbow.

"Thank you, sweetheart," she cooed as she laid her hand on the decades old cardboard, tied with a cloth strip. Glancing at it, her brow furrowed as she noticed one corner had broken open. She immediately became concerned that some of its precious contents may have spilled out.

"Oh no! Oh honey, help me get this untied," she requested, even as her arthritic fingers began picking at the knot in the cloth.

I obliged and helped, and together we removed the dusty old top to reveal her treasures inside. Her eyes anxiously scanned the collections of cards, letters, and old photographs, which were banded together in groups. "Oh, I hope none are missing…I couldn't bear that…" she whispered, her fingers lovingly touching image after image. Then, she touched the edge of a small wooden box, nodding as she assured herself it was still all right, not a mark on it.

Although I had seen the box many times over the years, I knew very little about the exact nature of its contents. Shaped like a miniature treasure chest, the jewelry box exhibited intricately carved designs on its sides, with the top displaying a picturesque scene of a village and people reminiscent of the 1600's.

Out of curiosity, I reached over and turned the latch, raising the top to find the mirror with its frosted edges I remembered seeing as a child. Then on the top of the items was an envelope with *To Louise From Vic,* written in a neat script. Under that, a black and white, well-worn photo of what I knew to be her and my father. They were sitting in the back of a big old black car with a group of other young people, each one laughing joyously.

For a minute, I stood staring at it, and then slowly lowered myself into the chair perpendicular to hers. Mom and Dad were so young in the photo…teens even, but obviously very much in love.

Throughout my life, mom had often regaled me with snippets

of her tumultuous young adulthood during the 30's and 40's…and of my handsome, dark-haired, dark-eyed father, whom she adored from their first meeting. My heart constricted a little…how I wished he were still with us.

My brothers, Tom, Bud, and Jim, brought in the last of the boxes and closed the storm door, and then wandered into the kitchen.

"Well, that's about got it," Jim murmured as he took a seat at the table to rest. My husband came up behind me and put his hands on my shoulders, leaning down to give me a kiss on the cheek, even as Bud paused next to her chair and laid a hand on Mom's shoulder.

"Whatcha got there?" Steve whispered, smiling softly as I met his eyes. Mine were a trifle misty. "A picture of Mom and Daddy," I whispered back and he nodded.

Mom looked up from several photos she was holding and saw my expression. "Let me see that one," she requested softly, reaching for the photo. I handed it over and she gazed down at it lovingly. Pressing her lips together, she shook her head once, and then drew in a slightly ragged breath. It had been a long and exhausting day and her emotions were quite fragile. "My Vic. He always was such a handsome devil," she murmured, and I could tell she was remembering the day the photo was taken.

The doorbell rang just then, and my oldest brother, Tom, went to answer it, bringing back several boxes of pizza and three two-liters of soda. I rose and began gathering paper plates and cups as we set about taking a well-deserved break.

As we milled around the kitchen, eating and chatting, Mom continued to stare at the photo, lost in the past.

"Mom, you really should eat something," I called, but she wasn't listening.

"Grandma," my youngest son, David, murmured as he slid into the chair nearest hers. "Don't you want some pizza? It's your favorite."

Mom looked up at David and smiled. Gazing at him, she could see a family resemblance, and something about him brought more memories. The way he held his head…the dimples, the long eyelashes, the perfect white teeth grinning back at her. Reaching out a shaky hand, she caressed his cheek and murmured, "Did I ever tell you how I met Grandpa Vic?"

He started to open his mouth to say that he'd heard the stories many times, but I caught his eye and managed a small shake of my head. He raised his eyebrows at me, and then grinned at Mom, answering, "No, Grandma…but I'd like to hear it," as he sank his teeth into a piece of pizza.

Mom smiled and nodded, excited to have an interested audience. It was always more fun to reminisce *with* someone, rather than alone. She'd been alone with her cherished memories for quite a while.

As all of us settled down to eat pizza at the kitchen table, Mom leaned toward my son and murmured, "It was a long time ago…just before the Great Flood…the winter of '37…"

PART I
SOMETHING'S GOTTA GIVE

ꕥ

CHAPTER 1

Vic and the Guys

Wednesday, January 6, 1937, Louisville, Kentucky

STEADY RAIN STREAMED down the blue and white striped awnings of the White Castle at First and Market as a young man sprinted to the door. Yanking it open, he ducked inside, and smoothed dripping locks of his hair back as he scanned the other patrons.

Seeing no familiar faces, Victor 'Vic' Matthews huffed a small sigh and approached the counter. Absently noticing line cooks flipping burgers and dipping fries into boiling oil, he pulled a handkerchief out of his pocket and wiped some of the rain from his face and hair as he waited for the person ahead to finish. Breathing in the aromas, he wondered for a moment what it was about White Castle hamburgers that smelled so mouthwateringly delicious. His stomach growled longingly.

As he stepped forward, the girl behind the counter, with short but attractive dark hair and a friendly smile chirped a practiced, "Welcome to White Castle. May I take your order?"

Vic nodded, choosing to focus on her nametag, 'Judy', as he tried to ignore the aromas wafting his way. Lamenting the fact that he was the first of the group to arrive and therefore had no one from which to bum, he rummaged through the pockets of his jacket and pants, and finally came up with one lone nickel.

With an embarrassed shrug, he rasped, "Jus' gimme a Coke."

Judy nodded, thinking *Big Spender,* and gave him the once over as she stepped to the side and shoved a cup under the nozzle.

Just then, two girls squealed raucously as they dashed in the door. Giggling, they immediately began to wrestle with an unruly umbrella.

Vic glanced over his shoulder at them as he placed the nickel in Judy's palm. Picking up the soda, he nodded again to the counter girl, and then his gaze shifted around as he headed toward the back corner to wait for his friends in their favorite booth. Once there, he shrugged out of his wet jacket and sprawled onto the seat with a tired sigh.

As minutes ticked by, more customers entered. Families enjoyed their meals…friends laughed together…lone patrons wolfed down food as they cast their gazes around at the other customers…bums wandered in hoping for a handout. All the while, Vic merely sipped his drink and stared out the window, his chin resting on his palm, watching as relentless rivulets of water crashed down from the awnings onto the already soaked pavement below.

Seated at a table across the dining area, the two young ladies who had arrived after him sipped hot chocolate and nibbled French fries as they cast furtive glances his way. The girls whispered privately about Vic's rugged good looks, his muscular physique outlined by the nice fitting dress shirt. One murmured about the 'dreamy' rich mahogany brown hair that crowned his head in thick waves, and wondered aloud what it would be like to run her fingers through it. Her companion sighed over the clean, square contour of his face and full, sensually curved lips, which seemed to her to be literally begging for a kiss. Surreptitiously watching him, they wondered what could be making such a 'swell' looking guy seem so down. As one whispered that she'd be glad to try and make him smile, they covered their mouths with their fingers to muffle the escaping giggles.

Preoccupied and restless, Vic took no notice of them as he

relentlessly drummed the fingers of his left hand on the table. Normally, the continual splashing of the rain outside the window would have lulled him into a peaceful state of mind. On this day, however, it was achieving the opposite, and adding fuel to his brooding dissatisfaction. The usual soft warm shade of his sepia-toned eyes had turned as hard and cold as rusting steel, the phenomenon reflecting his mood as his thoughts chased one another around in never-ending circles.

Is this rain ever gonna stop? It seemed to him as if it had been raining forever, as the sky had been dumping water on the city for over a month. He couldn't remember the last time he caught a glimpse of the sun. *It's sure been a beastly wet 'n warm winter so far,* he mused.

Shaking his head with a sardonic smirk, he thought back to six months before, during the record-breaking, extremely hot and dry summer of '36 – the hottest summer ever recorded in Louisville. Everyone in the city had wished and prayed for rain. *I guess the Man upstairs saved up and decided to dump on us now,* he silently griped. The constant rain they had been experiencing of late had transformed the simple task of traversing the streets of downtown into one of continuous aggravation. A prime example being that morning, when he had been forced to interview for a job in uncomfortably damp clothing.

Figures. Nothin' ever goes my way. He snorted softly as he pondered the fact that his life hadn't ever been the stuff of dreams. Like snapshots in an album, memories of losing his parents as a child and being shuffled from one relative to another made his mood sink another notch. He knew that none of them had wanted to take in a needy boy, and that everyone was struggling to make it in the lean times of the Depression. But was that *his* fault? Feeling as if he were wound tighter than a two-dollar watch, he muttered a few choice words under his breath. He was raring to go, to work, to laugh… and to love. But circumstances beyond his control always seemed to be holding him back, like the mooring ropes on a steamboat.

Shaking his head again and sighing in frustration, he ran a hand back through his damp, disheveled hair. Unconsciously, he was striving to somehow dislodge the shrill voice of his sister-in-law, which was stubbornly replaying in his mind.

"We can't keep on like this, Vic!" Liz had yelled at him the previous evening when he had dragged himself home after another day of his ongoing and unsuccessful hunt for a job. "Jack works. *I* work. And the fact is, we're tired of carryin' you! Sick and tired of it."

On that score, he agreed with her. He was sick and tired of it, too, like a pain in his very bones. Tired of waiting for his life to really begin. Tired of looking for work and coming up empty. Tired of sleeping on the living room floor of his brother and sister-in-law's small apartment. That certainly didn't make the situation any more tolerable. *Man, something's gotta give soon, or I'm gonna go outta my mind...*

Determinedly, he turned from the wet world outside the window and allowed his gaze to roam around the restaurant as he tried to push the feeling of utter hopelessness away. All he managed to do, however, was observe the gainfully employed enjoying 'life'.

*It ain't like I'm lazy...I go after every opening or rumor of one. Yet, somehow I'm always passed over. Always ignored. Just like today...*he fumed, thinking about how he had followed up a lead at the Belknap Warehouse, but fifty guys – the old and the young, the hungry and the desperate – had showed up hoping to fill one lousy opening.

And once again, he was passed over.

Between that and Liz' constant insults and harping, his self-confidence had really been taking a beating lately.

The smug look on that Belknap foreman's face as he had shown the 'losers' to the door resurfaced in Vic's memory. For a moment, frustration got the better of him and he slammed his hand down on the table in exasperation.

Several patrons, including the two young women who had been sending longing glances his way startled a little at the sound and turned to stare at him again, wondering the reason for his outburst. He noticed their attention then and raised the hand he had just slammed in a vague apology. They smiled and went back to their conversation as he returned his gaze out the window and back to his musing.

When will I ever catch a break? He wondered with a heavy sigh. *Somehow I've gotta show 'em all that Vic Matthews has what it takes. If I could just get half a chance, I'd run with it, full-tilt, like…like Bold Venture…* He sighed then, picturing the winner of the Kentucky Derby the year before. *That horse fought his way through the pack and charged forward to win, leavin' dislodged jockeys and a mess of startled horseflesh in his wake.*

A tiny smile graced Vic's handsome features as he remembered picking that mount to win because he had liked his name, *Bold Venture,* and a two-dollar bet meant he had walked away from the window with a cool forty bucks in his pocket. Closing his eyes for a moment and drawing in a deep breath, he relived the elation he had felt to actually be on the winning side that day. To be 'in the money.' That thought momentarily pushed away the fact that nothing about his life since then had resembled a 'winner's circle'.

Someday I'm gonna set out on a 'bold venture' of my own, he vowed silently, as his eyes warmed with oft imagined scenes of a successful future.

ꕤ

A FEW MINUTES later, two young men dashed inside the door of the establishment and out of the rain – twenty-one-year-old Earl Grant and twenty–two-year-old Alec Alder. Spotting their friend occupying their customary booth, they grinned and waved, making their way over to him while shaking the excess water off their clothes.

"Blasted rain!" Earl grumbled as he slid into the seat across from Vic and smoothed a lock of his straight, dark hair back from his face with one wet hand before wiping it on his jacket.

"Hey Pally, how goes it?" Alec asked as he flopped down onto the seat next to Vic and gave him a teasing punch in the arm. He took off his dark gray cap and, holding it by the bill, whacked it a few times against the table's edge to dislodge the excess water as he swiped back a few strands of his thin brown hair with his other hand.

"It *goes*," Vic mumbled with a shrug.

"Ahh, another negateevo, huh?" Alec offered with a sympathetic pout. He totally understood his friend's mood, as he had also come up with a losing hand that day.

Vic merely rolled his head toward his friend and gave him The Eye, Alec's customary fun-loving personality grating on his nerves.

"Well guys, guess what *I* heard," Earl began, his green eyes sparkling with suppressed news. "Ford's hirin' for a special project. They're payin' five bucks a day, and the first ten guys that show up, they'll let work. Sweepin' the floor and haulin' junk around. Maybe hammerin' a nail or two. I'm goin' over first thing in the mornin'. Ya'll want in?"

"Better than nothin', I guess," Vic shrugged again, although his mood brightened some at the prospect of making a little money. Liz had hinted during her tirade that morning that he might have to find another place to flop if his 'luck' didn't change soon. His brother Jack, as usual, had just sat there mute. *Maybe this will please the old so-and-so…*

He checked that thought as soon as it occurred. Liz wasn't an old so-and-so. She was right; he *did* need to hold up his end. It was just how she went about it – the constant harping – that stuck in his craw…and the fact that she couldn't seem to see how hard he was *trying*.

Glancing across the table at Earl, Alec raised his eyebrows in question, before shifting his eyes back to Vic. He studied for a moment the side of his friend's face as he stared out the window at the wet gloom. *What he needs is a pick-me-up, as in a woman,* Alec thought with a smirk.

Gently elbowing Vic in the side, Alec offered with a chuckle. "Hey ol' man, guess who I ran into today?"

Vic glanced at him and shook his head before reaching for and downing the rest of his soda.

"Remember that girl I took around for awhile last summer?"

Vic narrowed his eyes as he tried to remember. "Mary somethin' or other?"

"Yep. Well, her and another girl were strollin' down Fourth, see, and I met up with 'em. One thing led to another and…" he paused with a snicker and glanced around as if he were divulging state secrets. "Anyway, they're up for a good time on Friday. That is, if you're *interested*," he added, nudging his friend with a shoulder.

Mildly intrigued, Vic eyed his jokester pal closely, having been the victim of Alec's 'blind' date set-ups before. "This one's a *looker*?"

"She's a real babe," Alec acknowledged with uplifted hands as he pictured the girl. "Dark hair… cute figure…great gams… real perky. Name's Edna Hoskins. Says she's nineteen."

"She got good teeth?" Vic asked with a doubting smirk, picturing the worst.

"Yep, sure does. I made sure 'a that for ya," Alec grinned, knowing his friend's pet peeve regarding girls with less than pleasing hygiene. He reached into his pocket to retrieve a small scrap of paper. "Here's her address. I told her you'd pick her up at seven and we'd meet at the Cozy," he added, indicating one of the neighborhood theaters.

Vic took the slip and read the address. "I guess," he somewhat reluctantly agreed. "That is… providin' I make some dough

CHAPTER 2

Louise, the Girls, and The Family

TWO DAYS LATER, the rain still had not let up. The sky above the tall buildings of downtown Louisville continued to drench the area as three young women made their way down First Street late that afternoon, huddled together under a large umbrella.

"You guys want to catch a movie tonight?" asked Fleetwood McDougal, affectionately known as 'Fleet.' Her chestnut brown eyes sparkled with merry anticipation as she eyed her friends, Eleanor Mabley and Louise Hoskins.

Removing one hand from the handle of the umbrella, Fleet tucked a strand of her wavy, honey hued hair inside the edge of her red scarf. She clamped her thin lips in a grimace against the brisk wind, accentuating her somewhat angular face.

"What's playin'?" Eleanor wondered aloud, her hair blowing across her face in the wet breeze. She reached up to brush it away. Her mother being part Cherokee, Eleanor had inherited her black hair and eyes, but she had received her complexion from her Irish father. Normally, this would have been a pleasing combination, but on Eleanor, it somehow seemed incongruous. Most of the time, she just looked pale and sickly.

"*San Francisco.* It's got Jeanette MacDonald and *Clark Gable* in it," Fleet added with a grin, knowing both girls couldn't help but swoon at the dashing matinee idol.

"I thought you had a date with Frank?" Louise replied, puzzled. As the wind blew gusts of rain aggravatingly under their umbrella, she drew the wool lapels of her dark gray hand-me-down coat tighter around her chest. Reaching up with one hand, she adjusted the light blue scarf covering her smooth, sable hair. The gentle arch of her brows over her rounded almond eyes as well as her creamy complexion conveyed the innocence of youth, yet her solemn and watchful countenance projected wisdom beyond her years. Her eyes, mostly brown with a trace of mossy green, seemed to shine like a glittering star through a forest of trees on a dark night, as if they were hiding a mystery that was waiting to be solved.

"I *did.*" Fleet sighed, huddling closer and hunching her tall, slim frame down a bit to equal her shorter companions. "But he got a chance at snaggin' a little cash, helping their neighbor do something or other, so he jumped on it."

Louise and Eleanor nodded in absolute understanding. Times were lean, and nobody in his right mind would turn down a chance to make a little dough.

"Well, I can't anyway. Daddy told me and Billy this morning he wants us to stay in tonight," Louise replied to the original question as she carefully negotiated around a puddle and cast an apologetic look toward her friends.

"Well, that stinks," Fleet griped, as always itching to have some fun. Then she glanced at her friend again. "Wait…your Dad's back from Bowling Green?"

"Yep, he got in last night," Louise answered, her hazel eyes warming as she thought of her beloved father, Willis. Oh how she missed him when he was away.

"He's still working, though…right?" queried Eleanor the worrier, as she watched Louise's face closely.

"Yeah, this is just a visit for the weekend," she assured her friends quickly, as each knew how hard it was for Louise's father to secure and keep employment. It was the same story for everyone struggling to emerge from the aptly named, 'Great Depression' – no work. Fathers, brothers, and husbands all seemed to have the same thought – *try another town, maybe there's work there.* However, most of the time they found conditions *there* the same as they were back home, and the men sooner or later came dragging back to their loved ones in defeat. Louise's father was especially affected as, at sixty-four, he was way past his prime in the opinions of most employers. Unfortunately – bosses could afford to be choosy.

Reaching the welcome refuge of the "Neighborhood House" just then, the girls hurried up the three concrete steps and fumbled with the knob on the large door. Dashing inside, they giggled merrily as they shook water droplets from their hands.

The center, run by Laura Herndon, was housed in a large brick-veneered building on First, between Walnut and Liberty. It consisted of two separate structures, a large two-story house on the right, in which lived the stern Mrs. Klapheke, the director, and a larger gym/auditorium on the left. This building sported a stage at the far end, and basketball goals on the sides. A large open area fanned out behind the structures, which was perfect for baseball or football games, and also included slides, swing sets and horseshoes.

Neighborhood kids spent many evenings out there as a group, listening to boxing matches on the radio, as such greats as Joe Louis or Max Baer battled for the title. The girls in the group enjoyed the camaraderie of those times as much as the boys. Sitting on the edges of their chairs, everyone stared at the old Philco radio as they listened to the boxing announcer's eager voice describing each blow. Good-natured arguments would sometimes ensue over whom would win the match, although everyone knew Joe Louis was practically unbeatable.

"Come on in here out of that rain, girls!" Mrs. Herndon affectionately ordered as she ushered them inside and closed the door against a damp gust. Giving each of the girls a quick hug of welcome, she asked about their day at school, and exchanged other pleasantries. The girls smiled at the friendly woman as they answered her questions and hung up their damp outer wear on hooks next to the front door.

Although Mrs. Herndon had been assigned by the state to run the Neighborhood House, she truly loved her charges as if they were her own children, a bit like a second mother. Louise was especially fond of her, as the kind lady had taken the girl under her wing. Over the past several years, she had taught her how to file her nails properly and even wear a bit of makeup – things Louise's mother never seemed to have time to share.

"You're just in time for rehearsal," Mrs. Herndon encouraged. Seeing several others already on the stage at the far end of the large open space rehearsing for the center's upcoming play, the girls quickly joined them. Thoughts of money troubles and the incessant rain immediately took a back seat to their world of make believe.

Louise, with her smooth creamy skin, twinkling hazel eyes, petite figure, and beautiful soprano voice, was undeniably the center of attention. On top of that, she was a natural on the stage. Many of her friends secretly thought she had star potential, and Laura Herndon had wasted no time in picking her for the lead role of Annabelle in the musical. It was an original work she had entitled 'Song of the Old South'. The center's director, Mrs. Klapheke, had even somehow procured costumes for the young actors, including hoop skirts and top hats. It was shaping up to be a large production, and they had been working on it for months.

Fifteen minutes later, the main door opened as another youngster entered. Louise paused in her song and turned her head in response to her name being called.

"Mama wants you to come home," Billy Hoskins, Louise's younger brother, bluntly informed her as he skidded to a stop at the edge of the stage. At eleven, Billy was small for his age, having been born prematurely. Yet, he was a clever, cheerful boy with dark hair and bright blue eyes – and he and Louise shared a close relationship.

"How come? I just got here," Louise groused, crossing her arms on her chest as she wondered what chore her mother wanted her to do now. Silently, she wished her older sister, Edna, would help out more. *She's probably out gallivanting around somewhere in this rain. Then she'll come down with a sore throat and Mama'll make me take care of her,* she silently fussed.

"I don't know," Billy shrugged. "She just said go get ya."

"I don't get a minute's peace," Louise muttered as she turned to Mrs. Herndon, apologizing for the interruption.

"That's quite alright, Louise dear. You have your part down pat, we'll just continue without you – Fleet can be your stand-in. You run along and obey your mother," she added warmly.

"Yes, Ma'am. See ya later, guys," Louise mumbled to her cast mates as she turned and made her way quickly down the stage steps.

"Come on, Billy," she ordered with a sigh of resignation, grasping his arm to tug him along.

"Aw shucks, I wanna stay and watch," he mumbled.

"If *I* can't stay, neither can *you*," Louise growled, exercising her 'older sister' authority.

Reaching the door, Louise draped her coat over her head and dashed with her brother out into the still pouring rain. They ran the two and a half blocks home to the cramped apartment shared by the six family members – their mother and father, Mary Lilly and Willis, along with four siblings, a pair each of boys and girls.

Five minutes later, and soaking wet, brother and sister quickly clomped up the steps and scurried inside the large two-story duplex near the corner of Second and Chestnut. The family's diminutive apartment was on the first floor toward the back of the building.

Mouth watering aromas filled the abode. "Louise, help me get supper on," her mother, Lilly, instructed as soon as the girl stepped foot inside.

Lilly Hoskins, a short, stout, hard-working woman, had lived through many a tough time in her fifty-five years. She wore her long, straight, light brown hair in a bun, and her roundish face and creamy skin accentuated the shine of her sapphire blue eyes. If picturing their mother, all four siblings would have undoubtedly seen the same image in their minds – dark blue sheath dress, its white buttons done up to the rounded white collar, black sensible shoes, and the inevitable apron tied around her waist as she labored at keeping their two-room apartment orderly and spotless. Like most people during the lean years from twenty-nine until the War began, they didn't have much, but what they did have she made sure she kept neat as a new pin.

A proud woman, Lilly sometimes let that pride get in the way. An example of that was her unusual penchant for refusing to stand with everyone else in the neighborhood 'soup' lines. Insisting that one of her children ask for an extra helping for their homebound parent – when she was anything but – Lilly just couldn't stand the thought that others might realize they were as 'needy' as the majority of the population.

"Where's Edna?" Louise asked curiously as she removed her coat.

"In bed with cramps," her mother replied in a tone that brooked no more questions.

Louise sighed wearily, but made no fuss, knowing that her sister did have extremely miserable cramping during the first day of her monthly. Moving toward the kitchen area, she bent to press a kiss to her Daddy's cheek as he sat reading the newspaper in his worn, but comfortable, easy chair.

Willis was a tired looking, lanky man with thinning salt and pepper hair and faded blue eyes. He smiled lovingly up at Louise, reaching up to give her cheek an affectionate pat, as he mused how proud – and blessed – he was to have such a beautiful, obedient daughter.

"I'm so glad you're home, Daddy," Louise murmured softly, grinning as she was rewarded with one of his cheery winks, visible behind his wire rim glasses.

"I'm glad to *be* home, Sweet Pea," he murmured affectionately. "It was a long, wet trip this time."

Billy kicked his wet boots off and dropped his jacket on the floor before flopping down on a chair near his father. Willis gave his son a glance and with a tiny grin, separated the comics from his paper and handed it over to the youngster. This had become a ritual between father and son, looked forward to by the boy more than the father would have imagined. Billy grinned back and flipped the paper open, intending to immediately immerse himself in the world of Popeye, Buck Rogers, and Tarzan, while arrayed on his chair in the exact pose of his parent – one leg crossed over the other, face set in concentration.

Lilly, without looking up from her task, instructed her youngest to pick up the discarded article of clothing and hang it on the hook by the door.

"Billy, don't you have homework?" the mother astutely added, casting a knowing glance at him as she stood preparing supper at the old Magic Chef stove in the corner.

"Yes, Ma'am," Billy muttered as he turned from obeying her order about the jacket and chanced a peek at his father, whom he hoped had become thoroughly engrossed once again in his paper. No such luck. Willis Hoskins, ever alert and nearly impossible for any of his children to fool, cast The Eye at his youngest over the top of both his spectacles and his newspaper. No words were needed – Billy grudgingly folded the paper and reached for his schoolbooks.

Louise grinned at Billy's antics before glancing over at her other brother, Joseph "Sonny Boy" Hoskins, a tall, handsome young man of sixteen with an unruly shock of blond 'sunshine' hair and cornflower blue eyes. Ambitious and hard working like his parents, he was busy placing a stack of newspapers into his shoulder bag in preparation for his shift of hawking the evening edition of the Louisville Times at the 'magic corner' of Fourth and Broadway. Sonny's small job played a large part in keeping food on the table for the family of six. He was an excellent salesman, and his father often affectionately joked that his son could sell an icebox to an Eskimo.

"Sonny, how you gonna sell papers in this rain?" Louise asked her brother pointedly as she reached up on the shelf over the sink to retrieve the plates and glasses for the meal.

He shrugged and leaned over to pick up his hand-me-down jacket and quickly slipped his arms into the somewhat tight sleeves. From one of the bunched flapped pockets, he withdrew his traditional newsboy's flat cap, and placed it firmly on his head. "It'll stop soon. But I can always stand in the big entrance of the Heyburn and wait for some of them top floor executives to come out. They're always good for a sale."

"Sonny, now you take those things right back off," Lilly fussed. "You're not going till you eat a hot meal. It's wet and cold out there and you need your strength."

"It ain't been cold all week, Mama, and today it got up to sixty-five. That's what the paper says," Sonny refuted, pointing to the top story on the front page.

"Sure is *crazy* weather," Billy agreed, looking up from his history book.

Just then, Edna emerged from the bedroom and eased into a chair at the table. "It sure is *crazy*. I don't remember ever seein' January so warm like this…and what's with all this rain? I hate it! It's makin' my hair frizz," she griped, curling her lip in a characteristic pout as she impatiently pushed back a lock of her hair that she had dyed red the day before.

"Well, warm or cold, it doesn't matter *Joseph Robert* – you still need to eat to keep up your strength. Hauling newspapers around is heavy work," Lilly insisted.

"Aw Mama…" he muttered, but Willis cast him the 'mind

your mother' look. It was enough. Sonny sighed and removed his cap.

"Alright, but I gotta get *goin'* soon. I gotta beat Jim and Harold," he added, referring to two other newsboys who had, as of late, been vying for first dibs on Sonny's lucrative spot if he happened to be running late. They knew he had it down to a science, catching patrons in their mink coats or top hats coming and going at the luxurious Brown Hotel, and late toiling office workers from the Heyburn Building directly across the street. Providing he got there before rush hour was over, he never failed to sell out.

After several minutes, the family sat down to a hot, delicious meal of fried potatoes and onions sprinkled with bits of hot dog, and served with creamed peas. Lilly was a good cook and had a knack for fashioning a filling meal out of whatever was on hand.

Settling in, they continued talking about the events of their day and the subject that was on everyone's mind – the aggravation caused by the seemingly unending rain.

After a few minutes, the soft music playing on their Westinghouse cabinet-style radio was interrupted by yet another report predicting more of the same – and possible flooding. The family took little notice.

At the conclusion of the weather report, the announcer calmly intoned in his smooth baritone 'radio' voice, "And now, back to our program of Dance Band favorites."

ꕥ

CHAPTER 3

The Meeting

TRUE TO EARL'S word, Ford had indeed allowed a group of men to work all day, both Thursday and Friday, and paid cash at the end of each day. Earl, Vic, and Alec had managed to be the first three in line on both days. For Vic, it sure felt good to have money in his pocket again – and he had enjoyed placing five whole dollars in Liz's hand at the end of the second day. That even earned him a grudging half smile from his sister-in-law.

Later that evening, Vic pulled up to a two-story brick duplex on Chestnut Street in a large, black, '33 Studebaker, and quickly checked the address on the small slip of paper.

Rain was coming down steadily, with no end in sight, and it made Vic grateful that Earl's father had allowed him to borrow his car for his date. Turning off the motor, he glanced around at the black and chrome interior of the vehicle, with its extended back end, long side windows, and low roof. *Hope Edna's got a sense of humor...and don't mind ridin' in an old hearse...* he mused with a grin as he turned in the seat and laid a hand on the backrest of the worn and faded horsehair seat cover. Spying the torn places in the headliner and knowing the damage had occurred from the sharp edges of wooden coffins sliding in and out, he emitted a tiny chuckle. *I think this car's nifty, with its big round headlights, old-fashioned running boards and spare tire on the side.* He remembered Earl's father acquiring the vehicle for a 'song' when the Coots Funeral Home in Jeffersonville had purchased a new one. The big old car, now a familiar site in their neighborhood, had come in handy for many things, such as taking kids to school on rainy and snowy days, or transporting injured neighbors to the hospital.

Reaching up to tilt the small, mottled rear view mirror to the left to check his appearance one more time, Vic attempted to quell the butterflies flapping their wings in his stomach. Cursing the incessant rain and mumbling of his aversion to blind dates, Vic flipped up the collar of his worn leather aviator jacket and slipped out of the vehicle. Sprinting to the door of the building, he quickly ducked inside the main entrance. There, in the dim light from a single bare bulb high up in the ceiling, he checked the paper again to make sure it was apartment number two, before making his way down the shadowy hall to the large door.

Through its scratched, dark walnut surface, he could hear music and people talking, though he couldn't determine how many were inside. The thought made him, for a moment, somewhat uneasy, as it was always a little unnerving to approach the unknown. At his knock, he heard scuffling noises and what sounded like urgent whispered instructions. When no one immediately came, his brow furrowed as he cocked his head to one side, trying to decide whether he should knock again.

Man I hate blind dates…who knows who's gonna open this door… If Alec has fixed me up with another dog…I'll have his hide, he smirked, shaking his head at his own thoughts. Mentally, he prepared himself to maintain a neutral expression no matter what the girl's appearance might be, not wishing to hurt the poor thing's feelings…

Just as he raised his fist to give the door another rap, he heard the lock being turned and the entry opened about a foot.

The delicious aroma of fried potatoes and onions, still permeating the warm abode, came floating out to tickle his senses. His mouth instantly watered, reminding him he'd only downed a quick bologna sandwich when he returned home from work, since Liz had not saved him any supper.

Then his eyes widened and a slow smile made his handsome face beam with charm.

There in the opening stood a lovely young woman in a tea length dress of embroidered netting over champagne satin. Rich sable hair softly floated around her shoulders…creamy smooth skin on a heart shaped face made it seem as if an ever-present light shone in her countenance, like the flame of a candle…lips like the wispy curve of a butterfly's wings stretched slightly over a perfect line of pearly white teeth…and beautiful hazel eyes twinkled behind gently curling black lashes as she stared up at him enraptured. Vic's breath caught as he stared back, momentarily stunned. He felt his pulse speed up as he took in the girl's radiance.

Finally, he cleared his throat and unconsciously ran a hand back through his hair, which had been made slightly wavier by the rain and the damp evening air.

"Umm…Edna?" he murmured, the damp weather making his warm baritone sound husky. The words served to break the spell into which the two had been plunged.

The young woman blinked several times as if trying to gather her thoughts. Then one delicate hand unconsciously moved to the neck of her dress as she slowly shook her head.

"No…I'm Louise…Edna's my sister. Are you Vic?" she managed. Unconsciously, she moistened her suddenly dry lips; slightly afraid he could hear the thunderous thumping of her heart.

Vic nodded and chuckled self-consciously, feeling like a fool for not introducing himself at once.

"Yeah, sorry. I'm Vic Matthews…I'm here to pick up Edna…she ready?" he added, silently hoping the sister was as much a looker as this one.

Glancing back over her shoulder at someone Vic couldn't see from the doorway, Louise turned back to him apologetically,

"Oh…I'm sorry. She's…not feeling good tonight," she murmured. She seemed to be hedging, as if scrambling for a reason other than the truth. "She won't be able to go on the date with you. She's sorry you made the trip for nothing…she didn't have a way to reach you." Her voice was kind and gentle, and seemed to glide into his ears and take up residence in the center of his chest.

Vic digested this for a moment. He was being stood up by a blind date. *Great,* he silently fumed, wondering if she truly 'didn't feel good.' He thought for a moment that maybe the lovely Louise might want to go in her sister's place, but negated that idea, figuring she already had a date for the evening – since she appeared to be dressed for it.

Vic had no way of knowing that Edna had borrowed the dress for their date; however, now that she couldn't go, Louise had tried it on… and it fit her perfectly. Just before Vic had arrived, Louise had been modeling the lovely dress for her father and brother, the elder commenting that it made her seem much more mature.

The two at the door heard a muffled voice from the other room and Louise nodded in answer, relaying to him, "She asked if she could take a rain-check." As soon as the words were out of her mouth, she realized the unintended pun. Biting her lip, she attempted to stop herself from chuckling. Vic caught the joke and nodded, his lips pulling into a half grin. His eyes dropped to her mouth as her lips rounded into a smile that seemed somehow, in his unconscious opinion, to fend off the gloom of the rainy night.

Glancing back up to meet her eyes again, he murmured with a shrug. "Yeah, sure." He waited a few beats more, staring at the girl as she returned his gaze. "Well…goodnight then," he finally added, nodding to her as he turned to retrace his steps back down the hall. *So much for a hot date to 'keep me warm on a rainy night,'* he mused wryly.

Louise watched him until he disappeared out the front door and into the rain, then slowly stepped back into the cozy apartment and shut the door. Leaning her forehead against the cool hard wood, she could still smell the heady scent of Old Spice aftershave that had emanated from him…could still see the twinkle in his eyes, and hear his smooth voice intoning, "Good-night." Her knees felt weak.

*My gosh! That has got to be the most gorgeous man I've ever seen in my **life**!* She reflected as she turned to rest her back against the hard surface of the door. Staring straight ahead as though in an enchanted stupor, she allowed every second of the encounter to replay in her mind. Pressing a hand unconsciously to her chest, she felt her heart still pounding fast.

*Those eyes…that wavy hair…those dimples…his voice was so smooth and deep…it was like living a scene from a movie…*she dreamily contemplated, totally immersed in his enchanting memory.

"Louise, is he gone?" Edna's edgy voice interrupted her rever-ie.

Distracted, Louise called back, "Yeah."

"Well…what was he like?" her sister impatiently inquired as she came to the bedroom doorway. "Was he cute?"

Louise glanced at her sister, her gaze taking in the habitual sour expression, the brassy red hair, the cold blue eyes and the stubborn set to her chin. It occurred to her that Edna always seemed to get everything she wanted, while Louise 'performed' like Cinderella. Edna snuck around, drank beer, and did all kinds of things she never seemed to get in trouble for, while Louise was called on the carpet for 'looking' at someone wrong.

Louise's eyes narrowed slightly as she made up her mind right then and there. *If **any** Hoskins girl snags handsome Mr. Vic Matthews, its gonna be **me**.*

Fibbing to her sister for the first time in her life, Louise shrugged nonchalantly and moved away from the door. Purpose-ly, turning her back to her sister's shrewd stare, she murmured, "He was…just okay."

"Just okay, huh?" Edna snorted, decidedly unladylike. "Well

good, then I'm *glad* I couldn't go with him," she added as she turned back into the room to recline on the bed with the hot water bottle and a well-worn copy of Hollywood magazine.

"Louise, come help me," their mother instructed just then, beckoning the girl to come and assist with drying the dishes. "And you better take off that borrowed dress before you get something on it."

Louise automatically obeyed, her mind only half on the task…the other half was firmly occupied with a pair of warm brown eyes and dark wavy hair.

Somehow she knew something significant had just happened…and she would never be the same.

ജ൦ൽ

BACK AT THE car, Vic dived in through the driver's door and shut it quickly against the deluge, muttering an expletive or two and taking out a worn handkerchief to wipe his hands dry. *Won't this beastly rain ever stop?*

He started the motor, yet merely sat staring straight ahead as he tried to decide what to do on a lonely Friday night with three dollars and change burning a hole in his pocket. A *rainy*, lonely Friday night. He thought about meeting up with Alec and his *date*, but that just didn't appeal to him. He considered for a moment catching a movie at another theater, but he nixed that idea, as well. Going to the movies solo was definitely not his idea of a good time.

Glancing back at the large brick duplex, he could see light shining from one of the rear windows and he wished now that he had asked the lovely Louise if she wanted to take her sister's place. The raindrops glittering on the glass in the muted light of the street lamp faded from his view as sparkling hazel eyes and a breathtaking smile swam across the screen of his mind. He'd never felt so *drawn* to a girl before…

Finally, Vic sighed as his hand settled onto the ball-shaped knob of the shifter and put the car into gear. "*Ehhh*," he grumbled with a whispered expletive. "Guess I'll just head on over to Lucky's and shoot a little pool." He sighed as he glanced over his shoulder to check for traffic before maneuvering out and on down the wet street.

For the rest of the evening, Vic couldn't shake the memory of the girl in the doorway…

ℵ

CHAPTER 4

Something is Coming

LIFE WENT ON for the inhabitants of Louisville the following week. Life…and rain.

Vic went back to pounding the pavement, or more accurately 'dodging puddles', looking for work. Having heard through the grapevine that Colgate, over in Clarksville, might be hiring, Thursday found him completing an employment application in the main office of the large plant; although, he knew it would be a long shot at best.

Placing himself at the tollgate of the Second Street Bridge, he begged the favor of each driver that paused to toss in a quarter. Finally a Colgate employee – an old man in a rusty Ford pickup – took pity on him. Vic gratefully sprinted around to the passenger door and climbed in out of the elements. He and his benefactor then headed to the huge former Indiana Reformatory-turned-soap making facility, with the famous, forty-foot wide, brightly lit clock.

As the wheels of the old pickup rolled along with the flow of traffic on the wet bridge, Vic stared at the gleaming lights of the huge timepiece on the opposite shore. Its red radiance appeared distorted through the raindrops on the windshield and the dim glow of the thickly overcast dawn. Somehow the large, slowly ticking hands of the device intensified the sense of inescapable urgency and doom he had been feeling for weeks. It was as if the hands themselves, stroking by the minutes on the clock's huge illuminated face, were somehow dragging him closer to the brink...of *what*, he didn't know.

With a shudder, he turned his head away from its looming presence. Through the rain-dotted side window of the old truck, the swiftly moving brown water below the bridge appeared thick with mud, and rife with grayish flotsam and floating debris – evidence of flooding upriver. Bits of splintered wood, brush, rusty metal, and even an old car, bobbed up and down in the swift current. With a grimace, he pictured it all jammed up against the dam or floating through the locks.

All the way across the bridge amidst the slow moving traffic, the old man's conversation consisted of nothing but dire predictions about what he considered the inevitable. *Flood.* A *BIG* one. "We're due. No doubt about it," the bewhiskered old gentleman intoned as he rolled the driver's window down and spat out the juice from a wad of chewing tobacco. "Livin' in a river town, the question ain't *if* we'll get one, but *when*."

Vic merely nodded, staring downriver as they crossed the center of the bridge. He tried to fathom what it would mean to the city...and its people...if a *big flood* did indeed happen.

Ah, the river...The Ohio...Gateway to the West, Vic mused. *Ohi-yo' – Good River* – the Iroquois had named it, or so an old Indian he had encountered once on the riverbank had told him. Vic had lived near the river his whole life and had always taken it for granted. At times, during the long hot months of summer, the river seemed so peaceful, cool, and calm – kind of like a wise, trusted friend. As a boy, he had gone swimming in it, fished along its banks, and hunted for fossils on the Indiana side of the 'falls'. He even worked on it the summer he was sixteen, lucking out with a job as a seasonal worker on the steamboat, The Idlewild.

He knew the river is what had made Louisville a town to begin with, since the 'falls' forced the flatboats and steamboats to stop and offload their cargo. It's where they got their drinking water, and most of their electric power. But now…it seemed more like a sleeping monster just awakening and stretching its massive limbs. As he stared through the rain-speckled window at the murky, swiftly flowing water below, he wondered how far those limbs would stretch…

An hour later, Vic handed his completed application to the girl behind the desk in the Colgate office. She smiled up at him and he noticed she had wavy brown hair and hazel eyes, making him think once again of the lovely Louise.

I wonder what she's doin' on a wet Thursday morning like this…

ꕤ

LOUISE WAS GOING about her daily life, attending school, running through the rain to rehearsal at the neighborhood house, and fulfilling her duties at home. Now, however, her mind would drift often to the handsome Vic Matthews, wondering if she would ever see him again. Louisville was a big city, and it was impossible to know everyone in it. Several times, Louise prayed she would be able to find out more information about him. She had no idea where Vic lived or worked, or the places he frequented. Louise had casually asked her sister, but Edna knew nothing about him other than his name.

All these thoughts kept her preoccupied, to the extent that she hadn't really noticed the slowly worsening situation and impending emergency. Nor could she have imagined just how it would turn her world, and the world of her loved ones, upside down.

On Sunday, the tenth of January, the Red Cross began warning people in the lower flood areas to be prepared to move if the rain continued. Old timers that had been through floods before began packing things to take with them, if they couldn't be moved to an upper floor. However, just as the river seemed determined to rise, it halted at 1.9 feet above flood stage. This gave the people hope that the warnings were yet another false alarm, and that the harbingers of doom were once again mistaken.

The water level in the river remained stationary for five hours, prompting the people to begin unpacking. This set them to griping about the inconvenience of the situation, the stupidity of the forecasters, the Red Cross, and everyone down at WHAS – their main source for news and information.

However, after those five hours, as if a large unseen switch had been magically flipped, the river suddenly began creeping further and further up from the confines of its banks. Those of the older generation, while heaping plenty of wisecracking 'I told you so's', continued moving their belongings and furniture to the second floors of their homes. Or should circumstances demand, to their vehicles for transport to higher ground. All the while, the river rose higher and higher, seeping ominously closer to the heart of the city.

By Thursday the fourteenth, the unending rain and the rising river were the primary topics of conversation across the entire Ohio Valley.

Thursday evening, as Louise and her mother set the table for supper, the steady rain kept up a continuous cadence outside the kitchen window.

Sonny was once again packing his satchel in preparation for another evening of pushing papers and dodging raindrops. Pausing for a moment as he actually read the main headline, he let out a low whistle.

"It says here that over the last two weeks…165 *billion* tons of rain has fell!"

"Good heavens!" Lilly blustered. Pausing in the act of placing silverware on the table, she stared at her son as she tried to comprehend such a thing. Shards of fear regarding a flood that could actually affect their family began to zip through her consciousness for the first time since the marathon showers had begun. A ritual from her childhood resurfaced and, with a shudder, she unconsciously make made the sign of the cross over her face and chest.

Billy stopped in mid action of bouncing a rubber ball against the door. "*Dang* that sounds like a lot."

"How do they *know* that? They *weigh* it or somethin'?" Edna snorted as she wandered over to the stove and lifted the lid on a pot of meatless spaghetti – her face immediately registering a pout of disappointment.

Sonny shrugged and continued loading his bag. "They got ways of knowing that kinda stuff, I guess." Pausing again as he stared at the article, the young man read the names of the different meteorologists working for the National Weather Service, such as J. L. Kendall. Musing for a moment, Sonny wondered just what it took to become a 'meteorologist.' *Probably college,* he mused downheartedly, knowing there was no way he or his parents would be able to afford such a costly academic pursuit. *But it sure seems like interesting work…*

Just then, the soft music on the old Westinghouse was interrupted by yet another news and weather report. This time, swallowing with nervousness, the family crept closer to the large radio. Staring at the apparatus, they listened in rapt attention as the newscaster delivered an updated report on the crisis.

"The river has breached its banks in most of the towns along the Ohio, and Louisville is no exception," informed the nasally voice of the WHAS announcer. "According to officials minutes ago, the Upper Gauge measured 2.3 feet above flood stage, with the Lower Gauge measuring 1.2 feet above, but it is rising steadily," he intoned, speaking of the gauges set above and below the rapids erroneously called 'falls'. "Rain has continued, non-stop, up and down the Ohio Valley, with no end in sight. National Weather Forecasters are predicting many more days of unending rain if the unusually perfect conditions do not begin to change in the immediate future. The Red Cross is urging everyone within broadcast range of this station to begin preparations for eventual evacuation." The urgency in his voice set the nerves of everyone in the room on edge.

With a shudder, Lilly lowered herself into her husband's favorite chair, fervently wishing that he were with them. She hated being without his calm, reassuring presence and being responsible for making such monumental decisions for the family, such as whether to stay or go – and what to take with them if they did indeed evacuate. The thought of leaving their home and belongings to the greedy fingers of a passing looter was simply unacceptable. Biting her lip, she began to unconsciously clasp and unclasp her hands in her lap as she stared out the window at what now seemed like *menacing* rain.

The newscaster's voice droned on, concluding with a report on a business having already been looted in the lowest section of The Point, the area opposite Towhead Island and Jeffersonville.

As the family hovered around their connection with the outside world, they gazed nervously into one another's eyes, each one reaching to grasp the hand of the one next to them.

"Mama…?" Billy murmured, gazing at his parent for reassurance, as all children will do in a crisis situation. "Will the water get up this high?"

"I…I don't know, Billy," Lilly whispered, reaching to draw the boy to her side.

Louise, now wide-eyed, turned her gaze to the eldest male in the room – sixteen-year-old Sonny.

"Sonny? You think we'll have to leave?" she murmured nervously.

Striving to be the man-of-the-house, as per the promise he made his father each time Willis left for Bowling Green, Sonny drew himself up to his full height and flashed his sister a brave smile.

"Nah," he assured with more bravado than he felt. "That ol' river's rose lots 'a times, but I ain't never seen it flood all the way in here."

Louise nodded in meager relief and hopeful faith in her brother's wisdom. Just then, the newsman on the radio paused in his narrative, mumbled some unintelligible words to someone on his end, and then cleared his throat.

"This just in. Elderly man reported stranded in riverfront shanty at the edge of The Point. The Red Cross has requested this be broadcast to anyone within hearing...*Send a boat.*"

ꙮ

VIC STEPPED DOWN from the trolley as it slowed to pass through the intersection at Fifteenth and Market. Crossing the street and jogging through the rain, he hastily managed the fifty or so yards to the door of his brother's apartment house. Taking the front steps two at a time he immediately disappeared inside. He unzipped his jacket, removed his hat, and tried to rub his hair dry as he slowly climbed the dimly lit internal stairs, his posture one of defeat. Reaching the door of apartment four, he paused and took in a fortifying breath before he turned the knob and entered.

Dispirited after another long day of slogging around in wet clothing while remaining frustratingly unsuccessful at obtaining gainful employment, he began to shed his damp jacket. Glancing toward the kitchen area, he saw his sister-in-law washing up the supper dishes, the sleeves of her dark gray wool sweater pushed up to her elbows. Her thin lips were clamped in a firm disagreeable line, which was her usual dour expression. She wiped at an errant strand of auburn hair with one shoulder as she sent him a smoldering glance.

The fragrant aroma of fried chicken hung tantalizingly in the air of the small apartment, but once again, no food had been saved for him. He sighed tiredly and closed his eyes as his stomach rumbled in reaction. *Great! That's a perfect cap on a lousy day...*

"Hey Uncle Vic!" a small voice interrupted his melancholy

musings, and he opened his eyes to see his eight year old auburn-haired nephew, Timmy. The boy smiled up at him from the floor, where he'd been playing with his set of Lincoln Logs. *At least somebody's glad to see me.*

"Hey, Tim. Whatcha building?" Vic asked the boy, sending him a tired smile.

"Hey Uncle Vic!" echoed six-year-old Shirley, Tim's sister, as she came skipping over. He instinctively reached down and lifted the tiny carrot top into his arms, glad for the affectionate welcome. She wrapped her petite arms around his neck and kissed his cheek.

"Hello sweetie. You been good today?" he asked the little girl. She nodded enthusiastically.

Just then, their mother turned from the sink and reached for a dishtowel with which to wipe her hands.

"Timmy, Shirley, go and get your nightclothes on, its time to get ready for bed," she ordered. Snapping her fingers, she pointed toward the room the children shared in the small two-bedroom apartment.

Vic put the little girl down and the kids immediately obeyed, knowing from earlier that their mother was definitely not in a good mood. Neither one relished testing her volatile temper.

Jack, ten years Vic's senior, with similar coloring and build, glanced up from his paper. Offering no greeting to his younger brother, he merely resumed his reading.

The tension in the air was palpable. Vic could tell *he* had recently been the topic of discussion.

Liz crossed her arms over her chest, eying her brother-in-law as he stood near the door. An uncomfortable feeling made him grit his teeth, as she seemed to be centering him in her 'sights'.

"Well?" she asked crisply.

"I put in an application at a few places, includin' Colgate," he answered. Liz raised her eyebrows in interest.

"But…they all hired somebody else," Vic added quietly. He

glanced at Jack, then back at Liz, hoping for a little sympathy. *Can't they see this is hard for me, too?* He felt as though he were standing at the bottom of a deep empty well, reaching up begging for a rope with which to climb out, but no one would toss him one. Worse yet, the people at the rim merely looked down at him, hundreds of feet below, and berated him for not 'picking himself up by his bootstraps.'

Liz threw up her hands in frustration, her mood already half way to anger due to a hard day at work, the rain…and the anniversary of something heartbreaking.

"*Again*! Why are *you* always passed over? What're you doing wrong?" she griped accusingly.

"I wish I *knew*…I wish somebody'd just give me a chance…"

"If you were *worth* giving a chance, they *would*!" she shot back, her face reddening with unreasonable anger. "Your *brother* never had any trouble finding work," she added snidely.

"*Lizzie*…" Jack murmured with a quiet sigh as he folded and laid his paper aside. Jack knew the underlying reason his wife flew off the handle so easily. The truth was, their first child had been stillborn, and Liz had suffered tremendously, both physically and emotionally. The anniversary of their first baby's death seemed to hit her harder and harder each year. As a result, he tended to remain silent most of the time when she went on a rampage; however, he had never shared that rather private information with his brother.

"Well, it's *true*!" Liz shot at her husband, though at his potent stare she had the decency to feel a tiny spark of guilt for her unprovoked attack.

"I'm trying, *really*," Vic defended himself, but she cut him off.

"Well, obviously you aren't trying hard *enough*."

"Liz, now just calm down a little. It ain't all Vic's fault," Jack began, pausing as his wife shot him a piercing look. Turning to his younger brother, he added, "But Vic…you been with us for four years, since Aunt Peg died. You're a man now. You should be on your own."

"Don't you think I *wanna* be on my own?" Vic shot back, his own frustration rising to the surface. "Don't you think I *want* a job and a place…a wife and kids of my own? I DO! But I can't help the stupid stock market crashed and messed everything up!"

"Me and Jack both work, and *you* shoulda stayed in the C's," Liz tried to interrupt, but Vic fired right back, "You and Jack were workin' *before* the crash hit! Jack took a cut in pay to keep his maintenance job at the Heyburn Building – and you lucked into *your* job at the cotton mill 'cause your uncle was a *foreman*, or did you forget that? I ain't got no foreman uncle I can get favors from."

Knowing he was right, Liz clamped her mouth shut and turned away, rolling her eyes and huffing a sigh.

Unable to resist, Vic added with a touch of bitterness. "Besides, what've I got to show for slavin' all summer in the C's, diggin' ditches in the California heat?" he asked, referring to the nationwide 'Civilian Conservation Corps', in which he had served a stint when he was eighteen. "I sent all my money to you to save for me, and you went out and bought a car with it! A car you wouldn't even let me *drive* when I came back!"

"Now hold on…you know the reason for that," Jack backpedaled, feeling only a trifle guilty for splurging with his younger brother's nest egg…but Liz had convinced him at the time that Vic somehow 'owed' it to them.

"That's over and done with," Liz argued, refusing to back down. "And besides, we went back to lugging the kids around on buses and trolleys after somebody stole that car, so you should be happy."

Vic sighed tiredly and moved to drop down in a chair, resting his head in his hands as he stared at the floor between his still wet boots.

"It didn't make me happy," he mumbled, his momentary defensive anger dissipating as quickly as it had arisen. He felt bereft and hollow, sunken like a cake after someone slammed the oven door.

The three fell silent, each submerged deeply in their own thoughts, and not paying attention to the now familiar rain and the ever-present drone of music on the radio in the corner. If they *had* been listening, it might have given them at least a bit of a chuckle. The deejay had, perhaps a bit tongue-in-cheek, chosen to play Guy Lombardo's latest hit, *September in the Rain.*

Finally, Vic dispiritedly raised his head, meeting his brother's similar mahogany brown eyes, and then his sister-in-law's moss green gaze.

"Believe me…I want outta here just as bad as you *want* me outta here. And just as soon as possible, I'll make tracks," he vowed in quiet seriousness, but added with narrowed eyes, "That is…unless you want me ta join the ranks of the hobos and sleep under the Second Street bridge…"

Liz winced a little at his words, and had the grace to feel a pinch of guilt that she was making such a fuss again.

Meeting Vic's wounded stare, her eyes finally softened some as she whispered, "No, of course not."

Their gazes held for a moment as Vic struggled to let go of the stab of hurt her earlier words had caused.

Clearing his throat, Jack offered wryly, "If it ain't under water yet."

Then, as if the radio announcer had heard his words, he chose that moment to break into the song. Just as the Hoskins were listening thirteen blocks away, the announcer reported on the river's levels at the upper and lower gauges, then mentioned the Red Cross' predictions regarding the eventual evacuation of the city.

Glancing at his brother and wife, who were looking to him questioningly as the 'master' of the home, Jack again uncomfortably cleared his throat and swore quietly.

"I wish they'd quit with all the flood crap. I've lived here all my life and I ain't ever seen it flood like they're saying. This rain'll stop soon."

Raising his eyebrows and remembering the swollen, debris-filled river earlier, Vic murmured, "I hope you're right, brother. I hope you're right."

ꕤ

CHAPTER 5

Flood!

THE NORMALLY CLEAR blue skies over the Ohio Valley had been drab and gray for weeks. Living under the heavy, ash-colored clouds for so long, the people had truly forgotten better days. Puddles of cold murky water, disagreeably damp clothing that never had the opportunity to get fully dry, and musty abodes…these had become their norm. Fireplaces and coal stoves couldn't quite cut the dampness – and steam registers only added to the overall heaviness in the air. Despairingly, it seemed as if the world would never be 'dry' again. Many a Reverend thought himself quite clever to base his sermons on Noah, and drive home the point with the current feeling of impending doom.

Indeed, there seemed no escape.

Everyone in the rain-soaked city attempted to carry on the best they could, keeping one eye on the river and one ear to the weather reports. Men and women continued to go to work, spending every free moment discussing the rising river with their fellow employees. Men gathered in doorways and other dry places, muttering about the rain. Women dashed through the wet streets, juggling babies, small children and umbrellas, and fretting about the weather as they descended upon the local groceries in an effort to stock up – bracing for 'the worst'. Predictably, the food markets soon began running short on stock. Children continued to attend school, nervously repeating what they had heard their parents discuss the previous evening – the very real possibility of a flood. The whole city was in a constant state of alert.

Mrs. Herndon reluctantly halted rehearsals for the play until the precarious conditions in the downtown area stabilized. Louise, Sonny, and Billy, slogged their way to school and back each day. Much like the early days of the Depression, the residents of Louisville found themselves in the same 'boat' – wishing, hoping, and praying for a speedy end to the incessant misery. The unseasonably warm temperatures had steadily dropped, to hover within a degree or two of freezing. This turned the rain at times into a mixture of sleet and wet, sloppy snow, although no accumulation occurred. It had become the most miserable January anyone could remember in years.

The unfathomable river, that 'Old Man,' remained a mystery to which no one knew the explanation. As the song said… *That Ol' Man River, he must know somethin', but he don't say nothin', he just keeps rollin' along.* Indeed, the river seemed to have a mind of its own, and had continued rising steadily, at a measured rate of a half inch per hour. River Road and many of the outlying streets on the fringes of the metropolitan area were slowly flooding. Shawnee Park and Cherokee Park quietly began to submerge. Unlike a flash flood, however, the slowly rising water almost had a numbing effect, so that no one could quite grasp the seriousness of the threat. At each new level, the general consensus always seemed to be, "It'll stop soon…"

Residents of The Point were given evacuation orders by the County Welfare Department, to which inhabitants of single-story abodes willingly complied. However, positive they could make it through, the poverty-stricken residents in second story refuges refused to leave. County police had to work for forty-eight hours coaxing them into boats for their own safety. By eight o'clock Tuesday night, January nineteen, the last stubborn straggler climbed down into a rescue craft. By then, the surface of the water was mere inches below his second story window.

Clutching a meager armload of possessions – all he was allowed – silent tears slid down the elderly black man's wrinkled face as the oarsman rowed him away from his home.

He feared he would never see it again. Sadly…he was right.

ꙮ

THE NEXT MORNING, the Hoskins family awoke to the now familiar sound of rain pattering against the windows of their apartment.

Willis had returned home on the previous Saturday, unsure of when he would be able to return to work. The man with whom he normally caught a ride advised him that he would forego attempting a return until the waters receded, as his truck had nearly stalled multiple times en route to Louisville. Indeed, the encroaching water was increasingly submerging every road leading south. Although they needed the money, Lilly was very glad her husband would be home during such uncertain times.

As the family began their day, a shout was heard from the front part of the building. Glancing at each other in alarm, Willis wrenched open the apartment door and the six of them rushed down the hall – to be soon joined by the other residents of the apartment house.

Gertrude Higgins, occupant of apartment number one, a tall, gaunt-faced, gray haired, cantankerous widow and owner of the building, stood at the window next to the door. Repeatedly murmuring, "Good Heavens!" she kept wringing her hands as she gazed outside. A man from the front apartment on the opposite side threw open the outer door, which elicited a collective gasp from his fellow residents. None of them could believe what they were seeing.

The pressure of the backed up sewers had blown off every manhole cover in sight, leaving the open holes resembling geysers, spouting water twenty feet high. But as the shocked tenants watched, the height of the geysers became shorter and shorter. The pressure eventually equalized, and the water settled down to merely gurgling and bubbling up. Slowly it began to fill the street, inching toward the curbs on both sides.

"Oh Will…I've never seen such a…" Lilly murmured, clutching her husband's arm as they stared at the spectacle.

"Nor I," Willis murmured, moving his arm to encircle his wife. Although the city had suffered a major flood in 1884, neither Willis nor his wife had been around to experience it. The truth being that Lilly had been born and raised in Bourbon County, while Willis had hailed from Wisconsin. They were both, to coin a phrase, in 'uncharted waters.'

Billy was the only one in the doorway enjoying the spectacle. "Oh boy, that was neat! I hope they do it again!" he gushed, prompting the others in the large foyer to glance at the little boy and shake their heads.

After a few minutes, Lilly turned her gaze from the menace in the street up to her husband's face.

"Will…what should we *do*?"

Glancing at the others, who were nervously dashing in and out of their apartments – not a soul knowing what their next course of action should be – Willis tried to be calm and reassuring for his family.

"I think we should just try to go about our day, Lil. The water'll probably fill the street and then stop until the sewer pumps can drain it away." Then leaning to press a kiss to her cheek, he added, "Don't worry."

Turning, he smiled at the rest of his family. "Come on," he encouraged as he reached both hands out to usher them back down the hall.

"Aww Dad!" "Do we hafta?" "What about the water in the street?" they responded simultaneously, even as they obeyed.

"Never mind, just do as I say," Willis ordered gently.

"You think I should go on to work?" Edna asked with a frown, referring to her job at Fleischman's Delicatessen at Sixth and York.

"I think we should carry on with our lives the best we can until...well, until *whatever*," her father answered. Giving her a little nudge on the back with his large hand, he encouraged, "Go on, honey. Get dressed."

The family did as he bid, eating a quick breakfast and going their separate ways. Leaving the house at the same time, Edna turned east while Sonny, Louise, and Billy headed west. Each one stared apprehensively at the slowly creeping water in the street, which by then was about six feet from the curbs on either side.

ꙮ

VIC AWOKE TO the now familiar splash of water falling down the drainpipe outside the wall of the apartment. He turned onto his back and yawned.

Observing a fast moving cockroach skittering past his pallet on the living room floor, he moved quickly and smashed it with a shoe, muttering a curse of disgust for the revolting creatures.

Sitting up, he stretched the kinks out of his back with a grimace, then stood and padded to the bathroom to attend to his morning business. After a few minutes, he could hear the muffled sounds of the others in the apartment as they began to stir. Finishing quickly, knowing there would soon be a line waiting outside the door, Vic hastened his shave.

At the sound of an alarmed shriek from somewhere on the building's first floor, he jerked the blade, lightly nicking the skin along his square jaw.

Everyone emerged from their apartments, including the Matthews family, and converged downstairs in the foyer. The group gawked, laughed, and squealed excitedly about the sewer 'geysers' in the street.

Realizing this did not bode well for the city, Vic scowled at the jokesters and made his way quickly back upstairs. He knew his friends, Earl and Alec, both lived with their families in first story residences on flatter ground, and he wondered how they were faring – and if the sewer 'volcanoes' had erupted on their streets as well. Having been such close friends since grade school, he knew Alec's widowed mother frightened easily. Earl's mother and father had many times made him feel like family, and the three young men were like brothers. Worried, he hurried to finish dressing and go over to see if they needed a hand. Jack, Liz, and the kids would be all right, he reasoned, since their apartment was on the second floor…

Ten minutes later, with the encroaching inundation covering the sidewalk at least an inch, Vic took off sloshing through the frigid water to Earl's house three blocks west. When he arrived at 16th and Cedar and turned the corner, he grimaced to see the flooding even deeper there than back at the apartment. It was already lapping at the stoop leading into the Grant's home, which was a one floor, wood frame, shotgun style house. The old black hearse was nowhere in sight.

Wading to the door, Vic could hear Earl's mother fretting over the situation. He knocked quickly, letting himself in before they could answer.

"Oh Vic!" Mrs. Grant gasped upon seeing him, her long dark hair still mussed from sleep. She was a tall, big-boned woman with a loud voice and an easy laugh on most days. Now, her arms were full of what appeared to be clothing and linens. Her wide set green eyes, which both of her children had inherited, were fraught with the beginnings of panic. "I'm so glad you're here! Help us get everything up off the floor!"

Vic glanced around at the chaos. Furniture and belongings were stacked willy-nilly in the front room. Earl's ten-year-old sister, Bernice, came rushing from the next room, her arms full of clothing and her favorite doll. Tears of fright welled in her large green eyes, spilling over and wetting her face. Earl paused in the act of placing cinder blocks under the legs of the couch, hoping it would be enough to keep the furniture out of any water that might find its way in. He didn't even want to contemplate the water rising any higher than that…

"Where's Frank?" Vic wondered aloud.

"He left last night to go check on Grandma. Guess the water rose too fast and he couldn't make it back."

With a nod and a hope that Earl's dad was not in harm's way, Vic immediately joined in the family's efforts. Lifting smaller pieces of furniture up onto larger items, the young men strove to leave as little as possible touching the linoleum covered wooden floor.

An hour later, with the Grant family's possessions stabilized as well as could be, and Earl's mother and sister awaiting news from Mr. Grant, the two friends headed over to Alec's family's abode. On the way, sloshing through four inches of water as the sky continued to drizzle rain; they cut through the road dissecting the Western Cemetery on Cedar Street.

Tall, majestic cedar trees, the reason for the naming of the street and the city's oldest yet smallest cemetery, surreally appeared as if they were rooted in water. Viewing tombstones partially submerged, the two exchanged glances and grimaced. Vic, with a shudder of foreboding, realized the Alder home was situated in a low area. Mentioning this fact to his friend, the two stepped up their pace.

Turning the corner at 17th and Market, they stopped in their tracks as the enormity of the situation met them head on. This area was already under at least a foot of cold, murky river water. Three houses down from the corner, they could see a rowboat at the Alder house. Alec was struggling to help his panicked mother step from their front stoop into the unsteady craft, her arms full of as many possessions as she could carry. Losing her balance in that instant, she dropped the armload into the muddy water with a frightened squeal.

Seeing this spurred the two young men into action, and they rushed to aid their friends. With difficulty, they gathered the now sodden sacks of clothing and household goods, and placed them in the boat. Alec's two older sisters were already aboard, huddling under a large black umbrella. Though shivering from the damp cold, both of the young women seemed dazed, as if they couldn't quite believe what was happening.

"Where you gonna go?" Earl inquired as the girls numbly reached to comfort their weeping mother and Alec sat down to take up the oars.

Alec flashed his friends a twinkling glance, smirking lightheartedly, "Higher ground!" as he placed the oars into the water. Always brimming with confidence and bravado, he was nevertheless scared witless. The fact that his mother and sisters relied upon him, as the only male in the family, weighed heavily upon his shoulders. He couldn't let them see the cracks in his characteristically jaunty shell, as he knew that would frighten them even more.

Just then, two men in a small, shallow-keeled boat paddled over to their location. The men, wearing policeman's caps and rubber rain gear over their uniforms, leaned toward the group.

"I'm Officer Kelly," one of them spoke up. "This' my partner, Officer Richards. You folks okay?"

At their nod, the policeman trained his eyes on Earl and Vic, who were still standing on the shallow stoop of the house. Without mincing words, he stated, "Fellas, we got us an all out emergency here. The Red Cross is callin' for boats. We need manpower. Lots of it. There's folks gonna be stranded all over this city before nightfall."

The enormity of the situation hit Earl in the gut, and he stammered, "I…I oughtta get back to my mom and sister…my Dad…he went to Oldham County last night to check on my Grandma…he ain't back yet…"

Vic glanced at his friend and then met Alec's eyes. "You guys need me…?"

Alec answered with his customary flash of white teeth. "Nah, go on. I got this covered. We'll float Junior here on back home," he added as he motioned for Earl to climb in.

Turning back to the men in the boat, Vic offered with a shrug, "Count me in."

Officer Kelly, with a relieved nod, motioned toward the back of the small craft. "Climb aboard."

Vic waded to the back of the boat and hoisted himself in. As Officer Richards pushed off against the side of the house, and began paddling down the street, Vic turned and watched Alec skillfully maneuver his craft toward the opposite direction. Earl turned his head, and the two long-time friends lifted a hand in farewell.

For a moment, Vic was torn as he wondered if he had made the right choice. An empty feeling settled in the pit of his stomach. As his boat turned the corner and continued on, Vic faced forward, his gaze focusing on evidence of the magnitude of the encroaching disaster. The street headed downhill and Vic watched in awe as the boat smoothly glided past a street sign, rising just four feet above the water line.

Somehow he knew the 'adventure' on which he was about to embark would be hugely instrumental in changing the course of his life. The only thing was…would it be change for the good…or for the bad?

ഇരു

AS THE DAY progressed, WHAS interspersed bits of music between 'flood' reports of street closings and gauge levels, as the unstoppable river continued to rise.

Nervous schoolteachers, tense bus and trolley drivers, worried business owners, and the general public, wondered deep down if this time around…*this* flood, would be different. An ominous portent of gloom seemed to be hanging above the city, hiding within the ever present, thick dark rain clouds.

Although they had heard of flooding in other river towns up and down the Ohio, the thoughts on everyone's minds were, "It can't happen *here*. Not *that* bad." Nevertheless, many people, the Hoskins family included, heeded the Health Department's suggestion to fill their bathtub with fresh water…just in case the pumps at the pumping station shut down.

By noon, Mayor Neville Miller issued the order that all schools be closed early, much to the delight of the youngsters, including Billy Hoskins. A typical kid, any time he could get out of doing a little schoolwork, he jumped at the chance.

Donning their rain gear and traversing the route from three different schools, the Hoskins siblings met at the corner of Second and Chestnut. They couldn't believe the depth of the water – it was now up over the curbs and sidewalks.

"Oh my gosh! Look at the water!" Louise gasped as she looked up at Sonny through the drizzling rain, shifting her umbrella to try and also cover their little brother.

Sonny placed his hands on his hips, looking first at the water, then around toward downtown, clearly pondering a decision. Finally, he murmured something unintelligible and set off in the direction opposite from home.

"Where you goin'?" Louise hollered after him.

"Tell 'em I'll be home later," he tossed over his shoulder as he took off in a trot toward downtown, his footfalls splashing with each step.

"But…*Sonny*!" Louise squealed, taking a step toward him, one hand outstretched.

"Just do it!" he hollered as he disappeared around a corner.

Billy glanced up eagerly at his sister, already beginning to move out from the protection of the umbrella as he offered, "I'll go see where he's goin'!"

"Oh no, you won't," she returned with a stern glare as she reached out to clamp a hand on his arm and keep him still.

Not wishing to get any wetter, Louise shook her head in exasperation and tugged at Billy's wet jacket.

"Come on, we better get home."

Splashing through the water on the sidewalk, the two made it to the four steps on the slight hill in front of their building. They hurried up to the front walk and then up four more steps to the covered door. Louise glanced at the houses across the street, aghast that the water was now up to the second steps of the stoops, as the land was much flatter there. A shiver ran through her as she quickly opened the door and practically pushed her brother inside.

Reaching their open apartment door, they each hesitated as they saw their parents and sister moving furniture and raising items off the floor.

"Where's your brother?" Lilly barked as they came on inside, not surprised to see them so early due to having heard on the radio that all the schools were closing at noon.

"He said he'd be home later."

"Oh that boy! Where did he *go*?" she asked in frustration.

Louise gazed at her mother, who normally made sure every hair was neatly in place, her clothing well groomed, and wearing a modest array of jewelry. Louise almost hadn't recognized the woman standing before her, as her hair and clothes were disheveled, and no jewelry could be seen, save her wedding band. Although her mother was customarily high strung and did not handle stress well, she had never seen her quite so bad.

Louise and Billy both shrugged. "I dunno, Mama." "He wouldn't say."

"He'll be home soon," Willis assured his wife, handing Louise and Billy large cloth sacks with orders to help pack.

"What's goin' on?" Billy asked as the magnitude of the situation began to sink in. This 'flood' business of exploding manhole covers and school closings was suddenly not so much fun anymore.

"We're getting ready…just in case the worst happens and the water gets this high," Willis patiently explained as he looked around, trying to decide how to protect his large easy chair from the creeping menace.

"But…where would we go if the water comes in?" Louise asked, her fear and uncertainty ramping up a few notches.

"Upstairs with the Anderson's. They said we could stay in their apartment until things get back to normal."

"But I don't wanna stay up there…" Billy began to whine, but his mother cut him off.

"Willis Junior, you just do what you're told!" she hollered with more aggression than needed, her arms full of sheets and towels.

In the act of helping her sister place chairs up on the dining table, Louise looked nervously over at their father as he paused to take his harried wife in his arms.

Unnerved, the others went about their tasks. The soft strumming of a guitar on the radio, and Bing Crosby's smooth crooning baritone warbling, "South Sea Island Magic," went along quite well with the sound of the rain outside. But for once, the amusing choice the deejay Foster Brooks had made had no calming effect on the frantic atmosphere inside.

Moments later, the WHAS news announcer broke into the song to make a report concerning yet another street closing, and mandatory evacuation for the residents and businesses there.

Stopping in her tracks, Louise fixed her eyes on her father. Softly she asked, voicing the question that had been on each of their minds since the eerie sight of the sewer geysers that morning, "Daddy…will we have to evacuate?"

Her father cast her a look and shook his head. Then, he glanced at the others in the room who had stopped their activities to stare at him and await his words of wisdom.

"I don't think so, honey. I'm sure the water won't get this high."

Although Willis had made his statement as though it were fact, in truth, he was plenty worried. In all his sixty-four years, he had never seen a weather system like the one they had experienced since the first of the year. Willis was afraid he would be proven wrong in the eyes of his children and wife – the people who looked to him to be the soul of knowledge.

He would have been even more afraid had he known just how wrong his statement would prove to be.

ꙮ

CHAPTER 6

B-13 and The Rescue

"THERE. HOPEFULLY THAT'LL slow it down," Willis murmured as he climbed to his feet from stuffing rags under the back door of the apartment house's common hallway. At the rate the water level was raising, he knew it wouldn't be long before it found its way under either the front door or the back.

The others stretched around one another to gaze out the door's window at the turbid water, now lapping up against the stoop. It was an eerie sight, as the unstoppable progression now covered the ground as far as they could see. Houses seemed to be floating, vaguely resembling pictures they had seen of the city of Venice, Italy – only much less grand. It was as if they were looking out the door of a houseboat.

Edna opened her mouth to make a wry comment, but at that moment loud, forlorn weeping was heard from a neighboring building. With the doors and windows shut, it was hard to make out the direction, which only added to the feeling of hopelessness.

Billy suddenly shouted from his 'post' at the front window in the foyer, "There's a boat goin' down the street!"

The residents of apartments one and three came out of their doors, arms full of personal items they had been moving up off of the floors, as everyone hurried to view the sight. A boat? Going down their street? Unreal…it all felt so surreal, this couldn't be happening!

At that moment, the music on the radio in apartment number three was once again interrupted. This time the announcer's voice was fraught with tension as he urgently began, "This is WHAS, owned and operated by the Louisville Courier Journal and the Louisville Times. The time is exactly 3:15 pm. We have been asked to broadcast the following announcement: *Warning to all river lowland dwellers. Already above flood stage, the river is expected to go at least two feet higher by morning. If your home is anywhere near the rising water, make plans to leave it at once*!"

"Two feet higher! Oh Will! Our Sonny! He's out there somewhere!" Lilly exclaimed, bursting into tears.

Willis took her in his arms, doing his best to soothe her. "Sshhh, honey. He'll be all right. He's a smart young man. He knows how to take care of himself." He hugged her tightly. "Don't you worry, now Lilly. Hush now…" he added, one large hand cradling his wife's head to his breast, his fingers gently patting and smoothing her hair across her forehead.

Sniffling against her husband's chest, Lilly removed a hanky from the pocket of her apron and dabbed at her nose as she murmured, "I know…I just can't stand it if I don't know where one of the children are…"

Edna, in a rare moment of family camaraderie, offered, "Aw, don't worry Mama. I bet Sonny's down at the Courier building right now, trying to sell the morning paper with front-page pictures about the flood. Once he gets done, I bet he'll hitch a ride on a boat if he has to, and come on home, his pockets full of money…"

"Yeah," Louise agreed, reassuringly taking her mother's hand in hers as Lilly used her other to wipe her eyes. "You know how he is…he don't wanna miss a good opportunity to make a sale. Right Daddy?" she added with a trembling smile.

"Right as rain, Sweet Pea. That Sonny Boy, he'll be walking in that door real soon, with his pockets jinglin' and whistlin', 'We're in the Money', just like he always does," Willis agreed, sending his daughters a wink at his pun and a grateful smile as he felt his wife relax a bit.

He just hoped they were right…but he had a feeling, somewhere deep down, that much time would pass before they would see their 'Sonny Boy' again.

ཀྵ

THE HOURS STRETCHED on as Vic, and several other volunteers, labored to save stranded citizens from their quickly flooding homes. They had also been instrumental in rescuing people in downtown Louisville; employees had gone to work that morning without a clue regarding the imminent danger, only to emerge from their jobs to find the streets shin deep in water. 'Rush hour' was a crazy experience of people yelling, crying, and wailing – or laughing and joking – as they tried to make their way home. Buses, of course, were unable to make their runs. Cars flooded out. Only high axle trucks could make it through.

Vic had joined a group of men in a larger boat with a motor, and had participated in one rescue after another. The policemen that had recruited him had been right; by late afternoon there were so many people stranded and yelling for help, it was impossible for the boats to keep up. City police, fire, and rescue crews were soon stretched to their absolute limits. Word had passed down that the mayor had been busy calling all around for help, and the Coast Guard was on its way.

Slumping down on the seat in the boat after helping a some what heavyset woman on board, Vic shook his head in wonder. How quickly everything had changed since that morning with the gushing sewers!

The young man looked over to another boat motoring past them, a large Red Cross logo hastily painted on its side. With a tired smile, Vic acknowledged that the mayor had done his work well, having coordinated with the efficient relief agency regarding detailed plans. If a rescued citizen had nowhere else to go, boatmen had been instructed to transport them to the old Armory at Sixth and Walnut. Utilizing the radio tuned to WHAS, they responded to call after call of, "Send a Boat…"

Many temporary rescue stations had been hastily placed to dispatch or receive boats near the water's ever-expanding edge, each one given alphabetical and numerical designations. Vic had been assigned to the B-13 station, located at the O.K. Storage Warehouse at Broadway and Barrett, which afforded an immediate uphill route to safety.

As his boat motored up to the building, Vic gazed at its seven-story limestone and brick façade. Wrought iron bars covered the lower windows and decorative moldings graced the doorway. Lights from inside beckoned warmth and relaxation to the rescuers, but what caught his eye at that moment were the large block letters spanning thirty feet across and four feet high. The crisp light from their bright red bulbs beamed in the gloom, 'O K STORAGE'. Somehow it seemed so strong and permanent in the midst of what had become an unstable, quickly changing world.

Once at the base camp, as he assisted yet another family of refugees from the boat, the wife gave Vic a quick hug. She thanked him for his instant reflexes and fast thinking in saving her rambunctious four-year-old from tumbling into the dirty, chilly water. Pleased and humbled, he nodded his thanks and shuffled his way into the building with his fellow rescuers as the woman's gracious words warmed his heart. It felt mighty good to be appreciated… Indeed, for Vic, it almost made up for the fact that at the moment he couldn't even feel his cold, waterlogged feet. He hoped for a brief respite and perhaps a few minutes to thaw out.

Glancing around at the seemingly impenetrable eighteen-inch thick walls of the large warehouse's main floor, he took comfort from their solid strength. Twenty feet up, sixteen by twelve inch raw wooden beams supported the second floor. The brick walls were strewn with dusty wires running to the lights, with bare bulbs hanging from the upper beams. Vic took in a deep breath, thankful that the delicious aroma of fresh brewed coffee overpowered the damp musty air inside the structure.

"Oh good," greeted the station's commander, Harold C. "Doc" Latham. He was a large, charismatic, hip-booted, raincoat wearing man, with a shock of red hair and a booming voice. "Bob – headquarters just radioed that they need your boat to transfer some supplies from City Hall to the relief center," he informed the captain of Vic's crew, Bob Gibson. "Said they need you A.S.A.P."

"Ahh dang it. No rest for the weary," Bob grumbled, albeit good-naturedly. He grabbed a sandwich off a tray and made an about-face, signaling to one of the men to accompany him. The two returned to the large craft Bob had left tied to the corner of the building and started up the motor again, quickly reversing and speeding off on their mission.

Vic and the remaining man from his crew – a tall and lanky, affable fellow by the name of Gerald – sat down on some chairs and began gulping down sandwiches and hot coffee provided by volunteers from a nearby church. One such volunteer – a sweet looking little lady wearing a kitchen apron over a dark blue sweater and skirt, her gray hair in a neat bun – introduced herself as Irene Waller. She hovered close, fussing over the two young men as if they were her children. Vic gave her a weary smile, his heart drawn by the gentle matronly attention.

Vic stared tiredly at the worn wooden floor beneath his feet, absently noting the scars and marks from many a wheeled cart hauling miscellaneous freight around inside. As he chewed on a sandwich, his gaze slowly lifted and he scanned the interior, including the small office area against the left side. Its walls only rose about eight feet into the expanse. He smirked as he took another bite, remembering when he had sat inside the small cubicle and filled out an employment application. *Man, that seems like another lifetime…but what was it…a month ago?*

After just a few minutes, the radio across the large room crackled with another distress call for a boat. With no other team available, Doc Latham cast an apologetic look their way.

"Better take this, night's approaching fast," Doc offered as he handed Vic an oil lantern.

Cramming the last of their sandwiches in their mouths and gulping down the rest of their coffee, Vic and Gerald grabbed some supplies from piles by the door.

Once outside, Vic fastened the lantern to a pole sticking out six feet from the bow of a small craft sporting an aged outboard motor. *At least we won't have to paddle,* he observed with a grateful sigh.

As they jumped into the vessel and headed out again into the still drizzling rain, the evening sky was just beginning to dim.

ℵℶ

"WELL, THERE'S NO stopping it now," Willis murmured as he stood from trying to stop the flow of water determinedly finding its way in under the back door of the apartment house. Mrs. Higgins stalked away down the hall to her door. Cursing under her breath about the coming damage to her property, the inconvenience of it all, and the situation in general – her tirade muffled slightly as she crossed her own threshold. The only one in the building with enough money to afford a telephone, Mrs. Higgins picked up the receiver and grudgingly asked the operator to connect her to WHAS, joining the throng of other citizens with the plea of, "Please, send a boat to…"

Though the residents of the two large apartments on the top floors of the structure were determined to tough it out, the first floor occupants had held out as long as they could. Two had already vacated the marooned building and headed uptown to stay with friends. The Andersons had been inundated with family and had callously rescinded their offer of hospitality to the Hoskins, which left Mrs. Higgins and the Hoskins family to fend for themselves.

"Come on then, let's grab what we can and go…" Willis began as he headed into the apartment.

"But how? Where?" Lilly fussed, her hands shaking as she slipped into her green woolen coat. "And what about Sonny! He'll come home and find us gone!"

"Can't be helped, Lil. We have to do what is best for the other children," Willis reminded his wife, the burden of responsibility for the family weighing heavily on his shoulders.

"Daddy! Another boat's comin'!" Billy yelled suddenly from the window in the foyer where he had stationed himself hours before to watch the comings and goings of the other residents on the street.

"Flag it down, son!" Willis returned, ushering the women out and securely locking the apartment door before making his way quickly down the hall. This last act was done partly out of habit, and partly out of a desire to at least slow down any looters that might aim their thieving sights on their building.

The boy struggled to lift the heavy wooden window and support it with the prop stick. "Hey! Hey, over here!" he yelled, waving his arm energetically.

The others hurried to the window, relieved to see the dim light of a rescue boat and hear the smooth thrup-thrup-thrup of its engine as it maneuvered up to the completely submerged front stoop. Its movement caused waves to lap at the sandbags that had been stacked at the base of the door to try and prevent the inevitable.

With the help of the porch and interior lights, plus the light from the lantern, the boat's honorary captain reached out to grasp the window's ledge and steady the craft against the brick wall. "Okay folks, one at a time, ladies first. Take care not to fall in the water," he advised as he reached a hand upward. "Sorry, but only one bag of belongings each," he added as he saw the myriad of bags and household goods stacked by the window.

Mrs. Higgins elbowed her way forward, practically shoving Lilly out of the way. Lilly gasped at the rudeness and stumbled a step backward, but Willis caught her against his chest, biting back a retort to the rude woman. Ingrained manners were all that stopped him from returning a scathing rebuke. Their landlady impatiently reached to grasp the boatman's outstretched hand.

Quickly, Willis and Lilly had to make the decision of what to leave and what to take of their packed necessities.

One by one, Mrs. Higgins, Lilly, and then Edna, were lifted into the vessel. Finally, Louise sat down on the windowsill, swinging her legs out as the man stepped forward again and lifted his hands.

Taking the bag of possessions from her grip, he deposited it into the boat, and then easily lifted her from her perch as she slid down his body.

The soft light of the lantern cast a hazy glow on their faces. In spite of the cold wet breeze, they both felt hot sparks of attraction as they recognized one another. A strange phenomenon occurred – as if they were holding onto the ends of bare telephone wires – each seemed to feel tiny shocks reverberating from fingertip to core.

Louise's heart surged as she realized their rescuer was none other than the man who had occupied her dreams and thoughts since that dark, rainy night two weeks before. Her eyes grew large in the shadowy setting as she gasped in recognition. Instantly, she was aware of a myriad of sensations…the strength in his hands and arms as he held her… the firm muscles bracing her body…the cold damp leather of his jacket under her hands as she held tight to his shoulders…even the pleasant musky tang of coffee on his breath from his hastily consumed supper, which ignited her own hunger…

As he held her suspended against his chest and hips, Vic realized the instant the lantern illuminated the girl's features that he was actually in the act of rescuing the young woman who had captured his imagination and haunted his dreams. All day he had wondered how she and her family were faring, and more than once had nearly steered the boat past the house, only to be rerouted to another rescue. Now as dusk had settled in and they were on their way to another address, Vic hadn't even realized they had motored down her street. To suddenly find her in his arms…he was shocked. Usually his luck didn't run that good.

Tiny droplets of rainy mist dotted their lashes, sparkling in the light like diamond dust. Hazel eyes stared, unblinking, into a potent maple brown gaze. Words were not necessary, nor would they come, each one too caught up in the total surprise of the occurrence. Time seemed to shift down to slow motion, like one of those old Kinetoscope hand crank movie machines at the fair.

Then, as quickly as it had happened, the moment was over.

Vic, recovering his poise with a jolt, swiveled in place and deposited Louise on one of the boat's benches. With a half grin and a small nod in acknowledgment of her startled expression, he turned back to grasp Billy and heft him into the boat as well, but the boy had scrambled down on his own. Lastly, Willis managed to climb down out of the window frame by himself. Vic gave the two an awkward smile as he turned back, his eyes irresistibly seeking Louise.

"You folks got somewhere to go? Family on higher ground?" asked Gerald from the back of the boat, grasping the rudder handle of the outboard motor in preparation of turning it where they needed.

"No, sir, we do not. At this point, we are not sure what to do or where to go." Willis answered as he settled on a bench next to his wife.

"Alright, well, don't worry. They got everything set up down at the Arm'ry for folks. Just sit tight. We'll have ya there in a few minutes."

"My family and I are much obliged," Willis wearily returned.

As Gerald prepared to turn the boat toward Sixth & Walnut in order to transport the displaced family to the armory, Vic reached under a tarp to grasp a supply of dry blankets. He hurriedly passed a few around to be shared by the family members. Saving Louise for last, he braced his feet on the floorboard of the boat as it turned east.

Louise looked up at his face, shadowed by the lantern behind him, and offered a shy smile. She leaned forward, allowing him to place the blanket around her shoulders as she murmured a soft, "Thank you." His reply was a short nod.

She was intensely conscious of the warmth exuding from his body just inches from hers, despite their cold surroundings. Conversely, he was acutely aware of the fresh scent of a lock of her hair peeking out from her hastily tied blue scarf.

He cleared his throat and made his way to his customary seat in the bow, watching for hidden obstructions in the water on the six-block ride.

As the boat glided through the dark water and navigated the streets-turned-canals, Vic often turned his head back toward the passengers. Time and again he found himself staring at the young woman as she huddled with her incessantly chattering younger brother.

Silently, Vic questioned why he had the compelling urge to go to her…to wrap his arms around her. But, of course, he didn't. He merely observed her shivering under the rough woolen blanket, and occasionally casting furtive glances his way.

What were the odds that *he* was on the boat that rescued *her* family?

Maybe my luck's about to change…

ꕤ

LOUISE CLUTCHED HER bag of belongings to her chest as she stood with her family before the sign-in table at the Jefferson County Armory Flood Relief Center. The massive stone and brick structure was serving as a temporary holding station until the people could be transported out of harm's way by train or truck.

As Willis gave the relief worker their information, the others glanced around with surprise at how many people were already there. Indeed, no time had been squandered or wasted. The Red Cross had been Johnny on the Spot, making plans and arrangements for speedy, effective help for the citizens even before the water had reached the flood mark. Boxes of supplies, blankets, food rations, and more were ready for distribution. Cots were spread out in neat rows, and people were huddling in small family groups. Several people were sitting alone on makeshift beds, staring straight ahead as if in shock.

The Hoskins had no idea how long they would be out of their home, and needless to say, the thought was not a pleasant one.

One thought was pleasant, however. Louise still couldn't get over the fact that Vic Matthews had come to their rescue. Impressions of those moments in his arms, as well as sitting within his line of vision in the boat, with his dark, hooded eyes staring penetratingly her way, kept swirling in her head until she felt practically giddy. *It was like a rescue straight out of a movie at the Rialto*...she mused with a dreamy smile.

Then the boat had arrived safely at the armory, and Vic had bid them a polite goodbye and good luck, though he had lingered the longest in saying farewell to Louise. How she had wanted to ask him...oh anything! Where he lived...if there was a possibility they would see one another again...but she hadn't. She had just clammed up and couldn't say a word, other than managing a small smile as he had murmured a last quiet, "G'bye." She could only watch as he had climbed back in the boat and set off to look for more stranded citizens.

"Here, Louise, pay attention," her mother's voice interrupted her thoughts. With a start, Louise realized the family had already been assigned places to sleep for the night, and were making their way into the larger, domed area of the building. People were milling around, trying their best to get comfortable, although in the forefront of everyone's mind, lurked the question of whether the water would reach even there. The thought of their homes and possessions being at the mercy of the encroaching muddy water, and the possibility of thievery by looters, would keep many of them awake long hours into the night.

ꙮ

VIC AND GERALD completed three more rescues before they were forced, by sheer exhaustion, to call it a night. These included an elderly, bed-ridden man and his thick-furred dog that had smelled none too good after it had jumped in the water. Vic had been forced to retrieve the poor animal and haul it into the boat.

After depositing them at the Armory, another rescue crew mentioned they'd been forced to pass by the plight of two middle-aged women who shared an apartment deep in the west end of town. Vic and Gerald immediately headed to the location. Unable to maneuver the boat past a wrought iron fence, Vic was obliged to wade waist deep into the frigid, muddy water. Doing his best to quiet their frightened weeping, he transported each one out to the awaiting boat, along with their two heavy bags of belongings.

By the time they made their way back to the base camp on Baxter, Vic had been 'on duty' a continuous twelve hours. For the last few hours, he'd been running on adrenalin and determination, and now both of those stores were down to the dregs. His skin, indeed his entire being, felt numb from hours out in the elements; he was wet and cold, and his nose had begun running like a sugar tree.

Gerald stopped by the food table for a late snack, but Vic –

although he was, in fact, quite hungry – decided to forego a hot meal, and dragged himself over to the freight elevator.

Exhaustion weighing down every bone in his body, he made his way inside. In a fog he accidentally pulled the lever inside the box first, before closing door, and had to rush to slide it shut as the lift began its climb. His hand numb from the cold, he reached for the strap hanging high in the center of the doorway and tugged hard. The heavy plank horizontal doors appeared and clanged together in the middle. As the antiquated pulleys and cords squealed their aggravation, the rattletrap box shimmed as it slowly rose up one flight to the next level.

Vic rested his forehead against a worn and splintered plank. With his eyes shut he allowed the slight imbalance in his stomach to quell the sudden spook he'd given his heart. Opening his eyes again when he felt the conveyance jostling at floor level, he righted his weary body and hurriedly pulled the lever. The lift stopped a foot higher than floor height, but too tired to adjust it, he pulled the strap to open the doors once more and stepped up over the high threshold.

Squinting in the dim light from the elevator, and with the faint light of a street lamp shining in through one of the large windows, he began to thread his way through rows of crates and boxes to the back section. This had been set up with bunks and pallets for the exhausted rescuers, many of whom where already occupying the space.

Quietly finding an empty cot, Vic wearily pulled off his shoes and socks, stripped down to his still damp undershirt and skivvies, and crawled under several layers of woolen army blankets. Normally this would not have been especially comfortable, but compared to the accommodations he was accustomed to at his brother's home, it was actually more so.

With an exhausted sigh, Vic gratefully closed his eyes.

Renewed dreams and visions of dark hair, creamy skin, and bewitching hazel eyes were his companions for the night.

CHAPTER 7

The Shots and Dove Creek

"NO!!" BILLY SQUEALED, twisting and turning as he attempted to loosen the grip of the hands that held him fast. A Red Cross nurse huffed an impatient sigh as she held a large hypodermic needle aloft. Several other refugees waiting in line for the shots grimaced at Billy's outburst, wishing he would just shut up and get it over with.

"It's alright, son," Willis comforted as he tried to still his frightened offspring. "It'll be over before you know it. This is a necessary precaution against typhoid and…"

"No! I hate needles!" Billy interrupted as he violently writhed to and fro. Suddenly, he broke free and took off running, dodging people, bags of belongings, dogs, cats, and birdcages, as he headed for the outer doors – and freedom.

"Billy!" Louise squealed, taking off after him as their father followed.

"Oh that boy!" Lilly fumed, wrapping her arms across her chest. She exchanged glances with Edna, who only rolled her eyes and shook her head in disgust as she popped her chewing gum, before returning to browsing a borrowed copy of Hollywood Stars Magazine.

Billy burst through the doors and emerged outside. He ran only a few steps before colliding rather solidly with the sturdy chest of a man. Strong, muscular arms immediately encircled the boy as a voice soothed, “Hey, hey! Hold on there…”

“Lemme go!” Billy hollered just as Louise burst through the door of the building in pursuit.

“Oh please, sir! Don’t let him go!” she called to the lowered, cap-covered head of the unknown man. Louise could see he was tall and muscular, and she was glad he had been at the right place to intercept her fleeing brother. Unconsciously, her eyes registered the thick fabric of his pants and the bulky warmth of his coat, and she knew instantly he must be one of the rescuers. At the sound of her voice, the head came up, the eyes connecting with hers…familiar maple brown eyes…

A wry smile graced Vic’s face as he watched her hurry forward…the very girl he had hoped to ‘accidentally’ run into again. “What’s he done?” he called to her jovially.

Reaching them, Willis not far behind, Louise smiled shyly and reached out to grab hold of Billy’s arm as he wriggled and fought. “He don’t wanna take the shots.”

Having just submitted to the ordeal himself back at the base, Vic could certainly sympathize. Nodding and glancing down at the boy’s frightened, tear moistened face, he grinned engagingly and immediately hunkered down to his level – though wisely not releasing his hold.

“Aww now, little buddy…there’s nothin’ to it. Really. Matter ‘a fact, I just had ‘em myself,” he confided, as if they had no audience. Louise immediately felt a tingle rush through her at the sound of that smooth, warm baritone voice.

Billy sniffled and turned his head, raising a shoulder to wipe his nose. “Really, mister?”

“Yep.” Then glancing up at Louise and Willis, he leaned his head closer to Billy’s and confided in a pseudo whisper, “Tell ya what I do when I hav’ta take shots…”

Drawing in a trembling breath, Billy whispered, “…What’s that?”

Vic grinned, his straight white teeth gleaming under the bill of his cap. However, intent on comforting the boy, he was totally unaware of the effect he was having on his female observer. "I jus' close my eyes, grit my teeth, and hold my breath. It's over before I know it." Totally void of deceit, Vic's eyes met those of the young boy. He watched as the youngster visibly relaxed, believing he now knew a way to at least survive the coming ordeal.

Willis stepped forward then, gently taking charge of his son. As Vic rose to his full height, the older, slightly shorter man nodded and smiled gratefully. With an answering nod, Vic smiled back.

"Come on, son," Willis encouraged, turning back toward the building. He draped his arm around Billy's shoulders as the boy now willingly acquiesced, though trembling and wiping his eyes on his sleeve. Willis bent his head a bit, murmuring words of comfort and encouragement to add to those Vic had offered.

Louise paused, glancing at Vic. Finding him gazing back at her with unabashed interest, her knees threatened to give way. *Oh my lord, he's just so…* she couldn't find the appropriate word, for *handsome* could not even begin to do him justice; what with his smooth chiseled features, the dimple in his cheek, and especially those magnificent eyes. Louise felt as if she had no choice in being irresistibly drawn to him. His eyes seemed to capture and hold her spellbound.

Smiling shyly, Louise forged ahead in an attempt to try and have a conversation with the man before he would once again be whisked from her life. Wetting lips suddenly dry from nerves, she murmured, "Thanks. Billy can be a handful sometimes."

Vic grinned and nodded. "Aww, he's alright. Reminds me 'a my nephew. And heck, nobody likes havin' ta get shots. But I sure wasn't gonna tell him my arm hurts like I been kicked by a mule," he added, chuckling as he gingerly rubbed the muscle of his right arm.

Louise laughed at his description, and the sound of her happy giggle seemed to permeate Vic's entire being. To him, it was as if she was so full of happiness and the joys of life that she wished to spread them around and sweep everyone along with her for the ride. *Am I crazy or somethin'?* he mused in wonder.

The two stood together awkwardly, each one feeling that undeniable pull of their attraction, and reliving a bit of the sparks they had felt during that moment of recognition the previous night on the boat. Indeed, each wondered if the other were feeling the phenomenon, but then dismissed the notion as unlikely. As the moment stretched on in silence, they both became a tad uncomfortable and each strove to think of something to keep the conversation going. She was hoping he couldn't hear her heart pounding. He was thinking she was even more beautiful than he remembered.

Finally, Vic spouted, "Your name's Louise…right?" at the same time that she stammered, "D…did you bring more people…?" They immediately chuckled together, making note of the other's obvious shyness.

"You go ahead," she offered, drawing her light blue sweater tighter around her chest as a gust of damp wind blew strands of her hair across her face. In spite of the havoc the rain and flood had made of their surroundings, the air seemed somehow fresh and clean, although heavy with moisture. She was glad it had temporarily stopped raining – and was secretly thrilled that he had actually remembered her name.

"No, you…"

Smiling, she swept the strands behind one ear and shook her head as she cast her eyes downward, so he went ahead and answered her question. "Yeah, we caught a few hours of sleep, got up at the crack of dawn and been rescuin' people. Seems like nobody believed the water would get so high…nobody obeyed the order to evacuate before it did…"

At that, her eyes snapped up to meet his. Guiltily capturing her bottom lip between her teeth, she cringed. That was *exactly* what her family had done. He immediately realized his mistake and quickly put up a hand. "No offense…I didn't mean nothin'. The water rose so fast, hundreds of people got stranded at work…"

"That's okay…you're right…" she admitted, still feeling a trifle embarrassed in spite of his qualification. "My dad kept saying the water wouldn't get as high as it did…"

"And gettin' higher by the minute," he added with a grimace. Nodding toward the low side of the armory building, he intimated how much higher the waterline had risen since the night before.

Louise glanced that way, hunching her body as a shiver rifled through her. "My brother, Sonny…we don't know where he is…he took off for downtown after we all got out of school, and we haven't seen him since," she confided.

Vic's heart immediately went out to her, somehow absorbing some of her sadness. "Well, I can try to find out for ya…what's his name…what's he look like?"

She turned back, meeting his eyes in hopeful surprise. "His name is Joseph Hoskins. He's sixteen, and he's got sunshine blond hair. He sells newspapers…"

Warmed at her unique description of her brother, Vic felt ten feet tall from the look she was sending his way…as if he had suddenly become her knight in shining armor. With unwavering assurance, he promised, "Okay, I'll keep an eye out."

Louise wrapped her arms tighter around herself, glancing back at the door to the building. "Thank you…and thanks again for helping with my little brother…Mama and Daddy have enough to worry about…Mama's been goin' on and on about Sonny, plus she thinks looters are gonna break in and steal everything we've got since we had to leave behind…"

"Aww don't worry none about that," Vic interrupted. "I'll go by your place and keep an eye on it – and somebody said the National Guard is comin' to help out, too."

Shaking her head in amazement, Louise murmured, "It's all

like a bad dream…I can't believe the water…" She turned to glance again at the low side of the building, which truly resembled the large island mansions in Venice she had seen in newsreels at the movies. Louise had wished she could see them in person…but now, it didn't seem so glamorous…

"Yeah, me neither. I bet we rescued…"

At that moment, his boat mate, Gerald, called from the vessel, "C'mon Vic! Time's 'a wastin'!"

Vic swung his head around, waving an arm at his friend. "Yeah, yeah! Comin'!" he groused, catching the other men of the four-man crew chortling at him and ribbing one another. Downright blushing, he turned back to Louise again.

As their eyes met, she huffed a small giggle as he cleared his throat and rolled his eyes. Awkwardly, they softly chuckled and began slowly backing away from one another.

"Well, I…"

"I guess I…"

Then Vic flashed his most charming smile her way; unknowingly making her heart jerk and her pulse speed up even faster. "You better get on back in there and get your own shots…"

With a laugh that seemed like sweet tinkling music to his ears, she backed up some more before answering, "I don't have to – I took all those shots last summer so I could go camping." With that, she pivoted on her heel and with a happy skip to her step, hurried toward the door.

Vic watched her pause at the door and glance back at him with a tiny wave, before disappearing inside.

Adjusting his wool cap more securely on his head, he shoved his cold hands in the pockets of his leather jacket. Spinning around, he headed toward the waiting boat, his steps accompanied by a jaunty whistle.

Louise would have giggled if she had heard – he was whistling, *I've Got You Under My Skin.*

ഇ൴

THE RIVER HAD continued its steady, unrelenting rise all night. After just a few hours respite that morning, the rain started up again in earnest around 10 AM. By that afternoon, the flood seemed truly like the days of Noah, with nothing but unending rain in the forecast. The volunteers manning the rescue boats would not have been a bit surprised to know that in a mere forty-eight hours, six full inches of rain fell on the already water-logged area.

Vic and his crewmates stayed on the job all day. They scarcely took the time to eat or escape the wet for warmth, as it seemed the radio at the command post continually crackled with another request of, 'Send a boat to…' Despite the fact that he kept so busy, Vic still wondered about the lovely Louise and her family… Had the boy taken the shots? Had the family been evacuated? However, each time his boat dropped off another load of frazzled, shell-shocked refugees at the armory, he had no chance find out.

Later, the guys in the crews of station B-13 would be shocked to discover that they had made more rescues at the peak of the flooding than any other rescue station – a staggering 200 refugees transported every *hour*. Boats of every size had been commandeered by the city and the Red Cross; a staggering four hundred powerboats operated by 700 volunteers – a good many of them based out of B-13. Those stalwart men made unremitting excursions to the 'Venice' that Louisville had so quickly become.

Thanks to the expert leadership of Doc Latham, the pastor of the First Lutheran Church, B-13 station immediately became organized and efficient. He commanded with the swagger and confidence of a general, perhaps due to the fact that he held a pilot's license on the Great Lakes and a first mate's license on ocean-going ships. Doc was good at a great many things – including judging character and recognizing leadership ability.

These he saw in young Vic Matthews.

By the end of that marathon day, the 21st, Doc had realized that Matthews could be trusted to go the distance, no matter the odds, circumstances, or conditions. In the next few days, the commander was proven right time and again, as he watched the young man quickly grow into a responsible and on the-ball crew chief. More than once, Doc witnessed Vic encouraging his crewmates when the going got tough. He saw him going the extra mile to ensure the safety of the refugees in his care, and observed that the other men with whom Vic served just naturally seemed to respect him and follow his lead.

Though Vic wouldn't think about it until much later, it seemed the Man upstairs had indeed heard his plea that rainy day, while sprawling so forlornly in the back booth of a White Castle – for a chance to prove his worth. And prove it, he did.

ꟾ

WITH HER FOREHEAD resting against the cold damp glass of the train window, Louise gazed through the raindrops at the sodden landscape rushing by. The family had been allotted two seats in the passenger car, so she and Edna were sharing a space, with Billy perched on Louise's lap. Lilly and Willis were seated directly across the aisle. They were on their way to the Dove Creek Country Club, located in another county.

With the drama of Billy and the typhoid shots…coupled with seeing Vic Matthews again and actually talking to him…standing in long lines with hundreds of other people for handouts from the Red Cross…and waiting for the decision of where they would be taken as refugees fleeing the inundated city, it had been quite an eventful morning.

The passenger car rocked gently as it rolled along. Packed in somewhat like sardines, the train car – equipped to carry forty passengers comfortably – was transporting fifty-five. The muffled sound of the wheels making contact with the metal tracks was not quite loud enough to drown out the nervous mumbling and occasional weeping of the other passengers. Families were being sent together to the far away club; a kindness appreciated by the refugees. Still, each family unit had its own set of worries – their homes and belongings…their friends back home…their jobs for those who were lucky enough to have them…and just the familiarity of their lives – would things ever be the same again?

Billy was quiet for once, absorbed in a borrowed copy of the comics page. Hugging her brother a little closer and turning her head, Louise glanced past Edna to their parents. Her father sat with his arms around their mother, her forehead snuggled against his neck. One of his large hands held hers consolingly to his chest as he whispered to her. The daughter knew, without having to hear the words, that Willis was comforting Lilly regarding Sonny. Their mother had been beside herself with worry over her boy, as no one had been able to tell them where he was or if he was all right. Lilly was the worrying kind. It was habitual, and one of the ways she showed her love. However, Louise knew in her heart that her brother could take care of himself.

For Louise, her mind seemed too full, packed with a confusing swirl of fear, excitement, dread, and expectation. What would this Dove Creek place be like? How long would they have to stay there? What was happening to their home and belongings? How deep was the water now – and would it get any higher? Her friends Fleet and Eleanor – were they and their families all right? Everything had happened so fast, and since very few people she knew had telephones, she had no idea what was going on in the lives of her friends. The Neighborhood House – was it under water? Would their lives ever get back to normal again?

But the main thought permeating all others…Vic Matthews. Would she see him again?

Returning her gaze to the landscape outside of the rain spattered window, Louise thought back to their departure from the relief station. Huddled under large black umbrellas, the family, along with roughly a dozen other people, had made their way out to a high-axle military transport vehicle. Gazing out the back flaps of the truck as they rode through the submerged streets toward the train station, it was as if they were sequestered inside a large canvas-covered gondola. Their travel mates ranged from the very poor to a well off couple with two children that complained about everything. But no matter their stations in life, all were treated the same, much to the delight of some and the chagrin of others. At least they had been given a passenger car to ride in; others had been relegated to boxcars and sent off to more distant destinations.

Just then, Louise caught a snippet of a conversation from the wealthy family.

"I'm still so angry at those two imbeciles," the woman fumed.

"I know, dear. As they say, good help is hard to find these days," the man returned.

"And the audacity of that one, telling me I couldn't take my minks! I still want you to report them!" the wife added as she regaled the details regarding their overloaded rescue boat. How it had capsized and spilled the rescuers, themselves, and their belongings, into the cold dirty water. She was absolutely livid regarding the 'clumsy' volunteer crew. The passengers nearby flashed the ungrateful couple looks of disbelief and annoyance.

It appeared that the woman did not want to accept the fact that she had most likely been responsible for the accident, because she had insisted on taking too many possessions in the boat. Not only that, but clearly, she did not appreciate the efforts of the two-man volunteer team.

Louise immediately bristled at the woman's tone and words, while wondering if it had been Vic's crew...

She certainly hoped not, and shut her eyes to send up a heartfelt prayer for his safety.

ഌറ

FORTY-FIVE MINUTES LATER the train car shimmied, the wheels emitting a soft squeal as the engineer applied the brake.

Louise and the rest of the passengers sucked in deep startled breaths, as they were jarred from the mesmerizing serenity of their own thoughts. The refugees began dazedly reaching for their belongings as the train slowed to glide into the station, knowing they had arrived at the small railroad terminal in Anchorage.

Emerging from the train car, they glanced around at their surroundings, which were, thankfully, sans dark murky water. Although it had been raining it felt more like a normal January day. The sun was even attempting to peek through a thin place in the clouds. Such a feeling of freedom this brought to the passengers! It was as if they had just been released from a long stint in prison. The very air seemed lighter and easier to breathe…

"Right this way, folks," a voice called, prompting the emerging refugees to turn their heads. A small man with a round face and a jolly expression motioned from the window of a bus parked at the edge of the platform. "I'm gonna take the women and children out to the country club."

"The women and children? But…" Lilly immediately blustered, turning toward Willis in near panic.

"Don't worry ma'am," the driver assured. "The men'll be stayin' right down the road at the Presbyterian church. They'll visit every day," he added kindly. The ladies, though not entirely happy at this prospect, nevertheless acceded to the inevitable.

The beleaguered travelers hoisted their meager belongings and trudged toward the waiting transport. The friendly man introduced himself as Jack Bayford, and informed them that he was one of the custodians at the club. As he pulled the bus away from the brick two-story depot, he chattered on about their accommodations.

"Now, the ladies of the local Presbyterian Church are already makin' plans on how we'll get you folks fed, and we've been workin' on sleepin' arrangements. Don't you folks worry, we'll take good care of you."

Several of the travelers thanked him, as he went on, "So, is it really as bad as they say? Buildings under water, bridges washed out, people drownin'…?"

Willis spoke up from the family's seats in the center of the bus. "We didn't see any of that, though the water looked to be about four feet in our neighborhood. I haven't heard of any drownings yet…"

"Well that's good!" the animated man exclaimed. "Cause I was tellin' my brother that they're gonna have to rebuild the whole city at that rate!" Switching subjects as if he had turned a page in a book, he then launched into telling the refugees a little of the history of the country club.

Louise allowed her mind to wander, gazing out the bus windows at the landscape of gently rolling hills. Later, she would realize they had been passing the many golf courses of the country club's massive grounds.

Finally, the bus turned into an entrance road and the passengers got a glimpse of their accommodations for the coming days – and none of them knew how long that would be. The clubhouse resembled a sprawling white brick mansion nestled in the midst of a stand of mature evergreen trees. Two massive stone chimneys rose through the steep, gray-shingled roof. Something about the structure seemed to exude gentle strength and security…

"Wow, look Edna…isn't this beautiful?" Louise breathed as she took in the sight. She had never been privileged enough to stay anywhere so luxurious. Louise wasn't alone, as the other passengers were uttering similar opinions. Even Edna murmured agreement that it was, indeed, a lovely place.

Soon, the driver pulled the conveyance up to the main front door and the weary women bid goodbye to their husbands and older sons.

Willis hugged the girls and Billy, before taking his wife into his arms for a comforting embrace. She held on tight, her fingers clutching at the fabric of his coat.

"Now, don't worry. I'll be over to see you tomorrow. For now, we just have to make the best of things," he reassured, as all five Hoskins stood together for a final farewell. The calm patriarch added, "We'll get through this. Come summer, we'll look back on some of this and laugh, you'll see."

"I hope so…" Lilly murmured, her pale blue eyes seeking her husband's reassurance.

He gave her one of his trademark winks and murmured, "Lilly girl, you know I keep my promises…" For a moment, years of privately shared memories passed between their locked gazes. Lilly's eyes softened as she silently admitted that her wonderful husband always did keep his promises – no matter the personal cost.

With a quick kiss, Willis reluctantly disengaged from her embrace and re-boarded the bus with the other men.

The women were quickly ushered inside the club and out of the cold January wind by a man who introduced himself as C. L. Bearden, one of the club's trustees. He was a tall man who carried with him an air of confidence, that of the privileged class. A bit eccentric, however, as evidenced by his fine, but somewhat worn clothing and handlebar mustache. He gave the impression of being of a bygone era.

"Come right in, ladies. We've been expecting you," Bearden informed them as he led the group to a large room decorated a pleasant light green. Large lace-curtained French doors allowed a good amount of light to filter in. A massive stone fireplace, in which burned an invitingly cheery fire, took up a third of the interior wall. The women and small children immediately headed toward it, lugging their possessions. Several of the ladies, including Lilly, showed some displeasure that the beds they would be sleeping on were actually straw-filled mats on the floor.

"But…surely we will be afforded private rooms…" the wealthy woman immediately complained, her nose wrinkling at the sight of the mats. "…And beds."

Bearden cast her a disparaging glance, noting the rumpled clothing and watermarked suitcase. He quickly deduced the woman as the type who maintained an air of the upper crust, without the means to back it up.

"Madam, this is a golfing club, not a *hotel*." Dismissing her with a turn of his head, he once again addressed the group, leaving the woman clutching her children and sputtering about the man's rudeness.

"Make yourselves comfortable. Some women from a local church will be here soon to bring food." What he didn't include was, although the club was known for the excellence of its cuisine, the refugees would not be partaking of any such fine dining. When contacted by the Red Cross, the owners *reluctantly* agreed to provide a place to stay for their unexpected boarders, as all club activities would need to temporarily cease.

"In the meantime, get settled the best you can. And…ladies, please see that the children respect the club's property," he pointedly added as he stared at a child of two or three who was, at that moment, tugging on one of the lace curtains. The embarrassed mother immediately took charge of the child.

With that the man inclined his head and left them to their own devices.

Lilly, Edna, and Louise looked around and chose a group of four mats as close to the fireplace as they could that the other women hadn't already claimed.

"I'm hungry, Mama," Billy complained as he plopped down on his mat. Lilly smiled sadly and leaned to caress his hair, before placing her belongings on the lumpy surface of her straw 'bed'. "I know, sweetheart. Hopefully the ladies he mentioned will be here soon…"

Edna and Louise shared a look of resignation – or for Edna,

more like aggravation – and set about making their temporary lodgings as comfortable as possible.

Before long, true to the promise, a group of ladies from the church arrived, their arms laden with cold cuts and bread for sandwiches. The friendly Mr. Bayford carried in a pail of fresh milk from the club's own cow, while another man brought in a large pot of delicious smelling soup. The aroma filled the kitchen and filtered out into the dining room where the refugees were milling about.

With worry on her mind about her husband and her missing son, Lilly fussed with making a filling meal for the remaining three members of her family. They spent the rest of that day acquainting themselves with their lodgings, which included amazingly luxurious bathrooms. Finally as the sun set, the group retired for the evening to spend an uneasy night trying to sleep, and taking turns keeping the fire burning in the fireplace.

Each woman there felt mixed feelings about the situation. True, they were out of harm's way and basically well cared for…but with little news filtering in to the secluded club, they couldn't help but wonder and worry over their homes and the friends they had been forced to leave behind.

If some had known what would eventually happen at home, they would have spent a truly sleepless night, as several of their own relatives and friends had been sent to tent cities holding as many as 1,200 refugees – just as the situation would take another turn for the worse.

Sometimes, ignorance is actually bliss.

ƐƆ(Ʒ

CHAPTER 8

Black Sunday

TEMPERATURES STEADILY DROPPED throughout the next day. Rain continued to fall, which helped to plunge more of what was already over forty percent of the area under water. As the day went on, snow and sleet began to pelt the waterlogged city and the high ground began to freeze. Ice formed on stagnant pools or pockets of water. All of this only made the job of the rescuers that much harder.

Broadway, normally the center of commerce and activity in the city, became a turbulent stream clocked at over 6 mph. Only powerful motorboats with experienced crews were capable of crossing the wide and dangerous avenue. Indeed, several smaller crafts had become deluged and capsized in the attempt. Several times during the day, Vic's four-man crew traversed the wide waterway on assignments in the 'Mary Lou', one of the larger boats assigned to B-13. No one wished to find out just how cold the water was; needless to say, they were extremely careful.

Medical officials had direly predicted 15,000 cases of pneumonia due to the extreme conditions, and Vic was determined they would not become part of such a statistic. After one of B-13's own men – 53-year-old John Shore – died of exposure and exhaustion, Doc Latham sent an urgent appeal straight to the mayor in support of his crews. As a result, the rescuers had been supplied with warmer coats, gloves, warm caps, and hip boots to aid in their efforts.

Irene and the other ladies from Doc's church stayed on duty, providing sustenance and warmth each time teams of 'their boys' returned to the station. They were all treated as the heroes they were, of course, but Irene quickly became quite attached to young Vic and Gerald.

The love and concern of Irene and the other church ladies had inundated the young man with a feeling he couldn't put into words. Indeed, the wall Vic had built to protect his heart from further hurt had begun to slowly erode, much like the banks of the muddy Ohio. As the hours and days of the crisis wore on, Vic felt more and more at home with his newfound friends, and cared for and accepted in a way he had never before experienced.

This was made painfully clear to him when he stopped by in his boat to check on Jack, Liz, and the kids that morning. He ordered his crew to motor down Fifteenth to the apartment's front stoop and made his way up the stairs to their door. However, for some unknown reason, he didn't feel the freedom to just walk in like he normally would. Everything seemed to feel different somehow. He felt vaguely detached…a bit like an outsider. So, he paused at the last second and knocked, half hoping they wouldn't be there.

The reception he received was a bit frosty, to say the least. His sister-in-law, who regarded him with a mixture of dislike and disinterest, opened the door as she wiped her hands on a towel. The kids ran to see him and Jack came to the door and shook his hand. However…the whole thing felt quite odd, as if he were a long lost stranger.

"Uncle Vic! Boats are goin' up and down the street!" Little red-haired Shirley squealed as she lifted her petite, sweater-clad arms for him to pick her up.

"They sure are, sweetie," Vic answered, giving his adoring niece a kiss on the cheek.

"Mr. Fred, downstairs, got sick last night – a big boat with red lights on it came and got him," Timmy informed his uncle, with large round, innocent eyes.

"That right? Musta been the Coast Guard…" Vic supplied, imagining the elderly gentleman bundled up and taken to the hospital.

The family stood awkwardly at the door, never moving inside to sit down or visit. Vic cleared his throat and self-consciously ran a hand back through his hair, scrounging for polite conversation. Jack moved to lean against the doorframe, his eyes now and then shifting to his wife.

"You best go on back to where you've been staying, 'cause we don't have enough food to last if we're stranded for very long," Liz made a point of saying when the children excitedly asked Uncle Vic if he were staying for lunch.

Vic turned to leave a few uncomfortable minutes later, realizing neither his brother nor his sister-in-law had even asked what had been occupying his time, or where he had been since the morning the flood had begun. And neither had he volunteered any information.

He clomped back down the steps and made his way out to his waiting friends.

Gerald eyed him as he stepped back on board. "You okay, man? The family alright?"

Vic huffed a small downhearted sigh and raised his eyes to his friend, noticing all three of the guys were staring at him in concern. One corner of his mouth lifted in his trademark smirk as he acknowledged silently that these guys, whom he'd only known for a few days, cared more for him than his own 'flesh and blood'.

"Yeah, they're alright. Let's just…get outta here," he mumbled with a dismissive shrug.

Glancing at one another and wondering just what had gone on upstairs that had affected their friend in such a way, they wisely said no more as Gerald gunned the outboard, and they moved on down Fifteenth.

Vic stared back at the apartment building, brooding. He wondered if he would ever call that place 'home' again.

Somehow it seemed unlikely…

However, his melancholy thoughts soon receded to the back of his mind as the business of rescuing people and the responsibility of his position as rescue boat captain took precedence.

As the day wore on, Vic and his crew navigated past both Earl's and Alec's homes and he was saddened by what he saw. Both families were, of course, gone to places unknown. Though discovering Earl's family's home was flooded, Vic could see in the windows that the water had only covered the floors a few inches. Alec's home, however, built in a much lower area, had already sustained quite a bit of damage – broken windows were allowing clothes and personal items to be taken away by the current.

Vic was afraid his friends would end up losing everything. Scooting over to the boat's edge, he reached down and retrieved an item out of the water. As he turned it over, his lips parted with the shock of realizing it was the sepia-toned photograph of the family that normally resided on the mantel in the front room. He'd seen it there dozens of times…he'd watched Mrs. Alder dust it, and lovingly trace the images with her finger. With a sigh, he stashed it in the bow of the boat.

"Hey guys…" he began, intending to direct his crewmembers to help gather items into the vessel, when a fully loaded rescue craft journeyed by with an urgent request for help.

Sighing, Vic regretfully abandoned the Alder's home and gave the order to proceed to the emergency, ten blocks to the west to the address of a large older home. There, Vic and the crew of the Mary Lou came to the rescue of a family of five, as well as a Doctor Morris Edwards, who had gone to the home to render aid. Five of the people were nearly unconscious inside the residence, but one had stumbled out onto the porch to feebly shout for help. Concerned neighbors had summoned assistance.

Vic and the others acted quickly, managing to carry the victims out onto the porch and into the waiting boat. Disregarding the fact that they could be suffering from Typhoid Fever and thus contagious, the team delivered the ailing people to the Louisville City Hospital. The front steps were serving as a dock for boats to deliver sick and injured people. Vic glanced up and smirked at someone's obvious sense of humor, as an impromptu sign had been strung across the wide sidewalk leading to the front doors. Made with red paint on a bed sheet, perfect block letters proclaimed, HOSPITAL BOAT LANDING.

Doctors at the hospital confirmed what Dr. Edwards had gasped before passing out; the family had suffered carbon monoxide poisoning, the culprit – a faulty furnace. A short article with an accompanying photo in the newspaper that afternoon read, "Thanks to the sure actions of a volunteer boat crew from station B-13, all six victims survived what could have been a tragedy." For the first time in his life, Vic felt almost famous. The Courier had even spelled their names right when they listed the members of the team.

However…their euphoria didn't last long.

As the weather worsened throughout the day, snow and sleet pelted the water, the boat, and the men inside. The temperature steadily continued to drop, on its way to a staggering 18 degrees. The rest of that day and the next, Vic's crew, like many others, patrolled the streets, a.k.a. waterways, on the lookout for anyone who might need help. The cold, but hardy, volunteers huddled under blankets in their crafts, each man keeping warm with a heated brick wrapped in a cloth and tucked inside his union suit.

By the time Sunday evening rolled around, all of the crews of volunteers were exhausted. As twilight descended, and not having encountered anyone out and about in several hours, Vic eyed his tired crew. Two were so exhausted, they were yawning and wiping their eyes. Gerald, at the rudder, stared blankly, then shook his head and wiped a gloved hand over his face to try and wake up.

"Fellas, whadya say we make tracks for the cave?" he muttered, stifling a yawn. The others nodded listlessly.

"We ain't doin' much good out here, no use freezin' our buns off," another member of the crew, agreed.

Nodding, Vic ordered, "Go ahead and turn down Fillmore, we'll head back that way." Gerald turned the craft and they began to make their way back to base for a much-needed night's rest. The water was deep in that area, nearly up above the windows on some buildings.

"Get a load 'a that!" Gerald laughed a few moments later, pointing with a gloved hand to a lighted billboard at the edge of the street. The others looked to where he had indicated and burst out laughing.

It was an advertisement for some off brand of cigarettes. Pictured was a man with a jaunty hat cocked to one side, his mouth open as he happily allowed smoke to escape, as if he had not a care in the world. The cigarette held in his fingers also had smoke rising. The water line ran right across his mouth, effectively making the unknown man appear to be swallowing water and the smoke the resulting steam. It couldn't have worked better if it had been planned.

"Remind me never to buy that brand," Vic joked as they motored past it and on up the street.

"Yeah, I'd say they're 'all wet', wouldn't you?" Gerald snickered, referring to the common phrase meaning, 'no good.' The pun made all four of the guys chortle. Turning the corner, they continued onto a main thoroughfare, heading east.

Suddenly without warning, the streetlight several feet above their heads, along with every light in sight, went out as if someone had pulled the plug. It plunged them and their boat into a cold, watery darkness. No moon or stars were visible to give light – it was almost like falling into a large cave, and it struck fear into each of the young men's hearts.

"Jumpin' Jehoshaphat!" Gerald sputtered as he accidentally steered the boat into an unseen obstruction in the darkness. The others yelped and grabbed the edges of the craft in an instant of panic. Thankfully, the unknown object toppled away, only causing the boat to rock, but not capsize.

"Oh man, this ain't good," Vic mumbled. Instantly, he knew what had happened. The fear of the possibility of it had been lurking in the back of his mind all day. He had tried to push the thought away after he had heard some old-timers predict that it was bound to happen. Then he had chosen to downplay the rumors he'd heard during the day, that several sections of the city had been rendered powerless. There was no ignoring it now. Now, it was a reality.

Seeing large sections of the city already darkened, with only a few areas remaining electrified, Vic declared in barely controlled panic, "The power plants…their generators are gettin' flooded…they're droppin' off the grid." The thought of that was enough to send shivers of dread through his entire body. *Water everywhere was one thing, but…temperatures well below freezing– and no heat or light…or radios?*

"We better step on it," Vic ordered, reaching for the oil lamp stashed in the bow. Gerald gunned the motor, heading toward the base. Phil and Eugene, the two other men in their crew, immediately began watching over the sides for anything that could potentially plunge the four of them into the cold, murky water. As they passed by another rescue team heading to their own base, the crews slowed and called warnings to one another in the flickering shadows of the bow lamps.

The four young men in Vic's boat gazed about at the eerie landscape as the vessel glided through the choppy water. From a break in between two buildings, they could see the whole western section of the city had gone dark, where before lights had been burning brightly in every building. *What next?* The young men lamented. The crisis seemed to be getting worse…and worse. Four hearts pounded anxiously as they made their way along.

Minutes later, as Vic's eyes focused on the welcomingly familiar bright red letters beaming on the O.K. Storage façade, he was about to make a comment that they had made it safely, when everything around them went dark – again. No more red letters, no welcoming lights of the station, no voice on the radio. The last power substation had gone down, plunging the remaining section of the city into total darkness.

Somehow, practically *feeling* their way along, the men made it to the base and filed inside after carefully tying the Mary Lou nearby.

The building, normally teeming with noise and activity, now housed subdued and hushed volunteers. *One good thing,* Vic mused, *the old building's coal furnace is still puttin' out heat on this cold night.* He made sure to shut the outer door securely against the blustery wet breeze.

The emotional nadir of it was the silence, because with an earlier power outage, WHAS had fallen silent. *WHAS!* Vic cringed. *Our lifeline!* Just when they had thought they had everything under control and it couldn't get worse… now contact with the outside world, not to mention between the citizens of their beleaguered city, had been eliminated.

It was 11:35 p.m. Sunday night. It would be forever immortalized as *Black Sunday.*

For Vic and the entire rescue force of B-13, things couldn't have looked bleaker. Several of the volunteer women, including Irene, huddled together near the food tables and tried not to weep in fear.

Vic stepped nearer, depositing the lamp from the boat onto a table. In spite of the tension of the situation, Vic's heart went out to the lady who had come to mean a great deal to him. Wanting to be a comfort, he placed a gentle hand on her shoulder, murmuring gently, "Aw, Miss Irene…it's gonna be alright…"

She nodded and reached into a pocket for an ever-handy lace hanky, and proceeded to dry her eyes.

"Alright everybody, I think it's past time for us to seek help from a Higher Authority," Doc Latham intoned as he moved to the center of the large main room of the warehouse turned control center and lit another oil lamp. The two-dozen volunteers and church ladies who were there moved toward him in the dim light, each one taking the hand of their neighbor. Their leader cleared his throat and tipped his head back in silent acknowledgment of the Eternal One.

"God in Heaven…forgive us for not first coming to You for help in this time of crisis in our city, but relying on our own strength and wisdom. Yay, dear Lord, our strength and wisdom as is nothing compared to your infinite power and authority…"

For the next few minutes, the preacher-turned-base commander sent up to the Almighty a heartfelt plea for help. Each person in the large room, regardless of the strength of his or her own convictions, heartily hoped that the unseen deity was listening.

When he finished, he pronounced a firm, "Amen," which the others echoed. They stood silent in the soft flickering light of the oil lamps for a few moments, each one hearing the rush of the water outside.

Finally Irene, with her soft soprano voice, began to sing Annie S. Hawks' beloved spiritual, *I Need Thee Every Hour…*

I need Thee every hour, most gracious Lord;
No tender voice like Thine can peace afford.
I need Thee, O I need Thee;
Every hour I need Thee;
O bless me now, my Savior,
I come to Thee.

Most of the others joined in the best they could. Vic, having never attended church, could only stand and listen to the strangely comforting song. He wished at that moment that he were familiar with the Savior of which she sang…

When she finished, Doc murmured a heartfelt plea into the stillness, "Hear us, oh God. Don't leave us without hope..."

Then just, 90 minutes after it had gone silent, the battery-powered base radio sprang to life as the familiar voice of WHAS returned to the airways.

"Praise the Lord!" Doc shouted amidst the cheers of his crew.

"Sorry about that folks," intoned the announcer. "We went down temporarily, but we're back. Somebody up there must like us," he added with an attempt at levity, explaining quickly to his listeners that a company called Kentucky Utilities had found a way to supply them with emergency power.

The others hugged and laughed with relief to hear the familiar voice of announcer Foster Brooks, as he once again began broadcasting messages of public service, missing persons, important information, and of course, pleas to, 'Send a Boat'.

But outside the rain, snow, and sleet continued to fall on a darkened Louisville.

ട്രൂ

"OKAY, LISTEN UP everybody," Doc called out, as about twenty of his volunteers were milling about the base station the next morning. No one relished the thought of going out in the frigid weather, although thankfully – mercifully – the rain and sleet had stopped during the night. The sun was actually shining for the first time in days – so many days, no one could remember.

"I just came from a meeting with the mayor at city hall. With the power out and temperatures so low, its gonna force thousands more folks to need another place to stay until the water decides to go down. They're saying might be as many as 75,000 more refugees."

The men and women nodded understandingly, very glad that they had heat in their building, despite the fact that they were depending on candles and oil lamps for light. Two of the ladies,

Irene and a younger woman named Mae, had elected to stay the night in the warehouse, on cots fixed up in the small office on the main floor. Each of them lived alone and neither relished the thought of spending a powerless and heatless night alone.

Doc continued, "So he's called the governor and asked to declare martial law. Ft. Knox is rushing 500 soldiers here to help keep order and give aid to the victims. They're gonna use Bowman Field to fly in tons of supplies – that is, if the rain'll hold off long enough to let the fields dry. And get this – even the White House is in on this – we heard that President Roosevelt is operatin' on a 24-hour wartime basis, and he's receiving continual updates." The others glanced at one another in mild shock at this revelation. Observing this, Doc continued explaining, "Louisville ain't the only town hit by this flood, you know. They're sayin' the entire Ohio Valley, and much of the lower Mississippi Valley's been affected – every town along the waterways…including Pittsburgh and Cincinnati…are flooded, too."

Amazed, Vic and the boat crews and volunteer ladies of B-13 shook their heads, each one swallowing nervously or unconsciously wrapping their arms across their chests. Until that moment, the thought had not occurred to them that the disaster might be affecting people in other areas, as well. They truly hadn't been able to see or even *think* beyond the massive amounts of water in their own streets. It was odd… but somehow, knowing others were affected triggered splintered responses of both relief that they weren't alone – and fear that the disaster was on such a grand scale. It felt like the end of the world had come…

"That means we're gonna have to redouble our efforts at evacuating," one boat captain murmured. The others nodded, musing that they thought they had completed at least that part of their mission.

"Not necessarily," Doc quickly intoned. "Seems that an architect, a Captain Ironsmith, and an engineer named Wyse, had an idea for building something they're calling a pontoon bridge. They started building it about an hour ago, recruited 300 workers – one of the local whiskey distillers donated something like 1,400 barrels to provide the ballast. Danged if it just might work, too!" he added with a laugh.

"A bridge? How in the world…?" Gerald murmured, reaching one hand up to scratch his head in confusion. "A bridge to where? *From* where?"

"They're gonna make it run about 1,800 feet, a floating bridge, from somewhere on East Jefferson all the way to Baxter Avenue. All folks will have to do is get to the start of it and they can walk out to dry ground."

"But…why do they need *that*? We can take 'em out in our boats, just like we been doin'…" Vic pointed out, the others nodding agreement.

"Good question, Matthews. But…morale has really plummeted since the power went out last night. The mayor's afraid people will panic thinkin' they're gonna freeze to death, and maybe even try to wade through the water to get to higher ground and warmth. With the temperature of that water, I don't have to tell you how long a person would last. Not to mention catching pneumonia or whatever. The bridge'll give 'em something to do other than just sit shivering, waiting for a rescue boat, I guess," Doc shrugged. Although he thought the bridge an ingenious idea, interesting and inventive, he actually agreed with Vic that it did seem a bit unnecessary.

"But it won't make *us* obsolete," he grinned at their suddenly crestfallen expressions. We're one of the stations the mayor's picked for a new assignment – delivering food rations to stranded folks around the city."

The men nodded, some murmuring to their fellow crewmembers as Doc continued, "Any volunteers? Just to let you know, I ain't putting all my crews on distribution duty. There'll still be rescues and transports needed every day, folks needing to get to the hospital or other places – for however many days the dang water stays where it is."

When no one immediately spoke up, Doc put his hands on his hips.

"Matthews? How 'bout your guys?"

Vic and Gerald exchanged glances. Phil and Eugene had not yet come down for breakfast, but it didn't sound like backbreaking duty to the crew's chief.

"Sure, Doc," Vic answered with a shrug. Their commander nodded and scanned the remaining men, calling out several more choices before moving on to other subjects.

ᘓᘐ

VIC AND HIS guys spent the day delivering Red Cross food supplies to those stranded in second floor refuges. Now that the power was off, for many, these food rations would mean the difference between starving and surviving.

During one pass down Chestnut, Vic ordered the boat be brought up to the Hoskins' apartment house. Upon hearing the sound of the motor slowing nearby, Mr. Anderson raised the window of their second floor dwelling and looked down below.

"Hello, down there!" he called down.

"Hello, sir," Vic answered. "How is everything? Noticed any looters tryin' to get in?"

"Nope, we haven't heard a thing," the man responded.

"What about…the Hoskins' son, Joseph – you all seen him since the family evacuated?"

Mrs. Anderson, her bundled head sticking out of a different window, spoke up, "Sonny? Yes, he came by two days ago, and asked if we knew where his folks were, but we told him we didn't know."

"Well, where is he now?" Vic asked, excited to have found out some news about the missing boy.

Mr. Anderson shrugged, totally unconcerned. "Don' know.

He was in a boat with some other people, and they headed off that way," he pointed west.

"He leave a message for his folks or anything?" Vic questioned, aggravated at the couple's uncaring attitude. "The family's been worried sick about him."

"Nope. Just waved and went on," the man answered. Then noticing the foodstuffs loaded in the boat, he added, "Whatcha got there?"

"Are ya in need?" Gerald called up. "We're out deliverin' food to the stranded. How many ya got with ya up there?"

"There's six stayin' here, countin' my wife and me," the man answered, as other heads began to jostle for position to look down and see who he was talking to. "And yeah, we could sure use some of that food."

It stuck in Vic's craw that the couple seemed so blasé about the fate of Joseph Hoskins. Nevertheless, he and the crew set about tossing a rope up to the man, and spent the next few minutes lifting cans and jars up to him, tied in a basket. When they were finished, they gave him and his missus a wave and continued on, the sound of their outboard motor echoing against the sides of the houses.

Hours later, their cartons of can goods and bags of potatoes and onions given away, the men turned the boat toward base, anxious to get a bite to eat and warm up for awhile before setting out on another mission of mercy.

Turning down Fourth, and cruising past the city's main library branch, the crew couldn't help but muse at the fitting sight they beheld. The library's very lifelike statue of President Lincoln seemed to be kneeling in the water. The murky brown liquid lapped at the tails of the President's long coat, which ended at the statue's knees. His hands were clasped in front at his waist, his expression somber, as if he were saddened by the calamity.

"Looks like he's prayin'," Gerald murmured as they motored by.

"Yeah," Vic agreed with a nod before cupping a hand at his mouth and calling out, "Atta boy, Honest Abe! Send up a prayer or two for this waterlogged old town!"

The guys knew that would be one flood memory that would never fade with time.

As they motored slowly on along the Venice-like streets, the four young men lapsed into silence. Gerald pondered the fate of the city itself and wondered if things would ever really be the same again. Phil and Eugene both lapsed into a kind of detached state, mostly thinking about the hot food they hoped to eat once they got back to base.

Vic, in his customary seat in the bow, watched the water for obstructions out of habit, while his mind pictured a girl…brown hair blowing in the breeze…hazel eyes twinkling with mirth…tinkling laughter as she slipped inside the door and out of his sight…

ꕥ

CHAPTER 9

Life at Dove Creek

LOUISE TURNED ONTO her back on the lumpy straw mattress and stretched her arms above her head, as the club's rooster let out another loud cock-a-doodle-do. With each new sunrise, she gained more of a dislike for that bird.

The swanky Dove Creek Country Club, like most establishments during the depression, had fallen on lean times. Although an enterprise geared at recreation and not a necessity, they had managed, by frugal management, to stay afloat and not close their doors. The owners had discovered quite prudent ways of allocating the club fees their members managed to pay. One such way was producing their own milk and eggs to supplement their food budget, while maintaining their air of luxury. Thus, the rooster.

Levering onto one elbow, Louise shivered and reached for her sweater as she glanced at the cold remains of the previous night's fire in the massive fireplace. She shook her head, musing that the others had been right to predict that Mrs. Geldhaus, their resident 'Queen of England', would not fulfill her turn to keep the fire burning.

Glancing over at the woman, snuggled with her small daughter within a mink coat, Louise shook her head as she remembered the 'scene' from the previous day.

The other ladies had gathered around the woman as she

lounged in a chair near the stone fireplace, her mink draped over her shoulders. She was curled comfortably, reading one of the magazines she had brought along. As usual, she was not attending to her children, Trudi and Hubert, who at that moment were chasing one another from room to room and making quite a racket.

Lilly and another lady, Mrs. Haddaway, exchanged glances as Lilly cleared her throat to get the woman's attention. Disinterestedly, Mrs. Geldhaus glanced over the top of the magazine at the assemblage of ladies, and droned, "Yes, what is it?" as if she were addressing a downstairs' maid.

Mrs. Fieldstone, the mother of a small, rambunctious boy, spoke up, "We wanna know if you're gonna tend to the fire tonight. We've all took our turns, goin' practically without sleep like I did last night – and me with a two-year-old ta' look after during the daylight hours," she'd added with a huff.

The snooty woman lowered her magazine with an air of superiority that would put Greta Garbo to shame. "I don't see how that is *my* responsibility. I didn't ask to be brought here in the first pla…" she argued, but Lilly cut her off.

"*None* of us wanted to leave our homes. But the water rose and there was nothing else for any of us to do, unless we had family or friends on the high side of town. Now, *however*, we're stuck out here together and we simply *must* be civil to one another – and *work* together." Lilly's anger had arisen half a notch with each word, as she could tell by the woman's expression she wasn't 'receiving' it.

The other ladies were all nodding in agreement and crossing their arms on their chests. On a roll, Lilly continued, "It stands to reason that we should all take a turn. And not only that – but you allow Trudi and Hubert to run wild, while the rest of us keep a firm hand on our children. It's only fair that…"

"All right, all right," Mrs. Geldhaus huffed with one hand upraised. "I'll get up and *'tend'* to the fire tonight," she drawled, deliberately mocking Mrs. Fieldstone's Kentucky twang. "Happy?" she added with a sneer, before waving a hand at them dismissively and raising her magazine once more, effectively terminating the conversation.

Somewhat satisfied, although each one noticed the woman had ignored the reference to the children, the ladies turned away. They headed back to what they were doing before Mrs. Fieldstone had talked the others into confronting Mrs. 'Geldawful', as she had named her.

Across the room, lying side by side on their mats, Louise and her sister had observed the exchange. Edna paused documenting it in her diary to glance over at her sister's face, noting the pleased smile and nod.

"Ten to one she don't do it, she's such a pill," Edna commented with her trademark snort.

"Nah, she'll do it," Louise immediately countered. "She sure don't want Mama to get after her," she added with a giggle.

Edna turned her head to watch as their mother, sitting with some of the other ladies, had already plunged into an animated conversation that had quickly arisen as to the best recipe for cooking Chop Suey. *Mama's recipe for that could win an award,* Edna mused, as she watched her mother lean forward and rattle off ingredients, ticking them off one by one on her fingers. Trading recipes had become a daily activity the ladies used to pass some time.

"Turning back to her sister, Edna snorted again. "Yeah, but Mama can't take a switch to Mrs. Geldawful."

Both girls dissolved into giggles as they pictured the scene – the woman shrieking in fear and dashing around the dining room, mink flapping in her wake, as their mother charged after her with a switch raised high in one fist, hollering, "You come back here and take your whippin'!"

"Hey Edna," murmured Suzy Flynn, a young widowed mother of four-year-old twins, as she paused by Edna's mat. "The iron's free now if you want to use it. Better hurry before somebody else gets it, though," she added before walking on to put away her freshly laundered and pressed clothing.

With a grunt and a mumbled 'thanks', Edna closed and locked her diary and shoved it under her pillow. Climbing to her feet, she grabbed the pile of clothes she'd been waiting to iron, and took off toward the laundry room without a backward glance.

Louise watched her go, shaking her head and musing over her sister's quaint oddity of ironing, to flawless perfection, every stitch of clothing she wore – right down to her undies.

Lying back down on her mat, Louise glanced around before reaching underneath and pulling out a carefully folded newspaper clipping. Tenderly smoothing out the folds, she stared at the grainy black and white image of four smiling young men in a motorboat. But it was only one smile that she cared about... a young man with dark eyes, and dark wavy hair under a jaunty cap. The heading of the article read, "Hometown Heroes Save Six Lives."

Louise's hazel eyes twinkled as she read again the short article. *The death toll in this continuing crisis nearly increased by six this morning. A family of five, as well as Doctor Morris Edwards, who had come to render assistance, nearly succumbed to carbon monoxide poisoning after the furnace in the family's home malfunctioned. However, thanks to the timely actions of a volunteer boat crew from station B-13, all six victims survived what could have been a terrible tragedy. Help was summoned, and the crew from B-13 sped across the waterlogged streets to the aid of their fellow Louisvillians, transporting them to Louisville City Hospital in the nick of time. "The crew obviously knew just what to do," stated John Stratton, M.D, who treated several of the victims. "And despite the fact that they didn't know what these people were suffering from – in other words, they could have been contagious – they wasted no time in getting them here," Pictured from left to right are the heroes: Gerald Gutterman, Phil Drexler, Eugene Banks, and Victor Matthews.*

Several days after the refugees arrived at the club, Louise had looked over the shoulder of Mrs. Haddaway, who was reading the only copy of the newspaper they had yet to receive. The young woman's heart had jolted as if she had stuck her finger in a light socket when she glimpsed the photograph. Nearly breathless, she had waited for the woman to finish. Then tucking the paper under her arm, she dashed down the hall to the ladies' restroom, and quickly hid in one of the stalls. Using her fingernail to crease the paper, she had hurriedly removed the small article and refolded the newspaper. Later after placing it on a table in the main dining room, she'd played innocent when the next person picked it up and squawked about the hole in the center.

Little did she know that article would become a prized possession…one that she would treasure in years to come. Indeed…even more than she could ever imagine…

*Vic Matthews…*Louise had sighed as she stared at the photo. *I wonder what he's doing this minute…is he on his boat, rescuing more people? Did they write any more articles about him?*

For the remainder of that evening after the ladies confronted Mrs. Geldhaus, Louise lay on her mat, listening to the soft conversations of the other refugees and daydreaming of the man who had completely captured her emotions.

There was no one with whom she could share her fascination…she knew she had to keep it quiet because she had happened to read an excerpt from her sister's diary the day before. Edna had carelessly left it open to a page where she had talked about her plans to try and find Vic Matthews after the flood was over, *and just see if 'Little Miss Goody Two Shoes'* had told the truth about him.

Edna's more experienced with men… she knows how to talk and flirt with them. The thought of Edna using her charms on Vic sent shards of dread into Louise's heart. *What would I do if Vic decided he liked Edna? I'd just die!* She'd lamented, and unconsciously grimaced at the thought. But a moment later, determination arose. *No, dag nabbit! This is one time Edna's not gonna take something I want!*

Louise vowed, as occasions and items in the past came to mind…dolls, books, and toys, even slices of cake or pie. *I've got to come up with some kind of strategy…*

Now wrapping her arms around her body, she stared into the cold hearth, deep in thought until another shiver in the early morning chill brought her out of her musings. She climbed to her feet, slipped into her shoes, and shuffled off for a few minutes of privacy in the club's luxurious ladies' restroom.

The restroom…funny how it had become the most enjoyable aspect of their stay.

The sparkling white and silver marble walls, white tiled floor, and lovely gleaming chrome had taken the refugees' breaths away upon first inspection. Louise, indeed, most of the women, had never seen such luxury. The large bathroom also boasted two shower stalls, complete with arched doorways and chrome and glass doors. Three pristine pedestal sinks of white porcelain adorned one wall, each accompanied by a large, round, brightly lit mirror. Two private commode stalls stood on either side of the showers. Two white padded stools sat before two mirrors, which allowed female patrons to freshen their makeup and hair after a hot day on the courses, or a steamy time on the dance floor during an event. Elegant chairs, surrounding a low table, adorned the left side of the room in a mini seating area that completed the opulent décor.

The restroom's crowning glory, however, was a round, multi-colored stained glass window. Mounted high above the sinks near the arched ceiling, it depicted a dove in flight over a lovely meandering creek.

The elegant ladies' room was so very different from what the Hoskins women were accustomed to. Back home in the large pseudo duplex building, each side had one bathroom – on the second floor. Mrs. Higgins, the cranky old woman who owned the house, never spent any money on improvements or maintenance. The bathrooms were old fashioned, cold and drafty. The one on the Hoskins' side had a chipped claw-foot tub, one bare light bulb in the ceiling, and the sink was stained with rust under constantly dripping faucets. The mirror over the sink was spotty and dark, and the wooden floor creaked loudly, especially in the middle of the night. Bare pipes ran down the wall over the top of wallpaper that had once been elegant, but was now faded, stained, and torn.

It was a decidedly unappealing room, and one in which you concluded your business and vacated as quickly as possible.

But this...this lovely restroom in the club was truly that...*restful.*

Louise made her way inside the quiet room and up to one of the sinks, washed her face awake, and brushed her hair. Pausing to stare with a grimace at her reflection, her hands came up to smooth the ugly dress she was wearing. Although the family had actually spared a few moments to grab items to take with them when they evacuated, their father had given assignments. Louise had retrieved items of hygiene, while Edna had been instructed to grab clothing for each family member, from a rack in the corner on which articles had been hung to dry. Edna had managed to pack items for herself and Billy, but very few for Lilly or Willis – and only one dress and a pair of socks for Louise.

Most of the refugees had been forced to vacate their homes rather quickly, leaving with few necessities. Therefore, the kind ladies from the churches in Anchorage had gathered some used clothing for them and brought the items on one of their food trips. However...before Louise could secure something suitable for herself, the other women had quickly snatched up the offerings, leaving only one item on the table – a dark green and tan dress two sizes too large for her petite frame. The previous night, she had had no other choice but to don the hated article while her own dress was being laundered.

Oh well...it's not like I'm going for a beauty contest or anything... she mused with a smirk. *But, dang that Edna! She always seems to land on her feet like a big ol' cat. I noticed she managed to bring* ***herself*** *more clothes...*

With a sigh of resignation, Louise pinned her hair back from her face and glanced around at the lovely bathroom, which was kept spotlessly clean by each of the lady refugees...*well...except that snooty Mrs. Geldhaus...* The fine, self-respecting ladies of the group had decided amongst themselves that they would show their appreciation for their more than generous accommodations. They made sure that when the time came for them to return home, they would leave the club looking as good or better than when they arrived.

I wonder what it would be like to live in a place as wonderful as this... Louise pondered with a soft sigh. *I'll probably never find that out.* The chrome gleamed in the sparkling light and Louise smiled, her mind going back to that first afternoon when all of the young people and children 'explored' their temporary lodgings. She and Edna had opened the door to this room marked *ladies,* and gasped in awe.

"This is the *bathroom*?" Edna had gaped.

"Geez..." Louise had breathed in fascination. "I've never seen anything so beautiful..."

"What you two gawkin' at?" a voice asked an instant before Billy came pushing past them, his eyes bugging nearly out of his head at the sight. "Wow this is keen! This is for you girls?" he had asked, then made a beeline down the wide hall to a door marked, "Gentlemen". He then had come back to report that the men's facility was just as swanky – only more for 'gents' and not so 'girlyfied', as he'd put it.

Indeed, the whole club was 'keen', clean, bright, and quite comfortable...if not exactly entertaining. It was, after all, meant to serve the immediate needs of its patrons who were availing themselves of the golf courses. There was no radio at the club, no piano, nothing to use for entertainment – those items were brought in if a member used the facilities for a party. As a result, after that first day, life at the elegant establishment had quickly settled into a rather boring routine of trying to find ways to make the hours between meals go by faster.

True to their host's word, the daddies were able to come for visits – but only for a short time – and never for meals. The reason for that was a mystery that no one could or would answer. The same Presbyterian ladies, who came each day with food for the mothers and children, and shared the work with a group of women from a local Methodist church, also fed the men. One would think that if everyone were in the same place for meals it would be easier, but…

Sometime after breakfast on the second day, the bus had pulled up out front and the exiled fathers had emerged, much to the thrill of their families. The Hoskins enjoyed the joyous reunion, and Billy had dragged his chuckling father around to view all of the special places he had discovered the day before. Then the family drifted into the large dining room-turned-sleeping quarters and sat together in chairs off to the side, feeling a bit like visiting inmates, and just tried to enjoy one another's company.

The hours passed quickly. Willis regaled them with stories of the fathers trying to sleep on army cots in the basement of the church – eighteen men in close quarters – his descriptions of the cacophony of most of them snoring at different and changeable decibels was quite comical. Billy entertained them with his innocent excitement over what had become an adventure for him – time away from school and chores and other drudgeries.

At one point, Edna lamented the fact that there was no radio, and she was missing her favorite shows, such as, The Guiding Light.

"Yeah, but I miss *Edgar Bergen and Charlie McCarthy*, and *The Shadow*," Billy had argued. "They're a lot keener than that ol' soap opera junk you listen to," he chided his sister, to which she leaned over and gently tweaked his nose.

"I do miss *Our Gal Sunday*," Lilly mused thoughtfully.

"And the news…right now, I'd even settle for a series of 'Send a Boat' messages," Willis added with a twinkle, causing the others to chuckle.

"I miss eating supper and listening to dance band music," Louise mused, picturing scenes that had been commonplace and taken for granted mere weeks before. It seemed so odd that so much had changed in such a short time.

After that, they had drifted into mentioning things they missed 'back home', and wondering how long they would be forced to remain away.

All too soon, Mr. Bayford apologetically informed the men that they needed to bid their loved ones goodbye for the night.

"But…so soon? My lands, he only just arrived…" Lilly had blustered, but the man had shaken his head with a sympathetic smile. "I'm sorry ma'am… I'm just followin' orders."

Knowing that they needed to be grateful for small favors and not take a chance on being asked to leave their lodgings, the family once again bid a reluctant goodbye to Willis, and watched him board the bus for the return trip to the church for the night. *He couldn't even stay and eat supper with us…* Louise lamented with a sigh and a sad shake of her head, as she missed her wonderful father very much when he was gone.

After that, the time seemed to crawl by. The second day, Louise and Billy ventured out quite far on one of the golf courses, mainly just to have something to do. The manicured grass-covered grounds, dormant for the winter, seemed to stretch on and on. Being born and raised in the city amongst tall buildings, concrete, asphalt, and neon lights, the wide-open spaces seemed almost unnatural. They both, however, soon came to enjoy the differences.

The next morning, the weather turned colder and forced the brother and sister to stay indoors. One of the refugees had brought along a deck of cards, and friendly games of Old Maid,

Go Fish, and Gin Rummy were enjoyed. The children played hide and seek and hopscotch. The exiles spent time drawing, or writing letters on stationary provided by the club, or playing charades. Several girls had brought their diaries along – including Edna – and wrote volumes, although Louise couldn't imagine what they found to document. Several of the ladies had brought books to read, and turns were taken reading them aloud in the evenings after the chores were completed.

The days passed a trifle more quickly for the women when it was their turn to help in the club's kitchen with cooking the meals or cleaning up afterwards. However, the room wasn't large enough to accommodate all of them at once. Another vied-for pastime was washing clothes. The owners of the establishment had granted the ladies permission to use the club's electric washer – a luxury some of them had never seen – to keep what few clothes they had clean. This also helped to provide a much-needed relief from boredom.

Nineteen families, complete strangers, were being forced to live together for the duration; and the various parenting styles sometimes caused agitation. Some of the ladies were quite permissive and refused to believe their 'little darlings' could do anything wrong, while others screamed and yelled over the slightest infraction of the rules. Those times were a bit nerve racking, but for the most part, the days passed with relative calmness.

And then, there were the meals. The kind, wonderful ladies of the church had taken the 'poor refugees' under their wings, determined to provide them with sustenance for the tenure of their stay. Supplementing the emergency rations being distributed by the Red Cross, they took turns and came three times a day bringing various items for meals. The mothers quickly set up a rotating schedule to help with the cooking, and after each one had their turn, favorites were soon chosen. However…it was plain fare at its best. Lilly's talent for making a scrumptious meal with varied ingredients proved quite welcome. Then there was Mrs. Geldhaus…but that was another matter. Louise sometimes wondered what the woman's husband ever saw in her. *The money musta been hers,* more than one of the other ladies mumbled over the course of their stay, as a way to explain the mystery. Mr. Geldhaus, himself, was quite nice, and not bad looking. From bits and pieces learned from floating hearsay, they were a wealthy couple that had lost the bulk of their money in the crash – everything but the 'attitude' of the wealthy.

With no radio, the only news received from 'outside' came from the church ladies, or the truck drivers who delivered the rations. When the two-day-old newspaper had been brought, the refugees had been shocked to hear that all electric power had shut down in the beleaguered city, except for some emergency generators for the hospitals and WHAS. Everyone wondered the fate of friends and relatives they had left behind, having believed them to be warm, safe and dry in second-floor abodes. Now, the people 'stranded' miles from home had no idea if their loved ones had stayed, or had to vacate as well.

The truck drivers reported rumors, gossip, and 'predictions' such as the possibility of epidemics of typhoid or cases of pneumonia. This news caused Lilly quite a meltdown, as the family still had no idea as to the whereabouts of their beloved Sonny, and the girls were very relieved when their father had arrived shortly after. He had, as always, known just what to say and do to alleviate his wife's fears.

The flood victims housed at the far away club felt so helpless and disconnected. One distraught woman, who had been worried sick over her brother and his family, had to be restrained from leaving to try and get back to Louisville.

The days stretched on and it seemed that the pendulum of their lives would never swing back to center again. It was an odd feeling…to be marooned so far away from all things familiar. Though their surroundings were for the most part opulent…it was like living in a 'golden prison', about which they felt a mixture of love and hate…

"You're up early," a voice broke into Louise's reverie and she blinked several times to focus.

"Yeah…was cold, I guess," she responded to Edna's reflection in the mirror.

Edna smirked and rolled her eyes. Yawning as she shuffled into one of the stalls, she remarked over her shoulder, "Told ya she wouldn't hold up her end. Wish I woulda bet money on it."

Louise nodded ruefully. Checking her reflection once more, and staring disgustingly at the dress with its hideous black leaves and large garish print, she retied the cloth belt to better fit her slender waist and buttoned the top button on her sweater. *I'll be glad to get my own dress back on,* she grumbled silently.

Then with a shrug, she turned and headed out the door, calling over her shoulder, "Better hurry up, the ladies'll be here soon with breakfast."

ᘓᘐ

"DADDY!" LOUISE CALLED as she watched her beloved father walk through the door behind several of the other men, not long after breakfast. She noticed he seemed a little more tired than usual, and she figured the sleeping arrangements at the church were taking their toll on him.

Willis flashed a large grin at his daughter, his cheeks pushing his wire-rimmed glasses a bit higher on his face.

"Hello, Sweet Pea," he murmured as she sailed into his arms for a hug.

As Louise's arms surrounded her father, she shut her eyes, so glad to have him back among them again. He felt so good and solid, and filled the lonely space that always remained so empty while he was away. She noticed a bit of mist just resting on the outer fibers of his jacket and she mumbled, "Is it raining again?"

"Nah, just heavy fog," he returned, his eyes closed as he cherished a moment of having his precious daughter in his arms.

When they pulled back to smile at one another, his grin turned into a confused frown.

"What's this you're wearing?" he asked as he indicated the oversized dress he'd never seen his daughter wear before.

Louise looked down with a grimace. "Oh this…my dress is in the wash. The church ladies…they gave us all some clothes to get us by – but after the vultures swooped in, this was all I could get."

Willis grinned again and stepped back, motioning for her to turn around for his perusal. The style of the dress was that of the twenties, with the low hung waist and V-neck– and designed for a much older woman. "Seeing you in this sure makes me realize… soon you won't be my Sweet Pea anymore. Someday you'll leave me. You'll get married and go off to make a home of your own with your husband, leaving your poor old Dad behind," Willis lamented, albeit teasingly.

Louise grinned up at him and threw her arms around his neck, feeling his embrace close tight about her again. Turning her head, she whispered, "Daddy, I'll always be your 'Sweet Pea'…and you'll always be my 'Daddy'…no matter how old I get." Pulling back again, she added with a twinkle, "Even when I'm an old married woman with six kids, I'll still be your 'Sweet Pea'…if you want me to."

Willis chuckled and gently tapped her nose with the tip of one finger. "That's my girl," he murmured as the rest of his family came to greet him. One by one, he hugged them all, and they meandered over to a group of chairs for their daily visit.

"It feels so good to be together," Lilly sighed as she sat near her beloved husband and tucked her hand within the crook of his elbow. He nodded, smiling at her lovingly, as he patted her hand.

Striving to push away thoughts of the fact that he would be leaving again in a scant few hours, Lilly turned her head and smiled as she gazed into the faces of her children. Her lovely daughters, who were sitting close to their father and grinning at him happily, and her precocious son, who had already begun to entertain them with his antics. But her smile faded a bit as her own words made her realize they weren't 'all' together…her precious Sonny was still *out there*…somewhere…she could only hope that he had enough to eat and a place to take shelter. She wished, and not for the first time, that she had the faith of the church ladies who came with the food. They always prayed and seemed so sure and confident in God's care and provision.

Lilly sighed quietly as she thought about her life. Decisions she had felt she had no other choice but to make…decisions that went against the teachings of the church. She had been raised Catholic, and thereafter had felt she couldn't come to God with needs or problems. Therefore, worrying and fretting were all she could do when a crisis arrived…

Louise sat back on her heels, giggling at a joke Billy had just told, and glanced at her mother. Immediately noticing the downcast expression slightly marring Lilly's smooth complexion, the girl figured that her mother was thinking of Sonny. She was worried too…but not as much as Lilly. Somehow…Louise knew that once the crisis was over and they could all return home, they would enjoy hearing about all of her daring brother's escapades.

For now, she would just enjoy small favors and snippets of joy when they came. As the others laughed at yet another funny story, Louise turned her attention back to the 'joy' at hand.

ꕥ

CHAPTER 10

The Surprise

IN THE MIDST of the noise and chaos of cleaning up after lunch, a knock was heard on the door of the club's kitchen. One of the ladies scurried over and opened it, allowing a deliveryman to come in with boxes of rations for the refugees.

Billy and several of the other young boys came running, excited to see 'Mr. Dobbins' on his third visit to the club.

'Hi, Mr. Dobbins!" the young boy called as he rounded the corner, just missing one of the mothers as she crossed the room to put away some of the breakfast dishes.

"Hey there, sport!" the kind older, gray haired gentleman responded with a grin, raising his burden up over the heads of the youngsters as he made his way through to the pantry. As usual, the kitchen was bustling with ladies, old and young, toiling like worker bees on their chores. With the kids buzzing around, it was nearly chaotic.

"What'dya bring us today, Mr. Dobbins?" a little girl named Sally asked bashfully, clutching a baby doll under one arm.

"Aww, we got some turnips, and some black eyed peas, and some lima beans…" the man responded, chuckling as the girl turned up her nose with a grimace. "But…I think I might have somethin' that'll put a smile back on your face," he added, producing a handful of hard candies from the pocket of his jacket. The kids all squealed in excitement and clustered around him as he chuckled and distributed one to each child, ending with the cute little girl. Thinking once again that she reminded him of his daughter at that age, his faded blue eyes shimmered as he bent down to her level. He gave her an exaggerated wink when he slipped her a second piece. She giggled and leaned to give his cheek a peck.

Then another man crossed the threshold, the load of heavy boxes in his arms stacked higher than his head.

"Put 'em right in there, son," the man gestured with his head to the younger man with him, his relief driver.

The other man came through the pantry door and placed his load on a shelf. Looking around, he spotted young Billy Hoskins, and his heart kicked into high gear.

"Hey! I know you…" Billy squawked, stepping up to the man who looked very familiar.

The man grinned and reached out a hand to ruffle the boy's brown hair, his eyes scanning the kitchen eagerly. Just then, a girl in a light blue sweater covering a green and tan dress, standing at the sink washing dishes, turned her head. Her hazel eyes opened wide in shock as she dropped the plate she was holding into the water with a splash. *Oh my gosh…it's…it's…HIM!*

Vic couldn't believe his eyes – or his luck. *It's her…so this is where the family's been all this time…*

"Louise, watch what you're doing, honey," Lilly fussed, wiping suds from the front of her dress with the towel she had been using to dry the dishes.

"Sorry, Mama," Louise mumbled, unable to tear her eyes from the most unexpected sight she'd had in some time. Vic Matthews – standing right there in the club's kitchen – staring back at her!

Riveted to the spot, Vic's lips parted in surprise and his dark, hooded eyes drank in the sight of her. She seemed even more beautiful than he remembered, and for a moment everything else faded from view as their eyes remained locked. He vaguely noticed her mouth move as she answered her mother.

"Hey, mister," Billy interjected, tugging on Vic's sleeve to regain his attention. "I did just what you tol' me, and that shot didn't hurt like I thought…but it did the next day," he added with a shrug. "But them nurses came here one day and wanted to give us all more shots, so me and my sister ran out on the golf course and hid!"

"That right?" Vic mumbled, clearing his throat as he continued to stare across the crowded space at Louise, who was reaching for a towel to wipe the soap from her hands.

Mrs. Haddaway reached for two plates with a friendly grin. "Can we get you fellas somethin' to eat?"

"You bet," the older man replied, nudging Vic's arm. "The club's our last delivery. The ladies always feel sorry for me and feed me," he chuckled, motioning for Vic to take a seat at the kitchen's prep table.

Vic doffed his cap and stuffed it in the pocket of his jacket, thoroughly pleased with this development.

"We've not seen *you* before, young man," Mrs. Haddaway commented as she set the plates in front of the men.

Jeb Dobbins spoke up as he removed his jacket and hung it on the back of his chair. "Young Caleb fell off the dock this mornin' at the warehouse and broke his arm," he explained regarding his normal co-driver, to a chorus of "Oh dear!" and "My Lands!" from the ladies. "So this young man was kinda in the right place at the right time, and he agreed ta help."

"Name's Vic Matthews," Vic added with a smile, glancing up as several women hovered around, placing items of lunch leftovers on the men's plates.

"Pleased to meet you," Suzy Flynn nodded to him, echoed by the others in the kitchen.

He nodded back, noticing the interested look in her gaze, but then his eyes flashed back to the girl at the sink. Louise hadn't taken her eyes off him, and she sent him a shy smile and a tiny nod.

As the men began to eat, Louise drifted over to the table to hover behind a chair that had been quickly occupied by one of the women.

"Wow, you got real butter!" Billy suddenly exclaimed. The little boy's eyes were round with amazement as he noticed the men smoothing pads of what looked like rich creamery butter on their rolls. "All we get is that margarine stuff," he added with disdain.

"That right?" Mr. Dobbins commented, glancing around the kitchen and wondering why.

"…And *prunes,*" Billy added with disgust.

"Yeah, prunes at every meal!" another child chimed in, causing everyone in the kitchen to nod in agreement. "Prunes, prunes, prunes!"

Louise snickered at Vic's grimace, vowing, "If we ever get back home, I swear I'll never eat another prune the rest of my days!" The others laughed in unison.

Vic chuckled too, in full agreement. He couldn't stand that particular fruit.

Catching Louise's eye, Vic offered, "Hey…got somethin' to tell ya… a couple 'a days ago I went by your place, checkin' on it, and the people that live upstairs said your brother, Sonny, came by a day or two after you folks left."

Louise opened her mouth in pleased surprise, squealing, "Really?"

Lilly, listening at the sink nearly dropped the glass she was drying, spinning with a gasp to view the young man at the table. Taking a closer look at him, she realized it was the same young man who had rescued their family the night they evacuated. She hurried over to him and put her hand on his arm, which caused him to stop chewing and look up into her eyes.

"My Sonny? He's alright?" she murmured, almost afraid to believe it. "But…where is he? Is he at home? Is he with the

Andersons?" She pressed a hand to her chest, her heart pounding.

Vic swallowed the bite of food he had taken and nodded. "I believe he's alright, Ma'am."

"You *believe*? B…but…" Lilly sputtered, not understanding.

"Well…they said he came by there in a boat with some other people and asked where the family went," Vic hastened to explain, hating that he couldn't give her more definite information. "When the Anderson's couldn't tell 'im, they said he went on back toward downtown in the boat with the others." As Lilly's face crumpled with disappointment, Vic added, "But he's with friends, it seems, Ma'am…I'm sure he's alright."

"Pfft, yeah," Billy mumbled. "Who knows what he's been up to. Most likely startin' trouble."

"Billy, that's no way to talk about your elder brother," Louise admonished. Moving to put an arm around her mother's shoulders, Louise soothed, "Sonny's okay, Mama. I just know it. Maybe they took him to the armory and he got sent to someplace nice, like *we* did," she added encouragingly.

Lilly gathered her composure and raised the edge of her apron to her lips as she nodded. The unexpected information had taken the wind out of her sails. Taking a deep breath, she patted Louise's arm, managing a small smile when Louise pressed a kiss to her cheek. Glancing at Vic, she sent him a tiny trembling smile as she turned back to continue her work at the sink.

Vic watched her go, feeling like a heel. He had meant to share what he thought would be encouraging information for the family; that Sonny was, at least, all right. Yet it seemed Mrs. Hoskins had not received it in that manner. Louise turned back, and seeing the look on his face, hastened to assure him, "Thanks for checkin' for us…at least we know *something* now."

Their eyes met and his slowly softened in relief. He sent her a silent nod.

"So…what are you doing here?" she asked, hastening to add, "I mean, I thought you were on a boat…I read something in the paper…" She blushed a little when his eyes sparkled happily at the knowledge that she had not only seen the article, but also remembered it. He had hoped that wherever she was staying, she would see it.

Vic resumed eating, explaining between bites, "I was. But once the water started goin' down and they got that pontoon bridge built, the boats were needed less and less. And since I drove a truck before, and I was over at the warehouse with Doc, it seemed like a good idea to go along with Jeb and help him out." He'd kept to himself that a big incentive for him to help was the possibility that he would find out where *she* had been taken. The whereabouts of the lovely Louise had been a mystery that had been bugging him for nearly ten days.

"You were on a boat?" one of the children asked excitedly. "Did you rescue anybody?" gushed a boy with two missing front teeth and a shock of red hair. Suddenly, everyone seemed to have questions for him…Had he been to a certain street…had he seen so and so, some family member or friend…had he had any close calls? They fired questions at him like cannonballs. Vic sat back with a grin and thought for a moment, enjoying the attention.

Just then, Edna wandered in the door, her curiosity aroused by the raised, excited voices in the kitchen. Grabbing an apple from a bowl on the counter, she drew up behind Louise to see what the commotion was all about.

Vic noticed the newcomer and nodded her way as he began to regale his audience with 'flood' stories. The children and ladies hovered in rapt attention as Vic intoned, "You wouldn't of believed it if you'd seen it yourself, the broad thoroughfares of downtown – they seemed like they were part of the river itself, with dozens of rowboats cruisin' the waters."

"Just like Venice, that place in Italy! Right, Mr. Vic?" Billy supplied, having heard that description from the adults many times. He grinned as Vic nodded and winked. "You're right about that, son. It looked just like what I've seen in those newsreels."

Continuing, Vic recalled catching a glimpse of an entire house floating down the Ohio, and of animals standing on small rafts or on the tops of stables. These were the first stories the displaced group had heard from actual witnesses, and they were utterly amazed.

Vic related about the funny billboard, which had them all chuckling, especially the kids. They immediately began to act out their vision of the spectacle, complete with 'glub glub' sound effects. Laughing with the others, Vic continued that memory, recounting how it felt to be in the boat when the electricity went off; and the awe inspiring moment when, after prayer and song, WHAS came back online, as if in direct answer to that prayer. Louise and several others felt shivers upon hearing that and glanced at one another, wide-eyed. One lady made the sign of the cross and shook her head in wonder.

When Vic paused again to take a few bites of food, Jeb offered his experiences of watching over 200,000 pounds of rations being offloaded from big airplanes on soggy runways, and army trucks lined up and ready to be loaded for delivery. "And the Red Cross, they had to really scramble to find places for everybody. You ladies here were lucky. Why, some of your fellow refugees have been stayin' in tent cities, if they weren't lucky enough to be taken in by a family with room to spare…" he mentioned gently. The ladies all nodded in agreement. Each one knew that, in spite of the boredom of staying at the club, they were, in fact, fortunate.

"The Red Cross turned some barber shops and storefronts into emergency health centers to dispense typhoid shots and basic first aid," he added, recalling when he had stopped by a barbershop-turned-clinic to see to a cut on his hand.

Vic picked up the discourse again, divulging how his boat had been chosen to escort Phil Harnden, the Universal Movietone Newsreel reporter. "The man was a wonder. You shoulda seen him, holdin' the camera and balancin' like a circus performer ridin' bareback on a trick horse – in a rubber raft towed on a rope behind our boat, no less," he crooned, giving a shake of his head and shoving another bite of food in his mouth.

"Are you gonna be in a newsreel, Mr. Vic?" Billy gushed, his blue eyes oozing with hero worship.

Vic flashed him a smile and reached to ruffle his hair. "I mighta got in a few shots."

"Wow…" the little boy whispered, feeling as if he were in the presence a movie star.

Chuckling, Vic spent the next few minutes apprising his listeners of where he and his crew had taken the photographer. How the man had snapped a picture of the statue of Lincoln 'standing on the water', and how Mr. Harnden had wished he could have been there to witness it as Vic and the crew had seen it – a praying Lincoln. "We took him down into the worst hit areas, like The Point, and floated by the Heigold House," he continued, shaking his head sadly.

The ladies 'awed' in empathy, as everyone considered the Heigold House one of most elegant mansions in town. It had frequently been the scene of swanky parties reported in the society section of the paper. "I just hope they can fix all the damage done to it by that ol' river."

He went on, describing how he'd watched as one man in a rowboat, paying too much attention to what the photographer was doing, had come too close to a traffic light hanging just above the waterline. It had actually knocked him into the current. "You never saw anybody scramble back inside a boat faster in your life!" he joked with a teasing glint in his eye, as his audience chuckled.

Then he paused for a moment, thinking of someone else who had fallen into the water, but the results had been less fortunate. As if hearing his thoughts, seven-year-old Hubert Geldhaus, spoke up, "The boat that took us from our house, it turned over and everything fell in the water."

His mother, standing to one side of the group, added disdainfully, "Due to the sheer incompetence of the men. Clumsy fools."

Vic turned his head and stared at her, his eyes taking on the hue of charred wood. "I only know of one rescue boat that capsized ma'am…the reason I heard was that the family insisted on takin' way more of their possessions than was allowed," he murmured quietly, controlling his tone.

The woman had the grace to appear uncomfortable at his words, muttering, "It was a ridiculous limitation – one bag per person? Why…I would have been forced to leave behind my furs…my jewelry…simply unacceptable—and now all but one are ruined…" she paused at the look on his face.

Vic took a deep breath, a muscle in his jaw flexed as he clamped his teeth and lips together. In a quiet voice, he returned slowly, his words measured. "One 'a those 'fools' was a friend 'a mine, ma'am. His name was John Shore. He was 54, married, with four kids." Recognizing at least a spark of reaction in her eyes, he drove home the point. "His wife hadn't wanted him to help, but he'd insisted, sayin' he couldn't sit by in a warm, dry house and do nothin' when there was people out there who needed rescuin'. Heck, he lived up in the Highlands, blocks away from the water." Then leveling his mahogany gaze at her he added, "He got pneumonia from bein' out in the weather too long after he fell in tryin' ta save your fur coats… he died two days later."

Mrs. Geldhaus' eyes had grown large and for once, she was rendered totally speechless. For the first time, she was forced to glimpse her attitude and actions through the eyes of someone else – and they were not a pretty sight. The other women turned to stare at her also; their opinion of her dropping even lower than it had been before. Mortified, she grasped hold of the arms of her children and exited the room without another word, as the kids fussed that they wanted to hear more 'flood' stories.

Vic shut his eyes for a minute, lowering and shaking his head in disgust. *What a self-centered woman…* Visions of John's funeral –

and the agonizing grief of his wife and children – floated through his mind's eye.

"Will you tell us more about the flood, Mr. Vic?" requested little Sally with a shy smile, shifting her baby doll to her other hip. Vic opened his eyes and glanced down into her large, baby blue gaze and smiled. Taking in a breath, he gave her a wink.

"Well, we saw stuff I'll never forget as long as I live…" he murmured, recalling movie houses, the waterline nearly up to the once glittering, but now dark and silent, marquees, reminding him of a ghost town. He related how the boats could just barely make it underneath the wooden railroad bridge that crossed Main Street; the water level was so high. "You had to duck down, or you'd hit your head for sure."

"Golly!" one of the boys gushed, wishing he was grown and could have been out having 'fun' like Mr. Vic and his crew. Indeed, all of the boys were riveted to Vic's side, trying to imagine the scenes he was describing. Mr. Dobbins sat back in his chair and lit a pipe, enjoying the stories himself. The older man had, for the most part – been out of the 'loop' delivering daily supplies, and had not experienced much of the actual flooding.

After a few bites of food, Vic paused to sort through the occurrences of the past ten days. He related to the group the frightening sight of seeing tanker train cars bobbing like corks in the deep water, even floating over to the high power lines and bumping into their poles. His audience gasped in wonder. "We were all thankin' God that the power was off, or this whole city woulda' gone up like the Fourth of July," he mused. He went on, trying to convey to them the absolute terror he had felt the night the Louisville Paint & Varnish Company caught fire and burned to the ground. Everyone in the room had heard the news about the huge fire in Cincinnati. "I wouldn't have given a plug nickel for any of our lives then. The Cincinnati fire was started by oil and gas on the water from overturned storage tanks, and it burned for 48 hours." Shaking his head, he added, "I don't mind tellin' ya…we were all afraid that what wasn't under water here in Louisville, would end up burned to a cinder."

Louise smiled in quiet fascination and hugged her arms across her chest as she watched him; his eyes were sparkling as he vividly recounted his adventures. She mused that if she hadn't been totally smitten before, this would have cemented the feeling, for sure.

Vic continued, regaling them with details about the already famous 'pontoon bridge', how it seemed to stretch on and on; so long that one couldn't see one end of it from the other. "That'll be one for the record books, I'll tell ya. Thousands of people rode anything that floated over to the foot of the bridge. That thing was bobbin', swayin', and shimmyin' as the people made their way down it, haulin' everything they could carry." He paused for a minute recalling the images he had seen as he went by in his boat. "Seventy-five thousand people walked out of the city on that pontoon bridge in three days," he shook his head, still awed by the sheer number. "I saw people carryin' bird cages, armloads of pots and pans, suitcases, pillow cases packed with stuff – all while wearin' layers and layers of clothes and two coats, three hats, trying to transport as much as they could and not leave it for the looters."

"Looters?" one woman asked, suddenly worried. "But what about the Police? The National Guard…the Coast Guard?"

"They're patrolin' all the time, Ma'am," Vic acknowledged. "The Coast Guard sent hundreds of their guys to the city. Navy from the Great Lakes and North Carolina came and they patrol, too. But when people are up to no good, they seem ta find a way," he added with a shake of his head. However, seeing the worry that had replaced the mirth on their faces, he hastened to add, "But to be honest, the authorities catch most of 'em before they have a chance to do harm."

"It's helped, though, hadn't it, that the downtown was evacuated?" Jeb spoke up. "I heard there ain't a soul left from Fifteenth to the river."

Vic nodded. "I'm sure it has. Though there *are* folks left, in second-floor apartments or above stores or businesses."

"But where did all of those people go?" Mrs. Haddaway asked, thinking of her brother and his family, who lived in a two-story house on Eighteenth.

"Well Ma'am, I heard tell that the churches across the city opened their doors, people in the higher sections of town, and like Jeb here said earlier – store fronts, even theaters and schools – anywhere that had space." He went on to share how grocery stores and produce markets willingly donated all of their wares to help those in need, and milk companies had given free milk and dairy products to needy mothers with small children. "Sometimes the river herself contributed…me and my guys fished a barrel of pickled beets outta the water one day," he snickered. "'Course, that came from a warehouse that was all but washed away by the current…"

Waxing pensive, he glanced around at the ladies, reflecting on the sobering realization of the damage the city had sustained, especially in The Point. Vic made the prediction that the city might just declare that entire end of town condemned, no longer allowing any of the buildings to be occupied again. "It's the dangdest thing *I* ever saw…looked like some kinda strange lake…acres of water dotted with rooftops and the top branches of trees…maybe a telephone pole here and there. It's mighty sad down there…those folks lost everything…"

The people in the warm dry kitchen of the luxurious country club, so far away from the crisis, lapsed into silence. Even the children sympathized with the unfortunate 'West Enders'.

Suddenly… hearing the details didn't seem so amusing anymore. One by one, the ladies began to drift away from the table. Each felt a jumble of emotions, all the way from gratitude to sympathy; drawing from the information Vic had shared.

"Well son…I think it's time we be mosyin' along, 'fore we

outstay our welcome," Jeb intoned, pushing his chair back as he stood to his feet.

Vic nodded with a murmured, "I think you're right." He wiped his mouth on a napkin and stood as the ladies went on about their business.

Louise followed him to the door as he began to make his exit, Mr. Dobbins already half way to the truck.

"Well, I..." Vic began.

"I...um..." Louise started. Both fell silent, not knowing what to say. He toyed with the idea of asking her out.

"Do...do you guys know when you'll be comin' back to town?" Vic asked, raising his hands to replace his cap and adjust it on his head.

The air was cold outside the steamy kitchen, so Louise crossed her sweater-covered arms over her chest with a slight shiver. "No...they don't tell us anything..."

He nodded, his eyes roaming down her body, noticing the tiny waist and the soft swell of her curves in the oversized dress.

"Shut the door, Mary Louise!" her mother's voice called from inside. Louise quickly stepped out and pulled the door closed behind her.

Raising her eyes to his face, she noticed the direction of his gaze and wrapped her sweater tighter around her middle, feeling extremely self-conscious. "I hate this dress..."

At his look of confusion, she added, "The church ladies brought us some clothes the second day we were here...but this was all I could grab." She looked down at it with a shrug. "Be glad to have *my* dress back. Heck, I'll be glad to be away from here and back home. We call this place the 'Golden Prison'," she added as she glanced around. Bringing her eyes back to his, she found them just watching her, his expression thoughtful.

Louise smiled shyly at him, casting around for something else to say and wishing she could keep him there indefinitely.

His smile widened, deepening his dimples, as he stepped a bit closer to her, placing one hand on the doorframe.

Startled at this bold move, she held her breath, her heart jumping in her chest as she gazed up into his face. *Oh my gosh…is he gonna kiss me?* The winter sunlight was bright behind his head as he effectively backed her into the corner next to the door. Blindly reaching behind, she felt the rough surface of the unyielding brick against her fingers and back.

Slowly, his hand rose to touch her cheek, as he murmured, "So…your name's Mary Louise…" She gave a faint nod. He went on softly, "Reminds me of my boat…her name was the Mary Lou. Anybody ever call you that?"

Nervous, she unconsciously moistened her lips and shook her head.

His eyes and the edges of his hair seemed to sparkle. "They oughtta. It suits ya," he murmured, his voice soft and low.

She swallowed, managing a whispered, "It does?" as her eyes darted back and forth between his, so close…

Vic nodded slowly, irresistibly drawn to the sparkling hazel lights in her eyes. He glanced from them down to her mouth, and then up again. *What would she do if I tried to kiss her? Would she let me?*

Then from the corner of his eye he saw movement inside the kitchen – her mother, glancing toward the door with furrowed brow – and he knew he had to make tracks. Vic backed up half a step and in a low voice, he murmured, "Be seein' ya…Mary Lou."

Speechless, Louise watched him give her a wink as he turned on his heel, disappearing around the corner of the building.

ᏑᏍ

CHAPTER 11

Going Home to the Unknown

NINE PEOPLE RODE along in a black '33 Studebaker hearse, three on the front seat, and the rest on makeshift seats in the back. The car was packed to the rims with household items, some of which was even strapped to the roof. Each person in the back strained to get a peek at the landscape slowly rolling by. They had been on the road for about thirty minutes before they approached the first telltale signs of how high the water had risen.

"We truly appreciate the lift back to Louisville, Mr. Grant," Willis intoned. He nodded with a smile to the little girl sitting next to her father as she turned her head and flashed him a grin.

"Aww, it's no trouble," Frank Grant replied as he negotiated around an obstruction in the road. "Glad we could help out."

"Daddy says your mom's a real good cook, Mr. Grant," Billy piped up. The little girl in the front seat shifted her gaze in his direction. Across the vehicle, Louise pressed her lips together to stifle a smile as she watched her brother quickly turn his head and look away from little Bernice Grant's shy grin.

Meanwhile, Edna snickered as she watched Lilly give their father The Eye. Willis cleared his throat and shot a look of good-natured aggravation at his youngest, before crooning, "Second only to *you*, my dear." His wife pursed her lips and nodded, "Mmm hmm." The tiniest curve of a grin, however, was enough to put the lie to her 'angry' look.

"Although I missed being able to enjoy meals with the family, I must say, the ladies of the church took good care of us men during our lonely hours of enforced bachelorhood," Willis complimented.

"Yeah, Mom's always loved cookin'," Frank agreed. "And she was in her element being in charge of the food brigade. You shoulda seen her figurin' and refigurin' ingredients, issuin' orders, and tastin' all the dishes before she allowed 'em to be served to you men." Willis laughed softly, having witnessed the elder Mrs. Grant in action; she had run the operation with the precision that would have befitted a general in the army. "But her house is kind of small," Frank added, "and after havin' all of us under foot for eleven days, plus cookin' for the men housed at the church, I think she was glad to see us go back home."

"Do you know *why* the men couldn't take their meals with us?" Lilly inquired, the subject of the family's forced separation still a sore one.

The man pursed his lips and shook his head with a bewildered shrug. "Just orders from the Red Cross, from what I understand. When they arranged for the church and the club to provide lodgings for flood refugees from Louisville, they stressed that the men, for propriety's sake, had to be boarded separate. Didn't make sense to us, though, why you men couldn't eat with your families – at least lunch or dinner – but we didn't make the rules. And them Presbyterian ladies, they're sticklers for followin' the rules," he added with a soft chuckle.

Slowing down to maneuver through a deep patch of mud in the road, and seeing more and more evidence of the high water that had occupied the area mere days before, Frank shook his head with a sigh. "Don't mind telling you, I'm dreading seeing our place, though a family friend told us it didn't fare as bad as others…"

"That's good to know," Willis acknowledged, glancing at his wife. "I'm concerned about what we will face, as well."

"I always try to see the good in every situation," Mrs. Grant murmured from the front seat, turning her head and meeting Lilly's eyes. "But I confess, I'm having a hard time with this..." Lilly nodded as the two women, strangers in reality, shared common ground.

Lilly pondered the crisis in regard to her penchant for thinking that every bad thing which happened to her was yet another 'punishment' heaped upon her shoulders. Clamping her teeth and shutting her eyes momentarily, she fought back tears of hopelessness – her would-be constant companion and resident enemy. Only the love of her husband and family kept that 'wolf' at bay.

The occupants of the vehicle passed the next few minutes in silence, reflecting upon Mrs. Grant's words, as soft music coming from the radio was nearly drowned out by the crunching of debris under the tires. Then, almost as if their conversation had been heard, the mayor took that moment to interrupt the recently resumed airing of music on WHAS with one of his 'pep' talks for his beleaguered city.

"My fellow citizens," he began in his familiar, rich baritone voice. *"As the menacing waters of the Ohio have begun to retreat, and our fair city begins its arduous task of recovery, I implore you to be encouraged."* The members of the two families met one another's eyes as they listened. Frank reached for the knob and turned up the volume. *"Good things can be said to have come from the disaster, and there is much to make history in Louisville in those friendships that were built up when the rich and poor labored side-by-side to rescue their fellow men. When executive and truck driver jointly operated a truck in carrying food to the homeless, when Protestant, Catholic and Jew filled sand bags to protect the homes of those they had never before seen...I think we shall all thank God that we live in a city which has shown the resourcefulness to meet the catastrophe, the generosity to take care of the weak and the helpless, and the determination to work together for a greater Louisville."* Heads were nodding in agreement as Willis murmured a word of acknowledgement. *"Let us not now cease with this welcome atmosphere, but continue to reach out and*

help our fellow man as the clean-up begins. Neighbor, reach out and help thy neighbor. Let us all put into practice that old saying, 'You scratch my back and I'll scratch yours.' In this way, my fellow citizens, we will, together, beat that 'Ol' Man River', and put him in his place."

Adding a few community announcements and helpful information, the mayor signed off.

Once again, the soft music resumed as the Hoskins and Grant families murmured affirmations regarding their leader's words, and mentioned friendships that were made during the crisis.

"Look at that!" Louise suddenly gasped as she pointed to a ghastly sight off to the side of the road. All nine occupants craned their necks to see the spectacle.

"Ewww!" Bernice exclaimed as the others made similar noises, all of them viewing the carcass of a large dog – suspended in a tree ten feet above the ground. It had apparently gotten caught in the branches and drowned. Its mouth and eyes were open and staring, seemingly frozen in terror.

Lilly gasped at the hideous sight. "Oh my lands! I…I can't imagine the water being that high!"

"Yes, but from what they said, it got a lot higher than that, downtown…" Mrs. Grant murmured as her eyes darted from debris to debris – everything from small bits of clothing and paper to household goods – nervous in spite of Vic's assurance that their place was still intact.

"Yes…" Lilly agreed, shaking her head in amazement at the amount of mud and detritus strewn everywhere. Her stomach was in knots, dreadfully afraid of what they would encounter once they reached their home.

Turning onto a side street several minutes later, they saw it was closed, a collapsing of the sewers resulting in a huge hole in the center of the road. From their vantage point, the occupants of the vehicle could see past the barricade to several workers gingerly making their way around the jagged break in the pavement, and looking over the edge into the black unknown. Lilly shuddered in reaction to the gruesome evidence of the power of the flood's destruction, the frightful sight leaving her with an increased foreboding about what they might find at home. Perhaps they had lost everything?

Frank turned onto another street and they made their way around, eventually turning onto Baxter.

"Well, would ya look at that!" Earl Grant murmured from the back of the vehicle as he shook his head in amazement.

"Jeeze…it's just like he described…" Louise murmured under her breath as they drove past the infamous pontoon bridge, half of its length now fully visible due to the steadily retreating waters. They could clearly see its structure and quality of workmanship, the crossed boards housing three barrels each, now resting on the mud covered street.

Continuing slowly on as each occupant of the vehicle stared at the sight in fascination, they eventually turned onto Chestnut, and Frank negotiated the piles of sludge and other obstructions to pull up where Willis indicated, in front of their building.

Steeling themselves, the Hoskins viewed the debris-littered front yard, with mud caked on the foundation and the front steps. With a jolt, they saw that the front window they had climbed from had been broken out and they wondered when and how it had happened.

Frank put the car in gear and left it idling. Climbing out, he immediately noticed the heavy, musky scent of the air as he moved to help his son and Willis retrieve the Hoskins' belongings.

"Can we be of help to you folks?" Frank quietly offered, nodding when Willis politely declined with encouragement that they should continue on to see about their own home. He thanked them once again for their kindness and the families bid one another goodbye as the Grants continued on their way.

"My lands, what a mess!" Lilly moaned as she turned to again survey the damage.

With trepidation, they clasped their belongings and stepping gingerly, silently approached their home. Mounting the steps, Willis turned the handle on the front door, resulting in the girls squealing and jumping back a bit when muddy slime came gushing out.

"Who's that?" a voice called from inside before a face appeared at the door. It was Mr. Anderson from upstairs, muck covered broom in hand.

"Oh it's you, Hoskins. 'Bout time you folks got back. Where you been?" the man asked. Looking down, he added, "Oh, hang on. Was just sweeping up some of this sh…muck." The family stood back while the man hurriedly swept some more of the sludge from the foyer out onto the front stoop and then gave the steps a quick swipe, as Willis recounted where they had spent the last ten days.

Tentatively, the family filed inside. The man jabbered about one subject after another, such as the aggravation of trying to function without drinking water for the first few days, or electricity or heat, save for their tiny fireplace. Not to mention the phenomenon of being awakened at night by the sloshing of water against the sides of the house as boats motored by. Grabbing an oil lantern he had stashed on the steps, Mr. Anderson quickly lit it and followed them down the hall.

"I didn't realize the electric power would still be off…" Willis murmured, meeting Lilly's worried eyes.

Finding the door to their apartment stained with river slime and unlocked, they glanced at one another as Willis turned the handle and pushed the door open. Together they stood for a moment to survey the damage. Mr. Anderson stretched up to peer over the heads of the girls. Suddenly, everyone heard the noise of footsteps coming down the stairs and Mrs. Anderson squawking about the oddity of having an *old black hearse of a thing* parked at their front door.

Seeing it was her downstairs neighbors returning, and catching a glimpse inside their place, the woman had the grace to clamp her mouth shut.

Except for a thick layer of mud and silt covering anything on or near the floor, things were pretty much where the family had last seen them. The legs of the dining table showed signs of having stood in six-inch deep water for days on end, but everything they had piled on its top was still intact. The range would need a good cleaning and it looked like the floor would need to be replaced, as the retreating water had left the boards hopelessly warped. Moving cautiously to the bedroom doorway, Willis was relieved to see that only a few inches of water had gotten in there, as it had a raised floor. The edges of the bedspreads and room dividers were slime stained, as well as the bottom of the bureaus. Shoes and other items on the floor of the closet appeared to be ruined. Everything reeked of the musky smell of river water. Lilly's eyes filled and spilled over as she viewed the mess.

"Gertrude came back yesterday. She's fit to be tied, gripin' about needin' to have all of the floors replaced down here," Anderson reported, snorting as he added, "You know how tight she is."

"How we gonna stay here, Daddy?" Billy whined as the cold and damp of their unheated dwelling seeped inside his thin coat. As if on cue, all five Hoskins seemed to feel the cold and shivered, almost in unison. At that moment, their home no longer felt like home.

"We'll just have to set about giving everything a good scrubbing," Lilly declared, though her voice shook slightly. Louise and Edna exchanged glances of doubt – it looked like they had a huge job in store.

Feeling charitable, Mr. Anderson glanced at his wife, and at her nod, gallantly offered, "You folks can sleep on pallets up in our place until things get back to normal."

Turning to meet his normally self-centered neighbor's eyes, Willis drew in a strengthening breath and gave the man a nod of gratitude.

"We'd be much obliged."

ꟷ

MR. GRANT MANEUVERED the car over and allowed it to slowly roll to a stop at the curb. His green eyes narrowed as his mouth fell open in dismay. The yard, much like the Hoskins' place, was a mess with the unsightly evidence that the river had been making its 'bed' there for many days. Each family member held their breath as they surveyed their home – and some unexpected activity – as four young men were hard at work sweeping and mopping.

At the sound of the motor, Vic looked over from tossing another muck-filled bucket out the door. Smiling, albeit with concern, he tossed the utensil aside and made his way toward the car as the doors opened and the occupants climbed out.

"Vic, what..." Mrs. Grant began, but he interrupted as he wiped his hands on a rag.

"Since you guys said you were comin' home today, thought I'd help you get a start on cleanin' up your place." Turning to survey the former crew of the Mary Lou, Gerald, Phil, and Eugene, as they paused in their tasks and waved, he added, "The fellas, well, they figured what the heck, they'd help, too."

Trembling, Mrs. Grant reached out to give Vic a hug as the others drew near. When Vic pulled back, his eyes met the worried gaze of his long time friend. Earl reached out and shook Vic's hand as Mr. Grant and young Bernice stared at their home.

"It's um...it's kinda bad in there, but I think it can be saved. At least everything is still there..." Vic added, prompting several questioning looks, which dissolved into understanding as they remembered what he had told them on his visit – their friend Alec and his family had lost nearly everything when three feet of water had inundated their house for days on end. Many of their possessions had floated away, as Vic had witnessed.

"Have they come back yet?" Mrs. Grant asked softly.

Vic shook his head sadly, the memory of cruising past the house still bothersome. "I went by there on the way here…" he stopped, unsure of what to say. "I don't even know where they went."

"Me either…they dropped me off that day and the last I saw of 'em, Alec was paddlin' on up the street and his mom and sisters were cryin'…" Earl mentioned, also stopping as he saw the expression on his mother's face. Neither young man wished to add to her burdens at that point.

Scrambling for something encouraging to say, Vic blurted, "I think if we get a good hot fire started in the fireplace, that'll help dry things out."

Mrs. Grant managed a small smile and a nod, holding her husband and son's hands, as she entered the door to their home. However, they stumbled to a halt as the enormity of the situation assailed her senses. The smell…a pungent odor hung heavy in the very air.

The odor of the river…earth and mud…and misery.

How would things ever get back to normal? For them? For their friends? For the city?

ꕥ

BUT THINGS DID get back to normal. Everyone pitched in and worked hard, cleaning, scrubbing, disinfecting with bleach and lye, deodorizing with baking soda, and demolishing and rebuilding where needed.

Two days went by and the Hoskins, much like most of the people in the city, poured themselves into the monumental task of cleaning up after the waters receded. Each day, the river retreated further back toward its normal confines, and with each foot of regained ground, the people of the city seemed to gather more determination and energy.

As Louise paused a moment from scrubbing and wiped her brow with the back of one forearm, she glanced over at the open doorway. Her eyes and mouth popped open and she let out a squeal as a voice asked no one in particular, "'Bout time ya'll came home. Where you been?"

"Sonny!" Louise cried, rushing over to throw her arms around her long-lost brother. Excitement erupted as Willis and Billy jumped up from their cleaning chores and Lilly and Edna hurried in from the bedroom. Each one bombarded Sonny with hugs and questions, until Lilly finally pulled back, fussing, "Joseph Robert, where have you BEEN? You're absolutely filthy!"

Sonny let out a chuckle and shook his head. "Man, have I got stories to tell."

"We were so worried about you!" "Where ya been? Tell us!" "Leave it to you to get inta some kind of mischief," Louise, Billy and Edna gushed at the same time. As the family gazed at their returning prodigal, each one unconsciously registered that he seemed thinner, and somehow different…as if his experiences had served to propel him further along the path to becoming a man, and not just a lanky teen.

"The first thing *you're* doing, young man, is taking those filthy clothes *off*. Take them off this minute! I declare they must be positively full of *lice*!" Lilly blustered, gingerly removing her son's cap from his head and grimacing at the smell. "Haven't you bathed these whole two weeks?" she griped, grumbling a few choice words about the condition of her returning lost sheep. This, in typical 'Lilly' fashion, came on the heels of wanting to squeeze and hug him, having been so overpoweringly worried for so long.

Sonny laughed again and headed toward the cupboard where his clothes were kept, even as Lilly followed him, fussing, "Now you get on upstairs to that bathroom and scrub yourself clean, you hear? You use that bar of lye soap and plenty of hot water.

Thank Heavens the power came back on to fire up the boiler..." she went on. Lilly clucked after him like the mother hen that she was and followed him up the stairs, fretting as they went, to wait for his clothes outside the door. She immediately marched herself outside and burned the lot of them, muttering about filthy lice.

Within minutes, Lilly came bustling in the back door with orders for Louise to run up to Hudson's Market for some more lye. It was a few blocks uptown and had reopened soon after the floodwaters receded.

Happy to escape a few minutes of scrubbing, Louise tossed her coat on and quickly tied a scarf around her none too clean hair, and set off at a brisk walk. Glad for the few minutes of quiet, she was actually humming a happy tune. She was just in the midst of daydreaming an outrageous scenario involving Vic Matthews knocking at her door, wearing a tuxedo and escorting her to a fancy ball, when she became aware of the sound of an automobile motor.

Turning her head, she couldn't believe her eyes – it was Vic Matthews – riding in what looked like the black hearse in which she had ridden home from the country club! Stopping dead in her tracks, her mouth dropped open as she stared.

Vic, riding in the passenger seat of the vehicle, had convinced his friend to take a detour after the guys had been sent on an errand to a local hardware. They were supposed to pick up items Earl's family needed in the restoration work on their home. When Vic had seen the girl walking briskly along Chestnut, he couldn't believe his luck.

"Hey man, pull over," he had requested of his pal.

"Why? Who's that?" Earl had asked, even as he maneuvered the vehicle toward the curb.

Then as the young girl turned to face them, Earl leaned over to see out the window.

"Hey there – you're Louise, right?" he called before Vic could get a word out. "How is everything? You guys have much damage?"

Vic and Louise both looked startled, each one wondering how the other knew their suddenly mutual friend.

"What are…" "How do you…" they both began, as they looked from one to the other.

"How do you guys know each other?" Vic asked, a fierce sensation of unreasoning jealousy suddenly suffusing his chest, making him grit his teeth at the rising emotion.

"My old man drove her family home…" "His father drove us home…" they both responded, stopping short as Louise giggled in reaction. She tentatively approached the passenger door so that she could see Earl better, to ask, "How about *your* home? Was it bad?"

"Not as bad as some, but oh man, the smell now…" he returned, still leaning over Vic.

"Yes! We've been scrubbing since we got home, but still that smell is there," she agreed, wrinkling her nose at the thought of it. Vic stared at her, fighting his feelings of jealousy. Everything about the girl seemed to draw him like a magnet.

After a few more exchanges with Earl, Louise's eyes switched to the other occupant of the vehicle, and the intensity of his gaze nearly took her breath away. Instantly, her mouth went dry and she swallowed nervously as the final moments of their last encounter…their 'almost' kiss…came rushing back to her memory.

"Hi," she said with a shy smile.

"Hey," Vic murmured, allowing his eyes to roam over her face and the scarf on her head. Its faded pink color seemed to bring out the healthy glow of her complexion.

Unconsciously she raised one hand to touch the unattractive object, acutely aware of her not-so-lovely appearance, and especially conscious of what she knew her hair must look like under the tattered scarf. *Drat it all!* She groused silently. *Why is it every time I see you, it's when I'm not expecting it!*

"You guys doin' okay?" Vic asked. "Did Sonny ever come home?"

"Yes today!" she immediately gushed, causing Vic's eyes to become alive with pleasure at her sudden animation. His feelings of jealousy forgotten, he laughed in delight.

"Where's he been?"

She laughed in infectious happiness. "I don't know yet. As soon as he walked in the door, Mama made him march right upstairs to take a bath – and she took his clothes outside and burned 'em, fussin' that they were full of lice!" she added as they both chuckled.

"He's sure got a lot 'a explainin' to do, huh?"

"Hey, uh…who's this 'Sonny'?" Earl interjected, feeling decidedly uninformed, and wondering how his friend knew this girl.

"Oh sorry, he's my brother," Louise explained, dragging her gaze from Vic to his friend. "He was gone the night we had to evacuate and we didn't know where he was the whole time we were away. Mama 'bout went crazy worryin'."

"I bet," he answered, imagining his own mother in that situation.

"I'd sure like to know where he was," Vic smoothly injected.

Louise met his eyes again, hers still bubbling with joy. Vic went on without missing a beat, "How 'bout I pick you up Friday night and you can tell me all about it?"

Her heart jumped in her chest, speeding up double time.

"You mean…a real date?" Louise asked, wide-eyed.

He grinned, thinking how cute she was, and so innocent. You'd think she'd never been on a date before.

"Sure," Vic answered smoothly. "How 'bout I pick you up about seven?"

Suddenly panic began to rise within Louise at the thought of Vic coming to the apartment. She feared that he would find out the one thing she wished to keep from him until she knew him better. Even worse was picturing Edna finding out that their hero rescuer and spinner of flood yarns was actually Vic Matthews, her blind date – and that he was more than 'just okay', he was downright gorgeous. Louise had suffered Edna's wrath more than once, and she was determined to avoid that as long as possible. Frantically, she scrambled to find a way…

Shaking her head, Louise moistened her lips as she thought for a minute. "Um…no," she began, but at Vic's crestfallen expression, she added, "I mean…Mama doesn't want anybody coming to the apartment right now, it's still such a mess. I…I could meet you somewhere…" she offered, hoping he would agree.

Vic thought that was a bit odd, considering the whole city was a virtual mess, but he merely shrugged. It didn't matter to him as long as he could spend an evening with this girl who had captivated his entire range of senses.

"Okay…how about…Luckert's on Fourth. It's on a bit of high ground and didn't take much water, so they've already reopened."

Relieved, Louise nodded, striving to hide just how excited she was that Vic Matthews had actually asked her to go out with him. "Alright. I'll see you there Friday night," she promised, though mentally she was already scrambling for something she could tell her parents. *Never mind…I'll think of something.*

Then realizing quite a bit of time had passed and her mother would be wondering where she was with that lye soap, she gasped, "Oh gosh, I better run. Mama sent me to the store for lye. She'll be sendin' out a search party for me."

Backing away from the car, she waved goodbye to the young men and turned, only then realizing she was within sight of the market. Hurriedly, she ducked inside the door as the big car pulled away and the screen door banged shut behind her. The interior was dim and shadowy, the walls lined with overly packed shelves. The familiar old and musty scents mingled with the aromas of fruits, fresh bread and bakery goods.

Rushing over the smooth, well-worn wooden floors with their accustomed squeaks, she circled the center product island of the quaint little store, heading right to the shelf she needed, and circled around to the counter, money ready.

"Well, little lady, it's good to see you again," Mr. Hudson greeted as he rang up her purchase. "This' the first time you been in since the flood. Your family okay?"

The jovial, gray-haired gentleman's eyes crinkled fondly behind his spectacles as he looked at her. Of all the neighborhood young people, sweet Mary Louise Hoskins had always been his favorite. Mr. Hudson felt like somewhat of a surrogate father toward her, especially so when Willis was away for extended periods.

"Hello Mr. Hudson," she replied, grinning at him, her happiness literally overflowing. She nodded in answer to his question, and told him briefly about where they had gone and when they'd returned. Then taking up her purchase, she bid him goodbye.

"I saw you talkin' with those young men outside. One 'a them your fella?" Mr. Hudson teased with a waggle of his bushy gray eyebrows.

She glanced up surprised, but realized she shouldn't be – Mr. Hudson always seemed to know all of the scuttlebutt and every who, what and where. He never missed anything happening out front of the big windows of his store. But a thought shot through her brain and sent a shard of electricity down her limbs – he might say something to one of her family members!

"Um…no, Mr. Hudson…they were just…askin' directions is all," she fibbed, dipping one hand inside a pocket and crossing her fingers.

The wise old man saw right through her ruse, but being so fond of her, he couldn't help but smile and nod. Nevertheless, he'd be sure to be on the lookout for anything going on when it came to sweet Mary Louise.

"Alright sweetie. You run along now, I bet Miss Lilly's

needin' that lye," he acquiesced, making a sweeping motion with his hand to scoot her on her way.

Plagued by guilt for putting such a deception over on sweet old Mr. Hudson, Louise bit her lip and nodded before slipping out the door. She wasn't good at lying. Everyone always told her they could see the truth plainly in her guilty eyes.

As Louise hugged the package to her chest and made her way down the familiar street, she had a feeling in the pit of her stomach that somehow this would all blow up in her face.

ꕥ

CHAPTER 12

Their First Official Date

HAVING BEEN ALLOWED a day to do as she pleased because the workers were finishing up the new floors in the apartment, Louise walked briskly along, scrunching down in her coat to fend off the sharp February breeze. She could barely contain the skip in her step as she thought about her upcoming date with the gorgeous Vic Matthews. The only drawback was…she still hadn't formulated a foolproof excuse to give her parents about where she would be.

Deep in thought, she turned the last corner heading toward the Neighborhood House and, upon spotting two familiar and welcome faces approaching from the other direction, she snapped out of her reverie and smiled.

"Hey you guys! I've been worried about you!" Louise waved and called as she hurried forward.

"Lou!" Fleet called and waved back as the girls quickened their steps, meeting with hugs in front of the building.

"Did you all stay in your place?" Eleanor asked as she pulled back from her friend's embrace.

Louise shook her head, "No, they took all of us out to a place called Dove Creek Country Club. All but Sonny, that is. We just got back this week," she added with a shiver, wrapping her gloved hands around herself in the brisk breeze. Turning toward the building to get out of the cold, she asked, "Did you stay here?"

Eleanor shook her head as she held the door for the other two. "No…they made us stay in a tent in what they called a 'tent city'." Her expression turned sad as she thought about the misery of it. The cramped conditions and contaminated drinking water. They had huddled around a blazing stove in the middle of the mess tent day after day, while the rain and sleet made the outdoors a morass of mud and misery. "It was awful…cold, rainy, icy, snowy…Mom and Dad both came down sick with colds…"

Louise looked at her friend as they all began to take off their coats and scarves. "But…your mom and dad are okay now?" The girl nodded with a grateful smile. There was, at least, that.

"We stayed here," Fleet volunteered. "Myrtle came upstairs with us and we toughed it out," she added, referring to her grandmother, whom she had always called by her first name. She did the same with her mother, Blanche. Louise knew that Fleet lived in a big old house, some blocks west from there, with her mother and grandmother. "We did okay, though. Had lots of candles, and wood for the fireplace when the power went off. Had plenty to eat…lots of men making deliveries," she added quite matter-of-factly, causing Louise and Eleanor to exchange glances and then look back at their friend. Fleet shrugged fatalistically. There was nothing she could do about her family situation. She knew what her mother – and her grandmother for that matter – did to provide food on the table. And she knew the reasons behind it. It was just something she normally didn't want to talk about, and it had become a tacit pact between the three lifelong friends.

Before any of them could say more, Mrs. Herndon came walking from the auditorium.

"Hello girls! Oh I'm so very happy to see you," she greeted, hurrying to hug each girl in turn. "I'm so relieved to see that 'Old Man River' didn't get the best of you."

The girls laughed, each one trying to tell the kind woman their story, all three talking at once.

Happily reunited with their cast mates, they spent the afternoon going over their parts and rehearsing the play, exchanging 'flood' stories and welcoming more cast members as they filtered through the door.

Looking at the clock and noticing the time, Louise gasped, "I gotta get going." Then as a worried look came across Louise's face, Fleet noticed and asked, "Somethin' wrong?"

Dying to tell *someone*, Louise drew her bottom lip between her teeth for a moment, glancing around. They were pretty much alone off to the side of the stage.

"Fleet…can you keep a secret?"

Fleet's eyes lit up. "Secret?" Then laughing, she teased, "What'd you do? Rob a bank?"

Louise grinned, but nervousness overshadowed the joke. "No…I…" she began, then leaned closer and whispered, "I got a date tonight."

Fleet grinned, but confusion made her eyebrows draw together. "Yeah…so?"

"So…" Louise hesitated, glancing around again, "so, it's with…well…" she paused, then rushed out with the whole thing. "He came by about a week before the flood, to take Edna out, only she had her monthly that night and couldn't go, so I answered the door, and she didn't see him, and I told her he was just *okay*, but…he's more than okay. He's…he's…" she paused, finally bursting out with, "The most *gorgeous* thing I've ever seen! And he asked ME out!" she finished, literally bouncing up and down on the balls of her feet, her excitement overflowing.

"Wow, girl! Why didn't you tell me about him before?"

"Well…I didn't get the chance, with the flood and all…"

"What's his name? What's he look like?" she queried, Louise's excitement beginning to rub off on her.

"Oh Fleet…" Louise sighed, picturing him with the sun to his back as he bid her goodbye at the club. "His name is Victor Matthews…he's the dreamiest…the most handsome…he's got wavy brown hair…and cute dimples…and his eyes are like…like milk chocolate, with sparkles," she giggled. "He's got big muscles…and the most dazzling smile…"

"So…what's the *problem*?" Fleet chortled, thinking *she* should have such a 'problem'.

"See…I just can't let him pick me up at home. I don't want Daddy to know about it, you know how he is…and especially Edna. She'll kill me. But…I gotta find some excuse to tell Mama and Daddy…"

Fleet curled her lip and shook her head, leaning to throw a conspiratorial arm around her friend. "Nah, no sweat. Just tell 'em you went to my house. Tell 'em…tell 'em we're gonna practice for the play."

Louise's eyes lit up excitedly, her smile a mile wide. "Perfect!" Leaning to hug her friend, she gushed, "Oh thank you, Fleet! I owe you one!"

"I'll take that in cash," she joked, causing both girls to erupt into chuckles. Louise made her excuses to Mrs. Herndon and bid her friends goodbye, hurrying out the door as she stuffed her arms into the sleeves of her coat.

Nearly five o'clock! She had to hurry!

✿

LOUISE HASTILY SKIPPED down the steps of the house, afraid she would be late.

It seemed that Lilly had thought of at least a dozen different chores she wanted done before Louise could make her escape to 'Fleet's' house for a few hours. And once again, Edna had gotten out of doing much of anything; having slipped out immediately after supper and even before the dishes were done. The new flooring was laid and the apartment was clean, and their furniture had been moved back in. Then Lilly had wanted to wash the curtains and a host of other things in preparation for their first night back home since that fateful evacuation night.

"Mary Louise, I just can't understand why you *have* to go to Fleet's, tonight of all nights," Lilly had complained as Louise had finally managed to remove her apron and begin to get ready.

"Because...because the play is gettin' closer all the time and we need the practice, Mama," she had responded – which wasn't a lie – they *did* need practice.

"Well, you just make sure you're back home before *ten*," her mother had snapped, turning to stomp out into the other room and muttering about having to do 'everything' *herself*.

Louise sighed and shut her eyes for a moment, then continued on, slipping into her best dress. A soft green shirtwaist with black buttons and belt and long tapered sleeves, that she had picked because someone had told her once that it made her eyes appear more green than hazel. Quickly, she stepped into what was now her only pair of shoes, which were ugly black leather with button straps. *Oh well,* she shrugged, *it can't be helped.* Then moving over to the dresser, she picked up her brush and ran it through her brown silken locks until they shone becomingly, finishing up the look by gathering the sides at the back with a large barrette.

Picking up her purse and, for effect, her copy of the play's script, she sailed out into the next room and grabbed her coat off the rack by the door.

Willis, once again ensconced in his comfortable easy chair – now all scrubbed and clean – looked up from his paper and gave his daughter a grin.

"You off, honey?"

"Yeah, Daddy. Gotta run...I don't want to be late," Louise gushed, and then realizing what she'd said, she turned her head for a moment and closed her eyes, hoping he wouldn't catch the slip.

He didn't. "Well, you run along and have a good time with your friend," he admonished, glancing down at her attire. "You look mighty pretty."

She smiled at him and crossed to his chair, leaning down and giving him a firm hug and a kiss on the cheek. "Thanks Daddy. I'll see you later."

Then before anything else could come up, she called, "Bye Mama," as she opened the door and slipped out, not waiting to hear a reply.

Dashing up the stairs to the bathroom, Louise hurriedly pulled the string for the light and removed several items out of her pocketbook. With shaking hands, she applied some powder, blush, and lip rouge, something she didn't normally do. In fact, she wore make up so seldom that she secretly 'borrowed' the items from Edna's large stash, hoping to put them back that night without getting caught.

Then giving her face one last critical appraisal, she snapped her purse shut and marched out the door, silently skipped down the steps, and out into the evening.

As she hurried on her way, her heart was pounding with such excitement that her fingers were tingling and she could barely breathe.

ꕥ

PEOPLE SCURRIED ALONG Fourth Street, anxious to get out of the chilly February evening breeze. Some were on their way home, while others were on their way to some other destination. Lights were just coming on in the shops. Voices murmured in unintelligible conversations as they passed by Vic, while he paced up and down the sidewalk in front of Luckert's. On every turn, he glanced up the street as he waited for Louise to arrive.

Laughing softly, he shook his head as he rubbed his damp hands down his hips before shoving them back in his pockets. He couldn't remember ever being so nervous before a date before, as if it was his first time taking a girl out.

His mind drifted back to the day before, when Earl had pulled the car away from the curb.

"Okay, man. Spill it. How'd ya know her?" his friend had demanded, dying to know the details surrounding his pal, whom he'd known all his life and never seen 'in love', now seeming absolutely smitten with a girl.

Vic had laughed, his grin flashing. "You remember the 'babe' Alec set me up with a few weeks back?"

"That's *her*? You mean he actually did you a favor?" Earl joked, casting a grin at his friend.

"Well…not exactly. See…Louise is her *sister*. She came to the door that night. Edna was the one I went there for, but she was sick, so they said. But man…I ain't been able to get Louise outta my mind ever since," he confided with a chuckle. "She…she really got under my skin…big time."

"Well…what about Edna?" Earl asked, trying to recall what she looked like the day they had ridden back from Anchorage.

"I saw her, when I went with that old man on the delivery truck that day – you know, when I came to see you guys? Plus…my boat was the one that rescued the Hoskins the night they evacuated. She's…cute and all. But *Louise*…she's special."

Earl laughed and reached over to give his friend a teasing punch. "I can *see* that."

Vic had laughed too, feeling on top of the world…

His mind came back to the present as he turned once again and saw her just as she was rounding the corner on Fourth and heading his way. *There she is.* He cleared his throat and began to jog toward her.

Holding her purse and the script clutched to her chest, Louise looked up and saw him at the same time, and quickened her pace. But when they reached one another, they were both struck with shyness for a moment.

Vic's gaze took in how lovely she looked, even more so than usual, he thought. With her hair pulled back, and the radiant pink windblown glow of her cheeks, she was exquisite. He noticed she was wearing make-up and for a moment, he couldn't remember if he'd seen her wear it before. Surely he had…

Louise allowed her eyes to take in every detail of her escort – his dark, wavy hair becomingly tossed by the wind, his freshly shaved face and jaw, the collar of his leather jacket turned up, with the jacket zipped up tight because of the cold. His hands were shoved deep in his pockets when she'd first seen him, but as he'd jogged toward her, he took one out to give her a jaunty wave.

"You're right on time." "Have you been waiting long?" they both began, only to break off and laugh self-consciously. It seemed they were always speaking at the same time.

"I just got here," Vic offered, then noticing she was shivering in the cold, he added, "Come on, let's go inside." Turning toward the establishment, he politely took her elbow to escort her down the street. Grinning with pure unadulterated joy, she glanced up at him as they walked.

The only thing spoiling the evening for Vic was the fact that he didn't have any money. He'd tried numerous times that day to borrow some, but no one seemed to have any, all of them in the *'same boat'* as he was. Mentally preparing to tell her that they could only sit at a table at the back of the malt shop, but not enjoy any refreshment, he looked up and let out a tiny gasp of relief.

Turning to her, he asked apologetically, "Um…this is gonna sound funny, but…could you wait right here for just a minute? I'll be right back," but before she could utter a word, he was jogging toward a young man who was heading in their direction.

When he reached him, Vic stopped, his back to the direction in which he had left his date. "Gerald, hey man!" Vic greeted. "How ya been?"

"Aw, can't complain, man, you know," Gerald returned, trying to glance around his friend at the girl he had seen him talking to.

Cutting to the chase, Vic admitted, "Man, I need a favor. I need some lettuce, real bad. Can you lend me a five spot? Anything? I'll pay it back as soon as I get it, I promise."

Gerald shook his head regretfully. "I'm sorry man. All's I got's some tin," he replied, digging in his pocket and coming up with two quarters. "I'll split it with ya, how's that?"

Sighing with acceptance, Vic nodded. "Better than nothin', I guess," and accepted the coin from him. "Thanks, man. Um…gotta go."

"That's the doll I saw you talkin' to at the armory that time, ain't it?" Gerald astutely asked.

"Yep, and she's cold, and she's waitin'," Vic answered, giving his friend a wink. "See ya later," he added as he turned and loped back to where Louise stood shivering. With a relieved grin, Vic took her elbow and escorted her into the drugstore, as if they were entering the Waldorf.

ᘓᘍ

"SO HE WAS at the Brown all that time," Vic murmured, shaking his head as he took a sip of his soda.

They were sitting together in the back corner of Luckert's Drugstore. It was a busy night, with patrons filling the stools at the counter and occupying every table, laughing and eating and telling 'Flood' stories. The bright lights in the ceiling reflected off the black and white diamond pattern of the tiles on the floor. Music blared on the big jukebox in the corner, at that moment, amusingly playing, "It Looks Like Rain in Cherry Blossom Lane" by Guy Lombardo. However, the two at the back paid no mind to anything or anyone but each other.

"Mmmhmm," Louise returned with a nod, wrapping her lips delicately around her straw as she took another drink of her malt. She had no idea Vic had borrowed the money for her treat, but only had enough to get one malt, which cost twenty cents. He'd had to settle for a soda. But he didn't care. He had lied and told her he'd had a big dinner.

"Sonny said when the water started to rise, he was with a couple of other newsboys. They'd been tryin' ta sell papers in the lobby, and he 'bout sold out!" she giggled, imagining her salesman brother doing just that – selling papers with a big headline about the record-setting rain to folks that just spent all day dodging raindrops. "He said the water all of a sudden started to come in the lobby, so him and the other fellas moved further inside. Hotel customers were callin' down to the main desk asking for newspapers to be brought up, so the manager let Sonny and one other boy take them upstairs 'cause all the bellboys were busy tryin' to sweep the water back out the doors. By the time they came back down, there was a foot of water in the lobby!"

Vic chuckled with her, his eyes never leaving her face – and her eyes, which were sparkling with pinpoints of hazel light. He was thinking that if he hadn't been smitten before, he sure would be now. There was something so…alluring about her that drew him in like a powerful magnet. Alluring…yet refreshingly innocent and down-to-earth. She wasn't one of those Dumb Doras like he'd dated before. Louise had brains and common sense, and he felt like he could talk to her about anything and she'd understand. *The kind that makes life worth livin',* his friend and boss, Doc Latham had mentioned as Vic had confided a bit about her earlier in the day. *She sure is…*Vic mused, mentally shaking himself as he realized she had made another comment and was staring at him expectantly for his response.

"Isn't that funny?" Louise repeated, suspecting that Vic had let his attention wander – but not realizing to where. She thought maybe he was getting bored with her 'Sonny' stories. "To think that my brother helped catch a fish in the lobby of the Brown! I can't imagine four feet of water there…and fish swimming in it!" she added, giving a tiny shiver of revulsion. "Ew, I'd hate to be the one to have to clean that up."

"Yeah," Vic agreed, having motored by the Brown on many occasions and witnessed the deep water. Matter of fact, he'd seen boys and men with fishing poles in the water. And to think – one of them had been her brother, but he'd had no clue.

"So where'd he sleep?" Vic asked, as much interested in the

story as he was just in hearing her voice tell it.

"He said the manager didn't want to give them a room, but a rich hotel customer felt sorry for 'em and told the manager to give 'em one and to put it on his bill. The manager let the boys work off their meals by takin' things up and down the stairs for the customers, since the power was off and the elevators weren't running. He didn't say why he didn't bathe all that time, though – and he sure stunk," she added, wrinkling up her nose at the memory.

Vic laughed amusedly, thinking how cute she was. They spent the next two hours just talking about anything that popped in their minds. Vic had no idea that Louise was painfully nervous the entire time, hoping she wouldn't say something that sounded stupid. She had no idea that Vic was hanging on every word she said and thinking he'd never had a better, more enjoyable time with a girl than he was having with her.

Several times, Vic had glanced down at her things beside her in the booth, noticing some papers. He wondered what they were. Finally, the suspense was killing him. "Hey…what is that?"

She glanced down, having forgotten she'd taken the script with her. "Oh that…it's the script for a play I'm in at the Neighborhood House. I play the lead," she added proudly, wondering if he'd like to go to the performance – but also wondering if she would even be able to sing and remember her lines if she knew he was in the audience.

"A play?" he murmured, impressed. "What's it called? What's it about?"

She took a quick sip of her malt and turned to pick up the script. "It's a musical called, 'Song of the Old South', and I play Annabelle. We've been working on it for a long time, before the flood happened. Our director, Mrs. Herndon, found costumes for us, like dresses with hoop skirts and suits and top hats for the boys. It's…it's a love story," she added, meeting his eyes shyly.

"Love story, huh?" he mused, putting two and two together. She was playing the lead. "You gotta sing to one of the boys?" he asked, trying to not to show he was actually feeling jealous of this unnamed fellow.

"Yes, especially in our big finish, when we sing, 'Song of Songs' together..." she paused, suddenly feeling very self-conscious.

"Yeah? Lemme hear ya," Vic urged, leaning to see her face, which she had lowered. "Sing a coupla' lines for me," he asked softly.

"Oh, I dunno," she stalled, wishing she hadn't brought it up. "I can't do it in here, with the music blarin' on the jukebox..."

Then glancing at the milk shake-shaped clock on the wall, she nearly choked on the last bit of her malt.

"Oh my gosh...I've gotta get home," she blustered. It was nine forty five. She began to hastily gather her coat, purse, and the infamous script as she scooted out of the booth.

Startled, Vic scrambled to slide out of his side. "Hey wait! Lemme walk you home..."

"Oh...you don't have to..." she stopped as he interrupted, "It's all right. I *want* to."

Acquiescing, as she didn't actually relish walking the distance alone after dark, she nodded, and they set out for her house. They walked briskly, both from the cold and the lateness of the hour. The weather was freezing, the damp air making their breath come out in cloudy puffs, and precluding much small talk.

Finally, feeling chilled to the bone, they arrived at her house. He reached to take her elbow and escort her up the steps, but she stopped him. Glancing around nervously, she gushed, "I...I had a really nice time. Thank you."

Confused, his brows furrowed. "You're welcome...don't ya want me to take ya in?"

"No! I...I mean, um...I've gotta...go upstairs first," she explained after wracking her brain for a reason. It was embarrassing, but it was a reason. He understood and nodded, accepting her excuse.

"Okay, well..." he began, then paused, stepping closer. "I had a good time, too. So…when can I see ya again?" he asked, his voice low. The streetlight nearby cast his face in half shadow, but the half she could see contained a glimmering brown eye that was focused on her in a way that made her toes tingle. Dazedly, she was barely aware that he had brought his hand up to softly graze her jaw line with the backs of his fingers. She knew she should go in. Anybody could come in or out of that door at any minute. But, she couldn't seem to break the spell he had quickly cast.

"Um…I…I'm not sure," she stammered, unable to form a clear thought. He was so close, he seemed to block out the very air and she suddenly didn't even feel cold anymore. In fact, she was downright…perspiring! The delightful hint of aftershave emanating from his cheeks and neck made her feel lightheaded…

"Sweet Mary Lou…" he whispered, leaning impossibly closer. "I wanna kiss ya…" he added, giving her a second or two to pull back. When she didn't, he bent his head further and touched his lips to hers. Oh, it was magical…she would have sworn she heard the soft shimmer of cymbals as he pressed just a bit firmer before changing direction and backing off, releasing her mouth. She'd never been kissed like that before. Sure, she'd been kissed, by a few boys at school…but Vic…she sighed with effervescent joy as he backed up an inch, smiling down into her face. Her eyes were closed and she seemed suspended just as he'd left her.

Then her eyes fluttered open and she gazed up at him. He thought she was the most beautiful girl that ever drew breath. It hadn't even been a passionate kiss, yet it had moved him more than any necking session in which he'd ever participated. He knew she had no idea the power she already wielded over his head. He was in deep with no way out. Somehow he knew his life had changed direction the moment she had opened the door that rainy Friday night. He just wondered where the road would take them…and how bumpy that journey would be.

Oh, if he only had known, what would he have done differently?

PART II
THAT ENCHANTING SPRING AND SUMMER

CHAPTER 13

Dating and Juggling Secrets

"THAT WAS GOOD you two, now let's go over the next part. I need all of you in this crowd scene to really look busy. Engage one another in idle chatter, just don't get too loud," Mrs. Herndon admonished as she motioned for the young people to come out from the wings.

Louise and Herman Schlasberg, her 'leading man', retired to the side to wait for their next scene.

"You did good, Louise," Herman complimented, smoothing back a lock of his black hair as his dark eyes gave her an admiring look. He was several years older than her, and up until that point had grudgingly thought of her as a mere necessity. Now, however, something about her seemed different, and the difference had caught his eye.

Louise, on the other hand, simply glanced up at him and smiled politely with a murmured, "Thanks. You were, too."

At that moment, Fleet came sidling up to her friend, tugging on her arm to put some space between them and the young man. He glanced over at them oddly.

"Whadya lookin' at, you twit?" Fleet sneered over her shoulder at him as she gave him a shove. "Keep your eyes in your head."

"Quit callin' me that, you b..." he sputtered, raking the taller girl a derisive leer.

"Fleet, what?" Louise gasped, dragging her friend further away. "Why do you hate Herman so much?"

"Aww, I just can't stomach know-it-alls, that's all. He's so full of himself," Fleet grumbled, her eyes shooting a few more daggers at the young man. Turning her back to him, she continued, "I can't wait a minute longer. C'mon, spill it, you're killin' me, here!"

Louise chuckled as she realized her friend's meaning, but she couldn't resist teasing her for a moment or two.

"Spill what, Fleet?"

"Oooooo," Fleet hissed, tugging her friend further away. "I ain't seen you in days and I'm dyin' to know how your date with your dreamboat went."

Louise grinned then, dropping her ruse. "Oh Fleet…I had the best time. He's so sweet. We talked and talked and talked…it was like we couldn't run out of things to say," she gushed.

"Yeah…yeah…" Fleet encouraged as Louise paused to savor the memories. "Well…where did he take you?"

"Luckert's over on Fourth," Louise sighed with a silly grin.

"Big spender," Fleet teased, chuckling when her friend shot her an offended look in instant defense of 'her man'.

"No, it was perfect. We sat in a booth in the back and gazed into each other's eyes," she crooned dramatically. "Just like they do in the movies."

"Did he kiss you?" Fleet probed, feeling both happy and jealous of her friend's obvious euphoria.

Louise shut her eyes, her lips moving into a dreamy smile as she pulled in a deep breath and let it out with a sigh. "Oh, yeah."

Fleet chuckled and looked around, softly smacking her friend on the arm. "You goof!" she whispered. "Be careful, or old Mrs. Klapheke'll be giving you one of her lectures on the *propa deportment of the well bred young ladae,*" she joked, mimicking the Boston accent of the center's director.

Louise pressed her fingers to her mouth, giggling in joyous

conspiracy.

"Okay…so when ya gonna see him again?" Fleet probed.

"This Friday…we're meeting at Luckert's again." They paused a moment while Mrs. Herndon called out some general instructions for the cast.

"He…he wants to come and see the play," Louise admitted, glancing at Fleet to see her reaction.

Fleet nodded and glanced back, wondering about the look in her friend's eye.

"Yeah…so?"

"So…just the thought of him being out there in the audience makes me feel all jittery inside. What if I forget my lines, or fall flat on my face, or something?"

Her friend reached over and took her hand for a moment. "That won't happen. You'll do fine. Just convince yourself that it's just another of these endless rehearsals," she added with a wink.

Both girls giggled softly, then straightened up as their cue neared. Watching the action – several of the cast in a plantation house parlor scene complete with antique furniture and pillars and a bay 'window' – each one smiled encouragingly as their friend Eleanor shuffled along with several other 'background' actors. Sitting down on a duvet, Eleanor, thinking quickly, reached out and caught an adolescent cast member before he slipped off the edge onto the floor. Even with the save, however, the cast burst out in snickers.

"Amateurs," Herman sneered softly.

ஐ

VIC STOOD UP straight, placing his hands at his lower back and stretching out the kinks caused by hours of bending and working to replace the warped floor boards in the Grant's home.

With every new day, Louisville got a little warmer, and cleaner, as the days and weeks rolled on. Hundreds of workers from out of state, including WPA workers, volunteers, and even guys from the CCC's and the Kentucky National Guard, descended upon the city in droves to help reverse the flood's destruction. Neighbor helped neighbor, friend helped friend, and little by little, the determined inhabitants regained a little more of their city, making headway toward normalcy.

Vic spent his days laboring right alongside the volunteers, and his nights bunking with them in lieu of going to the apartment and facing the frosty reception of his sister-in-law. First, he helped his friends, the Grants, with their labors and at that moment, he and Earl were working to finish up the floors in the living room.

"Shew! I'll be glad when this part of the job is done," he good-naturedly fussed, wiping sweat from his brow.

Earl stood up and wiped moisture from his own brow. "Me, too."

"Your dad go back to work yesterday?" Vic asked, though it was obvious since he wasn't there working on the house.

"Yeah, the factory finally got all the water out and got the machines runnin' again. Mom and sis are back at Grandma's," he added.

Vic nodded, and then eyed his friend with a half grin. "One good thing's come 'a this flood."

"Oh Yeah? What's that?" Earl asked as he reached for another board.

Vic stooped down again to help him hold the board while they nailed it in place. "Your Mom always used to complain about the floors squeakin'. Now you can be quiet as a mouse when you sneak in at 3 AM."

Earl chuckled in agreement. "Guess ya got a point there."

After a few minutes of working together in companionable silence, Earl cast a glance at his friend. "So…how'd your date with that little dish go the other night?"

Vic sat back on his heels, a slow smile taking over his face. "Great."

"Yeah?" Earl chuckled and leaned close with a wry, "*How* great?"

Vic met his eyes. "That ain't how it is."

"How *what* is?" Earl asked in mock innocence as he flopped down on his bottom for a break.

"She ain't like those Dumb Doras we've double-dated with before. She ain't some girl you take out just to see if you can get'n her pants."

"Ahh," Earl nodded with a knowing wink. "Couldn't get ta first base, huh?"

"Don't be talkin' about her like that," Vic immediately reacted, the need to protect Louise's reputation, even if it was just with his friend, suddenly rising up fiercely within him. "She's a *nice* girl."

Earl held his hands up in mock surrender. "Okay, okay, Chief. Take it easy. Don't get your feathers ruffled. I didn't mean no harm." He met Vic's eyes for a moment, watching him visibly relax until he smirked at his own reaction.

"Sorry man. I know ya didn't."

Earl shook his head at his friend. "Man, you got it bad, don't ya? I ain't ever seen you like this before."

"I ain't ever felt like this before," Vic admitted quietly. Then becoming self-conscious, he tried to make light of it before his friend started to relentlessly tease him. "Ahh, come on," he announced with good cheer. "We've only got a few more to do here and the living room'll be done." Leaning to take a playful swipe at his friend, he added, "If you'll get up off your lazy a…" but stopped as a shadow fell across from the doorway. The two looked over, wide grins immediately transforming their faces.

"Hey stranger!" they exclaimed simultaneously.

"Hey. Long time no see. Don't let me interrupt your work," Alec teased with a wink.

"Where you guys' been?" Vic asked, climbing to his feet and stepping over tools and sawed pieces of wood to get to their friend. "Yeah, man," Earl added, right behind him.

The three long-time friends exchanged quick man-hugs, joyfully slapping one another's backs.

"Aw, they put us up in a church way up in Prospect," Alec answered, hitching a thumb in the general direction. "Along with lots of other people," he added with a grimace. "But at least we had three squares and heat. Not much else, though."

"You just get back?"

"Yeah…we went by the house yesterday. Or I should say…what's *left* of the house," he added quietly.

Vic pressed his lips together and nodded, still feeling bad that he hadn't been able to do anything to help the relentless destruction. "I'm sorry man…are your mom and your sisters okay?"

Alec shrugged, trying to act nonchalant. "Yeah, good as can be, I guess." He turned his head to look out the door in the direction of his family's house, picturing his mother and sisters crying and wailing when they had seen the carnage the river had caused. Not much was left intact inside, though the building remained standing. Windows had been broken out and their belongings strewn hither and yon, some even hanging out the windows. A lifetime of memories…gone. All they had left was what they had managed to take with them when they evacuated. It was especially hard on his widowed mother, who had just barely recovered from his father's untimely death a year before.

Earl and Vic glanced at one another, unaccustomed to seeing their normally boisterous friend so subdued, not that they could blame him. Earl cleared his throat. "Um…so what's the plan, Stan?"

Feeling emotion rising, his eyes blurring a little with dewy moisture, Alec ground his teeth together and drew in a quick breath through his nostrils. "Well, the preacher at that church helped us find a furnished apartment to rent, and I guess we'll just start over from square one." Then turning back and seeing the downcast look on his friends' faces, he affected a quick pout and cleared his throat. With his characteristic bluster, he quipped, "Ahh, it could be worse. I could be havin' ta do manual labor like you two goons."

The three young men laughed together, play punching as they always had throughout the years of their friendship. Then, they got down to business.

Despite his comment, Alec pitched in to finish the job.

ഌര

THE WEEK CRAWLED by for both Vic and Louise. By Friday evening, Louise had managed to get permission to go to Fleet's again for 'play practice', and as she was getting ready up in the bathroom, she heard a knock on the door.

"Louise, Mama wants you downstairs," her little brother's voice informed through the door. He bent down to see if he could see through the keyhole, but she had hung a towel on the doorknob.

Louise sighed in aggravation. "What for? I did the dishes already."

Billy shrugged dismissively as he turned to head back down. "I dunno. Maybe it's cause Daddy's home."

"Daddy's home?" Louise repeated, suddenly torn. She adored her father, and always wanted to spend time with him when he was around, but they hadn't expected him to be able to come home again so quickly. Since he had resumed his job in Bowling Green that week, she had missed him even more, having grown accustomed to his presence during the crisis.

But…Vic… he would be waiting. She'd waited and longed for Friday night to roll around all week!

And to top it off, Louise had put on makeup, something she

didn't normally do, and she didn't know how her father would react. However, she didn't have time to take it off and reapply it… Oh, what should she do?

Racking her brain for an acceptable ploy, and feeling crushingly guilty about all of the skirting of the truth she had been doing lately, Louise hurriedly finished up. Combing and fixing her hair, she rushed down the stairs to greet her father.

Behind his wire rim glasses, Willis' eyes lit up when he saw his daughter, and he opened his arms as she came sailing into them.

"Hi Sweet pea," he crooned against her hair.

"Hey Daddy," she murmured against his chest, squeezing him tightly. Oh, it felt so good to be in his arms, as always. Louise loved her mother very much, but Lilly was a no-nonsense kind of woman, always working on some chore, and wasn't especially demonstrative with her children. As a result, Louise sometimes felt starved for affection. Her father, easy going and kind-hearted, was definitely the more affectionate of her parents.

Again against his chest, she mumbled, "I didn't expect you back this weekend." Steeling herself for his reaction, she pulled back a little to look up at him. Willis' pleased smile dimmed a little when he saw her face – and the unaccustomed makeup.

"I was missing all of you so much, so I twisted Mr. Collins' arm until he hollered 'Uncle' and said he'd give me a ride," he joked, adding softly, "what's this on that pretty face of yours, Mary Louise?"

Affecting surprise, she put a hand quickly up to her cheek. "Oh this? Fleet and I are gonna practice in our costumes, so I put on my stage makeup," she fibbed, superstitiously crossing her fingers behind her back as she smiled up at him, hoping he hadn't seen the guilt lurking within her eyes.

"Seems all she does anymore is go practice for that play. I'll sure be glad when it's over and done with," Lilly grumbled from the corner, where she was busy ironing a pile of shirts.

Louise cast her mother a wounded look. "You two are gonna

come see the play…aren't you?" she asked quietly, for the first time wondering about it. It hadn't occurred to her that her family might not even go. Lilly had the grace to look up from her work and send her daughter a tiny smile, although she was still a bit miffed at her that she hadn't wanted to stay and help with more chores. "Of course we will," she reassured.

"I wouldn't miss it for the world – seeing my daughter in the lead role in a musical," Willis added. "I know you're going to shine brighter than all of them."

Louise grinned and snickered softly. It never failed; her father always knew just the right words to say. "Aww thanks, Daddy. I wish I could stay, but I promised…" she worded carefully.

Willis nodded understandingly.

"You go on. Have a good time, honey."

"Thanks, Daddy," she answered, giving his cheek a quick kiss as she turned to go, nearly running into Edna as the girl appeared at the hall door.

"Where you off to in such a hurry?" she mumbled, then seeing her sister's face, she added, "Little sister's wearin' *makeup*? Who's the *boy*?" she sneered shrewdly.

Louise's heart somersaulted and she swallowed quickly, attempting an answering sneer. "*Noneya.* But if you must know, it's stage makeup."

"It better be – you better not have got into any of *mine*," her sister sneered back, in truth, a bit jealous of her younger, prettier sister.

Managing to appear affronted, Louise grasped her things and headed out the door, calling over her shoulder, "I'll be back by 10." *Oh I hope she doesn't go near her makeup drawer!* She silently prayed.

"See that you are!" Lilly groused.

Edna watched her go, suspicion glittering in her icy blue eyes. "Little miss goodie two-shoes," she muttered as she turned toward the bedroom, intent on checking her stash of makeup for any signs of pilfering.

However, Lilly called to her with an instruction and that took her mind off of it – luckily for Louise.

ജ്യ

HUDDLED IN HER coat, Louise rounded the corner and spotted Vic heading her way. Her heart skipped a beat – he was heading to her house to pick her up!

When they reached one another, Vic, grinning widely, leaned to give her a kiss on the cheek. "Hey."

"Hey," she replied. "What…what are you doing?"

"You were runnin' a little late, so I thought I'd come and get ya," he replied, his motives totally innocent. Truly, Louise knew he didn't understand the importance of her secrecy. She suffered a moment of fear that she wouldn't be able to keep all of her 'balls in the air' in the juggling act she had created.

Moistening her lips, she managed to smile sweetly, still scrambling to come up with excuses why he couldn't pick her up at the apartment. "Thank you," she murmured as she took his arm and they set out for the soda shop.

"So, you had a busy week?" Vic wondered as they strolled along. He looked down at the girl who had captured his heart. With her cheeks a comely shade of pink from the winter breeze, and her eyes sparkling, he couldn't stop his heart from flip-flopping.

Huddled against his arm, she nodded. "Yes, very. School started up again, practicing for the play, chores at home. Something going on every minute." With a shiver, she looked up at him, querying, "How about you?"

"Yeah, I been busy, too. Been helpin' my friends – you remember, Earl and his family…" she nodded and he continued. "They needed a new floor in their house, too. And a few days ago, another friend came back – his name's Alec Alder."

"Oh?" she asked, adjusting her gloves against the cold breeze. "Did his family have to evacuate, too?"

"Yeah…and…" he paused, the subject always causing his heart to sadden. "They lost everything. Their house was in one of the lower parts…"

"Oh…I'm so sorry!" she murmured, her eyes showing her sincere concern. "I can't imagine losing everything and having to start over…we were very lucky."

"Yeah…" he mumbled, lapsing into silence as they walked along.

Minutes later, they were warmly ensconced in what they were already thinking of as 'their' booth in the back of Luckert's. Having earned a bit of money during the week helping Earl's neighbor with some work, Vic offered grandly, "What would ya like? Anything you want, just name it."

Grinning, she replied, "I think I'd like something warm…maybe hot chocolate."

"That's all? You don't want nothin' to eat?" he probed.

"No, I ate at home," Louise answered. Vic's crestfallen look made her realize how that had sounded to him – as if she hadn't looked forward to their date. Thinking quickly, she added, "M…my Dad came home from Bowling Green tonight…"

That, thankfully for her, took his mind off and he smiled, knowing she loved her father very much. "He did, huh? He doin' alright?"

"Oh yes, he's fine," she assured, and nodded when he excused himself to go up to the counter and place their order. A few minutes later, he returned with her hot chocolate, and a burger, fries, and a chocolate shake for himself. Seeing her eyes open wider, he chuckled, "I ain't had nothin' since breakfast…hope you don't mind. You, uh…you can have some of it if you like."

Louise giggled at the look on Vic's face, as if the teacher in school had called him down. Nodding, she watched him slide into his side of the circular booth and begin to arrange his food. She slid closer, moving her hot chocolate, and reached out for a French fry, answering his grin with a twinkling smile.

Picking up his burger and sinking his teeth into it with a big bite, Vic savored its grand taste. "So, how's the play practice comin'?" he mumbled, wiping his mouth with a paper napkin.

"Oh fine. Mrs. Herndon says we'll be more than ready on opening night," she replied, reaching for another fry.

"You ain't told me when that is," he reminded as he opened for another bite.

"Well…she hasn't set the date yet. She's waiting for the city to get more back to normal, I guess."

He nodded as he reached for his shake. "Well, things are gettin' better every day, so…"

Louise nodded, settling back with her cup. She still hadn't figured out how to manage Vic attending the performance – with her family there, as well. *Oh man…the plot thickens, as they say…* she mused. *Fleet'll help me think of something,* she resolved, refocusing on her date and concentrating on having a good time.

He picked up a fry and motioned for her to move closer, slipping the tip in her mouth when she did. "Mmm," she responded as she clamped down.

"Yeah," he whispered, their eyes meeting as she paused her chewing for a moment. She swallowed and smiled into his eyes as everything else seemed to fade away…the music on the jukebox, the noise of the other patrons, the clink of dishes, the yells of the counter man back into the kitchen, and the scrape of chairs on the hardwood floor.

Then, Vic's stomach growled so loudly that they could both hear it, and they burst out in snickers.

"Guess I better finish eatin'," he laughed, tucking into his burger again.

They found it so easy to talk to one another, drifting seamlessly from one subject to the next, laughing and joking together. Just being with one another made them feel on top of the world.

Their two hours flew by.

Suddenly, as before, Louise noticed the clock and hastily began to gather her things. Vic slid out from his side as she moved to stand up, murmuring, "I'm sorry, but I have to go…"

"I'll walk ya," he automatically offered.

Nodding, she hoped it wasn't a bad idea, but was unable to think of a legitimate excuse why he shouldn't. He helped her with her coat and then shrugged into his leather jacket, before escorting her to the door and out into the cold. After the warmth of the diner, she shivered and he immediately slipped an arm around her, pulling her against his body. A bit shocked, her eyes widened and she looked up at him, but he merely looked down and grinned.

"Can't have you gettin' a chill," he murmured as they set off down the street.

All too soon, the walk to her family's apartment was complete, and she once again stopped him at the steps.

"Why can't I walk ya to the door?" he asked softly, a bit of hurt showing in his eyes.

"Um…Daddy's always real tired when he comes home, and I don't want to wake him up…" she hedged, guilt making her feel sick to her stomach. That reason seemed plausible, so Vic nodded and reached to wrap his arms loosely around her back.

"So…you busy next Friday?" Vic murmured, gazing down at her as he had the time before, the streetlight making his eyes and hair seem like they were sprinkled with stardust.

"No…" she hesitated, trying to decide how much to tell him.

"Yeah ya are. With *me*," he grinned with a teasing wink.

Louise chuckled. "Um…actually, it's my birthday, and I was going over to my friend's house after dinner…you could pick me up there," she suggested, giving him Fleet's address.

"I can do that. Seven o'clock? And…if your friend wants to come along, it's okay. Me and the guys thought we'd just kind of ride around – you know, in that crazy old hearse…I don't have a car of my own," he added, a bit embarrassed to have to admit that to her.

Biting her lip for a moment, she wondered what Fleet would say. But knowing her friend was always up for a good time, she answered, "I think she'd like that."

He met her eyes, his mouth moving into a half grin. "So…how old ya gonna be?"

Louise's eyes flashed and she drew herself up, grasping the neck of her coat and preening like a movie star, answering mysteriously, "A lady never tells her age."

"Oookay," Vic acceded with a grin, his eyes concentrating on her mouth. "But a lady can let a fella kiss her goodnight…right?"

She nodded with a smile and held still as he slowly neared, allowing his lips to touch hers softly. Once again, the phenomenon of sparks assailed her senses and she unconsciously sighed as he leaned in to press firmer, pulling back enough to nuzzle her lips and take her bottom lip between his, suckling ever so gently. Her hands had wandered to his jacket and for a moment she was lost in the heady sensations of his lips and the wonderful scent of aftershave emanating from his jaw and neck.

The sound of footsteps coming up the sidewalk behind Vic made her slowly begin to open her eyes, only to have them pop open when she saw who was approaching, with a wide knowing grin on his face. Louise wrenched away from Vic with a gasp.

Vic straightened a bit, brow furrowed. "What's wrong?" he began, but a young man was just then arriving at their sides.

Louise, her eyes wide with shock, mental wheels whirling, swallowed nervously and managed to rasp, "Um, Vic…this is Sonny…my brother. Sonny…this is Vic Matthews."

Vic immediately grinned and turned to stick out his hand. "Well, I'm glad to meet you, Sonny. I've heard all about your flood adventures down at the Brown."

Sonny shook his hand, his eyes cutting to Louise's guilty expression and back to her escort's cheerful and guileless gaze.

"Good to meet ya. You're the guy that had the boat that rescued my folks, right?"

"Yep. What a wild night that was," Vic answered, oblivious of the unspoken tension between the siblings.

"I bet," Sonny answered smoothly. For a moment, the three young people stood silently. Vic began to feel the tension then, and looked between the other two. He opened his mouth to say something, but Louise interrupted with, "Well…I really need to get inside. Um…thank you, Vic. I had a real nice time."

"No problem. Uh…next Friday, then…right?" Vic answered, a bit perplexed. *Maybe she's uncomfortable with her brother knowing her business,* he reasoned.

"Yes. Friday. See you then!" she answered brightly, turning to jog up the stairs. Sonny nodded at Vic and followed his sister.

She paused at the door and turned to wave at her date. He waved back, watching with a puzzled expression. Slipping inside as Sonny shut the door and leaned against it, she watched as he crossed his arms on his chest. He stood there, his blue eyes alive with mirth, and grinning like the proverbial cat with canary feathers in his mouth. "So, how long's this been goin' on? And…I'm assumin' nobody else knows…"

Louise swallowed nervously and cast her eyes around the foyer, making sure all doors were closed and no one was coming down the stairs. Then she whispered, "Oh Sonny, you gotta promise me you won't tell a soul!"

Sonny cackled softly, unable to resist teasing his sister. Truly, he wouldn't think of ratting her out, but…what were brothers for if they couldn't tease their sisters? "What's in it for me if I keep quiet?"

"Listen…you don't understand…he came to the house to take Edna out one night right before the flood, but she couldn't go. I answered the door…and when she asked me what he was like…I lied…" she explained with a grimace.

He laughed again, shaking his head at her predicament. Sonny had been on the receiving end of the wrath of Edna more than once himself and he knew she could be vicious. "Edna finds that out, she'll skin you alive."

"I know!" she hissed, looking around again. "And besides that…well…you know how Daddy is…he wouldn't let Edna date 'till she was eighteen and…" she paused, her eyes pleading for his understanding. "But…I think Vic likes me, Sonny…and I jus' think *he's* a livin' dream."

Looking up into her brother's eyes, hers softened and she stepped closer, reaching out to gently grasp the front of his jacket. Being the two middle siblings, they had been through a lot together growing up and Louise had covered for him many times with their parents. She hoped that would sway him to her side. "Please, will you help me, and keep my secret? I'll pay you back any way you say," she implored, gazing up at him in supplication. She looked so adorable, he couldn't have been mean to her if he'd wanted to.

After letting her stew a few moments, pursing his lips as if he were considering it, Sonny finally relented with a chuckle. Leaning forward, he wrapped a conspiratorial arm around her shoulders and whispered, "Yeah, I'll help ya out, sis." She immediately relaxed and grinned.

Turning toward their door, he paused and looked at her again. "Hey, um…how old is this guy, anyway?"

Grinning up at him, her eyes twinkling mischievously, she bit her lip and murmured, "Twenty."

"Twenty!" he reacted, blowing out a low whistle. "You sure you know what you're doin', sis?"

Louise pressed her lips together and nodded. "Yep. Someday, if I play my cards right, I intend on bein' Mrs. Victor Matthews," she declared determinedly.

He nodded and raised his eyebrows thoughtfully. "Ya know…it takes a mighty good poker player to run a full-on bluff all the way to the end and win," he murmured sagely. Touching a finger to the tip of her nose, he added softly, "Hope this plan 'a yours don't backfire on ya."

"Me, too," she admitted softly.

"You just be careful," he added as he leaned to place a quick kiss to her forehead.

Louise nodded, determinedly quashing the ever-present feeling of dread, and gave him a soft smile as they continued on to the apartment door.

CHAPTER 14

Fleet, Louise, and The Hearse

FEBRUARY MARCHED ON. For Louise's birthday, the family had a quiet dinner with several small presents and a plain chocolate cake. Her father hadn't been able to make it home again, but he sent Louise a telegram wishing her a happy birthday and that he was so very sorry he wasn't there to help celebrate with the family. The telegram touched her heart, and she put it carefully away in her memories box.

Then, free from chores for the evening, and thrilled that Lilly had actually given her permission to have a sleepover at Fleet's house, Louise grabbed the bag she had packed and bid a hasty goodbye to her family. She couldn't wait to get to Fleet's and get ready for what would be her third date with Vic Matthews. It didn't matter to her that they wouldn't be alone on this one. As long as she was with *him*, nothing else mattered.

Fleet lived about ten blocks away, in a big rambling house in the bad part of Seventh Street. Her grandmother, Myrtle, lived downstairs, and Fleet and her mother lived on the second floor. Lilly had never asked Louise where her friend Fleet lived, and Louise had never volunteered the information. Thus, the mother had no idea she had allowed her daughter to go and spend the night in a house that sported a red light on the front porch…

But none of that mattered to Louise. She vaguely knew what Fleet's mother and grandmother, who was in her early fifties, did for a 'living'. She knew they 'entertained' men, but beyond that, she had no idea of the details. Fleet was Louise's friend, and that's all she cared about. The rest…well… It was 1937 and the Depression had been raging for eight long years. A person had to do whatever they could to survive. At least, that's what Willis had always taught his children. Louise knew, however, that he had not intended the definition to stretch to that extreme.

Hurrying up to the door of the house, and pointedly dodging the leering looks of several men walking down the street, Louise clutched her bag and knocked briskly. After waiting a minute, she was about to knock again when she heard the lock being turned and the door opened to reveal Myrtle standing there in a faded blue robe. She was a tired looking woman, and despite the carefully applied, overdone makeup, seemed years older than she was. Her hair, like Fleet's, was the color of pale honey, her eyes a faded blue.

"Oh, hello Louise. Fleet's waiting for ya, you can run on up," she greeted in a friendly manner as she allowed the door to swing wide. "How ya been? And Happy Birthday, honey. Fleet told me," she added in answer to Louise's surprised glance.

"Thanks, Ma'am," Louise answered as she scampered on up the narrow, dimly lit staircase.

Upstairs, Louise cast her eyes around at the mess. Clothing lay strewn around on chairs and the couch, and dirty dishes occupied the sink and the table. Fleet's mother stood scrubbing a piece of clothing at an antique ringer washer, in preparation for hanging it on a sagging wire line stretching across one end of the kitchen. Worn, dusty draperies hung at the windows, and virtually no pictures or 'pretty things' adorned the rooms.

Heaviness seemed to hover in the atmosphere. It was so different from Louise's own home, which Lilly made sure was always clean and orderly, with sunshine streaming in the windows and something delicious cooking on the stove. For not the first time, Louise felt sorry for her friend, having to live in such squalor. She knew Fleet slept on a narrow cot in a tiny bedroom not much bigger than a closet. Not that she herself lived at the Ritz, having to share a bed with Edna, but still…

"Hello Louise. Happy birthday," Blanche greeted as she smiled at her daughter's friend, pausing to swipe straggling bits of hair away from her forehead with the back of her wrist. Observing the girl, who was standing awkwardly with her overnight bag clutched in front of her, Blanche glanced around ashamedly and mumbled, "'Scuse the mess…ain't had time to clean up in here…" Louise nodded uncomfortably.

At that moment, Fleet opened the bathroom door and grinned as she saw her friend. "Hey girl. So, wha'gya get for your birthday?" she asked as she made her way to the cluttered vanity table in her mother's bedroom. As she began to brush out her hair so that it lay in natural waves, she glanced at her friend expectantly.

Louise shrugged, "Oh…Mama crocheted me a real pretty scarf…Billy made me a card…Edna and Sonny went together to get me a sweater, though Edna said it was so I wouldn't be askin' to use her new one," she added with a chuckle.

Fleet nodded. "Your Dad make it back?" she asked, glancing at Louise's crestfallen expression. Instantly, she knew the answer.

"No…but he sent me a telegram," Louise responded, smiling softly as she thought of his thoughtful gesture. It was almost as good as having him there. *Almost.*

"Oh. Well, that's good…" Fleet mumbled, silently thinking she herself would be thrilled and overjoyed if her own father – whoever he was – were to contact her on her birthday. She could hardly imagine how that would feel… Shaking her head, she grinned and whispered, "Well…it's gettin' late…you better start gettin' ready."

"*We*, you mean. Don't ya wanna go?" Louise asked as she placed her bag carefully on the unmade bed and opened it, taking out her new sweater, which was a soft, baby blue, square necked, short sleeve creation. She laid it on the bed and removed the scarf from her bag, holding it up for Fleet to see. It was a lighter shade of blue than the sweater, with black around the edges.

"Well…" Fleet hesitated. "If you're sure you want me to…"

"Of course I do!" Louise blustered, pausing to gape at her friend. "Vic said there would be other guys going…I don't want to be the only girl!"

Fleet laughed, as she'd only been half teasing about her hesitation. "Okay, okay, I'm goin'. But we better step on it, it's already past 6:30…"

They set about changing, with Fleet helping Louise to artfully arrange the sweater around her neck and secure it with a pin at the back, under her hair. Then giggling together, they shared the blotchy, speckled vanity mirror, Fleet urging Louise to apply more makeup on top of what she was already wearing.

"Oh Fleet, not too much!" Louise gasped, but her friend just chuckled.

"You wanna catch his eye – and hold it – right?"

Louise blushed as she held her lips firm for Fleet to apply lipstick.

A few minutes later, Fleet squinted at the tiny bedside clock and quickly finished her preparations. Stashing Louise's bag in her tiny room, she grabbed her friend by the arm, and murmured, "We better get on downstairs." Louise nodded, barely having time to grab her purse before she was tugged out of the room.

"You girls have a good time," Fleet's mother offered nonchalantly. Louise noticed that Blanche hadn't even asked Fleet where they were going, or with whom, and the thought occurred that despite griping about her own family's over protectiveness at times, it did make her feel that they at least cared.

Fleet muttered something unintelligible as they passed the woman, who was still scrubbing bits of clothing, and started down the stairs. The girls glanced at one another, as they paused to let a man pass by on his way up. No one said a word, although the man cast a rather lewd look at both of the young women on his way by.

Louise shivered with disgust and rushed down the stairs, only then beginning to wonder if this had been such a good idea – staying overnight at her friend's house. She swallowed back the sick feeling she had when she thought about the ever-growing list of lies and half-truths she had been telling lately. It wasn't like her at all, and it still didn't sit right. Staying in Fleet's house wasn't quite sitting right, either.

Both girls hurried out the door, Fleet allowing it to slam behind her, and casting a look back at it over her shoulder. In truth, she hated where she lived…and she hated what her mother and grandmother did for a living. But, she never let on that she was ashamed, preferring to just shrug it off and pretend she was immune to the looks of the other girls and the whispers of the boys at school. She knew what they all whispered about her, but *they can whisper all they want, it still don't make it true.*

"Look, uh…" the willowy young woman said now, "I think it'd be better if the guys don't come here and see the house." She gestured toward the porch light. "Let's start walking toward the corner and let 'em pick us up off the street. It wouldn't do to…give 'em the wrong impression…"

With a relieved nod from Louise, the two took off, strolling slowly up toward Breckenridge. The girls had purposely dressed to get attention, especially Fleet. She was wearing one of her mother's dresses, topped with a short jacket. Along the way, several cars rolled slowly by, their drivers emitting wolf whistles at the two young ladies, along with some not-so-nice remarks yelled out their windows. For the most part, the girls steadfastly ignored them, except for one exceptionally rude man who added the action of laying on his horn as they were in the middle of crossing a side street.

"Aw, blow it out yer ear!" Fleet yelled, adding a quite not-so-nice gesture along with it. Louise clamped her lips and blushed scarlet, fervently wishing Vic would come to her 'rescue'. *What have I gotten myself into?*

Just then, from up ahead, she saw the now familiar long black vehicle turn the corner from Breckinridge and head their way. Immediately, her heart sped up.

"There they are," she murmured to her friend, both girls striving to look as nonchalant as possible as they strolled.

The vehicle rolled to a stop alongside them as the passenger window rolled down.

"Hey! Where you two headed?" Vic asked, a bit confused as to why Louise would be walking down the street when he had told her he would pick her up at the address.

The girls exchanged looks. "Um…" Louise began, "the house felt kinda stuffy…so we thought we'd get some fresh air. I knew you'd be coming from this direction," she added quickly. Vic grinned and nodded, accepting the explanation as he opened the door and climbed out.

"Vic, this is my friend, Fleet McDougal. Fleet, this is Vic," Louise made the introductions. Fleet smiled at the man, thinking he truly was every bit as gorgeous as her friend had said. "Nice to meet ya."

Vic nodded a greeting and turned toward the car. "Girls, that's Earl behind the wheel, and Ruth next to him," he explained as the two nodded and waved. "That's Alec, Gerald, Phil, and Eugene in the back, plus uh…" he paused as he tried to remember the names of the girls he had just met. "Barbara and Thelma."

Alec and Gerald had begun climbing out the back doors as Vic was speaking, both of them heading toward the girls with huge grins on their faces.

The girls smiled at the two guys and nodded. Louise recognized Gerald as the man Vic had spoken briefly with on the street during their first date. Vic had moved to Louise's side and gently took hold of her elbow in a silent show of 'ownership' as Alec and Gerald rushed to flank the taller of the two young women.

"Hey..." "Hi there," they both greeted with wide grins, suddenly launching into competition. "You can sit with me if you want..." "There's room in the back..." they each tried again, nearly tripping over themselves, each one holding out a hand toward her. Fleet laughed, totally enjoying being the center of attention. She sized them up quickly, thinking they were about equal in looks, but there was a special spark in Alec's eyes as he grinned at her that made something inside of her respond. With a ladylike chuckle, she glanced at Gerald with an apologetic smile and a murmured, "Thank you," before reaching to place her hand in Alec's.

"Aw man, that makes me the odd wheel," Gerald good-naturedly grumbled as the five climbed into the vehicle.

Vic sat down on the passenger side of the front seat and patted his lap as he looked up at Louise. "I'm afraid we've got a car full...you mind sittin' on my lap?" he asked innocently, though in truth he had hoped it would work out that way.

Louise grinned shyly and shook her head, proceeding to climb carefully inside the car and settle herself onto his legs as she greeted the other occupants. She shivered a bit as she felt his arms immediately encircle her. "Comfy?" he murmured in her ear, and she nodded a bit self-consciously.

Alec and Fleet settled themselves in the back and Gerald managed to close the back doors securely.

"Everybody in?" Earl called out as he put the car in gear. To a rousing chorus of "Yep!" he chuckled and off they went.

ꙮ

THE HEARSE SLOWLY rolled along Marion Street in the Point, its stunned occupants nearly speechless as they viewed the destruction first hand. The condition of the once elegant mansions along Louisville's 'Frenchman's Row' was positively shocking. The grand old homes had battled against Mother Nature many times, but sadly, they had finally lost the fight.

"I ain't been back down here since the water went down," Vic murmured, gazing at the sadly majestic structures now reduced to ruin. They had been magnificent in their heyday, each one a different design from the next, tailored to their owners' specifications. No detail had been spared in their elegance. The only thing no one seemed to have taken into consideration was their close proximity to the river. It was the age-old story of man thinking he knew better, and that he was the 'master' of his universe.

Earl steered the car around a large obstruction and Thelma let out a shocked gasp from her place in the back. "Look at the Heigold house!" she exclaimed as the others emitted low murmurs of sympathy. "I went there for a party on Derby day last year." At the incredulous looks from her fellow passengers, she clarified, "I mean, my mom cleans houses for a livin', and she was hired, along with a couple of others, to serve the guests drinks and such. They let me work, too. Man, what a night that was...I never saw so many diamonds and minks in my life..." she added dreamily, her memory of the once elegant house in stark contrast to its present reality. To say it wasn't a pretty sight was a gross understatement. Green river slime covered most of the structure, windows and trim were broken, and dried muck and debris littered the grounds. The mansion had suffered so much damage during its submersion that the owners had decided it was too far gone, and too much of a risk to refurbish, as who knew if another massive flood was in Louisville's future. The carcass of the large home was still standing the way the water had left it upon its retreat.

"You know," Alec mentioned from the back, "I heard the Mayor has vowed that come Derby, the city'll be back on its feet and ready for out-of-towners."

"That'll take a boat load 'a work," Gerald mumbled as he gazed out the window to the slowly passing dilapidated estates.

Vic stared at the sad sight of the ruined homes and nodded.

"Yeah, you can say that again."

"Hey, all this is making me sad. I thought we were gonna have a good time tonight," Ruth suddenly spoke up, only half kidding. Her blue eyes shot a look at her boyfriend as she pushed back her bright red, wavy locks with one hand.

"You're right," Earl nodded as he turned the corner, heading south, and away from the devastation.

"So, where to, guys? Any suggestions?" he called out to the vehicle at large. "We got about half a tank," he added as he checked the gage on the dash, referring to earlier when all of the guys had pooled their coins to buy some gas.

"We could park down by the river for a pettin' party," Alec teased, prompting snickers from the rest of the passengers. All, that is, except Louise.

"Well, that leaves *me* out," Gerald pointed out with a chuckle.

Sitting at an angle on Vic's lap, Louise shot him a look that he correctly interpreted as confusion. She had no idea Vic's friend had just suggested that they all sit it in the parked car and 'kiss'.

Glancing back at Alec, Vic narrowed his eyes and mumbled, 'Nix it, Chief – the bank's closed."

Alec retorted, "Aw man, it ain't no holiday!" as he wondered what had gotten into his friend. The Vic he knew would never turn down the chance to neck with a pretty girl, and from what he'd seen, Louise was sure a looker. His eyes crinkled as he thought back to some wild dates they had doubled on in their teens.

Earl snickered again, prompting his girlfriend to give his arm a playful slap as the others in the vehicle began to good-naturedly argue between the options of what to do for the evening.

Vic, wishing to smooth the awkward moment, announced, "I think Louise oughtta decide…since it's her birthday."

"It *is*?" "Aw Happy Birthday!" chorused the gang. Immediately, Fleet took up the baton, and began to sing, "Happy Birthday to you…" to which everyone else joined in. Pleased and flattered,

Louise turned to gaze at each one, her infectious grin flashing as she blushed slightly at suddenly being the center of attention.

Vic, thinking she was adorable when she pinkened like that, tightened his arms around her as he joined in the singing.

As one round came to an end, Gerald piped up from way at the back, "I got another one!" and began the song again, changing the words to, "Happy birthday to you, squashed tomatoes 'n stew, bread 'n butter in the gutter, happy birthday to you."

The young people burst out laughing, including Louise.

"…And many moooooore," the group warbled loudly, ending in amused chuckles as each one tried to outdo the other.

"So, how old are ya, honey?" Alec called out. "Ya legal yet?"

Everyone began calling out speculations and telling their own ages as Louise cast her eyes around, meeting Fleet's. Her friend raised her eyebrows and tilted her head in silent communication.

Vic joined in the guessing game. "Let's see…your sister's nineteen…Sonny's sixteen…so are ya eighteen yet, or did ya turn seventeen?" Vic teased, watching her press her lipstick coated lips together as she tried not to squirm. He wondered if she knew how attracted he was to her…and just how appetizing those lips were to him…

Before she could answer, Vic put back his head and laughed, "Oh I forgot, ya told me a lady never tells her age."

"Well, alrighty then!" Earl chimed in with a laugh. Taking his eyes off the road and casting a glance past his girl, he added with a wink, "Keep 'em guessin', honey."

Just then, the big car began to drift across the line as they passed an old Model T coming around the bend. The other car's horn suddenly sounded a loud, "Aaaoooooooga!"

"Watch it!" Alec yelled from the back as the girls squealed in alarm.

Earl cut the wheel just in time, causing the hearse's tires to bump the curb on the passenger side. The other driver stuck his fist out the window with a not-too-nice gesture and yelled obscenities their way.

"Keep your eyes on the road, man," Vic cautioned as he tightened his hold on Louise. She and Ruth had both flung out a hand to steady themselves against the dash and now Louise was absently rubbing her wrist. Vic murmured in her ear, "You all right?"

She nodded, moistening her lips as her heart raced nearly out of control, from the near miss or Vic's close proximity, she wasn't sure which.

"Earl Franklin Grant, that was *too* close," Ruth gasped, pressing a hand to her chest.

Earl nodded, letting go of the wheel with one hand and wiping his mouth as he fought to get his own heart rate under control. "Sure was. Sorry guys!" he added louder to his passengers in the back.

The near miss sent a hush over the startled group and for the next minute, they rode along in silence, each trying to still their hearts.

Finally, true to form, Alec quipped with a few choice words, "Aw, what we need is some levity in this here overgrown taxi," and tipped back his head and yowled, "Oooooooooooh, he floats through the air with the greatest of ease…" as he launched into a rousing rendition of, *The Daring Young Man on the Flying Trapeze.* Immediately relaxing, the others joined in. Feeling just like the characters on the old bus in that famous scene from "It Happened One Night", which they had all seen multiple times, the young people took turns singing verses, laughing, and teasing.

In this way, they whiled away the miles as the old hearse rolled along.

Earl, however, did make sure he didn't get carried away in the levity and run off the road again, much to everyone's relief.

ꙮ

IT WAS LATE when the big black car pulled up to the house across the street from Fleet's – a house that didn't sport a red light on the porch. Louise had made the excuse that she had given Vic the wrong address. It was a double house, something like the one Louise's family lived in, with a foyer, and an unlocked front door.

Vic opened the passenger door and allowed Louise to swing her legs out and stand up, following her as Alec was helping Fleet climb out the back.

"Lemme walk ya to the door, this ain't exactly a good neighborhood," Vic murmured in Louise's ear, out of earshot of Fleet. Louise nodded mutely, feeling bad for yet another skirting of the truth.

The others had already been dropped off at their homes, leaving only Earl and Ruth in the front seat. The four young people strolled slowly up the walk, each couple holding hands.

For Vic, he hated that the evening had come to an end. It seemed to have flown by. Now, as they wandered to a stop at the porch steps and turned toward one another, he took Louise's hands in his, feeling her shiver as the cold evening wind ruffled locks of her hair.

"When am I gonna see ya next?" he murmured softly, holding her close.

Louise felt as if she had stepped into a scene in a movie. Never had she thought she would experience the same sort of enchanting activities as she saw played out on the big screen down at the theater. Gazing up at Vic, the breeze fluffing the waves of his hair and the streetlamp illuminating his features, she could barely speak.

"Um…next Friday, I suppose," she answered his question.

"Aww," he pouted. "That's a whole week…"

"I know…but Mama doesn't like us to be out on school nights," she answered, blanching as she said the word 'school'.

He huffed a soft, frustrated sigh. "Well…bet you'll be glad when you don't have to worry about *that* anymore, huh?"

She nodded numbly.

Vic looked over his shoulder at their friends. Alec and Fleet had hit it off quite well, and were talking softly, their heads close together. Vic turned back to Louise and smiled. Releasing one of her hands, he raised his to her cheek. Without another word, he leaned down, drawing her close as his lips touched hers. The familiar sparks occurred, making them both draw in tiny gasps as they simultaneously leaned closer, melting into one another's embrace, lips fusing together.

After several moments, Vic finally made himself pull back, watching as her eyes fluttered open. He smiled as his thumb touched the edge of her mouth. "Happy Birthday, sweet Mary Lou."

"Thank you." She smiled back, never having felt such sheer euphoric happiness in her life. "Tonight's been the best birthday I've ever had." Vic smiled fondly, glad that he'd been the one to bring that about.

Finally, the four said their goodnights and the guys watched the girls climb the steps and disappear safely inside the outer door before they ambled back to the car.

The girls waited, surreptitiously watching out a side window until the car moved on and eventually turned the corner. Feeling like fugitives, they quietly emerged and scooted across the street, slipping inside Fleet's home.

As Louise turned toward the stairs, Fleet stopped her with a hand on her arm, murmuring, "Let's not go up there." Louise nodded, and followed her friend on into her grandmother's living room. It was nearly midnight, and the house was dark and quiet.

Grabbing some blankets and pillows from a closet, they fashioned pallets for themselves on the floor in front of the small fireplace. Louise caught a whiff of the now familiar, unpleasant musk left from the water, but she steadfastly ignored it. Flopping down on their makeshift beds, she gushed in a loud whisper, "Oh Fleet, that was so much fun! I just had the time of my life!"

"Sure was," Fleet agreed with a soft giggle.

"So, whatdya think of Alec?" Louise asked, though she had a good idea.

"Oh girl, I think he's just the *bee's knee's*!" she exclaimed, causing both girls to giggle and clamp their hands over their mouths to keep down the noise.

"I'll say," Louise agreed, "he keeps the party goin', that's for sure."

"I 'bout died when he said he wanted us to have a pettin' party."

"Yeah…what did that mean, anyway?"

"Oh girl, you ain't been nowhere, have ya," Fleet teased. "It means neckin' – you know, kissin', huggin'…*pettin'…*"

Louise's eyes widened and her mouth dropped open. "You mean…*touching?"*

Fleet laughed, enjoying her friend's shock. "Yeah, but your man saved your virtue."

Realizing what Vic's comment had meant, Louise clamped her teeth on her bottom lip and grinned. "Yeah, he did, didn't he."

"I saw the way he looks at you. Girl, he's got it bad!"

"Oh Fleet, do you think so, really?" Louise gasped as she flopped over on her back to stare at the ceiling.

"Heck yeah! I got eyes, don't I?"

Louise giggled, her mind reliving every wonderful moment of the evening…riding all around the county, laughing and singing, and telling 'flood jokes', and most of all, sitting within Vic's embrace snuggled on his lap. The evening had been the most fun she'd ever had – and she hadn't wanted it to end.

Making sure they kept their exuberance to a lower decibel, they spent the next thirty minutes whispering about their adventure with the gang, and the prospect of what the future could bring.

Eventually, Louise fell asleep, her dreams filled with strong arms, brown eyes, wavy hair, and dimpled smiles.

ꟾ

CHAPTER 15
Song of the Old South

"HELLO THERE, HOW'VE you been?" Irene Waller asked as she stopped on the street to talk with Vic. "Haven't seen you since the water went down."

Pulling back from their hug, Vic smiled at the sweet elderly woman. Having just that morning been through something traumatic, he wished for a moment that she had been his aunt or mother.

"I'm fine, Miss Irene," he mumbled, but the astute little woman took one look into his eyes and could tell something was on his mind. With maternal concern, she smiled tenderly and gently touched the sleeve of his jacket. "Mmm hmm…would it help to talk about it?" Alone after her husband and their two sons had been killed in action in WW1, Irene thought how close she and the other ladies of the church had gotten with their 'boys' during the crisis. It was as if they all had known one another their entire lives. Just then, she was feeling particularly motherly toward Vic, her favorite. Having seen his care, courage, and potential first hand, she was thinking how proud she would be if he had been her son.

Vic clamped his teeth together and looked away for a moment, unaccustomed to sharing his emotions or thoughts. Indeed, most of his life he had been told to just 'suck it up' at each new heartbreak or rejection, to 'get over it' after each new instance of having the rug pulled out from under him. Once again, something unsettling had left him feeling as if he were spinning on ice…

With a grimace and a tiny shrug, he opened his mouth to deny there was anything wrong, but closed it again when he looked back and saw sincere concern in the old woman's faded blue eyes. The gentle wrinkles around them crinkled a little more as she smiled at him encouragingly.

Taking a deep breath, he murmured, "Nothin' much, just I'm homeless…again."

"Homeless?" she immediately responded, tugging him over a little closer to the building to allow people to pass by. "Good heavens, son, what happened?"

Glancing around uncomfortably and meeting curious eyes, Vic related to the kind woman that he had mustered his fortitude and gone to his brother's apartment that morning, having avoided it for the duration of the emergency. She nodded, remembering the bit of information he had shared before about his family. He went on to relate that no one had been home, but he had used his key to get in. There he had found that someone, probably his sister-in-law, had unceremoniously deposited all of his things – his clothes, duffle bag, and his few remaining personal items – into a not-so-neat pile out on the apartment's tiny balcony. The sight had hit him like a punch in the gut. The message was clear. He wasn't welcome there anymore. He supposed he was lucky Liz hadn't just chucked the whole lot in the trash bin. "And the real kicker is…today's my *birthday*," he finished with a wry grimace at the cruel quirk of fate.

Irene, her gentle heart aching, reached to take one of his hands in hers as she wondered what kind of people they, his co-called 'family', were to treat such a wonderful young man like that. "Oh Vic…to tell you 'Happy Birthday' seems almost harsh…do you have somewhere to go?" she asked softly.

Meeting her eyes again, he managed a tiny smile. "Yeah…a friend – you remember, I told ya about Alec Alder and his family…" he paused as she nodded, remembering the sadness he had displayed the day he had helplessly watched their home slowly being destroyed. "They said I could stay with them for a while." At her look of confusion, he went on, "They lost nearly everything in the flood, but somebody helped 'em get a furnished apartment so they could start over." His thoughts turned for a moment to the evening before, when he had visited the family in their new digs and he had had the pleasure of presenting Mrs. Alder with the item he'd retrieved that cold wet day on the boat – the sepia-toned photograph of the family.

Mrs. Alder had taken one look at it and with a gasp, practically burst into tears. Reaching out, she had clasped it to her chest and shut her eyes. "Oh Vic… I… I can't tell you what this means to me…" she had stammered. "I had thought all of our family mementoes were gone forever…" He had apologized that he hadn't been able to rescue more items, but she had tearfully shaken her head and reached out with one arm to draw him into a hug, thanking him profusely.

Irene nodded, relieved. "Well, that's good that you have a place to go. So, have you found work, yet?"

He shrugged again. "Not really, but I been makin' a little money here and there when I can, workin' on the clean-up." He paused a moment, his eyes twinkling when he thought of the other things he'd been doing.

Irene noticed and astutely asked, "Have you seen the girl again?"

He smiled and gave a chuckle. "Yep. We're datin' now," he acknowledged.

"That's wonderful! Louise…right?" Irene prompted, remembering when he had mentioned he was concerned about the girl and her family, and where they had gone.

He nodded, picturing Louise as he had seen her several nights before. "Yep."

"Well, I'll be praying everything works out for you, son. I'd say you were due some good fortune."

"Maybe," Vic responded a bit doubtfully. Changing the subject, he inquired, "You been doin' okay since the flood?"

Blessing him with her angelic smile, she nodded. "Oh yes. Busy as a honeybee in June. And speaking of that, I should get moving – I need to buy some ingredients for several dishes I'm making tonight, for a potluck supper at church. You're welcome to come – there'll be plenty of good food," she added hopefully.

He hesitated for a moment, wanting to go, but the thought of showing up and not knowing anyone but a couple of old ladies seemed uncomfortable. The truth was, he had never been to church, and had no idea what went on there. The only encounters he'd ever had with church people had usually turned out badly…except for Miss Irene and the other ladies during the crisis.

Irene watched his expression and guessed what he was feeling. With a gentle squeeze to his arm, she murmured, "Well, you think about it. Dinner is at 6:30. It's come-as-you-are," she added softly.

He pursed his lips and gave a nod. "I might," was all he would promise.

He watched as she gave an answering nod and a farewell before turning to continue on down the street to attend to her errands.

Deep in thought, he turned the opposite way and ambled on down the street to pick up something at the market for Mrs. Alder to make for his 'birthday dinner'.

*I'm finally turnin' twenty-one…**some celebration**.*

ꙮ

LOUISE SPENT HER days alternating between cloud nine, nervous anticipation, and the fear of discovery. She was in so deep by that point that she didn't know how she was ever going to unravel the crochet of lies she had fashioned of the situation. She'd even tried asking God's forgiveness, but since she intended to keep up the ruse, she felt like a low down hypocrite asking for 'permissive forgiveness'. But it was as if she were under the influence of a very powerful addiction that she just couldn't shake – like a wino that would do anything for one more drink. For her, that wine was Vic Matthews.

Preparations for the play had proceeded nicely, and Mrs. Herndon finally set a date for a Saturday in March. They even had tickets printed. Cost of admission was ten cents. The cast was assigned the task of selling the tickets, with the intended proceeds going toward new sporting equipment for the center.

Vic made sure he was Louise's first sale, followed by her family, their landlady, and the elderly man who lived in the apartment across the hall. She made the rounds to several of her teachers at school, and also Mr. Hudson, who gladly handed over a dime. The rest of her supply of tickets she talked her brother into hawking, for as Willis always said, Sonny could sell an icebox to an Eskimo.

Two Friday evenings were spent with Vic listening fondly as Louise regaled him with 'play' stories and her aggravations at home, and with her listening in turn to his frustrations over not being able to find gainful employment. Her ruse holding, everything was moving along at a nice pace.

Finally, the night of the play arrived…

"Are they here yet?" Louise whispered as Fleet peeked through the curtain. Having been too nervous to look for herself, she'd begged her friend to keep an eye out for her family…and for *him.*

"Nope," Fleet mumbled, allowing the curtain to fall back into place. Turning to her friend, Fleet smiled and gave her a quick hug. "Don't worry," she murmured. "You'll do fine. Remember, it's just another of those endless rehearsals," she added with a teasing wink.

"Oh don't say that, considering what happened last week," Louise returned, rolling her eyes. She cringed as she remembered being in the middle of the closing song and feeling her skirt drop to the floor around her ankles as the pin holding the waist had snapped open.

Fleet laughed and shook her head. Reaching out to tug on her friend's costume, a many-layered, hoop-skirted affair that was securely tied on, she murmured, "That won't happen with this get-up. Just concentrate on your lines and follow Herman's lead," she added soothingly.

They moved over as several youngsters rushed by behind them, frantically searching for props or parts of their costumes.

"Oh, what am I gonna do if he comes?" Louise breathed, swallowing nervously. "But then, if he *doesn't*…"

Chuckling, Fleet reached out to grab their friend Eleanor by the arm as she hurried past on her way to have a problem with her costume fixed. Fleet whispered to the raven haired girl, "Tell this goof that everything's gonna work out."

Eleanor, thinking the concern was merely the play, leaned to give Louise a quick hug. "You're gonna do fine, Lou. Don't worry. You look beautiful – and you sing like an angel!"

Louise smiled and reciprocated the hug, murmuring, "Thanks…if I remember to breathe."

The girls giggled nervously as Fleet turned to look through the slit in the curtain again, reaching out to touch Louise's arm. "Your family just came in."

"Oh good…where are they sitting?"

"Um…" Fleet paused as she watched until they decided on seats. "Over to the right, about middle ways back. I don't see Sonny, though…"

"Oh, he said he'd be late, but he'd come as soon as he sold all his papers. What about…" Louise whispered, but Fleet had scanned the faces in the folding chairs quickly filling the large auditorium. She shook her head. "Not yet."

Just then, Mrs. Herndon motioned to everyone to come over for a last huddle of encouragement and instruction before the play would begin. All of the kids and teens were brimming with nervous excitement, wishing it was over, yet thrilled to be involved.

ᘛᘚ

TEN MINUTES LATER, Vic jogged up to the outer door of the Neighborhood House, aggravated that he had been delayed. After slipping inside and giving his ticket to the girl at the table in the vestibule, he moved forward, viewing the action on the stage and looking for a place to sit. Empty Seats seemed to be a luxury, and other than a few at the very front, he couldn't see any. Opting to make the best of it, he settled for leaning against the wall by the door.

Contemplating the kids in the play, he wondered when Louise would come on and if he had missed any of her scenes. *The story's cute, I guess, but kinda hokey. But maybe that's because the younger kids ain't much on actin'*...he mused as he snorted quietly at a funny line delivered by a young boy. The audience laughed appreciatively.

Minutes went by...and then he saw her, wearing a beautiful antebellum long-sleeved costume of royal blue with black lace. Carrying a delicate fan trimmed in blue lace and ribbon, which she fluttered graciously as she talked, Louise strolled onto the stage and spoke a few lines to the young boy. *She's a natural. She don't seem nervous at all*...Vic reflected as he watched, totally spellbound. But for him, the scene was over far too quickly, and she continued on to the other side of the stage and disappeared behind the curtain's edge.

After another minute of action, the curtain closed and a young girl came out from the wings carrying a sign that read, 'Act 3'. Vic clamped his lips in a tiny pout of frustration, wondering if he had missed any of Louise's scenes. *I'll ask her to act them out for me,* he daydreamed with a half grin as the curtains opened and his attention was once again drawn to the stage. However, he couldn't have told you later what the plot was about, because the only thing that held his attention was Louise when she was featured. Throughout the performance, Vic watched closely as Louise smoothly handled her scenes with the boy he assumed was Herman, even when they danced a few moments of a waltz.

Sonny arrived mid way and took up a spot on the other side of the door. At one point between scenes, Sonny glanced around the large room and spotted Vic, his sister's crush, on the far side of the door. Eagerly, he scanned the audience until he spotted the family. *This could prove interesting…*he thought with a rakish grin.

ꕥ

FINALLY, THE LAST scene came and Louise walked onstage, having changed her costume for another hoop-skirted dress of deep emerald green. Even from the distance, Vic could tell the color set off the auburn tint in her brown hair.

Vic watched from the back, captivated, as the other characters left the stage and Louise wandered gracefully around the set, speaking her lines of pondering her future, while gazing out over the audience. She met her father's eyes, and tried to stifle her smile caused by the pride in his countenance. A soft lilting melody began to play and she started to sing a song entitled 'Song of Songs'. The lyrics were all about two lovers who had met on a night in June and spoke tender vows to one another. It spoke of magical moonbeams and golden dreams, summer roses, and vows that were made to be broken. The words, and her voice, were equally lovely, and she held the crowd of enthralled patrons in the palm of her hand. Her eyes scanned the assembly of familiar and unfamiliar faces. And then…

Vic moved, straightening up from leaning against the wall. Louise saw him in that instant, stopping dead as their eyes connected. Until that point, she had thought he hadn't come. The sight of him caused her to catch her breath for a second and pause, before she controlled her emotions and continued to sing. *He's here! He came!* She squealed silently as her heart kick-started into racehorse speed. It took great effort on her part to concentrate on the lyrics to the song.

Then Herman, her leading man, shuffled forward and joined her in finishing the number in what was the play's finale. Louise turned toward him and he took her hands as they had rehearsed dozens of times, and they harmonized perfectly as they sang of dreams of delight and nights of bliss. Allowing her imagination to take flight, and injecting much feeling into the words, Louise sang not to Herman, but to Vic. Totally caught up in the part she was playing, she had *become* Annabelle, and Vic was the ardent suitor holding her hands. As a result, she sang the song even better in performance than she had in any of the rehearsals. As the last note held and then ended, Louise's leading man leaned to place a kiss on her lips as the curtain slowly closed, revealing the words THE END written on a paper pinned to one edge.

The cast members assembled for their bows in front of the closed curtain, and the audience erupted in heartfelt applause. Louise dared not turn her head in Vic's direction, though she could feel his eyes on her – but if she had, she would have chuckled at his expression of almost comic jealousy stemming from the ending kiss.

Sonny applauded along with everyone else, and then suddenly remembered his promise to help his sister out. Looking around for ideas in case the need arose for him to run interference, he saw their father stand and begin escorting their mother and siblings into the center aisle. Looking to his right, Sonny saw Vic begin to make his way against the crowd as he headed toward finding Louise.

The brother quickened his step and intercepted the family. "Aw man, I missed the first half, but what I saw was great," he began, enthusiastically engaging Willis and Lilly in a lively conversation about how good they all thought Louise had been in her scenes. Out of the corner of his eye, he noticed Vic reach their position and hesitate. Apparently deciding not to interrupt a family moment, he went on, excusing his way through the crowd toward the front.

Edna rolled her eyes after a few moments of the family gushing about Louise, and casting her gaze toward the stage, saw the profile of a man she could have sworn was the one who had rescued them the night of the evacuation. Wondering his reason for coming to a play by a bunch of neighborhood kids, she observed him for a few moments, admiring his rich wavy hair and broad shoulders. *Mmm, I wish he woulda stopped to chat…* Just then, Billy got her attention as he mentioned a funny line in the play.

A few minutes later, Sonny offered, "Pop, I'll stay and walk Louise home if you want."

Anxious to get home and relax in his big chair, having had no time to do much more than grab a bite to eat before heading over to attend the play after his ride had let him off at the house, Willis agreed with a relieved smile. "Thank you, son. Tell your sister we'll see her at home." With that, he began to escort his family on down the aisle.

Sonny watched them for a moment, and then with a happy-go-lucky whistle, he turned and began to make his way down toward the stage.

❧

IT HAD TAKEN twenty minutes for Louise to remove her costume, as everyone in the cast, plus Mrs. Herndon, had wanted to congratulate her on her fine performance. She truly had been the star of the production, and she deserved every accolade they offered. Talking and laughing with her fellow cast members, she finally emerged from behind the curtain. Hoping Vic hadn't grown tired of waiting, she quickly scanned the few people left in the large area before spotting him talking with her brother Sonny.

Vic turned his head then and saw her, pausing in mid sentence. Noticing the direction of his gaze, Sonny followed his line of sight. He chuckled as he observed the other man, who appeared to be as 'smitten' as his sister.

As she came toward them, Vic couldn't take his eyes off her, his intense stare causing Louise's cheeks to pinken.

"Hi," she murmured as she reached their position.

"Hi," they both answered, and Louise grinned delightedly, then laughed as one of the kids in the cast bumped her as he ran past. "You were great, sis," Sonny offered, leaning in to give her a quick hug. Before he pulled away, he whispered, "I ran interference for ya with the folks. You owe me one." Their eyes met. Hers sparkling with gratitude, she nodded her thanks.

Sonny pulled back and added out loud, "I told Pop I'd stay and walk ya home. They said they'd see ya at the house, I think he was tired – he just got home."

Vic took a step closer to Louise, reaching out to cup her elbow. "I'll see her home…that is, if you've got somethin' else to do…" he offered, conveying his wishes as the two males met eyes.

Sonny tipped his cap at the pair and with a grin, turned and sauntered toward the door.

Vic reached out to gallantly take one of Louise's hands and place it in the crook of his elbow as he turned them toward the exit. They strolled along slowly. Neither spoke at first. The big room was alive with laughter and a dozen conversations going on at once.

Glancing up at him, Louise asked shyly, "Well…? What did you think?"

Vic's eyes twinkled as he gazed down at her. "You were great."

She smiled happily, feeling on top of the world. "Thank you.

What'dyou think of everything else? The play, the costumes…"

They had reached the vestibule by then and Vic paused in answering while he maneuvered them through the outer door. Once outside, he grasped her hand again as he directed them down the sidewalk and into the cool evening. Glancing down at her as she pulled the edges of her sweater together for warmth, he grinned and winked. "I don't remember none 'a that. All I saw was you."

"Vic!" she laughed delightedly.

"I'm serious. I didn't see nothin' else…'cept you and that twit at the end and how he couldn't keep his mitts off ya."

"Herman?" Louise giggled. "He was my leading man. He was Annabelle's true love," she added, unable to resist teasing him.

Glancing around to make sure no one was watching, he playfully growled as he pulled her close, "He was a *twit*, and he kissed ya."

"So?" She goaded, catching her lip between her teeth and gazing up at him. Still half in character, she fluttered her lashes at him in true Southern Belle form.

He allowed his eyes to roam over her exquisite features, attracted to her like a bear to honey. "So…I don't want *nobody* kissin' you…except *me*." The look in his eyes at that moment was so piercing, her heart skipped a beat and then sped up.

"…Oh…" was all she could manage. Her mouth went dry as she forgot to continue in her teasing.

Their gazes held for another few moments, but a family with a fellow cast member passing by made them separate.

They walked along in silence for a bit, just enjoying one another's company. After a while, Vic tightened his hold on her hand. "You really were good. You could be in the movies."

Infinitely pleased, she giggled softly. "Oh goodness, you can't imagine how nervous I was. I was scared the whole time that I'd forget my lines, or trip over my dress. Or even that something worse would happen…like my costume falling off," she added, remembering her embarrassment when her skirt had fallen down in rehearsal.

He snickered, and lifting her hand to his lips, he pressed a kiss to her fingers. "If it had, I'd a rushed up onstage and put my jacket around ya," he offered graciously.

She paused in their stroll and swept one arm out, bowing gracefully. "A gallant gentleman. I am in your debt, kind sir," she drawled one of her lines, with the more pronounced southern accent she had used in the play.

Straightening back up, they laughed together joyously as they strolled on down the street.

All too soon, the duplex where she lived came into view.

This time, Vic insisted he walk her to her door. Gulping and whispering a quick panicked prayer for help, she nodded and they walked up the steps and down the hall.

At the door, she turned to him and he reached out, touching a finger to her chin, whispering, "Goodnight, sweet Mary Lou. Lovely Annabelle," he added with a twinkle.

Her eyes fluttered shut as his head descended, his lips touching hers warmly. They lingered there for some seconds before he reluctantly released her.

"Goodnight," she whispered in return, reaching blindly behind her for the doorknob and hoping fervently that he wouldn't insist on waiting until she was inside. She smiled as he gently palmed her cheek with a grin, before he turned and sauntered to the door. There he looked back and lifted a hand in farewell before opening the door and slipping outside. Sighing in relief, she turned the cold brass knob on the door and slipped inside the cozy apartment.

Lilly looked up from her mending. "There you are. Where's your brother?"

Louise had to shake off the delicious enchantment of the evening as reality forced itself back upon her, and for a tense moment, she grappled for an answer. Then, hearing footfalls coming down the steps, she shrugged, "Upstairs," before she moved on into the room and enjoyed the compliments and proud congratulations of her father and younger brother.

"You were wonderful, honey," Willis intoned warmly and she sailed over to give him a hug. "I was so proud of you. We both were," he added, nodding toward Lilly.

"You were great!" Billy added. "All of that practice musta really paid off."

She gave them all a pleased, but secretive grin, thinking…*if you only knew…*

ꟗ

LATER THAT NIGHT, as she and Edna settled into the bed they shared, each one moving to the opposite edge as usual, Edna murmured, "You did okay in that play." It was the most complimentary thing she'd ever said to her sister.

"Thanks, Edna," Louise whispered, immensely pleased.

"Guess who I saw there tonight," Edna continued nonchalantly.

"Who?"

"That Vic guy that rescued us. Remember, the one that came out to Dove Creek and told flood stories?"

A feeling of panic immediately assailed Louise and she swallowed dryly. "Yeah."

"He's a looker, that's for sure. I bet he's hot to trot, too," Edna went on, with a few colorful phrases that made Louise blush. "Wish I knew more about 'im. I was too scared the night of the flood to pay 'im any mind. But now, well… Wonder what he was doin' there tonight. Think maybe he knows one a' the kids in the play?" she pondered, adding with a risqué snort, "He's got them dark handsome looks and big muscles that dreams are made of."

Louise's heart by then was hammering so loudly, she was

afraid her astute sister would hear it. "That right?" she managed, closing her eyes with a grimace, thankful for the darkness of the room so that Edna couldn't see her face. She wondered, and not for the first time, what punishment her sister would mete out when she found out the truth.

"*Mmmmm* hm. Anyway, like I said, you did good tonight," Edna returned, turning on her side and stretching out to get more comfortable.

"Thanks," Louise again whispered, silently wishing and praying that Edna would forget her sudden interest in Vic and move on to someone else. Some*thing* else. *Anything* else!

That night, her dreams of Vic and his charms were intermixed with disturbing images of arguments, yelling faces, and tears.

It was a long time until morning.

ꕥ

CHAPTER 16

The Brownie, The Stash, and The Derby

WEEKS PASSED, AND Edna's comments from the night of the play slowly faded with time.

For the young couple, the month of April floated by as if suspended in a sea of bliss. Louise dreamed her days away in classes at school. Vic pounded the pavement looking for steady work, and took every opportunity he found to earn money.

One low spot did occur for Louise when she came down with yet another case of tonsillitis, a malady that had plagued her for most of her life. As it happened every time she had been stricken, her mother became her caregiver, coaxing chicken soup and hot tea down her throat in small increments, and helping her gargle with warm salt water. Despite feeling downright lousy because of the illness, those were sweet times for her simply because Lilly treated Louise as if she were special, as if she were precious. Luckily for Louise, she was able to persuade Sonny to locate Vic to let him know she wasn't able to join him for their date.

One day in mid April, both Earl and Alec secured jobs at a local factory that produced wooden shipping pallets, but try as they might, they couldn't persuade the hiring manager to extend one more position to include their friend. This was quite a blow, which resulted in a few rough, uncomfortable days between the friends, especially since Vic was now residing with the Alders.

Although it wasn't the best situation, he did sleep comfortably on the couch in their living room.

That Friday night, the gang was once again cruising in the old black car, singing at the top of their lungs and enjoying one another's company. The young people had pooled their money and were heading to their favorite haunt, the White Castle on First Street.

As Vic and Louise cuddled near the back door, they heard Alec's voice say, "Hey you guys," and turned to face him. Their mouths dropped open in shock to find the lens of a black and silver, box-shaped 'Brownie' camera pointed their way as Alec crooned, "Cheese!" just before snapping the shutter.

"Will you cut it out with that thing!" Vic griped good-naturedly. "Before I crack you over the head with it." That was the third surprise shot Alec had taken of him since they had piled in the car and Earl had shown the gang his new toy. 'New' to him, since that afternoon when Mrs. Grant had gone to the pawnshop to buy back an item they had given as security for a small loan, only to find the shop dealer had sold it. Since it had only been that morning that her time had expired and he hadn't allowed her any extra days to repay the loan, the man felt sorry for her tears and allowed her to pick another item at a reduced price.

Alec, having immediately commandeered the device, just laughed at Vic's complaint, swinging around to snap a picture of Earl and Ruth cuddling in the driver's seat.

"You gonna pay for the pictures to be developed, huh pal? Since you're wastin' all the shots?" Earl retorted with a snort.

"Sure," Alec grinned, snapping a close up shot of Fleet posing for him. "I feel like celebratin'. Got me a good job, a beautiful gal on my arm, and headin' for some good chow. It don't get no better," he laughed again.

He swiveled around and turned the camera toward Gerald and his new love, a young blonde girl named Delores. Gerald swung an arm at him, so he shrugged and made to turn away, but surreptitiously turned back and snapped the photo anyway. After leaning to give Fleet a firm kiss on the lips, Alec tilted his head back and sang, "Aaaaaaaaannnnnd, 99 bottles of beer on the wall, 99 bottles of beer. Take one down, pass it around, 98 bottles of beer on the wall…." to which the other occupants laughingly joined in.

A few minutes later, Earl pulled the large hearse into the somewhat full lot of the White Castle and threw it into park as his passengers began to spill out the doors, laughing at the wide-eyed looks they received from other restaurant patrons.

"Whatsamatta wit' you? Ain't ya never seen a lively corpse before?" Alec teased one lady, prompting a reaction of, "Oh! Well, I never!"

"Maybe ya oughtta try it," Alec shot back, immediately followed by a, "Mmmph! Hey! What was *that* for?" as Fleet elbowed him in the ribs.

"Can't you behave?" she asked, only partly miffed.

"Noooooow, if I did, ya wouldn't like me as much, *would* ya," he countered, reaching out and softly tugging her to his side. Trying not to grin at his antics, Fleet chuckled and shook her head as she disengaged from him and grabbed at his arm. "C'mon, you goof. I'm starvin'."

He immediately doffed his flat-billed cap and bowed from the waist, one arm swept wide. "Your…*castle*…awaits, M'Dam."

Just then, Vic placed one foot against his friend's rump and gave him a playful shove. "Get thee inside then, you blaggard," he groused, causing Louise to giggle as she recognized a line from the play. The lot of them laughed happily and filed inside the establishment.

Once they received their orders, the playful young people trooped back out to the car and piled inside, leaving the doors open. Sitting on every available surface, they set about digging into their food. Louise found herself perched on the running board between Vic's knees as he made himself comfortable on the edge of the back seat.

Once again, Alec-the-camera-hound set about using the rest of the Brownie's film to capture his friends in comical poses of eating. As he rounded the car, he pointed the lens at Vic and Louise.

"Hey kids, last shot on the role. Make it good!"

Vic grinned down at his girl, murmuring, "I'll make it good. C'mere, babe," and slipping a hand to the back of her head, he pulled her toward him, his lips immediately taking hers in a fiery kiss, the hottest they'd had yet. Louise instantly melted. Unconsciously releasing the paper-wrapped burger onto her lap, her hands slowly crept up Vic's chest as she gently grasped fistfuls of the front of his shirt. Both were far too caught up in one another to notice the click of the shutter, or Alec's voice as he singsonged, "That'll be a good one."

Never had either of them experienced the flood of sensations and emotions they felt when they were together, especially when they kissed. It always made Louise sink into remembered images of scenes in the many romantic movies she had seen – and had always wondered if things like that happened in real life. Now she knew…yes, they did.

For Vic, he had never thought about finding such a love as he'd found in his delightful Louise. She was everything a young man could ever want, and he couldn't get enough of being with her, touching her, kissing her… He knew she had him totally captivated, but he didn't care one jot.

Mumbling a risqué word, Alec murmured with a snicker, "Okay you two, you can come up for air now."

Fleet cast a glance at her friend and shook her head in amusement, then reached out and grasped hold of her beau's shirtsleeve, chiding, "Leave 'em alone. You could learn a thing or two from them, you know."

Alec laughed and stepped close to his girl, immediately jumping into the challenge she had tossed out. With a naughty grin, he growled, "Oh yeah? C'mere," and pulled Fleet into a tight clutch. Immediately he lowered her backward in a dip that would have rivaled Valentino, as he kissed her hungrily. When he finally let her up, she giggled, crooning, "Then again, maybe not." The others chortled at their antics.

Finally, Vic and Louise slowly pulled back from their enchanted kiss, starry-eyed, totally oblivious to their friends' tomfoolery.

Neither one could think of any place else they'd rather be, than right there, together, spending time with one another. The future seemed bright with promise.

As Vic gave his girl an affectionate wink and brought his burger to his mouth for a hungry bite, Louise smiled lovingly at the man over which she was head over heels in love, thinking she couldn't wait to see that snapshot.

She knew it would be a memento she would cherish, although she had no idea at that moment just how much…

ꙮ

SOON THE DAYS flowed by and it was the first Saturday in May – Derby Day! As the mayor had promised, hard work, diligence, and neighbor helping neighbor, had paid off and the city was cleared of the evidence of the long-standing inundation. Proving the naysayers wrong, Louisville was once again ready for out of town visitors with money to wager and spend.

The evening before, during their customary Friday night date, Louise had quite a close call when Vic nearly invited himself to spend the day with her – at her family's apartment. Upon his inquiry as to her plans for Derby Day, she had mentioned the fact that her aunt, uncle, and cousins were coming for the day and that her father was home from Bowling Green for the weekend.

Studying the expression on her face when he mentioned dropping by, the old familiar feelings of not being welcome began to surface and he turned her to face him, asking in a pained tone, "What is it? You act like you don't want me to come around your parents…"

Louise's heart immediately lurched at the hurt in his eyes and the compounded problems she was causing herself because of the deceptions. She immediately responded, "Oh Vic, it isn't that!"

"Well…*what* then?"

"It…it's just…the apartment is small, you know? It's just two rooms. It gets crowded real quick," she answered, grasping at straws.

Their eyes met and held, and Louise swallowed uncomfortably. They'd been walking together along Main Street, eating ice cream cones as the sun began to set on what *had* been, up to that point, an idyllic date. Neither one spoke for a moment as Vic digested her excuse and tried to figure out if there was anything behind her actions. It dawned on him that in all the weeks they had been dating, he'd never once actually picked her up like a gentleman, speaking with her family and promising not to keep her out late. She had always insisted she would meet him somewhere…

Just then Eugene, coming from the opposite direction, stopped to chat. Totally oblivious of the tension between the couple, he asked cheerfully, "Hey pallie. What's doin'?"

Vic threw him a look, wishing he would move on.

"Ya got a light?" Eugene persisted, indicating the cigarette he had just bummed from another friend on the street.

Vic sighed in frustration. Reaching into in his pocket, he produced a lighter, one-handedly manipulated the horizontal flint to produce an instant flame, and held it to Eugene's cigarette. Drawing the fire in to touch off the tip, Eugene's eyes focused on the item in Vic's fingers. It was a silver plated Dunhill model. Vic kept it polished and in perfect condition.

"Nice lighter, man," Eugene commented, knowing the item's value as he had admired similar ones in the pawn shops. Touching the object, he turned it enough to read the inscription engraved on the side, *Daniel Elbridge Matthews*. "Where'd you get that?"

Vic turned his hand and glanced at the item, reading the name he'd read ten thousand times before. "Was my old man's. Only thing I got when he died," he added quietly, thinking of the item's history; it had been given to his father as a gift for his forty-fifth birthday – three years before he passed away. With a shrug, Vic pocketed the keepsake.

"You workin' the track tomorrah?" Eugene queried as he turned his head to grin and wave at another friend who tooted his horn as he drove by the trio. "I heard they still got a few two dollar windows that need tellers."

Vic had, indeed, been thinking about seeking a job for the day out at the Louisville Jockey Club, which had only recently been renamed Churchill Downs, for one of the world's most famous horse races, 'The Run for the Roses'. Matter of fact, Vic had not even thought about skipping the Derby, until he found himself asking for an invite to Louise's house.

Now, he looked back at her, noticing the nervous way she was fiddling with the napkin wrapped around her ice cream cone. With resignation, he shrugged and glanced again at Eugene. "Sure. Got nothin' *better* to do."

Although Vic had missed Louise's expression as she winced at his words, Eugene caught it.

The young man, finally realizing there was some sort of tension going on between his friends, cleared his throat and gave a short nod. "Okaaay. See ya there, then. Bye Louise," he added. She responded with a tiny wave and partial smile. With that, Eugene made tracks on down the street.

Moments ticked by, and Louise chanced a glance up at Vic's face. It was unreadable. Somehow she sensed that he was kicking different scenarios and reasons for her evasiveness around in his head. She was right. Her actions had unwittingly dredged up his old feelings of rejection caused by the hurts in his past. But in all of their time together, he had told her very little about his life.

"I'm sorry Vic. I…I don't want you to think…" she began, but paused, not knowing what to say. She couldn't think of any reason good enough. What would she say? *I can't have you come to the house and meet my family, because then everyone would find out I've been sneaking around behind my parents' backs…and keeping Edna from finding out who you really are…* She knew they would all have to find out sooner or later…but *later* would be much better. Reaching out a hand, she tentatively touched his arm.

Fatalistically, Vic finally just shrugged and murmured, "Ahh forget it. Truth is, I was gonna tell ya I was gonna work the track anyways."

Lamenting that their date had been spoiled, they both glanced around uncomfortably as they wished things to be the way they had been just a few minutes before. Finally, Vic touched her elbow and indicated they should continue on their stroll. He spent a few minutes catching up on his now dripping ice cream.

"So…Sonny gonna push papers at the track?" he asked, striving to sweep his feelings under the rug and go on as if nothing had occurred.

Louise swallowed a large bite of her treat. "He sure is. He worked the Derby last year and really cleaned up. One man bought a paper and handed him a ten – and told him to keep the change!" she confided in amazement.

Vic snorted with a nod. "Musta just won a big pot, had money ta burn." Fondly remembering the Derby the year before – and winning 'big' on *Bold Venture*, he added, "That's a good feelin'."

Louise nodded, relieved that their tiff had apparently been short-lived. "Yeah. Sonny's lucky like that. He can always spot the big spenders."

"He'll make good, then…" he responded, pausing as he noticed a commotion across the street. "What the…?" Several men had excitedly gathered at the remains of an old abandoned pub. Built in the 1800's, and unable to be salvaged after the flood, the building had been hastily torn down to the foundation and wooden floor.

Louise looked that way, brow furrowed. "What's going on?"

"I don't know…but let's check it out," he murmured. Grasping her hand and quickly checking both directions for traffic, he crossed the street at a trot, tugging her along with him.

When they reached the assembly, Vic asked the nearest man on his knees, who was pulling hard on one of the floor's planks, "What's doin'?"

"Man, there's all kinds 'a money under this floor!" the excited man responded, finally succeeding in prying the floorboard loose.

"You *kiddn*?" Vic asked, incredulous.

"Man, don't just stand there – *help* – before somebody decides to come and stop us!" another man returned.

Always game for ways to fill his pockets, Vic handed Louise the remains of his cone, murmuring, "Wait here," as he dove into the middle of the fray. As one board after another was pried loose, the eager scavengers dipped their hands down into the dried mud. Hooting in surprise and pleasure, they clawed at the treasure trove of old coins – some even solid gold. The money must have been irretrievably dropped through the wide gaps in the floorboards over the one hundred years the pub had been in operation.

Suddenly other people came running to see what the excitement was about. With a squeak, Louise moved back out of the way.

"Look at all this! It's like a gold mine!" one man exclaimed as he pulled a handful of booty from the dried mud under the rough sawed timber.

Vic straightened up and crammed his stash into his pockets, then turned to help the man to his right pull up another board. "There must be hundreds of dollars worth of coins under there!" he yelled over to Louise. Heart pounding with excitement, she tossed the forgotten ice cream cones to the ground behind her and nodded, joining with several other girls rooting for their men to get all they could. The girls – all barelegged and wearing skirts – held back from kneeling on the rough-hewn floor. Feeling like fast friends, they grasped hands, jumping and squealing with excitement.

As one man impatiently shoved another back, striving to grab the biggest amount for himself, the once friendly endeavor suddenly began to turn rowdy. The sore victim who was shoved righted himself and knocked the first man on his behind, taking his place at the opening. Vic dodged a shove himself as he reached down and grasped another handful of coins. Spotting two five dollar gold pieces, he quickly palmed the pair.

"I can't believe all of this is down here and nobody's got it out before!" he commented to the man next to him. The man nodded, murmuring, "That's my pal over there, Charlie," he indicated a man several feet away, hard at work pulling up a board. "He's the one who first saw it. We was sitting on the floor havin' a smoke and he noticed somethin' twinklin' down between the boards."

This has gotta be the easiest money I've ever made, Vic was thinking, when all of a sudden, everyone heard the unmistakable sound of police whistles. All heads snapping up in that direction, they looked up the street to see two uniformed patrol officers heading their way at a run.

"It's the heat! Beat it!" one of the men yelled. Panic erupted as every man scrambled hurriedly to his feet, taking off in all directions. Vic grabbed two more handfuls of coins and stuffed them in his pockets as he hastily jumped up from his knees. Grasping Louise's hand, they scurried down to the next cross street and turned. The evening air was pierced with the shrill sound of the whistles and shouts of, "Halt! Stop right there!" Hearts pounding furiously as they giggled with excitement from the rush of finding 'buried treasure' and nearly getting nabbed by the cops, they ran full-tilt away from the ruckus.

When they were about two blocks away, they ducked into in a doorway and peeked out to see if anyone was following, but thankfully there didn't appear to be.

"Whew!" Vic laughed as he caught his breath, leaning his head back against the door of the shop that was closed for the night. "That was close!"

"Yeah!" Louise gushed, placing a hand to her chest, as she too caught her breath. Her eyes sparkled with exhilaration, and her hair had come loose from its moorings and now framed her face in disarray. Vic glanced at her, adoring every nuance of the elation displayed on her face.

"How much did ya get?" Louise asked as she grinned up at him, gesturing at his pockets.

"I dunno…" he paused, trying to figure the best place to go to find out. "Um…c'mon," he said as he made his decision, taking her hand again as he set out for the Alder's apartment.

ꟸ

"OH VIC! THIS is so exciting!" exclaimed Rose, one of Alec's older sisters. She was rather large, nearly as tall as her brother, and a little on the plain side. Rose and Bertha, the two Alder girls, who were well on their way to being 'old maids', still resided with their mother and younger brother.

"Look at all these old coins!" added Bertha, the smaller, mousier of the sisters.

When Vic and Louise had arrived at the apartment, Mrs. Alder had been across the hall visiting a sick neighbor, and Alec and Fleet had gone to the movies. Rose had offered to rinse the dirt and grime from the coins as Vic had turned his pockets inside out, emptying their contents into a pan. Now, the five of them sat around the kitchen table, picking through the small stash.

"Silver dollars, five-dollar gold pieces, my goodness!" Louise murmured, fascinated.

"This one's dated 1880…this one 1902…" Bertha read as she

brushed through the coins.

"This one's a quarter...dated 1801..." Vic mumbled, jotting down the amount on a scrap of paper.

"Vic! This is a genuine Liberty twenty dollar gold coin – minted 1860...it could have been down there since the Civil War!" Mrs. Alder gushed, amazed at the amount of money that lay on her kitchen table.

"Oh I wish you could have gotten more!" Rose exclaimed, dollar signs in her eyes as if they belonged to her.

Louise immediately rebuffed, "He was lucky to get what he got – there were so many other guys there, all shoving each other, trying to get their share..." Meeting Vic's eyes, she added, "At one point, I was afraid that fat guy was gonna knock you out of the way."

Vic laughed. "He almost did."

"What are you going to do with all of this, Vic?" Mrs. Alder inquired, closely examining the Liberty coin.

Vic looked up from his notations with a thoughtful expression. "There's lots I wanna do with it... I'm gonna give you some of it for my board..."

"Vic, no, you don't have to..." Mrs. Alder began, but Vic interrupted, "Yeah I do. I can't stay here, sleepin' on your couch, eatin' your food, and not pay you nothin'. Why don't you take that piece there and see what Larry down at the pawn shop'll give ya for it."

Mrs. Alder smiled fondly at him, deciding not to argue for the sake of being polite, since she did need the money. "Alright, I will. Thank you, Vic."

Louise met Vic's eyes and they shared a smile.

ꕥ

THE NEXT DAY, Vic spotted Louise's brother as he made his way through the west gate of Churchill Downs. "Hey Sonny, how ya been?" Vic called, stopping for a moment to chat.

Sonny adjusted the heavy shoulder sack full of papers and grinned at his sister's crush. "Hey man. Louise told me about your windfall last night. I guess instead of sloggin' around in the infield you'll be sippin' mint juleps on Millionaire's Row as the band plays 'My Old Kentucky Home,' huh?" he joked, referring to the traditional start of the Derby.

Vic laughed and shook his head. "Weren't that big 'a windfall. Nah, gonna work a window, takin' bets from all the other stiff's tryin' to make a fast buck."

"I hear ya," Sonny nodded as he turned aside to hand a patron a paper and receive the payment.

Vic waited until he was through, and then reached out to tap Sonny's arm. "Hey…lemme ask ya somethin'. Louise…you got any idea of something I could get her? The kind of stuff she likes?"

With half a mind to tease him, Sonny grinned at the older man. It was obvious Vic was smitten with Louise. Thinking for a minute, he answered, "Well…I know she's always talked about things with her birthstone in 'em. It's purple I think."

Vic nodded, his eyes narrowing as ideas came to mind. "Her birthstone. Yeah, okay. Thanks, man," he added as he flashed his white smile. "See ya later. Hope you sell out today."

"I will," Sonny returned with a confident chuckle as another customer walked up and he reached in his bag to sell him a copy of the morning paper, which of course included the sports page with racing statistics and info about the horses.

ꟷ

AFTER VIC CHECKED in with the manager of the betting windows, he was assigned to one of the two-dollar stations.

Sitting down at the barred opening and acquainting himself with the other workers, he settled in for a long and hectic day. He knew that once the races began, men and women would line up at the windows, eager to place their money on the thoroughbred they felt was a 'sure bet'.

Vic couldn't quite make up his mind about betting some of the money he had found the evening before. Recalling the total, $67.52, minus the twenty-dollar coin he had given to Mrs. Alder, he wavered once again on what he should do. He wanted to buy Louise something pretty…but there were so many things for which he needed money. He could put some of it away to start building a nest egg for his future…or he could wager it and hope for a big pot – and a bigger start to his savings.

Having followed the scuttlebutt, he knew that War Admiral, whose sire was the famous Man of War, was by far the favorite to win the Derby that year. The problem, he knew, was picking the right combination – 'Win, Place, or Show'. A fellow could get messed up and lose everything just by picking the wrong position, even if he picked the right horse. It was such a gamble. Vic chuckled to himself as that thought occurred. *That's why they call it gambling.* He knew the chances were much better for losing than winning. But…remembering the feeling of walking away with forty dollars in his pocket after last year's win with Bold Venture, he knew he would end up betting at least some of his stash.

To keep from losing it all, Vic had purposely left the older coins in his duffle bag at the Alder's apartment. Patting the pocket containing his money, he hoped like everyone else, that when the time came, he would make the right choice.

Foregoing small talk with the other tellers, he gazed out over the vast infield, which was quickly filling up with revelers, as he mused over the history of the famous track. There was just something exciting about being out there, in the thick of things, experiencing the thrill of the chance to win big. The jostling about with all the other people…the aromas of the different food vendors…the sounds of the announcer on the overhead speakers.

The track, which he knew had been founded by Col. M. Lewis Clark, grandson of William Clark of the famous 'Lewis and Clark

Expedition', was *the* place to be on the first Saturday in May each year if you happened to be in Louisville. Celebrities, the rich, and those with connections to the rich, congregated there to experience the thrill of the wager, everyone with their eyes glued to a 1 ¼ mile dirt track as 15-20 thoroughbred horses battled for supremacy – the prize, a large amount of money, fame, and a garland of 554 red roses to be draped on the winner.

One thing Vic reminded himself, however, was that gambling fever could control a person, causing them to make foolish choices. As a twelve year old, he had seen it first-hand, when his own father had wagered his entire paycheck on a 'sure thing' – and lost. That one poor choice had resulted in the family losing their home. In shame and defeat, Daniel Matthews had taken the younger two of his three sons – Vic and his brother Alvin – and moved back to his boyhood home in Evansville, Indiana, where he had died less than six months later. He'd never gotten back on his feet. The day his father died had been the worst day of Vic's young life…

Just then, Eugene tapped him on the arm in greeting as he hurriedly passed by on his way to a teller station several places down. Jolted out of his musings, Vic realized that the first of the day's ten races was about to get underway, so he reached up and clamped his white 'teller' cap on his head and focused on his job.

As the day progressed, Vic saw men, and an occasional well-dressed woman wearing an outlandish Derby hat, come to his window and hand him money through the safety bars as they legally wagered on the 'ponies'. More than once, the man or woman received the betting slip from him and brought it to their lips for a kiss of good luck. Some of those came back to collect, some didn't. Some bet with confidence and lost, some bet with fear and trembling and came back a winner. Truly, there is no 'sure' method.

When finally the big race of the day was next, Vic knew it was now or never. He'd hoped for a 'feeling', but between two Derby horses – War Admiral and Reaping Reward – he had the same sense of excitement and fear. Voices in his mind battled for his attention – Louise had cautioned against betting on the horses, and his friend Irene had also mentioned the vice in a negative way. However, knowing he would kick himself if he didn't at least try, he decided to only bet a portion, keeping back enough to buy his girl a nice gift. Making his decision, he went with the name he liked best, as he had the year before, rather than the 'favorite'.

With one minute left to place a bet, he reached in his pocket and withdrew two five-dollar coins and tossed them to Eugene several stations down.

"Put me down for Reaping Reward, to win," he called in between customers.

Eugene called back, "You sure?"

Vic released an amused snort. "Sure as I *can* be."

His friend quickly completed the transaction and passed him his slip. "Good luck."

"Thanks," Vic answered as the announcement was made to shut their windows.

Tension immediately ensued across the thousands of Derby goers as War Admiral decided for some reason that he was frightened of the starting gate. This caused his handlers – and everyone else at the Downs – eight long minutes of frustration as they coaxed and wrestled the thoroughbred into the slot. Finally, they were off, and three breathless minutes later, Vic was shaking his head and lamenting his choice, yet so very glad he had erred on the side of caution. War Admiral had won. Reaping Reward had not reaped a reward for Vic, the horse had come in third.

As he left the grounds that evening, one hand against the pocket that still held the bulk of his 'windfall' and his wages from that day's work, the other waving at Louise's brother, he was very glad he'd had sense enough to listen to the voices of reason.

He couldn't wait to tell Louise about the day, when he gave her the gift he planned to purchase. He knew she'd be proud.

ജ്ഞ

CHAPTER 17

Fontaine Ferry Park

ON A BEAUTIFUL Saturday morning a week later, Louise dried her hands and quickly removed her apron, having hastily finished the family's breakfast dishes. Quickly, she checked the barrettes in her hair in the mirror by the door, and smoothed the skirt of her lavender flowered, v-neck short-sleeved dress.

"Bye Mama, I'm goin' now. I'll be home before dark," she called to her mother in the bedroom. She wanted to hurry and leave the apartment before the inevitable could happen. That wish didn't come true, however.

"Where ya goin'?" Billy asked as he came in the door from taking the trash out to the can.

Louise set about gathering her things, striving to answer her brother with care. She glanced at him with a small smile. "Me and Fleet are goin' downtown…"

"But where?" her brother insisted. A typical boy with an appetite to match, he leaned to grab an apple from the bowl on the table.

Lilly came into the room then, carrying the rag she had used to dust the bedroom furniture. "Now, make sure you girls conduct yourselves like ladies, and don't be riding that awful roller coaster," she instructed as she grabbed the broom from the corner.

Before Louise could answer, Billy squawked, "Roller Coaster!

You're goin' to Fount'n Ferry?"

Louise caught her lip between her teeth, wishing she had made it out the door before Billy found out. Now, she looked at him, scrambling for a reason why he couldn't go with her. He had always gone with her before. Fontaine Ferry Park, commonly referred to as 'Fountain Ferry', was one of the few places during the Depression that kids in Louisville could go to have fun. She, Billy, Sonny, and Edna, as well as their cousins, had been to it dozens of times. Louise's conscience smarted as she was faced with the realization that so much had changed since she had taken up with Vic. She and Billy had been inseparable before that. Now… Her heart clenched as he stared at her with his big blue eyes, the hurt evident. "I wanna go, too," he begged.

"The Velvet Racer got ruined in the flood, Billy," Louise reminded her brother, but he would not be detoured. "A house smashed into it and tore it up. Remember seein' the pictures in the paper?"

"I don't care! There's lots 'a fun stuff to do, you know that!"

Just then, a knock sounded at the door and Lilly moved over to answer it, revealing a smiling, smartly dressed Fleet. Lilly noticed the girl was wearing what looked like a new outfit – a red polka dot, flared skirt paired with a white short sleeve blouse with red dots, trimmed with a red bow and sporting a sash belt of the same color that accentuated Fleet's narrow waist. For a moment, the older woman wondered why the girl would be dressed so nicely to go to an amusement park and ride the rides.

"Hello Mrs. Hoskins. Louise ready?" Fleet asked cheerily as the girl stepped into the room.

Lilly had not been aware that Louise had planned to slip out without taking Billy. Now, she turned to her daughter, concern and a tiny bit of suspicion furrowing her eyebrows as she realized Louise had put on a nice dress as well. "You're not taking your brother with you?"

Oh no…what should I do…? Louise agonized for a moment as

she quickly weighed her options. Intending on the outing being a double date, the guys were going to meet them at the entrance, and she knew the first thing Vic would do when he saw her would be to take her in his arms for a kiss! Fleet's eyes widened at this unexpected turn of events and the girls locked gazes for a moment. Louise turned toward her brother, a gentle excuse on the tip of her tongue, but tears began to well in Billy's eyes as he stared at his sister, terribly upset.

It was more than Louise could bear. Billy didn't deserve to be hurt. With a small smile, she reluctantly acquiesced. Holding out one hand to him, she murmured, "Yeah, come on. You can go."

Relieved, Lilly nodded in satisfaction and reached into her apron pocket. "Here's fifty cents. It's all I have, but it'll pay his way in and on the streetcar, with a bit left over for a snack."

Louise nodded and dropped the coins in her purse with the nickels and dimes she had made washing dishes for grumpy old Mrs. Higgins.

"Now Billy, you behave yourself and mind your sister," Lilly instructed as she shooed the young people out the door. In truth, with Willis unable to make it home for the weekend, Sonny out selling papers and Edna at her job at the deli, Lilly was glad she would have a few hours of quiet.

Once out front, the girls exchanged glances, wondering how they would maneuver around this setback. With a shrug, Louise murmured, "C'mon, let's go."

ꟾ

THE MARKET STREET Trolley shimmied and shook as its metal wheels rolled over the tracks in the intersection. Three blocks from the park, Louise brushed back a windblown lock of hair from her face and turned to her brother on their shared seat. He'd been happily chattering on since they had boarded the old streetcar.

Over the sounds of other passengers carrying on conversations, and the noise of the rattletrap vehicle, she leaned toward him and murmured, "Billy…can you keep a secret?"

His eyes lit up with intrigue. "A secret? You got a secret, Louise?" He couldn't imagine what it could be.

Fleet turned in her seat just ahead to watch how her friend was going to handle the current subterfuge. Louise glanced at her and then back at her brother. Choosing her words carefully, she began, "Billy…you remember Mr. Vic, the man who rescued us the night of the flood?"

Billy nodded vigorously. "Sure I do."

"Well…now you can't tell a soul, you gotta *promise* me," she reasserted, her hand on his shoulder as he kept nodding. "Well…me and Vic…he's my boyfriend now."

Billy's blue eyes grew impossibly larger. "He *is*? Gee wiz! But why's that a secret?"

"Never you mind why. But you gotta promise me that you won't go tellin' Mama or Daddy – and especially don't say nothin' to *Edna*," Louise stressed, the hand on his shoulder tightening.

"Okaaay okaaay," he assured. Then waiting until she visibly relaxed, he added impishly, "But it'll cost ya. I get ta ride *all* the rides today…plus I get a corn dog *and* cotton candy," he bargained cleverly.

Fleet snorted and turned around in her seat, calling back over her shoulder, "End of line comin' up."

Louise chuckled and shook her head, thinking her 'little' brother wasn't so little anymore. He was taking after his older brother and becoming a shrewd wheeler-dealer. She stretched up to see the wide area in the street where the trolley made its turn around, one block from the entrance to the park.

"Ok, it's a deal. But you just remember to keep your trap shut, or I'll skin you alive."

Billy giggled and bobbed up and down on his seat. "But, I still don't understand…Mama and Daddy like Mr. Vic…and why don't you want Edna to know? Oh!" he added, bursting with a sudden thought which he couldn't resist using to press her buttons. "You think Mr. Vic might like Edna more than you?"

Louise rolled her eyes as Fleet giggled at the little boy's boldness.

"C'mon," Louise addressed her brother. Rising to her feet and gathering her purse, she tugged on his arm as the trolley stopped.

ഇ ര

VIC PACED BACK and forth below one of the massive towers at the park's front entrance, striving to tamp down his impatience. For the third time, he patted his shirt pocket, to make sure a certain item remained hidden there. He just hoped he wouldn't botch the moment when he could present his carefully chosen gift to his girl.

Alec strolled up to him and turned his head to the left, his eyes trained on the bustling intersection of Northwestern Parkway and Market Street. "Any sign of 'em yet?"

"Nope. Wonder if somethin' held 'em up..." Vic began, slightly irritated that Louise had insisted she and Fleet would make their own way there. *Why don't she ever let me pick her up at her house?* He wondered yet again. Pausing, he squinted as his eyes caught sight of a familiar dress and head of dark shiny hair darting around a slow walking couple.

As the three young people came within viewing distance of the entrance to the park, they saw the guys simultaneously. Fleet raised an arm and waved at their waiting beaus.

"There they are," Vic mumbled gratefully. The street outside the entrance busy with cars, he looked both ways threading cautiously through the traffic to rush up to Louise as she dropped Billy's hand. Taking her in his embrace, Vic wrapped one arm around her waist, the other hand gently grasping the back of her head as he greeted her with a murmured, "Hey babe," and a solid kiss just as Alec reached Fleet and proceeded to follow suit.

Billy giggled as he watched his sister and Mr. Vic smooching in broad daylight.

As Vic pulled back a bit to gaze at his girl, it was only then that he realized her little brother was standing near. Unperturbed, as he naturally figured her whole family was aware of their relationship, he grinned at the boy and reached to ruffle his hair.

"Hey Billy. How you been?"

Before the boy could answer, Alec asked, "Who's the kid?"

Louise glanced over at him, embarrassed. "His name's Billy. He's my little brother. Billy, this is Alec," she explained. Afraid that the guys might think this would ruin the double date they had planned, she turned her eyes to Vic, but he was grinning as he exchanged chuckles with Alec.

"Well, looks like it's family day," Vic murmured, turning slightly and indicating a group of young people gazing their way as they stood in front of one of the large pillars at the entrance to the park. On closer inspection, Louise recognized Earl and Ruth, along with Earl's younger sister Bernice.

In explanation, Vic glanced back at Louise, "Earl and Ruth wanted ta' tag along…and then Earl's mom insisted they take Neecee, too."

Louise grinned, thinking things seemed to be working out. "Same here."

Across the street, Bernice spotted Billy and remembering him from the long ride back to Louisville after the flood, the little girl grinned happily. Billy noticed her looking his way and he felt his face begin to flush. He remembered her, as well.

At first, Vic had felt frustration at the unexpected turn of events, as he had hoped for some romantic alone time with Louise. But now, he laughed amiably and turned, one arm slung around her shoulders.

"Ahh well. Let's jus' go have some fun," he murmured, deciding to be happy that at least he was about to spend the day with his girl.

꧁꧂

DODGING THE CROWD an hour later as they stood between a yellow ticket booth and a food vendor, the eight young people dug into sweet clouds of pink cotton candy. They had ridden the Ferris wheel, with Billy insisting he ride in the seat with Louise and Vic so that he wouldn't get stuck riding with Bernice. Next they spent an exhilarating time riding the Scrambler and something called Loop-O-Planes, which were two cars shaped like airplanes attached to a tall pole. Billy and Bernice spent several rounds riding the Kiddie Kars, after which the group had decided to stop and purchase a treat as they made plans on what to ride next.

Vic had plans of his own. He wanted to be alone with Louise, but with her younger brother stuck to her side like glue, that had so far proved impossible.

"This is fun. I love Fount'n Ferry," Bernice enthused as she licked errant sticky strands of fluffy spun sugar from her lips. She cast her eyes once again at Billy Hoskins, thinking he was the dreamiest thing she'd ever seen, as his big blue eyes glanced her way.

"Yeah, it's my favorite place," Ruth agreed, tilting her head to gaze up at Earl with a dreamy expression. He grinned and gave her a sexy wink as they shared a private look no one else could interpret.

"I want to go on the big slide next," Fleet offered, giggling as Alec shared a bite of his spun treat with her. He smirked teasingly, "Aw c'mon, I thought we'd hit the Whip next."

Fleet laughed and gave him a gentle shove. "*You* can. Last time I rode that, I got whiplash."

Billy squirmed under Bernice's constant stare, and he gripped the paper cone and swallowed a large bite of his candy. "I wanna ride some more stuff. C'mon Louise," he whined, reaching to tug on his sister's sleeve.

Vic turned his head and gave the boy a wink. "Hold your horses, son. We will."

Earl tore off a large hunk of his confection and stuffed it in his mouth as he cast a glance toward his long time friend. He knew Vic was straining at the ropes to get his girl alone, and he felt a tiny bit bad that he and Ruth had invited themselves along. He had been of a mind to tease Vic and let him stew a bit, but suddenly feeling generous, he swallowed the hyper sweet concoction and said instead, "Look Chief, we don't necessarily have to stay together. If, uh, you guys wanna mosey on, we'll look after the kid for ya," he added with a sly wink.

Vic grinned at his friend and slipped an arm around a silent Louise. She was wondering how Billy would react and if he would retaliate later as she met her brother's eyes with a silent plea.

"But..." Billy began to protest. Bernice's broadening smile was making him uncomfortable, though he couldn't have put into words just why.

Opening her purse, Louise retrieved the coins her mother had given her that morning, and handed them to her brother. "Here, Billy. You can buy what ever you want, okay?"

Before the opportunity could slip through his fingers, Vic grabbed Louise's hand. "That's settled then. See you guys around five at the carousel," he called over his shoulder as he tugged her through the crowd. In seconds they were out of sight. The group left standing looked at one another and laughed at Vic's exuberance.

Once out of sight, the two began to stroll down the main midway-like thoroughfare lined with game booths and lovely shade trees, dodging mothers pushing strollers, old couples walking slowly, and kids darting to and fro. After a few minutes, Vic chuckled and unexpectedly pulled Louise up next to a corn dog booth. Entwining his fingers with hers, he quickly pressed her back against the side of the structure and brought her hands up beside her head. Breathless, Louise giggled at the sheer excitement of it all.

Then, his eyes alive with risqué mischief, Vic leaned down, mouth open, and covered her lips with his as he succumbed to the undeniable urge he'd been tamping down all day. Both sets of lips were still sticky with spun sugar.

It was already the most enjoyable trip to Fontaine Ferry she had ever experienced; and now that they had escaped the watchful eyes of her brother, she was finally where she had wanted to be all morning – 'alone' in the crowd with Vic, and in his arms. With tingles of overpowering attraction to the man who held her captive zipping through her body, she sighed helplessly and allowed him to have his way.

Moments later Vic finally pulled back, bringing the kiss to an end, his brown eyes glittering merrily. Gazing down into Louise's own eyes, he was nearly overcome with the depth of his feelings for her. Pride alone kept him from letting her know just how tightly she had wrapped him around her pinky.

Clearing his throat, he murmured, "Okay, Miss Hoskins. Where to?"

Eyes twinkling happily, she shook her head to indicate she didn't have a preference. She felt absolutely on top of the world.

ജ൱

AN HOUR LATER, they walked by the entrance to the Tunnel of Love, its lighted words shining brightly over the domed entrance illuminated on the surface of the fast flowing water. Vic was surprised to see no line of people waiting.

He glanced over at his date. "Wanna ride with me?"

She nodded, and he grasped her hand, steered her over, and handed the operator two tickets. Holding on to one of the red painted safety bars at the edge, he helped Louise into a floating four-passenger craft.

Louise was a bit nervous. She had never ridden through the Tunnel of Love, and now to be doing so with Vic – completely alone, for at least the few minutes it would take to navigate through – it was sure to be high on her list of moments to remember.

Vic settled in at her side, immediately wrapping an arm around her shoulders as the operator used a long stick to push their boat into the flow of the swiftly moving water. In moments, they had crossed under the entrance and rounded the first curve into the winding tunnel, disappearing from sight.

The soothing sound of the water buoying their craft along helped to settle Louise's nerves. She noticed that the walls were decorated with white hearts illuminated by a string of lights at the center of the ceiling. The tiny bulbs gave off just enough radiance to alleviate the fear of 'sailing' into a dark abyss. Just as she turned to make a comment regarding how good the cool interior felt on such a warm summer day, Vic turned her way.

"I been waitin' ta get you alone like this all day," he growled.

Wasting no time, his arms surrounded her and he pulled her into a close embrace as his lips took hers in a fiery kiss. Overwhelmed, she surrendered at first, her hands rising to touch his chest, the fingers of one hand brushing against his chin. The kiss was more than she had ever experienced before, as his tongue forced its way inside her mouth. Her head was spinning with sensations, some enjoyable, some a bit disconcerting. The heady masculinity of him thrilled her in such a way; she wouldn't have been able to put it into words. His arms were so strong, holding her body against his. Louise could feel his heart thumping under her hands, and feel his warmth through the soft cotton of his shirt. Her senses registered that his jaw was pleasantly smooth from his careful shave that morning, and she could still detect the delightful aroma of the aftershave he had applied. Her heart pounded exhilaratingly.

But then Vic's hands began to roam a trifle too familiarly along her side. As he pressed one palm intimately against the side of her breast, she suddenly stiffened in his arms and with a tiny whimper, broke the kiss and pulled back.

"What's wrong?" Vic rasped, totally caught up in the moment.

Breathless, she tried to ascertain his expression in the dim light as the boat went around another curve, bumping into the wall as it went.

"Nothing…I mean…I…" she stammered, embarrassed that she had never 'made out' with a man before – at least not that passionately.

"The ride's almost over…c'mere baby," Vic murmured, leaning forward to try and engage her again in some serious sparking.

"Vic…*no*," she protested, turning her head and pushing against his chest.

He relented, pulling back to stare at her profile as he strove to dial his passions back down.

Afraid he was angry, Louise chanced a look at his face, and was relieved to see he just seemed puzzled. Knowing she should explain, she mumbled, "It's just…I've never…no man's ever…*touched* me like that," she finished lamely.

At that, he sat back a bit, chuckling at himself as he ran one hand back through his hair.

"I'm sorry, babe," he murmured. "I didn't mean to turn into a wolf on ya…" he added, reaching to steady her as the craft bumped another curve and water splashed within inches of their seat. "Or a water snake," he amended with a snort.

Louise swallowed nervously and smoothed her hair, catching her lip in a tiny grimace as she met his eyes. "Are you mad?"

Gazing at her as she sat there so prim and proper, how could he be angry with her? With a soft chuckle, he shook his head, reminding himself of what he had said to Earl just weeks before –

she's not that kind of girl.

"You were right to stop me…before ya needed ta slap my face," he teased with a grin.

Thinking she couldn't imagine *ever* wanting to slap him, for anything, she grinned back. She leaned into his side as he once again slipped his arm around her shoulders and pulled her against him, tilting his head to press his lips to the top of her head.

Just then, they rounded the last curve and saw the bright sunshine of the outdoors just yards ahead. For each one, the short ride through the Tunnel of Love had deepened their feelings for one another. For Vic, the few minutes had reinforced the respect and care he felt for Louise; and for her, it made her realize just how much of a hold this man had on her emotions.

Both knew they swimming in deep water, miles from shore. The realization was exhilarating, and even a bit frightening for the two young people.

ജ്ജ

THE REST OF the afternoon went by far too quickly for the fledgling couple. After emerging from the Tunnel of Love, they ran together, laughing and holding hands, to the Angel/Devil Slide. Vic insisted that they ride double on one mat, and ended up being Louise's hero when he stopped her from leaning too far over, resulting in him suffering a friction burn on his forearm. Gritting his teeth against the pain, he assured her it was *nothin'*. He was secretly pleased, however, when she fussed over it, insisting that he get a Band-Aid at the small medical aid booth in the center of the park.

After that, they wandered from one game of skill to another, Vic spending quite a few nickels trying to win his girl a big prize. He came close several times, before finally managing to win a small figurine of a white knight on a smartly decorated steed. Minutes before, several youngsters chasing one another had run by too closely, one of them knocking into Louise. She would have fallen against the hard edge of a concrete barrier, but thinking quickly, Vic had reached out and caught her in his arms, swinging around and setting her safely on her feet. Breathlessly she had thanked him for being her 'Knight in Shining Armor'. As Louise grasped the figurine to her chest, they laughed together over its unintended significance.

After that, they spent an idyllic time resting together on one of the many benches in the cool shade of the trees while feasting on corn dogs and red cream soda. It was an absolutely perfect summer day, with just the right touch of refreshing breeze. The best part, for Louise, was just being able to sit close to Vic, relishing in the comfortable feeling of his arm thrown around her shoulders as she snuggled against his side.

As they sat on the bench and watched children running by and others milling about, Louise turned her head to gaze at Vic's profile. A question popped in her head that she'd been meaning to ask him, so swallowing a bite of her corn dog and dabbing her mouth with a paper napkin, she queried, "Vic…why do Earl and Alec sometimes call you 'Chief'?"

His mouth formed a half smile and he let go a soft snort before taking a sip of his soda. "Aw, it goes back to when I was a kid. See, um…I'm the youngest of…three brothers," he paused as an indefinable look came into his eyes, but he moved on. "And when we'd play Cops and Robbers, or Cowboys and Indians, I never got to be the head honcho." He huffed a self-deprecating smirk. "I made the mistake 'a tellin' those two clowns that once, and after that Earl started callin' me Chief. Then Alec picked it up. Their way 'a showin' me respect, I guess," he shrugged, a bit self-conscious that he had bared some of his inner self to her, but she leaned into him and gave him a kiss on the cheek.

"I think that's sweet."

He cast her a mock affront. "*Sweet?* Babe, you know just how ta put a guy back in short pants, don't ya," he growled, albeit playfully. She giggled as he leaned over and gave her lips a quick smack.

They spent the next little while idly chatting, or observing the crowd. Vic glanced often at his watch. All through the day, he had been on the lookout for just the right place and moment to present Louise with his carefully chosen gift. Everywhere they had gone had seemed far too 'public', and the Tunnel of Love too dark…though truthfully, he had forgotten about it then.

Finally, at quarter to five, he suddenly stood up from the bench. Once again grasping Louise's hand, he murmured at her silent query, "Let's head on over to the carousel."

"Oh, but we still have a few minutes…" she started to argue, even as she allowed him to tow her along behind him, hating that the day was swiftly coming to an end.

Arriving at the huge carousel just in time to step onto its ground level surface for its next cycle, Vic tugged Louise through the maze of majestic, beautifully carved and painted horses to one of the stationary seats.

"But…aren't we going to ride a horse…" Louise began, but the intense look in his eyes stopped her protest and she followed him onto the seat. Gazing around at the dazzling lights and mirrors as the whistle blew and the large apparatus began to move, she marveled at how the carousel seemed like a work of art. It was beautifully painted and perfectly maintained, as all of its shiny surfaces gleamed and sparkled. The horses were so colorful and so gorgeously decorated as to appear quite regal. Glancing up for a moment into the open top of the ride, Louise was fascinated with the mechanics of the 'jumper horses'. As a child, she had been almost mesmerized watching the smooth workings go round and round.

It only contributed to the overall sensation of enchantment she had been feeling the entire day. Music played and children laughed and talked as Louise felt Vic take her hand and turn her toward him.

"I been wantin' to do this all day long," he murmured, gazing for a moment into Louise's eyes. Then with his free hand, he reached into his shirt pocket and retrieved a small, velvet covered box. Her heart jumped as she thought he was about to present her with a ring.

With a shy smile, Vic explained, "I wanted to get ya something nice, and especially since I didn't have any money to get ya anything for your birthday…so…well…I hope you like it."

Taking the box, she opened it to find a small, but lovely pendant on a simple silver chain. Her lips parted in surprise and pleasure, as she gasped, "Oh Vic! An amethyst necklace! It's beautiful!" He chuckled softly in relief at her pleased reaction, bending his head to see how to help her take it out of its moorings. Holding it up for her inspection, his eyes fairly glowed with affection as he watched hers sparkle with excitement. "I've always wanted a necklace with my birthstone in it. How did you know?" she asked, a large happy grin adorning her face as she switched her gaze to meet his eyes.

He grinned and snickered, the dimple in his cheek pronounced. "Aww, let's just say…a little bird tol' me."

Louise laughed softly in response. Never had she felt so cherished. It was as if all of her childhood dreams of finding her 'Prince Charming' had culminated in that moment. For a crazy second, she wondered if she were dreaming.

"Here, lemme put it on ya," he whispered, undoing the clasp and reaching around behind her head to fasten it. She gathered her hair out of the way and settled the pendant within the v-neck of her dress. It was as if she had dressed in anticipation of it, as the necklace coordinated beautifully with the purple flowers in the material.

Louise knew Vic had wagered on the Derby and lost, as he had admitted as much to her the day after. But she didn't know how much of his stash he had left, and now she worriedly drew her lip softly between her teeth. "Oh Vic, where did you get the money? This must have cost a fortune!" she murmured, gazing into his eyes as he sat back to view the pendant as it sparkled against her skin.

He pressed his lips together and gave a negative shake of his head. "Nah. Got it with some 'a the floorboard money," he explained softly, choosing not to tell her that Larry, at the pawn shop, had assured him it was a real amethyst, but Vic had his doubts because everyone in town knew the man was a bald faced liar.

She smiled lovingly, her eyes twinkling in the carousel's lights. "Thank you. But I…I feel bad that you spent money on me like that…" she insisted, knowing that without a steady job, his small cache of money would eventually be depleted.

Shaking his head again, he reached for one of her hands, brought it up to his lips, and grazed the surface of her knuckles with a soft kiss. He wanted to tell her that, if he could, he'd shower her with presents and gifts, but the words sort of stuck in his throat. Instead, he managed, "You're worth it. You're an angel. The sweetest, truest, most beautiful angel I've ever known," he added softly.

At his words, her conscience crimped sharply. *Oh my gosh…what will he think if he finds out all the ways I haven't been honest with him…*

The thought stilled in her mind as he leaned forward, sealing his words with a soft kiss. She melted into his embrace, as always. However, after just a few moments, the operator making his rounds passed them and tapped Vic on the shoulder to remind the amorous couple that they needed to comport themselves properly. After all, there were children nearby.

The two sat back and softly chuckled, for a moment resting their heads against one another. Vic gently stroked Louise's arm as she closed her eyes and held tight to her necklace.

Too soon, the magical carousel ride began to come to an end as the large apparatus began to slow down – along with their idyllic day.

They disembarked together, holding hands, just as their friends came walking into view. Billy ran up to his sister, launching into his day in the park and how the six young people had spent most of the afternoon in Hilarity Hall, enjoying the Barrel of Fun, the Sugar Bowl, and the Devil's Slide, along with the house of fun mirrors. Billy wanted his older sister to be proud that he had spent his money wisely. He did leave out, however, that he had grown used to Bernice and by that time had even begun to feel a bit of attraction to the sister of her friend.

Overflowing with happiness, Louise just couldn't turn Billy down when he pleaded with her to ride the carousel with him, just like they always did when they came to Fontaine Ferry. With a grin and a shrug to Vic, she took her brother's hand and together they ran up onto the glittering ride, both of them hopping onto brightly painted jumper horses.

Vic stood with his friends, arms across his chest, grinning from ear to ear and thinking one day soon he would gather his courage and tell Louise how he felt about her. However, for now he was content just to watch the angel he adored laughing and waving each time the big wheel came around.

By the time the group left the park that evening, the sun was almost to the horizon. The gleaming lights in the massive entrance were just coming on as they passed through it and when they reached the street, Louise stopped and turned, gazing back at the lovely sight. She knew she would treasure the memory of that enchanted day for the rest of her life.

She just didn't know how much.

ഗ്രെ

CHAPTER 18

On the Idlewild

VIC HELD LOUISE'S hand securely in his as they followed their friends ascending the wide partitioned staircase.

Reaching the top, they moved over to allow more people to crowd in as Alec pointed the way to some empty chairs along the side of the already quite full deck/dance floor of the Idlewild. The atmosphere bristled with electricity for not only the dance, but also the old boat itself.

There was a kind of magic about the old packet steamboat. It had been built in 1914, and sported the fancy embellishments of the Victorian era, including latticework and decorative tin ceilings with carved arched trusses. The distinctive sound of the steam calliope playing such catchy tunes as *Down By the Riverside, Camp Town Races*, and *Take me out to the Ballgame* added to the thrill; although the patrons did begin to tire of the repeated melodies on the thirty minute wait to board.

By the time the six friends had made it through the throng, any empty seats to be had were taken. With a shrug to one another, they gravitated to the edge near the railing to await the start of the cruise.

The band tuning up was a local ensemble that had already gained a regional reputation as being 'pretty keen'. Mere minutes later, conversation halted and the crowd reacted with gasps and chuckles as a jarring, overwhelmingly loud hum erupted without forewarning when the engineer released valves on the old steam engines in preparation for getting under way. The large craft gave an unsettling shimmy, and then the passengers felt it begin to move as the captain maneuvered the boat away from the dock. It took a moment for them to adjust and find their 'sea legs'.

"This is gonna be so much fun," Ruth squealed. Earl and Vic exchanged amused glances, and Vic silently wondered if Earl's girl knew he wasn't much for dancing.

"Yeah. I've been on the Idlewild lots of times, but never for a dance," Louise crooned, gazing around at the crowd and turning her head to check on what Vic was doing. He and the other fellas had their heads together, apparently engaged in 'Guy talk.'

Just then the bandleader, Charlie Raeburn – a tall, thin young man sporting a suit two sizes too big, black rimmed glasses, and his bright red hair an unruly mop – called out to get everyone's attention. His voice seemed a tad rough, as if he might be coming down with a cold, as he announced their first song, a rousing and well executed rendition of Tommy Dorsey's 'Marie'.

The group of friends immediately took to the dance floor, trying to crowd their way in and still have room to move.

"Sold too many tickets, looks like," Alec observed to Vic as he turned to take Fleet tightly into his arms.

"Yeah, moneygrubbers," Vic folded Louise into his arms as well, grumbling as he looked around and tried to calculate the number of passengers. Having worked one season on the boat, he knew its particulars, and he wondered if they were over their maximum allowed capacity of six hundred and fifty.

Louise had a bit of trouble trying to follow Vic, as other dancers kept unceremoniously bumping into them. Nevertheless, when the band began to sing the words to the tune, Vic leaned close and murmured, "Marie…it's almost your first name. It could be your song, huh?"

Vic mumbled the words with the band, including the lines regarding heartache and tears.

Louise laughed and shook her head. "I like that song, but not the words so much." Vic chuckled, "No, I guess you're right."

They finished the dance with Vic striving not to allow the crowded conditions on the floor to raise his frustration level.

The band immediately launched into popular songs of the day, including Benny Goodman's 'Stompin' at the Savoy', and other fast tunes. It wasn't long before everyone was feeling hot and sticky in the summer evening, despite being out on the river. Even the open-air deck seemed closed in. A Tommy Dorsey ballad, 'Alone', began, and the dancers seemed to breathe a sigh of relief as they could just shuffle their feet to the soothing tune.

Half way through the song, Alec tapped Vic on the shoulder and indicated he wanted to switch partners. With a scowl from Vic and a giggle from the girls, they did. Louise found that she could follow Alec's lead so much easier – though she would never voice such a thing to Vic – but it was almost as if she could anticipate Alec's moves. After about a minute, he grinned down at her.

"Hey, you're pretty good, Little Bit," he complimented, using the nickname he sometimes called her, which referred to the fact that she was quite a bit shorter than her friend Fleet.

"Thanks. You're not so bad yourself, Double A." They chuckled together as the song came to an end.

Vic was immediately at Louise's elbow. Gently taking hold of her arm, he tugged softly on it, mumbling, "C'mon. Let's sit a few out."

She nodded, and they began to make their way through the crowd. Before they made it to the side, however, the bandleader began explaining that they usually had a female singer with them, but she was out sick.

"But if there's any girls here who think they can sing and would like to give it a try, come on up."

The floor was immediately abuzz with chatter, people trying to convince one girl or another to go up and take the stage, but no one would. That was when Fleet came pushing through the crowd to Louise's side.

"You do it, Lou. Get on up there!"

"Me?" Louise balked, immediately nervous. Looking around at the packed deck, filled with hundreds of people she didn't know, she felt decisively intimidated.

"Sure honey," Vic encouraged. "You've got a great voice."

Louise looked up into his eyes, his belief in her abilities warming her and bolstering her confidence. Seeing her wavering, he prompted, "Go on, you can do it." Then without waiting for a reply, he quickly grasped her hand and began tugging her behind him toward the stage at the far end.

"Nobody game?" Charlie the bandleader called out as he scanned the crowd.

Vic and Louise broke through the pack a few moments later and Vic held up one hand.

"Yeah, here!" He escorted her to the steps at the side of the raised platform and as she turned to him, eyes wide, he kissed her cheek and whispered, "Knock 'em dead, babe."

Charlie met her at the steps and extended a hand to help her up.

"So, you can sing, honey?" he asked in a friendly manner, his engaging grin helping to put her at least a bit at ease. She nodded.

"Ok, what's your pleasure?"

Thinking quickly, Louise swallowed her nervousness and balled her hands into fists, pushing on through the fear and shyness. She'd always had the uncanny ability to hear a song once or twice and just 'have' it, remembering the tune and the lyrics almost verbatim. Thinking of one of her recent favorites, she answered, "Um…do you know, *Once in A While?*"

"Sure do," Charlie nodded in satisfaction and turned to his band mates. He tapped out the rhythm and the band began to play the smooth melody.

Louise walked to the center and looked out over the large

crowd. Most had begun dancing again as soon as the music started, but her eyes quickly found her friends – Fleet grinning from ear to ear, Alec, Earl, and Ruth giving her the thumbs up, and especially the warm, twinkling brown eyes of Vic. As she gazed at him, he winked and nodded encouragement.

About forty seconds in, taking a breath, she began to croon the lyrics. The song fit her voice perfectly, so that she didn't even have to strain to hit any of the notes. As she sang the words about wanting a lost lover to think of her after they were no longer together, a cold chill made its way down her spine, in spite of the hot, stuffy atmosphere of the wooden deck and hundreds of perspiring dancers. Determinedly pushing such thoughts aside, she pressed on as her smooth soprano floated beautifully on top of the melody created by the instruments.

Vic watched with chest-bursting pride as his lovely Louise stood up there on the stage, becoming more confident with each line. He could see her standing a little straighter, and singing a little fuller as the song went on. During the middle interlude, she even moved to the beat, flashing a smile over at the band as they confidently played. They grinned back at her, each one nodding support. The dance crowd reacted with scattered applause as they gave appreciative encouragement.

At the last time through the chorus, she took in a deep breath and sang out, her pitch and vibrato wonderfully perfect. Part of her consciousness registered that she had never sung better – and she was so glad for it, with so many witnesses.

Then, the song was over and Charlie was thanking her for volunteering. "You wanna stay up here and sing some more?" he asked with a grin. But suddenly shy again, she shook her head with a polite, "No thank you," and looked around for Vic. She found him at the steps, waiting.

"Let's give it up for the little lady!" Charlie yelled out, prompting the packed crowd to erupt in applause before the band started another number and everyone went back to dancing.

"Lou, you were great! Just great!" Fleet gushed, giving her friend a quick hug. "You're every bit as good as some of the girl singers on the radio. You could sing with the big bands like Goodman and Dorsey," she added with genuine affection. Although Fleet could sing as well, she wasn't nearly as good as Louise, but she had that rare gift of being truly happy for her friend and not harboring any petty jealousies.

"Ya done good, kid," Alec added with a wink as Louise grinned at her friends, feeling as if she could jump over the moon. Turning to Vic, she found him gazing at her with a mile wide smile. He didn't even need to say the words that he was immensely proud of her – she could see them in his expression.

The three couples went back to dancing, with Louise now and then being congratulated on her song by couples close by. As the band began to play a ballad, Louise and Vic swayed close together, trying to be lost in their own world in the midst of the crowd.

All of a sudden, Vic felt a tap on his shoulder. Thinking it was Alec again he turned his head to growl at his friend, but instead came face to face with a young man wearing a dress shirt, striped tie, and pants that were creased sharp. He had a squarish, plain sort of face, blue eyes, and wore his light brown, wavy hair slicked back.

He addressed Vic, but his eyes were focused on Louise. "Mind if I cut in, Mac?"

Vic opened his mouth to say something along the lines of *He** yea, I mind,* but somehow the other man took the hesitation as consent and grabbed Louise's hand, pulling her into his arms and whirling her away through the crowd. Stunned and wondering how the heck that had happened, Vic stood there dumbfounded, unable to do anything about it without making a scene. Moving over near the edge of the dance floor, he strained to keep sight of his girl.

Louise hadn't liked the fact that this unknown man had

horned his way into her dance with Vic, but being innately well mannered, she tried not to show her aggravation as she concentrated on following his lead.

"You sing real good," he complimented as he adequately maneuvered on the packed floor.

"Thank you." She gave him a polite smile, taking the opportunity of a turn to crane her head and look for Vic, as he seemed to have just disappeared.

They danced in silence for about a minute. "Ain't seen you around before. You from Lou'vll?" he inquired persistently, taking advantage of a sudden press of the other dancers to draw her closer into his arms. The action made her uncomfortable and she tried to pull back.

"Y…yes, I am," she answered, wishing she knew a ladylike way to tell him it was none of his business as she made a mental note to ask Fleet how to get rid of unwanted wolves.

"Good. Maybe I'll see ya around some time. Would ya like that?" he continued, slowing to a stop as the song came to an end.

"I…I really don't think so. Please, excuse me," she added, searching the immediate area for Vic, but not finding him anywhere.

"Your boyfriend seems to've flown the coop," he pointed out as the next song started. Reaching out, he clamped his hands on her arm and her side, but she resisted, something about him and his persistence making her extremely uncomfortable.

"I… I'd rather not…" she began, but he shook his head as if he wouldn't take 'no' for an answer. "C'mon, babe, don't be a cold fi—" He stopped in mid-sentence when an arm suddenly came from off to the side and separated the two of them. The hand attached to the arm clamped possessively onto Louise's elbow.

"The lady said '*no*'," Vic's voice murmured in a low, menacing tone. Louise looked up at him in gratitude, noticing the firm set to his jaw, and the dark glint in his eyes.

"Now, look, Mac," the stranger began, but Vic stepped between the man and Louise as his left arm smoothly swept her behind his back.

The two men stood eye to eye for a moment, Vic about an inch taller than the other man.

"The name ain't 'Mac'. And she's with *me*," Vic added as he touched the stranger's chest with two fingers and gave him a short, but firm, shove. "Got that?"

Unsure if fisticuffs were about to ensue between the two men, the other dancers moved back a bit. The stranger considered pushing the envelope, but something in Vic's eyes made him change his mind. Finally, he backed off another step and took his eyes from Vic's to nod to Louise. "Some other time," he ended, before turning to slip into the crowd.

For both of them, the incident had spoiled the good time they had been having. Vic turned and looked at Louise, and then took her hand. "Let's go get some fresh air," he mumbled, already towing her toward the bow of the boat. She gladly followed as they weaved their way between the throng of dancing couples, as the loud music began to fade with each yard they covered.

Reaching the steps, they climbed to the top deck, emerging out into the evening air and the cool breeze coming off the water. To Vic, it was much needed, as he had begun to get extremely hot under the collar back there on the floor – and not just from the heat. Inside he was near to reaching his boiling point, as something about that stranger sweeping Louise right out of his arms had stuck in his craw.

The breeze felt marvelous on their heated faces as they gazed out at the sun low in the sky, casting long streams of light on the surface of the river.

Both took in deep breaths.

"Ahh, it feels good up here," Louise murmured as they set out strolling along the weathered wooden surface of the deck. She slid one hand under the hair at the nape of her neck and allowed the cool breeze to flow through as she sighed with relief. Vic squeezed her other hand as he tugged her along beside him, and turned his head to gaze at her face.

"Sorry I dragged you away from the dancin'..."

She flashed a sweet smile at him. "Oh, that's okay. I was needing a break anyway..."

Each one wondered if they should say something about the altercation, but neither knew exactly how to start. Uncomfortably, they looked away from one another, turning their gazes to the houses far away on the Indiana shore, barely visible in the waning light. They passed quite a few other passengers, mostly couples strolling together.

When they reached the stern, Vic drew Louise up to the rail next to several other couples, each one gazing downward at the mesmerizing sight of the wooden paddlewheel turning swiftly through the water. The resulting micro-fine mist the great wheel generated added to the passenger's refreshment. Its large red blades produced a distinctive thumping and swishing sound, almost like a heartbeat, as they sliced determinedly through the choppy surface of the water, effectively moving the boat along at a good clip. After a while, the others drifted away two by two until Vic and Louise were left alone, arms touching as they stood together at the rail. The rhythmic rotations of the old stern wheel had worked its magic, and served to soothe Vic's aggravation.

After a few minutes, he turned and leaned back against the rail, gazing down the length of the deck as memories played through his mind.

"I ever tell ya I worked on this boat one season?"

Louise grinned, hoping he would tell her more. In all of the dates they had shared, Vic had never talked much about himself. She wanted to ply him with questions, but somehow she always held back, instinctively knowing he was a very private person.

Now, she leaned against his arm, and murmured, "Really, Vic? When was that?"

He smiled fondly. "The summer I was sixteen." Thinking back over those carefree days, he breathed in the damp river air again and sighed. "I used to come down to the river and fish, or just sit and watch the boats and barges go by," he explained softly, images of sitting by the river with his father coming to mind. "Sometimes I'd watch ships go through the locks. There was an old man…Clyde Bremmer…he was the Idlewild's Chief Engineer. He was a great ol' guy…knew this old tub inside and out." A grin spread across Vic's face as he recalled the man. "He took a likin' to me, and talked the captain inta takin' me on for the summer as a deckhand, even tho' I was only sixteen and you were supposed to be eighteen to work on it." He paused as images from those days rolled through his mind. Louise just watched his profile, not wishing to intrude on his thoughts.

"Ol' Clyde, he was a good ol' bird. He taught me a lot…"

"Yeah? Like what?" she challenged playfully.

Rising to the test, he pursed his lips for a minute. "Like about what makes it go. Now this is a Mississippi style, stern wheel steamer, versus a side-wheeler. See that paddle wheel?" he queried, tossing a thumb over his shoulder. "It's driven by two steam-powered, single-cylinder, double-action, reciprocating engines that are older than the boat itself, like from around 1870 or something. That paddle wheel is nineteen feet in diameter by twenty-four feet wide. It's got an eight inch steel hexagon shaft with six steel hubs. The hubs support ninety-six white oak radial arms and thirty-two 24-foot oak bucket planks, arranged in sixteen sets of two. They can push this old tub as fast as eighteen knots…" he paused, expecting a look of confusion to cross her countenance. He wasn't disappointed. "Which is about 20 miles an hour. That's pretty fast for a craft as big and heavy as it is. Takes a while to bring it to a stop from that speed. They don't usually run it that fast, though…unless they're racin' or somethin'."

Louise's eyes twinkled as she watched him, truly impressed

with his knowledge.

"Did you only work on it that one summer?"

"Yeah…I came down here first thing the next season…and they told me Clyde…he'd died," he paused again, remembering the pain that news had caused. "Heart attack. They had a new skipper…" he shrugged, indicating they wouldn't bend the rules for him a second time. "Wouldn'a been the same without Clyde anyways."

Louise nodded as they both lapsed into silence for a few minutes, enjoying the peace of motoring down the dark river, in spite of the sound of the music playing on the deck below. Up there, on the back edge of the large riverboat, it seemed like they were in their own little world.

Turning to look again at Vic's profile, Louise stated softly, "I don't really know much about you, Vic…I know you're living with Alec and his family and that you moved out of your brother's apartment, but…" she paused, hoping he would just decide to open up to her.

He exhaled slowly. Talking about his life and childhood always depressed him. But he knew Louise had to be curious. That was natural.

"My parents are both dead…"

Louise gasped softly. "I'm sorry, Vic. What happened to them?"

"My mom died when I was about two. Don't really remember her… I had two more brothers, too…but they both died as babies. My old man…he died when I was twelve."

"Oh Vic," she whispered, her heart breaking. "How did he die?"

"Heart attack, I think," he shrugged.

She could sense that it still hurt him to talk about it and she touched his arm gently. "Is that when you got your lighter?" she asked softly.

Vic gave a tiny imitation of a smile. "Yeah." Reaching in his pants' pocket, he drew out the treasured memento, and gazed at the engraved inscription. "When he died, he didn't have much left...had to sell most everything to pay off...some debts." He stared at the object as memories floated through. "He liked to smoke them Cuban cigars and he used to let me hold the lighter for 'im...so my brothers let me keep it." Closing his hand around the cool, smooth metal, he suddenly vowed, "I'll never part with it, even if it meant livin' on the street. Pop had his faults...but he was a good dad to us."

"I'm sure he was," she whispered, tenderly caressing his arm. "What happened to you after he died? And your brothers?"

He pressed his lips together for a moment. "Jack was already married and livin' here. Al was sixteen. We got shipped around for a while, stayed with aunts, cousins, a friend of Pop's. Then when Al got married, I went to live with him and his wife..." he paused, remembering the not so warm welcome that rainy night he'd gone to stay with them. "They live up in Indiana. That's where we were livin' when Pop..." he paused, not wanting to tell her all of the details, especially about the gambling. "So anyway, I lived with them for about a year, then I came here to live with Jack, my oldest brother. Then when I turned eighteen, I did a hitch in the CCC's."

"What was it like?" she asked, knowing that was the abbreviation for the Civilian Conservation Corps. "Sonny's been talkin' about signin' up, but Mama doesn't want to let him go. She's afraid he'll get hurt, I guess."

He nodded. "It can be a little rough. The CC camps are loggin' camps, mostly. But they're run safe. Plenty 'a good food, bed and board, plus you get paid for it," he smirked, thinking about how excited he had been to be saving up a nice nest egg at the time, sending it home to Jack and Liz...only to come home when his stint was up and find out they had spent his money. It was still a bitter pill to swallow. He shook his head, striving to turn from the old feelings of anger and betrayal.

Pivoting around to stare out at the river behind the smoothly moving vessel, he murmured softly, almost to himself, "Seems like something's got it in for me. Something always steps in and messes up a good thing." Then hesitantly, he admitted, "I…I never really felt wanted my whole life."

Hearing her give a tiny gasp of sympathy, he turned and took her hands as he stared down into her eyes. There were so many things he wanted to say, but his customary shyness kicked in and he was suddenly tongue-tied and a bit afraid. It bothered him that he wasn't sure if she felt the same way toward *him* that he had felt about *her* from practically the moment they met. One thing that held him back was the fact that she seemed determined to keep her life separate from him, and that realization smarted deeply. He couldn't understand why…

Louise gazed up into his eyes, wanting so badly to tell him *she* wanted him. The words were on the tip of her tongue, but that just wasn't something a girl could say to a man. Her heart ached for the hurt she saw reflected in those haunting eyes. She'd had no idea he'd had such a hard life up to that point – and life hadn't exactly treated him kind since she had known him. This new-found knowledge stirred the maternal instincts within her heart and she wanted nothing more than to be the one to make him smile…but she remained mute.

From down below, strains of another ballad drifted up, and looking around, Vic's mouth curled in a smirk as he took her in his arms.

"Lots 'a room up *here*," he murmured against her hair as they began moving slowly to the music. It felt so right to be there, together, in one another's arms.

They both wished the evening would never end.

ജ്ര

CHAPTER 19

Contests at the Knights of Columbus

"MAN WHAT *IS* it?" Vic mumbled to himself as he walked out of another unsuccessful job interview. He looked skyward for a moment, anger welling up inside. "You got it *in* for me, or what?" he fumed, frustration at his on-going joblessness knotting his stomach. The fact that his two best friends were gainfully employed only made matters worse, and made him feel…obsolete.

The woeful details of his life relentlessly tormented him as he walked along, hands shoved into the pockets of his best pair of trousers. His self-esteem was taking a constant beating, with no job and no money to make plans for his future. And to top it off, the past few days he had been playing a dodging game with one of Alec's sisters, Rose. He grimaced as he remembered her coming into the living room in the middle of the night and proceeding to kiss him awake, as he lay asleep on the couch. When he had tried to tell her, gently, that he wasn't interested, she proceeded to throw herself at him with the full intention of not taking 'no' for an answer. The only thing that saved him was Mrs. Alder getting up to go to the restroom.

Vic had managed to persuade Rose to go back to her bed and leave him alone, however since that night it had become increasingly uncomfortable for him to be in the apartment alone with Alec's sister.

“What a mess,” he murmured disgustedly. The frustration roiling within him burned hotter and hotter, like a steam boiler moments away from blowing its stack.

As he continued down the street, he glanced up to see a man coming toward him he hadn’t seen in months – Doc Latham from the B-13 flood rescue station. A tiny smile graced Vic’s lips as the other man’s face lit up in recognition.

“Vic Matthews! How’ve you been, son?” Doc greeted with a large smile and a rousing handshake.

“Aw, fair to middlin’ Doc,” he answered with a shrug. “How’s everything with you?”

“Can’t complain, can’t complain,” the other man quipped, his gregarious smile dimming a little when he noticed the downcast posture and pinched expression of his young friend. He guessed, correctly, that things had not improved for the young man in the area of steady employment. His heart softening, Doc stepped closer and placed an arm around Vic’s shoulders. “Where’ve you been keeping yourself, son?” he asked gently.

“Here and there,” Vic shrugged again, glancing around before meeting his friend’s gaze. Though Vic couldn’t form the words, his eyes spoke volumes. In many ways, he was about at the end of his rope.

The older man nodded knowingly. “You had a meal today?”

“It ain’t like *that*, really,” Vic hastened to assure his concerned friend. “I’m gettin’ three squares, stayin’ with a friend’s family. It’s just…” he paused with a soft huff of dissatisfaction. “I can’t seem to luck into steady work and it’s startin’ to really get to me.”

The man pursed his lips and nodded, racking his brain for anything or any opening he might have heard about, but nothing came to mind. Then thinking back over a conversation he had had with Irene, their mutual friend, he asked softly, “How ‘bout the girl…?”

At the mention of Louise, Vic’s face transformed. His eyes aglow, he nodded. “She’s the only bright spot in my life,” he admitted softly.

Doc nodded sagely. "You know what they say – if you have *one* bright spot, then your life isn't *all* bad."

Vic looked down at his shoes as irritation heated up again. "Sometimes I think…maybe the Man upstairs has it in for me or something."

Gazing at the young man, so down on his luck, the wise minister chose his words carefully. Though he didn't know Vic's whole history, he knew enough that he could connect the dots. "Are you on speaking terms with Him, son?" he asked softly.

With a wry attempt at a one-sided smile, Vic shrugged and admitted, "Not really. Don't really know all them 'thees' and 'thous' like you preachers use…"

Doc laughed good-naturedly. "Aw son, you don't have to talk to Him in 'thees and thous'. Just talk to 'im like you're talking to *me*. You know…He's a gentleman, and He likes to be *asked* for help. Over the years I've seen so many people that expect Him to be active in their lives, expect *miracles* even, but they never actually come right out and *ask* Him. He never forces His way into our lives…He waits for an invitation."

Vic thought for a moment and realized Doc was right – he hadn't ever really *asked* anything of God, half expecting that He was just a big, angry *something* somewhere in the sky that merely searched for ways to hit people over the heads and make their lives miserable. Or being set to yank the rug out from under you just when you thought things were on the rise.

Doc watched him, almost able to 'see' the wheels spinning in his mind. Turning toward the direction he had been headed – his church – he offered, "If you're not doing anything right now…there's a lady we both know cooking up a big feast for tonight. I know she'd love to see you. Wanna drop in for a visit?"

With a chuckle as he thought of sweet Miss Irene, Vic nodded and allowed the older man to bustle him along the sidewalk as he made small talk.

A few minutes later, they reached the First Lutheran Church. Its large, twin-steeple, Gothic-style limestone edifice was a bit intimidating, and Vic almost balked at approaching its stained-glass double front doors. Instead of guiding him in that direction, however, Doc ushered Vic around the back and through a service door into the building's large kitchen.

Several ladies, busy as bees and chatting happily, were overseeing the fixings for that night's community meal. They turned as one when the door opened.

"Ladies, look who I ran into just now," Doc chuckled, prompting Irene to grin from ear to ear. Drying her hands quickly on a towel, she hurried toward their visitor.

"Vic, my lands, it's so good to see you!" she gushed, taking him into her arms for a warm hug. The other ladies also remembered him from the B-13 crew and came forward to bid him welcome.

Vic returned Irene's embrace, mumbling, "Thanks Miss Irene. Good to see you, too." He nodded to the others with a careful smile, a bit bashful to suddenly be the center of attention. Not for the first time, he was swept with the wish that Irene had been his mother. How different his life would have been...

Steering Vic and Doc toward stools at the large work counter, the ladies bustled around, each one asking Vic how things were going and setting before the two men samples of the items they were working on for that night's dinner – for the men to 'give their opinions'. As he enjoyed bites of sauerkraut and bratwurst, various vegetables, and the filling for lemon meringue and chocolate cream pies, Vic felt himself relax and even begin to take pleasure in the loving care the ladies heaped upon him. His situation began to seem not so dismal.

At the mention of Vic needing to find employment, Irene turned to one of the ladies with an excited gasp. "Betty, we were just discussing needing help and here it walks in the door," she chuckled, proceeding to explain to Vic that she and her friend had decided to move in together to share expenses, and needed a strong young man to help with the task. They spent the next few minutes discussing the particulars and arranging a day and time and how much they would pay him.

An hour later, his spirits buoyed and his stomach full, Vic bid goodbye to his friends and left, his steps much lighter than they had been.

When Vic walked into the apartment, having stayed out until he was sure Rose wouldn't be the only one there, he saw Alec walking out of the bathroom running a towel through his hair from a quick bath. His job at the factory always left him covered in sawdust.

"Is that you, Vic?" Mrs. Alder called from the kitchen. "Supper's almost ready."

"Hey Pally, any luck?" Alec asked genially.

Vic met his friend's eyes for a moment and compressed his lips in a grimace, with a quick negative shake of his head. "'Cept a one day job helpin' a lady move her stuff." Trying not to let his earlier dejection overtake him again, he flopped down and sprawled onto the couch. "I gotta get somethin' soon. Somehow this drought's gotta break," he mumbled. With a tired sigh, he let his head fall back, eyes closed. "Louise wants to go to that big dance at the K.C. this weekend," he mumbled, referring to the Knights of Columbus hall on the corner of Third and Guthrie. "But…" he paused, his pride bruised that even the money for tickets to a dance was hard for him to come by.

Alec laughed, thinking of how excited Fleet had been on their last date, gushing about how *keen* that dance would be. "Yep, Fleet's been talkin' about nothin' else for weeks. Last big fling of the summer." Leaning over to give Vic a friendly punch to the shoulder, he added, "Don't worry about it. I got you guys covered. My treat."

Vic opened his mouth to argue, feeling a distinct pinch to his self-respect that his buddy had bailed him out so often, but Mrs. Alder's voice calling them both in to dinner interrupted.

Alec, however, seemed oblivious to his pal's angst. Playful as always, he reached over with one hand to give Vic a teasing smack on the back of his head, chuckling, "Last one there's a rotten egg," before he sprinted into the other room.

Vic rose slowly to his feet. He didn't know what, and he didn't know how, but *something* would have to change soon.

He just hoped it would be for the better.

ꕥ

"HOE'D SCHTILL, WI' ya?" Fleet mumbled, bobby pins clamped in her teeth as she held the wooden-handled curling iron to a section of Louise's hair. Louise fidgeted yet again, twisting to try and see the progress her friend had made on her hairdo. Fleet had curled the lower portion into large, full waves becomingly framing Louise's chin and neck the way Jean Harlow had worn hers in a movie. She was now working on curling the top backward into a loose, but controlled swirl and fixing it with the pins from her mouth.

"It just doesn't look right for some reason…" Louise murmured.

"Well, it won't if you keep messin' me up," her friend grumbled. "And remember, I still have ta finish my makeup, and it's gettin' late."

"You're right, I'm sorry. I just…I want everything to be perfect tonight. For some reason, I feel nervous," Louise admitted, wondering at the unsettled feeling she had been experiencing all afternoon. Edna had grilled her, giving her the third degree. While dressing, Edna happened to pick up a pair of her shoes and looking closely, spotted a scuffmark on one side.

"You been wearin' my stuff again, haven't ya," she had sneered, holding out the shoe right under Louise's nose. "This scuff wasn't there the last time I wore these. What'dya do? Play dress up or something?"

Louise had frantically placated her sister, suggesting that perhaps she had scuffed the shoe while moving things around in the closet. Edna grudgingly bought the excuse, but the incident had left Louise shaken. What would her sister do if she knew the whole truth – that she was using her makeup, her clothes…she had even borrowed Edna's clutch purse for that night!

Once again, she determinedly pushed aside the fact that she had racked up so many half-truths and outright lies in her relationship with Vic that she was starting to lose track of them herself.

Fleet chuckled and shook her head, standing back to admire her handiwork. "Honey, you got no reason to feel nervous. You're gonna knock his socks off."

Louise grinned at her friend's image in the mirror, and then looked back at herself, twisting this way and that as the edge of her dress moved against her calves like a soft mist.

As Fleet put the last pin in her friend's coiffure and lowered her hands, they both gazed for a moment at Louise's reflection in the old mirror in Blanche's room. Fleet had painstakingly applied Louise's makeup and the overall result was nothing less than stunning. The dress, a 1920's style party dress belonging to Fleet's mother, was made of champagne colored embroidered lace over silk, and was truly exquisite. Blanche had worn it to a party back in her younger days, and then never again. It had remained hidden away in tissue paper in an old trunk. The silk lining was sheath like, while the outer shell formed a scooped neck and short, capped sleeves. It hung in one piece straight down to the uneven hem, like that of a scarf, with the straight edge of the lining visible underneath. The soft color gave her alabaster skin a warm glow.

Louise felt as if she were about to step onto the big screen at Lowe's Theater.

"See, I told you that dress would look great on you," Fleet complimented.

"Thanks. You look good, too," Louise returned, switching her eyes to her taller friend's attire. Fleet had chosen a summer evening dress that fit her figure perfectly, with lovely pink and gold flowers on a black background. The low, scooped neckline rounded out to short draping sleeves where the soft material fell in tiny gathers. The skirt reached nearly to the floor, allowing a view of her gold cage-front t-strap shoes.

"Alec'll be followin' you around like a puppy on a leash," Louise teased.

Fleet wiggled her eyebrows at that thought. "That'd be somethin' huh? I don't think the boy knows how to be serious," she added, a momentary look of something flashing in her eyes.

Louise studied her friend's expression for a moment. "You really like him, don't you," she finally stated.

"I'm *crazy* about him…even though he's a goofy nut," Fleet admitted with a smirk. "But I'll be dogged if I tell 'im that. And don't you say nothin', neither," she ordered with a stern glance at Louise. "I have a feeling Mr. Alec Alder is just a Good-Time Charlie that don't want no ties…just like most guys," she added softly, thinking of her own long-lost father, and all of her mother's and grandmother's 'gentlemen callers'.

Louise reached over and laid a hand over Fleet's. "Oh honey…I don't think Alec is like that. I don't think Vic would be friends with him if he was…" she encouraged softly.

"Maybe…" Fleet pressed her lips together for a moment, and then determinedly stood up to her full height. Squaring her shoulders, she winked at her friend. "Ah heck with it. We're gonna have *fun* tonight, huh?" Hurriedly setting about applying the finishing touches to her own makeup, she gushed, "I been lookin' forward to this dance for weeks. Alec says the band that's playin' is supposed to sound near as swell as Benny Goodman..."

Louise stared thoughtfully at her own reflection in the pitted mirror as her friend droned on, wondering why she couldn't shake the feeling that something bad was about to happen. The *woman* staring back at her seemed like another person altogether, not the carefree girl who had played 'hide and seek' with her younger brother at the country club during the flood. Had she really changed that much since this 'adventure' had started?

Determinedly, she shook off a tiny cold chill and rubbed goose flesh from her arms.

Tonight, she would have *fun*. She would worry about details some other time...

ᘏᘔ

TEN MINUTES LATER, the girls had just made it inside the vestibule of the house across the street, their hearts pumping madly from nearly getting caught in their deception, as the black hearse rolled to a stop at the curb. Sporting jackets and ties, Alec and Vic immediately opened their doors and sprang out to go get their girls.

Comically, both young men skidded to a stop, emitting identical wolf whistles, when the young ladies opened the door and stepped out onto the stoop.

Louise giggled and Fleet struck a pose, raising one hand to flip a curl teasingly over her shoulder.

Vic whistled again as he stared at the 'vision' that was his honey. "Shew, girl, I'm gonna have to fight the other guys off with a stick, you lookin' like that!" he complimented as he moved forward and lifted a hand to Louise. Queen fashion, she placed hers within, and gracefully flowed down the steps. "Mmm mm, that's some dress," he added approvingly, his eyes taking in every detail, from her red, shiny lips to the gold high-heeled pumps she had secretly 'borrowed' from her sister.

"Thank you," she answered sweetly, her own eyes running over the handsome figure he made in his jacket and tie. Thinking the persistent wave refusing to lie down on his slicked back hair gave him a sort of rascally air, she purred, "You look really good, too, Vic."

He grinned and leaned forward to give her a kiss, but stopped an inch away. "Is it okay to kiss ya, or are ya gonna say I'll mess up your lipstick?" he grumbled teasingly.

"I'll freshen it up before we go in," she giggled, tilting her head back for his kiss and relishing the manly essence of aftershave clinging to his cheeks and neck.

Fleet had descended the steps and curled her hand around her escort's arm as he moaned, "Oh babe, you are looking *fine* in that dress. We might not even *make* it to the dance," he added with a naughty snigger.

Fleet's mouth dropped open and she gently whacked Alec's arm before raising her hand to touch her hair, her nose raised in a perfect imitation of a Hollywood starlet. "I *beg* your pardon. I didn't get *this* dressed up, and wait *weeks* for this night, just to end up in the back of a *hearse* doin' what we do every Friday night, Mr. Alder. We're *going* to that *dance*."

Vic and Alec both let out a chortle, followed by Alec inclining his head in acquiescence. "Yes *ma'am*."

The four laughed happily as they moved to the car and slid onto the back seat.

"Hi Louise, hey Fleet. You guys look real snazzy," Ruth chirped as she turned on the seat to look back at them while Earl put the car in gear. She glanced down at her own dress, bemoaning, "I didn't have nothin' that swell."

Earl glanced over as he negotiated a turn. "You look keen, Ruthie. You look good no matter what you got on," he added with a wink. She giggled with pleasure at his unexpected compliment and leaned over to give him a loud smack on the cheek. Her mood restored, she squealed excitedly, "This is gonna be a real wingding. I heard the band that's playing tonight is just aces!"

"Yeah. I'm so excited. It'll be just like a movie with Fred Astaire and Ginger Rogers," Fleet gushed in agreement.

Louise exchanged glances with the other two girls, nodding in accord. Picturing herself and Vic out on the floor, 'cuttin' a rug', as the saying went.

"You been talkin' about nothin' else since I took you to see those two *dance* movies," Alec griped good-naturedly.

"I got a feelin' it's gonna be a *long* night," Earl joked, prompting everyone in the car to laugh at his aversion to dancing.

Ruth couldn't resist teasing, "Well, maybe Fleet'll let me borrow Alec for a few turns. Or maybe somebody *else* might ask me…like that guy on the Idlewild cuttin' in with Louise."

"Hey, you just watch that stuff," Earl huffed with pretend affront, only to grin down at Ruth as she scooted closer to him with a giggle.

Louise glanced at Vic, noting his hastily concealed scowl. She pressed her lips together, deciding not to join in the teasing.

Thankfully Alec changed the subject and they rode the rest of the way in companionable conversation.

ꕥ

IT HAD BEEN a glorious evening. The six friends had arrived at the Knights of Columbus dance hall, spilled out of the car, and hurried into the building amidst some gawking from other attendees regarding their unusual mode of transportation. As they had entered the ballroom, the girls had 'oooed' and 'aaahed' as they gazed around at the stylishly dressed couples milling about on the polished tile floor. The large room's four brass chandeliers, with glass lantern-shaped globes, hung from arched beams high in the ceiling, giving the space an air of grandeur.

"Hey, look there," Ruth prompted, touching Louise's elbow and pointing toward a sign standing next to a small table holding a pad of paper. The sign read, "Singing Contest tonight. Prize awarded. Sign up here."

"Oh Louise, get in that!" Fleet encouraged, nudging her friend toward the table.

"Oh, I don't know…" Louise drew back, glancing up at Vic's expression as if for permission. Singing that night had been the farthest thing from her mind. Having no idea in advance, she hadn't warmed up her voice or picked a song, the normal things a person does to prepare for a contest.

He grinned at her, clearly proud. "Yeah, honey. Go on. You wowed 'em last time."

With a nervous giggle, Louise gave a tiny shrug of acquiescence and leaned to pick up the pencil next to the pad and quickly wrote her name.

ꕥ

AN HOUR LATER, the dance was in full swing. True to the ballyhoo, all of the attendees thought the band was A-1, and did sound amazingly like Benny Goodman's orchestra. The place was comfortably packed, but nothing like the miserable conditions they had endured on the boat.

Taking a break from their regular set, the bandleader, Jeff Treymer, stepped to the microphone. Flashing his pearly whites at the crowd, the dark hair and tanned skinned young man presented quite a handsome package. He prompted more than one young lady in the room to harbor star-struck hopes and dreams toward the locally famous musician as he announced that the singing contest was about to start.

Nervous and jittery, Louise turned to Vic. "Wish me luck?"

He grinned encouragingly and bent to kiss her cheek. "Go get 'em," he whispered.

Finding there were only three contestants, two girls and a guy, the bandleader motioned Louise and the other two to come up on stage. He had them introduce themselves, and they drew straws to see who would go first. First in the draw was Dale Venter, and he did a passable job singing Pennies from Heaven, although he didn't sound much like Bing Crosby. The audience gave him polite applause.

Then the other girl, a tall blonde named Jean Dragoo stepped up to sing, sporting a tight red dress that showed off her quite voluptuous attributes. Her choice, a Billie Holliday song, "A Fine Romance", was delivered with several markedly flat notes, but the men in the room didn't seem to notice and gave her a rousing response when the bluesy tune finally came to an end.

All that time, Vic had been gazing with pride at his girl up on the stage, standing demurely and waiting for her turn. He could tell she was nervous, but he could also tell that she was conquering her nerves and pushing through to just make herself *do it.*

When Louise stepped up to the microphone and the first strains of the same tune she had sung on the Idlewild, *Once in Awhile,* began, she raised her head and looked out over the audience for the twinkling brown eyes that always gave her courage. She found them, watching her with such confidence and affection that she took a deep breath and plunged into the song, delivering a performance that trumped even the one from the night on the boat. By the time she was finished, everyone in the house knew she would win.

Then, everything happened quickly. Voting by rounds of applause, Louise was declared the winner, and she was receiving her prize – an intricately carved wooden jewelry box, shaped like a miniature treasure chest. Amidst congratulations and pats on the back, Louise found her way back to her friends and flew into Vic's arms, feeling as if she were floating on top of the world.

The dancing began again with a rousing swing number and the friends crossed to the side of the room, laughing and teasing with their 'starlet'.

Resisting his girl's insistence for another dance, Earl mumbled, "I think I'll go on over to the refreshment counter and get me a soda. Anybody else want anything?"

When the others began giving their orders, Vic laughed at Earl's comical expression. "I could stand to skip a dance, I'll go with ya." Alec gave Fleet a quick kiss on the cheek and called out, "Hey guys wait up!"

The three girls left to their own devices turned to one another, Louise still giddy with leftover nerves.

"This has been some night, huh?" Fleet gushed, reaching out for her friend's prize and taking a closer look. "This is *nice*. You deserve it, you did great."

"Thanks, Fleet," Louise returned, glancing over her shoulder at the guys at the other end of the large room. "So…how goes it with you and Alec tonight?"

"Oh…he can't seem to keep his hands off me," Fleet replied, rolling her eyes. "I'm still waitin' for some 'a those tender words of affection, though."

Ruth laughed and shook her head. "Alec's all fun and games. I wonder sometimes if he's got a serious bone in his body."

The taller, willowy girl eyed her friend with a knowing look. "I *know*. That's what I'm afraid of."

"Well, *I* say…" Louise began, only to be interrupted by a tap on her shoulder. She turned around to find the same young man she had danced with on the Idlewild, standing there grinning down at her.

"Oh…hello," Louise greeted, and his grin grew even larger.

"So you remember me, huh? That's good – because I sure

remember *you*," he crooned confidently. "Congratulations on winning the contest."

"Um…thank you," Louise replied, her smile genuine.

Holding out one hand toward her, the stranger murmured, "Care to dance?"

"Well…" Louise glanced at her friends, eyebrows raised.

"Go on, honey," Fleet encouraged. "Vic said he wanted ta sit one out, right?"

"But…" Louise hedged, remembering the heated words between Vic and this guy that night on the boat. Truth be told, she was not in the least interested in dancing with him. Though passably nice looking, with wavy, light brown hair and blue eyes, nothing about him appealed to her.

He, however, took her hesitation favorably. "C'mon, I won't bite," he teased, boldly grasping one of her hands and pulling her into his arms before she could protest.

She gasped a bit at his forwardness and glanced over her shoulder at the girls, who were giggling and shaking their heads at her reaction. He maneuvered them into the mix of dancers.

"Name's Tom, but everybody calls me T.J." His eyes ran appreciatively over her lovely face, hair, and dress. "What's yours?" he added when she didn't immediately respond.

She glanced at him, while mentally calculating how long the song would last. "Louise," she answered politely. She smirked silently regarding the state of his memory, since the entire room had been informed of her name during the contest.

"Louise…pretty name," he complimented, striving to keep them pressed closer together than was needed for the faster tempo. "Seems like we're destined to keep running into each other," he pressed. "Can't say that makes me mad, though. I sure wouldn't mind taking a dish like you around. So…what are ya…twenty? Twenty-one?"

"Um…" she blustered, smiling with a light blush in spite of

herself. It felt good to be receiving such compliments. She hadn't truly realized just how the elegant dress had enhanced her appearance.

At the end of the large room, Vic turned from taking two sodas from the server, his brow furrowing as he looked down to the space where they had left the girls. At first he didn't see Louise, but then stopped cold as she turned while dancing – with what looked like the jerk from the dance on the boat! And she was smiling up at him!

Feeling his blood begin to boil with unreasoning jealousy, Vic started back toward them, memories returning of the other guy snidely calling him *Mac.*

"Hey Chief, wait up! What's your hurry?" Alec called, finishing paying for the drinks and hastening to catch up with his friend. Earl grabbed his and Ruth's refreshments and fell into step as well, wondering why the rush.

Stalking right up to the dancing pair, Vic stopped, his eyes glittering like charred wood.

Louise looked over and emitted a soft gasp as T.J. turned his head to look over at the other man, immediately recognizing him from the time on the steamboat. Noticing the two bottles of soda in his hands he quipped dismissively, "No thanks, Mac. We're kind of busy right now," as he moved to turn away from the interrupter.

"You're gonna be busier than *that* if you don't let her go," Vic growled, the frustrations of his life in general adding fuel to the fire. This fancy dresser looked like he had money, or at least money to spend, and it galled Vic, sliding under his craw and quickly festering.

"Look bud, the lady's not complaining, so just back off…" he began, as Louise tried to placate her suddenly angry boyfriend. "Vic, it's alright…"

Fuming, Vic knew he looked a bit ridiculous standing there

on the dance floor with two cold and dripping bottles of soda in his hands. That didn't make his temper any better.

The other man flicked his eyes quickly down the somewhat comical stance of his rival and back up again. Then switching his gaze to the girl in his arms, he drawled, "Babe, you need to trade this *boy* in for a man."

That was the last straw. Turning to his friend hovering at his elbow, Vic murmured, "Hold these," and handed the bottles to Alec.

Alec took the bottles out of his hands, but immediately swiveled to hand them to Fleet, who along with Ruth had gravitated over to the scene of the ruckus. "Calm down, Chief," Alec tried to soothe as he turned back. "Don't go blowin' your sta…" he stopped as Vic swung back around and landed a strong right cross to the interloper's jaw, causing him to stagger backward.

Louise squealed, her hands flying up to cover her mouth in shock, as other couples close by emitted squawks of alarm and quickly scooted back out of the way.

Alec and Earl immediately grasped Vic's arms and hauled him backward, each one knowing he was dangerously near letting loose. "Calm down, Vic! Take it easy," they attempted to appease as he strained against their control. The adversaries glared at one another as the competitor lifted a hand to rub his jaw.

Just then, the manager of the hall forced his way through the crowd and stalked up to the panting, volatile men as Vic shrugged out of his friend's grasps.

"I'm gonna have to ask you two to take your argument outside – and *don't* come back in. This is a *respectable* establishment and we do *not* condone such behavior."

Mortified that now half of the dance floor was gawking at them, Louise scurried over near the other girls as the manager unceremoniously 'escorted' them to the emergency exit on the sidewall.

Once they were outside and the door swung shut behind them, they realized that the antagonist had not chosen to exit with them and continue the fight.

All of a sudden, it was like the air had been released from a balloon and as the startled friends gaped at one another, Alec suddenly burst out laughing.

"Well, I guess we've had enough dancin' for the night!" he cackled, shaking his head as the others joined in with him.

The six turned dishearteningly toward the parking lot and their vehicle as Earl joked, "Aww, we might as well head on over to the W.C. Lounge. I hear the 'atmosphere' is better there."

"Aww blazes, I only got one lousy dance in there," Ruth whined dramatically.

"Don't worry baby, I'll drop a nickel in the jukebox and we'll cut a rug on the white tiled floor. How's that?"

Ruth glared at him, albeit playfully, allowing a half grin as he threw an arm around her shoulder. "Not the same, but better than nothing."

Vic glanced at his friends and then turned his head to look at Louise as she ambled along, her arms crossed over her chest as she hugged her prize close. She looked over just then and caught his eye.

"Vic, I'm sor…" "I'm sorry, Louise…" they began simultaneously, stopping short as Vic wrapped his arm around her. "Me and my stupid temper, gettin' us kicked out of the dance like that," Vic grumbled in self-disgust.

"I should have turned him down…he just kind of took me over…"

"It's okay," he reassured as he smiled down at her. "It's normal that somebody else would want to dance with ya…there's just somethin' about that guy that rubs me the wrong way."

"Well, we won't have to worry about *him* anymore," Fleet assured as they continued on to the car and finished out their evening at their favorite hang out.

Little did any of them know that circumstances were about to occur, setting in motion a chain of reactions that would turn the world as they knew it upside down.

PART III
MISUNDERSTANDING AND SEPARATION

CHAPTER 20

Shocks, Surprises, and Harsh Words

IT WAS A late summer, Sunday afternoon; the kind that usually leant itself to lazy hours of listening to the radio, or sitting around with friends sipping iced tea and swatting at mosquitoes.

Vic had been on edge all day, but couldn't for the life of him have told you why. It was like something illusive and menacing was in the air. The very atmosphere felt thick and heavy. He wanted to squirm out from under it and run – but there was nowhere to run *to.*

As he walked down Fourth Street, killing time before he went back to the Alder's apartment for the night, he looked up to see Eugene, who had been one of his boat crew from the days of the crisis. He hadn't seen him in weeks.

"Hey Vic," the smaller man greeted as he stopped to chat.

"Gene," Vic returned, stuffing his hands in his pockets and stepping back to lean against the corner of a building nearby. "Where you been keepin' yourself?" he asked, just to make conversation. He took out his lighter and lit Gene's ever-present unlit cigarette, then with a shrug, lit one for himself. It was a habit he had recently picked up.

"Still crashing at my folks'," Eugene responded, then glancing around as if he had a secret that was bursting to get out – which in fact he did – he looked back at Vic and murmured, "You hear what happened to Ger?"

Instantly alert, Vic straightened up, his brow furrowed. "Gerald? No, man – what happened? He alright?"

"Phh," Eugene puffed with a disgusted sneer. "As alright as he *can* be, I guess – if you call sittin' in jail bein' alright."

"In *jail*?" Vic burst out. "What'd he get arrested for?"

"Man, you ain't gonna believe this…you remember that girl he was taking around a couple of months ago?"

"You mean that little blonde…Delores?" Vic answered, brows furrowed.

"Yep. Well…seems she lied to old Ger. Told him she was eighteen. He's been thinkin' about marryin' her. Even tried it out for size, if you know what I mean," he paused to glance around, making sure of their privacy. "All the time, she was really only fifteen."

Vic's eyes and mouth opened round like saucers as he put two and two together. "They got him for statutory?"

Eugene nodded. "You got it." Then shaking his head he mumbled, "Man, what kinda girl does that to a guy, huh? One that ain't worth *spit*, that's what," he answered himself. "Like my ol' man always says, 'Any girl that'll lie to ya won't be true to ya neither,'" he added sagely.

Vic felt like the wind had been knocked out of him. Gerald had been a good friend; they had grown close during the flood and remained so afterward. Closing his mouth and reaching up to unconsciously run his hand through his hair, he murmured, "How'd they find out? She tell somebody?"

"Her mother found that photo Alder took a' the two of 'em. Seems she put two and two together and asked the girl."

Shaking his head, still reeling from the shock, Vic absently reached out and patted Eugene on the arm, murmuring, "Thanks for tellin' me, man…I'll see ya later."

Eugene watched him go, and then with a shrug, he turned and ambled on down the street.

ꕥ

UNWILLING TO RETURN to the Alder's apartment as he knew no one but Rose would be there until later – and needing to feel grounded again after the revelation Eugene had dropped upon him, Vic found himself standing outside of the Hoskins' abode. He needed to be with Louise, to talk to her, and to hear her thoughts about all of this.

Being that weekends were 'family time' and her father didn't want them disturbed, he had never just shown up at her place like this, unannounced. Yet, Vic told himself there shouldn't be a problem. After all, he was her boyfriend, right? They were a *couple.*

The hallway seemed stuffy and a bit dark, as the only light at the moment was coming from the front windows. Muffled conversation and a shout of laughter filtered down from upstairs as he paused before knocking on the dark wood of the apartment door.

Vic straightened the collar on his jacket and ran a hand through his hair. Taking a breath to try and steady his unusually jumbled nerves, he raised his hand, but hesitated. Somewhere in the back of his mind, something was urging him to back away. His brow furrowed and he almost turned to escape. However, figuring he was merely still reeling from the scoop on Gerald, he steadied his nerves and rapped his knuckles against the door before quickly plunging his hand into his pocket. Inside, he could hear music playing, and the family laughing and conversing. He felt so detached from Louise's family life that a miniscule part of him wondered if he might not be welcome.

Just as he was about to turn and go, the door swung open accompanied by a whiff of sauerkraut to reveal Sonny standing in the threshold. His eyes widened as he realized who it was, and why he was probably there.

Vic' eyes narrowed, unsure about the unusual reception. The last time he had seen Louise's brother, on Derby Day, Sonny had been friendly and accommodating…

"Um, hey Vic…how's it going?" Sonny asked hesitantly, trying to signal him with his eyes that this might not be such a good idea.

"It's okay…" Vic smiled at Sonny, and then tilted his head to see around him to the table across the room. Such a varied range of expressions greeted him that he was momentarily nonplussed; both Willis and Lilly were gazing at him with what could only be described as dumbfounded expressions…Billy had his hand covering his mouth as he seemed to be trying to stifle a laugh…Edna's expression seemed suspicious…and Louise, looking decidedly pale, was staring at him as if she had seen a ghost.

What is going on here? Vic wondered, unsure of his next move. Although he was interrupting Sunday dinner, he had expected them to at least be polite…

"Can I come in?"

"Man, what're you doing?" Sonny whispered, but far too late, as he heard his father say, "Tell the young man to step in, son."

Vic slipped inside, standing uncomfortably as the family continued to gape at him.

"What can we do for you…*Vic*, right?" Willis continued.

Vic met each pair of eyes, finally settling on Louise, who seemed anything but happy to see him. Indeed, she had the look of someone facing a firing squad that was cocked and aiming right at her.

Nevertheless, he requested softly, "I um…can I talk to Louise a minute?"

Lilly turned her head, just then noticing her daughter's expression. "*Louise*?"

Billy could take it no longer, bursting out, "Oh man, the jig's up sis, and you are gonna *get it* now!"

Edna also turned to gaze at her sister, her eyes switching from her guilt-ridden face to the man near the door. "Vic…you're Vic

Matthews, aren't you," she accused, for the first time connecting their 'rescuer' from the flood to the 'just okay' young man who was supposed to have taken her on a date one rainy Friday night – but he had never come back for that 'rain check'.

"Yeah..." Vic nodded, something unpleasant beginning to curl in his stomach. Nothing about this felt right and he was wishing fervently that he had heeded his inner warnings and fled the scene without knocking.

"And you're coming here to see *Louise*?" Edna continued, now staring at her sister with nothing short of murder in her glare as the pieces of the puzzle began to fall into place.

"And just what do you wish to see my fifteen year old daughter about?" Willis calmly inquired. Calm, that is, on the surface. Underneath his composed exterior, Willis was quite upset, for several reasons.

Seeing the remorseful look on her sister's face, Edna lost all reserve. "You been sneakin' around seein' him, haven't you? Wearin' my *clothes*, wearin' my *shoes*, wearin' my *make up*, wearin' my *perfume*! And *lyin'* to me all this time! AIN'T YOU!" she demanded, leaning over to grab Louise's arm and give it a yank hard enough to make Louise yelp out in pain.

Momentarily distracted by Edna's outburst, Willis' comment finally registered in his consciousness, and Vic's eyes widened. He stared at Louise, hoping against hope that this was all some kind of mistake or bizarre joke. Swallowing the lump of trepidation in his suddenly dry throat, he croaked, "Fifteen? You're *fifteen*? But..." he paused, racking his brain to remember what, if anything, she had told him about her age. He recalled the night of her birthday and how she had merely giggled and remained mute when everyone had tried to guess her age. Why had he been convinced all this time that she was seventeen...? *My God...that means she was FOURTEEN on our first few dates!*

Louise's eyes filled with tears of contrition, and then panic as she watched Vic's expression begin to harden. The moment she had dreaded, but foolishly hoped would never arrive, had unexpectedly come, and she found herself totally unprepared for the fallout.

"*Mary Louise*, what is the meaning of this?!" Lilly screeched. "*Have* you been doing all those things?"

Unable to believe she had committed such a blatant, continuous offense as to lie to them, and to this young man, Willis sat silently staring at his daughter. This was not the Mary Louise he thought he knew. His 'angel' girl…

"I…I…" Louise stammered, but truly, she had no defense. Every lie, every act of falsehood, had been done for the express purpose of catching and keeping Vic Matthews as her beau.

For Vic, it was too soon on the heels of finding out his good friend was in *jail* because of a girl lying to him in the very same way. Suddenly, the air in the room seemed too thick to breathe, and Vic began backing blindly toward the door.

Sonny, who had been standing back, at a loss of how to help his sister or stem the force of what he knew was sure to be an explosion of immense proportions, put out a hand as he murmured, "Vic, hold on…"

"And just what do *you* know about all of this, Joseph Robert?" Willis demanded as Vic turned, grasping for the doorknob.

"Vic wait!" Louise gasped, the prospect of the massive amount of trouble she was in with her family far outranked by the anxiety of Vic becoming angry with her, and possibly not wishing to see her again.

Shocked and recklessly angry, Vic turned back, piercing her with eyes so vexed, their normally soft brown tone had taken on a somewhat red hue. "Wait? For WHAT? So you can *lie* to me some more? Aaagghh, to he** with it," he growled in disgust, flinging one hand out as if to sweep the whole mess away, before wrenching the door open.

"No!" Louise erupted as she sprang into action. Leaping from her seat at the table, she took off after him, squealing, "Lemme explain!"

"Mary Louise! Come *back* here this instant!" Louise heard Lilly's shrill voice call after her as she made it into the hall in time to see Vic yanking the outer door open.

"Vic!" she called, running down the hall and out onto the porch. "Stop! *Please*!"

He spun at the bottom of the outer steps, lancing her again with his eyes as she skidded to a stop at the landing. His 'angel' was now revealed to have very dirty feet of clay, and he was actually sickened by the whole mess. Their eyes held, his glittering with rage, hers spilling tears.

Finally, she whispered, "I'm sorry! I…I did it because…I *love* you, Vic…"

He visibly recoiled. "*Sorry*? You lead me on for months, dressin' like you're a grown woman, actin' like you're gonna move out on your own soon, makin' out with me…and all the time, you're just a *kid*! I coulda got in trouble 'cause of you, don't you *know that?*"

"I'm *not* a kid! I…I…" she cried out desperately, gasping as he suddenly charged back up the steps. She cringed as he brought his face nose to nose with hers.

"What *else* have you lied to me about, *huh*? For all I know you been runnin' around with every guy in town!" Her shocked reaction to that only fueled his fire and he continued recklessly, "Maybe you ain't so *innocent* like you acted in the Tunnel of Love that day. For all I know you've flopped on your back for every Tom, Dick and Ha…" he stopped short, his head jerking to the right as Louise's palm forcefully connected with his cheek.

Bringing his hand slowly up to rub the offended area as he turned back, his eyes were glacial. Grinding his teeth together and raking her from head to foot in disgust, he turned and bounded down the stairs. He'd never felt so angry and betrayed in his life.

Shaking with emotion, Louise raised both hands to her face, tears flooding her cheeks as she watched him go. His reaction to finding out the truth had been a hundred times worse than she had dreaded or imagined.

"Hey, c'mon," came Sonny's voice from just behind her as he gently touched her elbow. Feeling sorry for the trouble his sister was in, and guilty that he hadn't been the big brother he should have been by trying to intervene or steer her in the right direction, Sonny gently took hold of her arm and escorted her back inside to 'face the firing squad'.

Sonny closed the door behind them as Louise slowly raised her eyes to encounter a room full of angry expressions. She swallowed as she tried to brace herself for the explosion.

ꕤ

VIC WANDERED THE streets, blindly fuming and muttering to himself, eventually ending up at the river's edge. He stood for the longest time, staring out at the expanse of the water and watching the setting sun reflect off the gentle waves.

He felt as if he had lost his best friend. Indeed…Louise wasn't just the girl he was in love with…she'd become his whole world. So many people in his life had lied to him, cheated him, rejected him…but he had been convinced that Louise was different, that she was honest, and good, and worth his trust. That she was truly 'the one' who would help him fulfill his dreams. Now, he wondered if he would ever be able to trust anyone again. He realized he had misguidedly placed his whole confidence in a girl who had done nothing but deceive him. He had let down his defenses and given her his heart. *How could I have been such a fool?*

Images assailed his mind…Louise up on the stage singing like an angel…Louise kissing him with fiery passion…Louise giggling and smiling like a schoolgirl on the carousel…

Like a schoolgirl. The words made him shiver as he pictured himself languishing in a cell down at the county jail. When he thought of how many times the two of them had been locked in a passionate embrace and how much he had wanted to do more than just kiss and 'pet', his mind reeled. *How could I have not known she was just a kid? How could I have fell for all the lies and half truths…all of her reasons why I couldn't pick her up at the apartment – Daddy wants to rest, Mama's in a bad mood, Billy's sick, I'll be staying over at Fleet's…*

Fleet! The thought made him suck in a breath. *Is she just fifteen, too? Oh man…I gotta let Alec know…*

Knocked totally off balance by the revelation, Vic's world had turned upside down. Just the day before, he'd had a clear plan…find a job, save up a nest egg, ask his girl to be his bride, and live 'happily ever after'. Now… Now one of his close friends was facing the possibility of prison, and he was teetering on the edge of falling into the same pit.

However, even as angry as he felt right then, he knew he was still hopelessly smitten with the lovely brunette. But therein lay the danger. Vic shook his head as he wondered fleetingly how many dumb saps were down there in the jail, shell-shocked and pondering how they had gotten themselves into such a mess.

The future had never seemed bleaker.

Finally, desperate for some kind of relief from the constant barrage of brooding introspection, he thought once again of his mentor and friend. Lifting his hands up to scrub at his face and rifle through his hair, he turned and trudged back toward town, hoping they would still be there by the time he arrived.

Some time later, he stood outside the tall, imposing edifice of the church, listening to the calming strains of what must have been a large pipe organ. The song seemed somewhat familiar, and it gave him a measure of comfort and reassurance, so that he stepped forward, grasped the door handle, and slipped silently inside. Stepping quietly on the slate floor in the foyer, he hesitantly entered the back of the huge, towering sanctuary, which was about half full of parishioners. He knew no one, and couldn't see Irene or Betty anywhere. Doc was at the pulpit, his rich baritone leading the people in worship.

Vic eased down onto the far edge of a back pew and sat with his hands folded reverently in his lap, his eyes closed. As the congregation sang the soothing old hymn, he realized where he had heard it before. *I Need Thee Every Hour*... Miss Irene had sung it that terrible Black Sunday, when the electricity had gone off during the flood and the world felt like it was coming to an end. It seemed to have brought about good things that night... He hoped it would have the same effect again.

As the song ended, Doc dismissed the congregation and the people began to gather their things and exit, quietly talking among themselves. Vic was aware they were leaving, but kept his eyes shut, half afraid he would see disapproval or judgment in their glances. Several minutes later, he felt a gentle hand touch his shoulder and he opened his eyes to find Doc and Irene sitting in the pew directly ahead, smiling at him softly.

"Do you need help, son?" Doc asked gently.

At the look in his eyes, the hearts of the man and woman blanched. They could tell he was quite upset.

"What is it, Vic? Has something happened?" Irene murmured.

Vic wasn't sure how to start. He wasn't even sure what he was doing there. All he knew was that he did need help sorting things out, making sense of his life that now seemed like pieces of a puzzle someone had tossed haphazardly onto the floor.

All at once, the words began to spill from his lips and he told them everything...his thoughts, his feelings, his actions – and hers. The pendulum of his emotions swayed wildly. At times his words were angry and bitter, filled with the emotion of her 'betrayal'. Other times they were soft and loving as he told them of his feelings for the young...*young*...brunette.

At last, spent, he sat with his elbows on his knees, his head in his hands, as his friends hovered on either side. As their eyes met over his head, they knew he was at a precipice and much depended upon the advice they would attempt to give him.

Doc closed his eyes and tilted his head back, one hand gently at the nape of Vic's neck, as he murmured a heartfelt prayer for help to the Almighty. His prayer was succinct, asking God to look down with mercy upon their young friend, and to show him the way, and show them how to help. He reminded the Lord that they were looking through the glass 'darkly', and asked Him to make everything clear and the crooked paths straight.

When the prayer ended, Vic took in a deep breath, finding that he did somehow feel a bit better, though he was afraid to put too much stock in that just yet.

"Son, what would be your heart's desire right now?" Doc asked him.

Vic thought for a moment, trying to analyze his own feelings. "I dunno…I guess I wish she hadn't done it…or maybe to just be able to forget her."

Irene spoke up just then. "Now Vic," she began softly, "perhaps this is not as black and white as it looks." He turned his head to meet her eyes as she continued. "Granted, what she did was wrong. Lying is wrong. But…from what you've told us, it seems her main reason was to keep you interested…to buy herself some time. After all…she won't be fifteen forever… For the most part, Louise seems to be a good girl…she loves her family…perhaps she got caught up in the excitement of the moment, meeting you, and once she started with the ruse of you thinking she was older, she didn't know how to get out of it. The fact that she broke down in tears when the truth came out, instead of reacting with belligerence, says a lot…"

Vic nodded, her reasoning making sense to his shattered thoughts. The main thing in his mind was that he was afraid to try to be with her again…and from the look on her father's face, that seemed a bit doubtful.

"Perhaps…" Doc murmured, pausing. "Perhaps some time apart would do you both some good. Is there anywhere you could go?"

"Well…I been thinkin' about…tryin' to go back in the C's,"

Vic admitted, and indeed, the thought had been playing through his mind since he had divulged some of his past to Louise on the boat.

The gregarious pastor flashed his infectious smile. "I might be able to help in that regard. Let me make a few phone calls and see what I can do."

After another prayer and several more minutes of conversation, Vic finally walked out of the church feeling his load was quite a bit lighter. With easier steps, he made his way back to the Alder's apartment.

ꕥ

THAT NIGHT, LOUISE cried herself to sleep. The harsh words and stinging reprimands refused to stop echoing in her mind, which added to her own voice of self-recrimination.

Lilly had been the angriest; she had grilled her daughter for what seemed like hours, with her voice raised to a shrill pitch, as she demanded details on how this subterfuge had been accomplished. Truthfully, part of Lilly's anger was because her pride was stung. She felt she had been made to look a fool, having believed all of the fabrications that enabled Louise to sneak around with a man six years her senior. Louise's friendship with Fleet, of course, would come to a screeching halt. She had been too trusting of her 'always obedient' daughter. Sneeringly she accused Louise of allowing Vic to take liberties, as 'all young men are prone to do', and stubbornly refused to believe Louise's vows that such a thing had not occurred.

Edna had managed a few more digs, even resorting to calling her sister an outright 'slut', to which Willis had quietly stepped in. He had ordered Louise's siblings out of the apartment while the parents dealt with their wayward daughter. So for the duration, Sonny, Edna, and Billy sat on the stairs, listening to muffled reprimands, and feeling a mixture of emotions toward their errant sister. Edna seethed with anger and not a small amount of jealousy that Louise, in her way of reasoning, had somehow managed to 'steal' Vic Matthews away from *her*. Sonny felt empathy toward his sister, as he had, on occasion, been in the 'hot seat' himself and he knew it wasn't a pleasant place to be. Billy mainly felt disenchantment. The little boy had always held Louise in such high regard, thinking she could do no wrong. Now, his sister seemed like a bad girl and he wondered if the family would ever be the same.

But perhaps Willis was the most disillusioned of them all. He had unfairly thought of Louise as his 'perfect' child, thinking he would never need to worry about her getting herself into trouble. Or ever need to discipline her as he had her older sister and brother on more than one occasion. He felt almost personally insulted, as if Louise's subterfuge had been aimed against him. Down deep, he felt a bit responsible, thinking that if he hadn't been working in Bowling Green, absent all week long, sometimes two weeks at a time, he might have been able to see what was happening.

Everyone seemed to think that Louise would soon begin to show her 'soiled' state and turn up pregnant. The only reason they didn't immediately march her down to police headquarters to swear out a warrant on Vic was Louise's passionate words in his defense.

Louise had never felt so humiliated, low down, and dirty. In spite of the fact that she hadn't done the worst of what they were accusing, she knew she had done quite *enough*. Her parents had never been angry with her before, at least not on this scale, and it was a feeling she never wanted to experience again.

Yet, her heart felt shattered in a thousand pieces and now, she had no one from which to receive comfort. She had lost her best friend in the process. Picturing the hatred and disgust in Vic's eyes made her feel physically sick. Naively, she had imagined that if she could just hold out long enough, even to her sixteenth birthday, that he would somehow think it funny that she had kept her true age from him all that time. That they would laugh about it together. Oh, how wrong could a person be?

Deep into the wee hours of the morning, she finally had managed to drift off to sleep, though sharing a bed with her sister had never been more uncomfortable. Louise finally had to resort to jamming her palms on her ears to shut out her sister's angry hissing comments. That surely didn't help her already lacerated heart, but added to her feelings of shame and remorse.

All in all, Louise was sure that her 'Prince Charming' would never darken her doorstep again.

And she had no one to blame but herself.

ഇന്ദ

CHAPTER 21

When it Rains it Pours

A WEEK WENT by. Then two. Then three. They had been the longest weeks of Louise's life. If she hadn't already felt remorse over the fact that she had done wrong, and sinned by lying and deceiving everyone, she surely would by the frosty treatment of her family. She'd been grounded to the apartment and basically relegated to a feeling not unlike Cinderella since the night Vic had knocked on their door.

Vic… Just the thought of him caused Louise physical pain. She hadn't heard from him. Not that she expected to…just hoped. But as angry as he had been, the things he had said, and the look of rage and disgust after she'd slapped him…Louise hadn't blamed him for staying away and washing his hands of her. She had deceived him. Deceived them all. Feeling like the lowest piece of scum on the earth, she wondered what, if anything, she could do to make amends.

School had started up again and all of her friends seemed to be having the time of their lives. But her 'life' was the farthest thing from exciting. She felt out of place and not like a 'schoolgirl' anymore. Mixing with the kids at the Neighborhood House didn't appeal to her either, and she hadn't even been by to see them once since the play. Now, she was an odd hybrid of girl and woman. No longer one…but not yet the other, either. As she sat at her desk in history class, barely listening to the teacher drone on and on about the Spanish-American War, she stared out the window, reliving her and Vic's enchanted summer.

Vic…those dimples…those mesmerizing brown eyes…the timbre of his voice when he murmured something risqué in her ear…the way it felt to be in his arms, dancing, snuggling…kissing. Oh the thrill of those lips meshing with hers, and the heady taste of his tongue sensually roaming her mouth. She even missed the simple act of breathing in the wonderfully familiar scent of him, a combination of his masculine essence and the brand of aftershave he always used. There had been many times throughout the long months when she had caught him gazing at her as if he had been on the verge of saying those treasured three words she had waited all summer to hear. Though they swam in his eyes, somehow they never made it past his lips. Did he love her? She sighed dejectedly. If he ever did, he surely didn't now. *It's my fault. How could I have been so dumb, so stupid, thinking I wouldn't get caught…thinking he would laugh when he found out…*

"Hey Louise," a whisper interrupted her mental chastising.

She glanced over at the teacher; a reed thin, bespectacled shrew named Agnes Glasscock, and then turned her head toward the girl in the seat behind her as she whispered back, "Yeah?"

"You wanna go to the malt shop after school? My older brother's gonna pick us up in his swell car. Some of the other kids are going," the cute blonde haired, blue-eyed girl, Helen Blankenbaker, whispered as she made sure the teacher wasn't looking their way.

Louise gave a small shake of her head, whispering back, "Can't. I'm gr… I gotta go straight home…help with supper. Thanks anyway."

"Suit yourself," the girl shrugged, thinking what a 'goodie two-shoes' Louise was, and sat back in her chair pretending to listen to the lesson.

Louise turned her head back toward the front, focusing on the open history book on her desk, but her mind was seeing a malt shop…the booth at the back corner…Vic eating French fries and listening in rapt attention as she told him about her day, the play, and anything that came to mind. She pictured his face up close as they shared a fry, and the moment when he tried to steal a kiss, but she was too shy and turned her head with an embarrassed giggle. He had chuckled good-naturedly and mumbled, "You're cute…"

Forcing herself to breathe in through her nose, she worked hard to halt the moisture that was threatening to fill her eyes. It wouldn't do to start crying right there in class! *You've cried enough tears to start another flood. Stop it, Mary Louise!* She scolded herself, determinedly training her eyes on the teacher and striving to commit to memory the dates she was mentioning. Slowly, the emotion retreated like the swollen Ohio after the inundation, and she was able to make it through the rest of the class…and the day.

ꟸ

THAT AFTERNOON, LOUISE walked along the street hugging her books to her chest as she headed home from school. Her hair blowing loose in the breeze, as she hadn't thought about tying a scarf over it, she allowed herself to once again get lost in daydreams. Billy was walking next to her, having met up with her at the juncture between their two schools, and was talking a mile a minute about something that had happened at recess.

"Hey! Louise!" a girl's voice jarred her consciousness, causing Louise to turn with a start toward a 1935 dark green Ford Phaeton convertible that was slowing down at her side. It was Helen Blankenbaker.

"Hey, Helen," Louise returned half-heartedly, glancing at the car full of schoolmates who just the year before had been her friends. Having grown up with most of them, they had shared many laughs and good times. She knew they were probably on their way to the malt shop and for a moment, the nostalgia of that weighed heavy.

"C'mere, my brother wants to say Hi," the girl urged, motioning Louise closer to the car's window. Louise acquiesced and stepped over, Billy hovering close, and bent her head a bit to be able to see the driver's face and utter a greeting. When she did, her eyes opened large and she stared, speechless. There, behind the wheel, sat the man who had twice insisted on dancing with her – the man who had identified himself as 'T.J.'

"We meet again," he commented smoothly, enjoying that she seemed to be tongue-tied.

"Y…*you're* Helen's brother?" she stammered, totally unprepared for such a development. She had thought she would never see the guy again. And *he* thought she was twenty-one! *Oh man, what a can of worms!* Louise realized that, once again, her actions were coming back around to bite her.

"You two know each other?" Helen queried, suspicious. Her mind was spinning as she tried to imagine how her brother and her classmate could have met, why T.J. seemed so interested, and why he had insisted on pulling over to talk to Louise just then.

"Yep," he answered both questions with a friendly grin. "Hop in, I'll treat you to a malt."

Louise shook her head, feeling a mixture of regret and relief that she couldn't. "I can't. I have to be home…"

"You're a real *Mama's girl*, aren't you," Helen purred. "I bet you never did anything wrong in your whole life."

Louise clamped her lips closed and shot the girl a look, thinking there was no way she would want that busybody to know her business. She thought of Helen as the 'Town Crier'. Telling her something was like publishing it in the Louisville Journal!

"Well, hop in and I'll take you home. It's a bit chilly out there to be walking," T.J. insisted. Upon her moment's hesitation, he added, "Open the door for them, Helen, and scoot over."

The girl did as her brother bid, but Louise hesitated for another moment. Quickly weighing the options, she didn't see any harm in it. Besides, it would be nice to have a ride and be out of the chilly breeze for a few minutes, as she had been running late and had not worn a sweater that morning.

"Okay…we live over at Second and Chestnut," she acceded as she climbed in, directing Billy to sit on her lap. She purposely avoided eye contact with Helen, as she could feel the other girl's eyes staring at her with unspoken curiosity about the situation.

A short car ride later, Louise bid them goodbye and the two hurried up the steps and inside.

As they entered the door of the apartment, they found their mother sitting in Willis' favorite chair, crying.

"Mama! What's wrong?" Louise gasped, immediately rushing to her, dropping down on her knees and taking her mother's hand. She feared the worst – had their father been killed in an accident at the factory?

Lilly sniffled miserably, dabbing at her tears with a damp handkerchief. She opened her mouth to try and speak, but no words came out. Louise glanced down, and noticing a letter and some cash on her mother's lap, she picked it up. Recognizing her father's handwriting, she glanced at her mother's face and then down at the letter, reading in a whisper:

My Dearest Lilly,

I bitterly regret having to send you this news in a letter, but didn't want to spend the money on a phone call. There's no way to say this gently, so I'll just say it. They let me go today. Said business was down, but I know it's probably my age. The new foreman's a young college boy, still wet behind the ears. He did give me two weeks severance pay and promised a letter of recommendation.

I'm enclosing all but a few dollars I'll keep for expenses. I'll stay here and look for another job. My board's paid up till the end of the month.

Now Lilly, don't let yourself get all tied up in knots over this. We'll make it. We always do. Don't go to pieces on me. You and the kids will be all right. Everything will be all right. If I don't find something else by the end of the month, I'll come on home and we'll go from there.

Your loving husband,
Willis

"Oh Mama," Louise murmured, meeting her mother's watery gaze.

"Just when I thought things were looking up...*this* happens! It's always *something!* Why can't we ever get *ahead?*" Lilly mewled, covering her face with her hanky and dissolving once again into tears.

Louise wrapped her arms around her mother, her own eyes pooling with tears as they met her younger brother's. His blue eyes were also filling, bewildered that his parent was so upset about the situation.

Man, when it rains, it pours, Louise mused sadly, gently rocking her mother back and forth and trying to be of some comfort as she wondered how they would keep going if Willis didn't quickly find another job.

"It's okay, Mama. We'll make it. Just like Daddy said. He'll figure something out. It'll be okay..." she tried to encourage, but deep down she felt as if a large guillotine was poised overhead.

Lilly nodded, knowing she should pull herself together, at least for her children's sake. She sat up straight, reaching to pat her eyes dry and straighten her hair. "Yes, you're right, Louise. This family has been through many tough times. Something will come along," she mumbled, though deep inside, the old familiar guilt from her secret past rose up like a dark, ominous shadow.

Minutes later, Sonny and Edna arrived home and the family shared a quiet supper. No one even remembered to turn the radio on for a little music. Sonny ate quickly and rushed out, determined to make sure he sold out of his papers. Lilly drifted over to sit once again in Willis' chair, rereading his letter over and over, while Edna and Louise cleaned up the kitchen, not a word shared between them.

Each Hoskins decided to retire to bed early, but none could sleep. A long night was spent with each one staring at the ceiling, hoping this wouldn't be a time like the last – when the family had to give up their apartment and beg to stay with relatives until they could get back on their feet.

Lilly lay in her bed, listening to the steady tick of the clock in the other room and feeling like the weight of the world was on her shoulders. Lamenting the seemingly never-ending *Depression*, she wearily wished they could go back in time to the 'Roaring Twenties', when everything seemed wonderful. Money and liquor flowed like water, and the future seemed to be paved with gold. Her husband had been a machinist, skilled at his trade, and his future – *their future* – seemed rock solid.

Now, she was once again adrift on the Ohio with nothing but a leaking rowboat – and the dam at the locks was straight ahead.

ꙮ

EVERY DAY AFTER that, T.J. was there in his car, waiting at the curb in front of the school for Louise to emerge at three o'clock. That first day, she had the unpleasant task of explaining to him that she was actually only fifteen. He had merely chuckled and shook his head.

"Well, you sure had me fooled, then," was all he said to that. Such a different response than Vic… But then, Vic had been much more involved with her… Wincing, she remembered the scathing way he had sneered at her, *"I coulda got in trouble 'cause of you, don't you know that?"* She'd known instinctively that he had meant he had wanted to do more with her than just kiss… She wondered if he had been thinking about, maybe wishing for, or even planning to do more. *But what would that matter*, she reminded herself. *I'll probably never see him again.*

T.J. drove her and Billy home that day, and although his attention made her a bit ill-at-ease, it did feel good to actually be in the company of someone who wasn't angry with her. From then on, she accepted his rides.

Helen, true to form, ferreted out the details and immediately spread the juicy gossip among their peers of how her twenty-two year old brother had met fifteen year old Louise at a dance, with her passing herself off as older.

Boys began watching Louise walk down the hall at school, giving her looks that made her distinctively uncomfortable. Everywhere she glanced, kids would chuckle and whisper to one another as she passed by. She could hear them whispering behind her in class and she guessed what they were discussing – that she had gotten herself in trouble by a grown man.

Even Eleanor had joined their ranks, miffed that she had been excluded from the secret Louise and Fleet had shared. Louise found that out the hard way one day after school.

"Eleanor! Wait up!" Louise had called as her friend neared the outer door.

The raven-haired girl stopped and turned, but cast a glance around as if to make sure no one was watching. Louise immediately picked up on the other girl's discomfort. Trying to get past that, however, she leaned in to give Eleanor a hug as she murmured, "Hey…been missing you…"

Eleanor only half hugged back, her eyes unfriendly as she pulled back. "Yeah? Surprised you had time."

"What do you mean?" Louise mumbled, surprised by the frigid response.

The girl shrugged petulantly, moving back a half step and drawing her books up to her chest in an unconscious air of separation. "I don't know…seems like you and Fleet had quite a busy summer."

"Well…we…" Louise began, but Eleanor quickly went on with a sneer, "After the play, all of a sudden the big star was too big for the rest of us."

"That wasn't it! I just…I didn't think you'd approve, I guess…"

"Phhh, yeah right," Eleanor scoffed, flashing Louise a glance full of pent up hurt. "We used to do everything together, like the Three Musketeers. Then, all of a sudden, it's just you and Fleet and you shove me out in the cold." Watching Louise's expression, she added, "How do you think I felt, huh?"

Louise realized for the first time that was, in essence, what they had unintentionally done. She crossed her arms over her middle, eyes downcast. "I'm sorry…we didn't intend to…things just kind of happened…"

"Yeah, well…" Eleanor paused, feeling a tiny bit sorry for her friend, but not enough to let her off the hook. "My mom says I can't hang around you guys anymore, anyway. She says you two are bad company," she added, although she stopped short of relaying that her mother predicted Louise and Fleet would both end up in Fleet's family profession.

Louise's eyes connected with Eleanor's again, shocked. "Bad company? But…listen El'…I didn't do that stuff the other kids are saying…we just…"

Raising a hand to cut her off, Eleanor gave a quick shake of her head. "Forget it. I gotta go. I got chores to do at home."

Nodding numbly, Louise watched her one time friend and confidant turn and hurry on out the door. With a heavy heart and dragging steps, she continued on that way herself.

Louise missed Fleet more with each passing day, but the older girl had graduated and was no longer there in Louise's everyday life. All in all, school had become pure torture. On top of all of this, she never had lunch money, or new clothes to wear, as hers were hand-me-downs from a cousin that didn't fit her right and made her feel conspicuous and ashamed.

The family still treated her like a black sheep and it was a feeling that hurt deeply. Well, all except Sonny. He merely looked at her with sympathy, which actually made her feel worse. She felt like a charity case. A redheaded stepchild. Her mother had settled into the habit of snapping orders at her, Edna shot stinging barbs at her every chance she got, and Billy withdrew from her, his lip sticking out in a pout whenever she looked his way. The weekend Willis had been home, he had virtually given her the cold shoulder. This hurt the most…finding she was no longer the apple of her Daddy's eye. How she longed to hear him call her his 'Sweet Pea' once more. Everyone she encountered made her feel like the 'soiled dove' they suspected her of being.

Grounded to home as she was, she hadn't been able to get out and try to see any of the gang, and she felt totally in the dark and forgotten…cast to the wayside. Was Vic still so angry that he didn't want to see her at all? Were the others disgusted with her? She toyed with the idea of sneaking out to try and see Fleet, or Alec, but the thought of doing yet another thing behind her parents' backs seemed totally unacceptable. At night, she tried to pray and ask forgiveness for the mess she had made of her life, but her prayers seemed only to rise to the ceiling and no higher. Hopelessness had become her life.

The joy of her enchanted summer as Vic's girlfriend was slowly fading from her consciousness.

ꕥ

ONE SATURDAY AFTER the upheaval, someone knocked on the apartment door. Lilly crossed over to answer it, wiping her hands on her apron and reaching for the knob.

There stood Fleet, a tentative smile on her face in response to the closed expression of her friend's mother.

"May I help you?" Lilly snapped in a tone that made it obvious she wasn't about to 'help' the girl.

"Hi, Mrs. Hoskins…can I come in?" Fleet faltered as Lilly positioned her stout little body in the doorway in such a way that she blocked entrance. The girl realized instantly that the atmosphere inside the Hoskins' abode was frostier than she had feared. *I guess I didn't give it long enough…*

"Um…is Louise around?" Fleet asked carefully, hoping to get a chance to tell her friend a few things she had found out from Alec.

Lilly drew herself up to her full 4'11 inches and answered, "I know all about the bad influence you were on my daughter. Louise will not be associating with you anymore. You need to just run along. You aren't welcome here."

Fleet visibly cringed at the unexpected attack. For a moment, she wondered if part of Lilly's vehemence had to do with Fleet's family background. A tiny tinge of anger flared because she knew she wasn't like that and had determined years before that she would never succumb to the 'family profession'.

The girls shared a quick look over Lilly's shoulder – Fleet's eyes sad, Louise's tear-filled. Fleet tried to signal Louise to try and get word to her, but she could see her friend had been totally cowed by the restraints her family had imposed. Deciding she wouldn't do anything to get Louise in further trouble, but would just wait and bide her time until an opportunity presented itself, the older girl swallowed nervously and nodded respectfully to Lilly, as she turned to go on her way. She knew it would do no good to argue or explain. What could she say? 'I'm sorry I helped my best friend deceive everyone?'

Pausing at the outer door to look back, she caught the angry look on Lilly's face before she firmly shut the door to the apartment. Fleet sighed sadly and hoped there would be a time when she would catch Louise outside. She also thought of her own mother, who had merely laughed and thought the girls' shenanigans were amusing. Both extremes seemed somehow wrong…

ꕥ

As THE DAYS went by, the money situation grew tighter and tighter for the Hoskins' family. Willis stayed in Bowling Green, much to his wife's chagrin, following up leads and promises of possible employment. He truly didn't want to give up and come back to Louisville, knowing the job market was shut tight as a drum to men of his age, and even young men across the city filled the ranks of the unemployed. Things like a good work record, skill, and years of experience had ceased to matter.

One night T.J. came to the apartment and knocked on the door. Louise was horrified when she looked up from some mending and saw who stood at the open portal. She wanted to run and hide. What would her mother think of this? Surely it would not bode well that she seemed to be cozying up to yet another older man. However, to her everlasting surprise, Lilly invited him in!

"Hello young man," her mother seemed to purr as she stepped back and allowed him entrance.

"Hi T.J." Billy greeted, looking up from his homework.

Speechless, Louise could only stare at her mother and wonder at her uncharacteristic behavior. Lilly seemed almost nervous, her hands fluttering about as she indicated for T.J. to take a seat – in Willis' chair. The girl wondered if she imagined that her mother was purposely avoiding her gaze.

"Thanks," he murmured as he made himself comfortable.

Not knowing what to say, Louise mutely glanced from him to her mother. Lilly sat down in another chair, one hand rising to pat into place her perfectly coiffed bun, and offered as an explanation to her daughter's unspoken question, "This young man has helped me several times, offering me a ride in his car as I walked along from the market with groceries. He tells me he is the brother of one of your classmates…isn't that right, Louise?"

Louise nodded, still dumbfounded.

"Well, he asked if he could come over and pay his respects. As a matter of fact…his father paid me a visit and asked if his son might be allowed to court you…" she added, resorting to the old-fashioned term from her girlhood in the late 1800's.

Louise's eyes widened. "*Court me*?"

Lilly went on hurriedly, "Yes…and I must say I appreciate the fact that he has been above board with his intentions…and quite helpful and generous…" she paused awkwardly, as if not wishing to divulge too much.

Louise swallowed dryly. *Intentions? Generous? Court me? Good heavens…does Mama want to marry me off like…like used goods or something? Does she really think I went and got myself in trouble?* Her heart pounding, she remained totally at a loss.

"But Mama…" Louise began, only to be interrupted by Lilly, "Why don't the two of you go to get a malt or something. It's all right. I'll let you off of restriction for the evening."

Louise didn't realize that Lilly, normally an extremely proud woman that wanted *no one* knowing her business, was in mortal fear of being unable to keep the family afloat financially. During Mr. Blankenbaker's visit, she had reluctantly agreed to at least allow her daughter to date his son, after the older man had made the generous offer to 'loan' them some money to tide them over. She had steadfastly refused to entertain the idea that what she was doing amounted to wholesaling her daughter. Instead, she comforted herself with the knowledge that many of her friends had 'farmed out' their children once the Depression had set in, sending them to outlying farms as what amounted to 'indentured slaves'. To her way of thinking, this wasn't *that* bad…

T.J. stood up, sporting a large satisfied grin, and helped Louise put a sweater around her shoulders. Before she knew it, she was in the car with him, heading toward the malt shop. Her head felt as if it were spinning.

ꕥ

THINGS HAPPENED QUICKLY after that.

T.J. began coming by the apartment every evening, taking Louise to the picture show, or over to his home. He lived with his parents and was the oldest of six siblings. His father made Louise extremely uncomfortable, as he seemed to leer at her whenever she was around, and made comments about her 'attractive legs'. His mother was a sour faced, extremely unfriendly person, who Louise privately thought of as 'Madam Pickle Face'. T.J.'s youngest brother Rory, a boy of about five, grated on Louise's nerves, as he was spoiled rotten and insisted on his own way in everything.

Louise felt as if she was on a train speeding toward oblivion, and she didn't know how to make it jump the track. Truthfully, she wished she could just opt out of the whole situation, but for some reason, it seemed to please her mother for her to keep company with T.J., so she continued. At least it took her mind off of lamenting her misery over Vic and wondering where he was, and it was a way to occasionally get out of the house and do something different. Each time she was out with T.J., she would be on constant alert, hoping to see one of her friends…but that never seemed to happen.

As the days went on, Lilly mellowed out and no longer acted angry with Louise. Matter of fact, she began treating her with extra sweetness, almost as if she hoped for something in return…

It was all so confusing for Louise. She didn't know what to make of these perplexing developments – and she had no one to talk things over with…she wasn't allowed to see Fleet…Edna had returned to her usual sullen self…Sonny merely shrugged if she asked his opinion…and her father was still out of town.

She felt completely alone…and most of all…*she missed Vic.*

ഗ്ര

CHAPTER 22

Evansville and the C's

VIC LEANED WITH one foot braced against a tree, his hands in his pockets, staring out at the river and pondering how different it looked there than it did back home.

Home… He realized with a smirk that he didn't really *have* a home. Hadn't in a good many years – only places where he hung his hat for a while. The 'home' he had just vacated had become increasingly uncomfortable. Alec's old-maid sister Rose was determined they should be a couple, and had come on to him relentlessly, trying every means at her disposal to entice or trap him.

Rose had really stepped up the pace after the debacle with Louise. That night she had snuck into the living room again, practically pouncing on an unsuspecting Vic as he lay asleep. His mind in turmoil, he had been in the middle of a confusing dream about Louise, where one minute they were arguing and the next they were sitting on the running board of Earl's car, kissing passionately. Unfortunately, Rose had chosen that moment to begin her 'seduction'. She'd been pleased, at first, when Vic began to quite ardently kiss her in return, but it ended quickly as he awoke to realize the lips he was kissing did not belong to the girl he loved.

"R…Rose, knock it off!" he had groused as he shot up straight and wiped his mouth with the back of his hand.

"Vic, please! I *love* you," Rose had whined as she plopped down on the couch next to him. Purposefully, she had allowed her robe to fall open, revealing the low cut negligee she had donned for her 'mission', thereby giving Vic quite a view of her more than ample attributes.

Boldly, she had reached out and grasped Vic's head in her hands, striving to pull him toward her for another kiss. Vic turned his face; repulsed not only by her forcefulness, but also by the fact that dental hygiene was not, to say the least, her strong suit.

Vic took hold of her hands and firmly pressed them into her lap as he said, as gently as he could, "Rose…I told ya…I don't feel that way about you. We're just friends…okay?"

Rose shook her head, tears welling in her large round blue eyes. "No, Vic…I'm crazy about you. I always have been. I'd do anything for you. Anything at all!" she declared, giving him such a piercing look she left no doubt as to her meaning.

Vic had closed his eyes and sighed, trying his best not to hurt her feelings. "Rose, I'm sorry…I ain't ever gonna feel that way about you. Try to understand…I love *Louise*…"

"But…" she began. However, before she could argue any further, Vic climbed to his feet and pulled her up with him. Deliberately, he closed her robe and tied the belt shut for good measure. "Now, you go on back to your room and we'll forget this ever happened… okay?"

With a sad sigh, she had nodded and turned to shuffle back the way she had come. However, Vic had known that night that she would try again at the first opportunity, and that he would absolutely have to find other digs in which to hang his hat.

Just then he was 'hanging his hat' one hundred miles to the west of Louisville – in Evansville, Indiana at the home of his brother, Al, and his wife Goldie. The couple lived in a third-floor apartment six blocks from the river, and he was staying there while he waited for official orders.

Shaking his head as he watched a boat go by, he mused that

lately it seemed all he did was wait and cool his heels. Just then, he was waiting for the letter telling him to report to the CC camp run by that friend of Doc's.

Every day he waited for the mailman to bring the mail, rifling quickly through the bills and correspondence belonging to Al and his wife, but so far, nothing had come for him. This concerned him on several levels. One, he was anxious to start his second hitch in the C's, so that he could begin building his nest egg for his future. Two…he wondered why *she* hadn't written to him.

I don't blame her for bein' mad, and even hurt, at me. I accused her of some pretty rotten things…but I thought what I did would have made up for it…

Tilting his head back with a sigh and watching a slow moving cloud, he thought back to those harried days after what he had come to think of as the *unveiling.*

He had intentionally stayed away from Louise's home after the chilly reception he had received from her family that terrible evening…and the slap Louise herself had administered in response to his verbal attack. Not wishing to be in the Alder's apartment any more than was necessary, he had spent his time roaming the streets, or sitting on the bank of the river, fishing. He'd even managed to catch a few catfish and brought them home for Mrs. Alder to cook. Figuring it was no use looking for a job, as was his normal daily routine, he merely passed the time waiting for Doc to give him instructions. Finally, the day arrived when he received a message that Doc wanted to see him.

Doc explained that his friend, Major Frank Connors, ran a large CCC camp at Beaver Ridge, Illinois, and that he could pull some strings to get Vic assigned to his unit. As Vic had confided in the reverend regarding the situation at the Alder's residence, as well as the stalemate concerning his girl, Miss Irene and Doc had searched for a solution to help their down-on-his luck young friend.

"Vic, is there any place you could go to for a few weeks, until

Major Connors sends you the paperwork?" Irene asked caringly.

Vic thought for a moment, and then looked his friend in the eye. "Well, I haven't seen my brother Al and his wife for years...they might let me stay a few weeks with them, only...they live in Evansville, Indiana."

The kind woman and the no-nonsense pastor exchanged glances, realizing what Vic was hinting at.

"Son, if you can get hold of them by telephone and they say it's all right...I think provision could be made for a bus ticket," Doc assured with a grin and a wink.

So, using the church's phone several minutes later, Vic had, indeed, made contact with his brother, who generously offered to send him the $3.75 for bus fare.

With his future seeming brighter than it had in weeks, Vic had made the rounds with his friends and even Jack and Liz, to say his goodbyes. It had been a somewhat uncomfortable time at Jack's apartment, although the kids were glad to see him, and Jack was warm – and Liz was polite. She did say that she wished him luck and was glad that he had found something he could do. The subject of the CC camps being a sore one for them all, the estranged family had carefully steered around it.

On his last night in town, Vic ate dinner at Doc's house, which was just down the street from the church. Doc's gracious wife Florence had fixed a wonderful meal and Vic's heart was light with hope and excitement for the future. Things were finally falling into place.

After he left, he had gone to Louise's apartment and walked down the hall to the large oak door. However, as he raised his hand to knock, he stopped.

From inside, he heard Lilly snap, "Louise, my lands! Haven't you started those dishes yet?"

Louise mumbled something indistinguishable, and Edna grumbled, "If you think *I'm* gonna do them for you, you've got another think *coming*! If it was up to *me*..."

"Edna, lay off her, will you?" Sonny's obviously aggravated voiced added to the mix.

Vic, hovering outside the door, was feeling a mixture of protectiveness toward his girl and awkwardness at hearing the exchange. But after a moment or two of hesitation, he lost his nerve. Backing off, he turned and left the building.

For the longest time, he watched from across the street, leaning against a lamppost where he could see the lights from their windows. Finally, as he realized his unconscious hope of Louise somehow coming outside in response to his nonverbal longings was for naught, Vic had turned and slowly made his way back to spend a sleepless night at the Alder's apartment.

Even if he had known that Louise was inside, crying herself to sleep – there wasn't a thing he could have done about it…

The next day, Saturday, Earl drove him to the bus station to catch a Greyhound to Evansville. All the gang, Ruth, Alec and Fleet, went along to see him off. Shaking Earl and Alec's hands, and giving the girls each a kiss on the cheek, Vic's heart had ached that the one person above all others he wished would have been there to bid him farewell was absent.

Looking his best friend in the eye, Vic murmured, "Check on her for me…I feel bad that I didn't get to see her before I left…to tell her I'm not mad…and tell her I'm sorry for the things I said…"

Alec, for once totally serious, mumbled, "But you put all that…"

Vic nodded, "Yeah…I just hope she got it."

Then, he had picked up his duffle bag with all of his worldly possessions inside and climbed aboard the large blue and white Greyhound bus. Quickly finding a window seat, he had waved at and watched his friends until the conveyance turned a corner out of the terminal and he was on his way – to his future.

Coming out of his daydream, he lowered himself to the ground at the base of the tree and took his wallet out of his pocket.

Reaching inside, he removed two pictures, handling them as if they were worth a mint. One was of Louise, wearing the pink and black print dress he'd seen her in many times, and though the picture was sepia toned, he saw her in living color through the eyes of his emotions… Her lovely complexion of peaches and cream…on her lips a soft rose lipstick as they curved into a gorgeous smile… and those dreamy hazel eyes… She was positioned sideways to the camera and looking over her shoulder, seemingly at *him.*

Gazing at it, it was as if she were right there with him – but that only made him miss her more. He stared into the likeness of her eyes, trying to 'connect' with her, to somehow get her to write to him and let him know how she was doing.

Vic almost didn't want to look at the other picture – but drawn as if by compulsion, he did. It was a copy of the one Alec had taken that crazy night that the gang had such fun eating sliders at the White Castle. In the photo, he and Louise were clutched in a tight embrace…kissing. He stared at their images, trying to transport himself back in time to that moment when the world seemed exciting and full of promise – and he was with the love of his life.

After long minutes of reminiscing and wishing, Vic sighed sadly and carefully returned the treasured photos to their safe place.

ꕥ

TWO WEEKS LATER, Vic walked through the door of his brother's apartment, shed his jacket and headed to the sink to wash his hands. He'd been trying to earn a little pocket money by helping a downstairs neighbor move their furniture. Moments later his sister-in-law came in the door, a pile of mail clutched in her hands and a big smile on her face. Tossing her blonde hair over her shoulder, blue eyes twinkling merrily, she grinned at him and purred, "Guess what I've got?"

He turned, about to admonish her not to tease him, but the look in her eyes let him know she was serious. Tossing the other mail on the kitchen table, she held out an envelope without a word. He could clearly see a round logo on its corner, with trees, water, mountains, and CCC in big letters – and it was addressed to him.

"Yeehaa!" he guffawed and practically ripped it from her hand as she laughed with him.

Tearing open the envelope, he read the words from his new boss quickly, grinning from ear to ear. Without looking up, he murmured, "I'm to catch the bus on Friday." Glancing up at her, he held up the enclosure, a Greyhound bus ticket. "The waitin's finally over," he grinned.

So bright and early Friday morning, Al and Goldie sent him off with handshakes, hugs, and a brown paper sack packed with a bottle of pop and sandwiches, which Goldie had made. Lugging his duffle, he walked the five blocks in a light misting rain from their apartment at 608 Chevy Street to the bus terminal, and was soon aboard and settled.

The four-hour ride was uneventful. He spent the first part of it staring out the window, through drops of rain, and daydreamed of Louise. At one point, he felt a stab of fear zip through his body, but he wasn't sure what had brought it on. Especially since, he had reminded himself, he was on his way to the start of *their* future, and things were looking up. It took awhile for that sensation to pass, however. But pass, it did, and settled into a feeling of numb resignation.

The bus stopped once for a convenience break, and Vic got out to stretch his legs, and partake of his sandwiches and drink.

The nearest town to Camp Beaver Ridge was a tiny hamlet called Dana, where the bus eventually let him off at the small post office. There he sat on the curb and waited twenty minutes until an army transport truck pulled up, its dark green canvas looking as if it had seen better days.

A young man peered down at him. His white teeth gleamed from a face a pleasant hue of café au lait. His round eyes, a rich dark coffee bean color, were fringed with dark lashes and twinkling merrily. His close-cropped hair, of which Vic could only see a small bit under a worn green cap, gave a hint of soft charcoal.

"You Victa' Matthews?" he asked with the friendly drawl of the Deep South, and Vic wondered if he was from Alabama or Georgia.

"Sure am," Vic answered, climbing to his feet and dusting off the back of his trousers.

"Well, climb aboard. Dis yuh o'fficial welcome, an' yuh transport out tuh the camp," he announced, his full lips curved casually into a jovial smirk that said life is fun and so am I.

The man swung the passenger door open as Vic picked up his belongings and climbed up into the high cab of the old truck.

The driver stuck out his hand. "Name's Floyd. Floyd Grimes." Vic took his hand in a firm shake and gave him a nod. "Good to meet ya."

The man grinned again and grabbed the wobbling gearshift, placing the cantankerous old truck in first gear. Fighting against it bucking and jerking, he maneuvered it around to head back the way he had come.

"So. Dis yuh first time in the C's?"

Vic grasped the safety strap above the door and watched the road as they lurched along. "Nope. Did a hitch in California a few years back."

"Cal'fornia, huh? Ain't neva been. Heard tell it's mighty pretty though…"

Vic flashed him a grin. "Mighty *hot*, too, at least where *I* was. Man, sometimes it'd get up to 110 – in the shade. I was glad to come back East where a body can cool off, know what I mean?"

Floyd's head tilted back as he let go a rousing guffaw. "Dat I do, man. Dat I *do*."

Chuckling, they bumped along in silence for a few minutes. Vic then glanced over at his companion, wondering what his story might be. The man's pursed lips whistled a soft, cheerful tune as large, strong hands gripped the steering wheel of the truck with confidence. "You been in long?"

Floyd flashed him his contagious smile. "One week. Dis heah's my first 'signment on my own. The Maja' said if I gets you to the camp in one piece, he'll gimme 'portant cargo next time," he joked. Vic knew he was teasing as they both chuckled.

Grasping the wheel just then, Floyd wrangled it to the left as he turned the truck onto what looked like an access road.

"I'll be sure 'n tell him you drive like a pro," Vic offered. "You uh…you *do* know where we're goin', right?"

Floyd threw back his head and laughed. "Dis heah road don't go no place but dah camp. Don'choo worry none."

Vic grinned and made a point to settle back in the seat, eyes closed, as he quipped, "In that case, wake me when we're there."

"Man, with the potholes in dis heah road, I don' think you gonna get much shut eye!" Floyd chortled just as the right front wheel hit a chuckhole that jarred the entire cab.

"Not if you keep hittin' chuckholes that could swallow an elephant!" Vic teasingly groused.

Both young men laughed together in instant camaraderie. Somehow they both knew it was the beginning of what would turn out to be a strong friendship that would last a lifetime…

ཀྱ

THIRTY MINUTES LATER, the camp came into view. It was a large encampment, with eleven buildings, including four barracks, a mess hall, recreation hall, infirmary, officers' quarters, garage, latrine, and shower building.

Floyd slowed the old truck to a shuddering halt and Vic climbed down, shouldering his duffle.

"Boss said tuh come see him when you gets heah," Floyd instructed as he came around the front of the truck. "He'll be in theah," he added, his southern accent drawing his words out as he pointed to a building on their right.

"Thanks, man," Vic responded as he hefted his load more comfortably on his shoulder.

"See's yah laytah," the other man replied, turning on his heel to head toward the mess hall, whistling Yankee Doodle merrily as he went.

Vic gazed after him for a moment with a small crooked grin and a shake of his head, then turned and found his way to the supervisor's office and knocked on the open door. A tall, handsome man with neatly combed black hair and a strong, square jawed face sat behind the desk writing. He looked up at the knock and smiled in a friendly manner, gesturing Vic to come inside.

"Come on in, son. I take it you're Doc's young friend," he stated rather than asked.

"Yes, sir. Victor Matthews, sir," Vic replied, automatically falling into the habit of addressing his superior according to military tradition – something his previous camp commander had insisted upon.

The commanding officer smiled again and stuck out his hand. "Major Frank Connors. I'm the Forest Supervisor and commander of Beaver Ridge," he explained, motioning for Vic to sit down. "Have a seat, son." Then after Vic settled into the chair facing the supervisor's desk and stashed his duffle at his side, the man added, "Your friends call you Vic, right?"

Vic folded his hands respectfully in his lap and nodded, "Yes, sir."

"Well, Vic, I understand that you served in the Corps before, at a camp in California, is that right?"

"Yes, sir. I served six months at Camp Havilah."

Connors nodded and opened a file on his desk, which was obviously Vic's paperwork. "I noticed you enlisted this time for the full two years. I know a few details about you from Doc, but tell me young man, do you have plans, and long-range goals?"

Vic smiled, relaxing a bit at the continued friendly attitude of his superior. "Well, sir…I plan to stay in the corps and save my money for my future…"

The other man grinned and sat back in his chair, meeting Vic's eyes with his own, which were a cool, light shade of sky blue. "A future that concerns a certain young lady, I presume?"

Vic sent the man a closed-lip smile and a small nod. "If she'll have me."

Connors laughed and nodded. "Ah women. Unpredictable creatures aren't they."

Vic raised his eyebrows, thinking that was an understatement. "This one sure is, sir."

The commander nodded again and rested his elbows on the arms of his chair, fingertips touching as he observed his newest enlistee. He could tell just from the intelligent glimmer in Vic Matthews' eyes that he was sharp, and would prove to be a hard worker, and an asset to the camp. His record from his previous hitch included glowing reports on the then eighteen-year-old.

"Well, Vic, I know that you were in the Corps before, but I'll give you my usual spiel that I dish out to all new enlistees, just in case some of the rules or facts have changed."

Vic nodded.

"As you know, you'll be paid $40 per month, $35 of which will be sent to the family member of your choice, which in your case you've chosen…" he paused as he consulted the file, "Your brother James Alvin Matthews."

"That's right, sir."

He went on, "In addition to your cash stipend for the five-day workweek, you will receive three full meals a day, lodging, clothes, footwear, inoculations and other medical and dental care, and – at your option, vocational and academic instruction."

At Vic's nod of understanding, the Major rocked back in his chair. "As you will remember, the CCC is modeled on the military – minus the guns," he quipped. "All enlistees wear uniforms, are stationed in military-style barracks, and are supervised by military brass, such as me. You won't be required to march or drill, but we do stand at attention every evening while the flag is lowered. If you do as you're told, be where you're supposed to be, and don't cause trouble, your hitch will…go off without a hitch," he snickered at his own pun.

Vic murmured his agreement, thinking that this camp seemed to be a tiny bit less like the military than the one he was at in California, but he liked the feeling of a well-run program. That was what he had enjoyed during the crisis in January – the way Doc had run the rescue station, with military-like precision.

The commander paused for a minute, as if weighing what he was about to say, then continued frankly, "Vic, most of the young men in this camp now are fairly new enlistees, inexperienced at or wholly ignorant of the fundamentals of the tasks they will perform. Just this past June, Congress changed the age limits for the CCC to 17-23 years old, and as a result, we had an influx of young enrollees. The stints of my older, more experienced residents all seemed to come to an end around the same time. My feeling, therefore, is that since you were in before – and from the glowing recommendation I received from Doc concerning your work ethic and overall reliability when the going gets tough, in a very short time I'll be promoting you to crew manager…and thereby increasing your pay."

That was great news to Vic, and his dimpled smile revealed his pleasure. "I'll work hard for you, sir. Just gimme a chance. That's all I'm askin'. I won't let ya down."

With a jovial smile, the commander stood to his full height and leaned to shake Vic's hand. "That's good enough for me, son. Come with me and we'll get you squared away."

ꟸ

THEIR FIRST STOP was the camp physician, who gave him a routine physical. He informed Vic of what he already knew – he was in perfect, robust health, except for being flat-footed. That particular malady had never given him trouble, so he just shrugged good-naturedly and replied, "Okay."

Soon after, Vic entered the deserted barracks, his arms full of uniforms, boots, bed linens, and other paraphernalia he had been issued, including a canteen.

Making his way to an empty lower cot, its mattress rolled up at the foot, he temporarily deposited his trappings onto the lid of the locker at the end. He made short work of making the bed, and had just finished storing all of his stuff when his barrack-mates came back from their workday. Laughing and shoving one another like the boys they were, each one gathered around him, introducing themselves. Names like Butch, Bobby G., Clarence, Marshall, and Spike were among the monikers.

One young man, Gary, made a derogatory remark about the bunk he had chosen being underneath 'the darky's bunk', but Vic shot him a disapproving look when he realized he meant Floyd. The young enlistee who had made the crack had the grace to look ashamed when Vic replied, "Yeah…*so*?"

Later after chow, evening chores, and the lowering of the flag, when the camp turned in for the night, Vic suspected that same smart-mouthed enlistee guilty of performing what must have been his 'initiation'.

Sliding into his freshly made bunk, Vic's bare foot encountered a cool, smooth wiggling object, and he let out a yell, kicking the covers back and jumping free. The others in the room burst out laughing, pointing and rolling around in their bunks as Floyd leaned over to see what happened.

Nodding, Floyd murmured, "Yep, they done the same tuh me on my first night," before rolling over and making himself comfortable again.

To a continued chorus of howls of laughter, Vic ran a hand agitatedly back through his hair and watched his temporary bunkmate slither further up the sheets. Recognizing the varmint as a Northern Ringneck snake by its bluish grey body and orange ring around its neck, he knew it wasn't poisonous. He'd dealt with them before while fishing back home. Reaching out and taking it by the tail, he hurriedly carried the twenty-inch long creature over to the door and out into the nearby woods a few feet away, where he released it back to the wild.

Upon his return, the boys were still laughing at his animated reaction, and he knew this first impression of him would set the precedent. In truth, he had been unnerved by the presence of a snake in his bed, but now he mustered his resolve and glanced around at them all in calm assurance.

"Glad you guys had some fun at my expense tonight. But its light's out and I don't wanna lose no points my first night in camp."

With that, he ambled to his bed, wiped his feet on the blanket, and – after a quick glance under the covers – climbed into his bunk to get some shuteye. The others were still cracking jokes about how high the new guy could jump; nevertheless, they silently admitted to a grudging respect for the new member of the crew.

Turning on his side, he stared at the photo of Louise he had wedged into the corner of the headboard of his bunk, which was illuminated by the soft moonlight shining through the window. Something was bothering him…tugging at him…about the girl his heart adored. As if she were in some sort of distress. Frustrated that there was no way for him to know or find out, he thought about praying…something he knew Irene and Doc would recommend. However, even in his mind he felt tongue-tied when it came to talking to God.

Finally, Vic's eyes drifted shut and he slipped off to sleep, hoping there wouldn't be any more surprises.

CHAPTER 23

Louise! Don't do it!

"SIS, ARE YOU crazy? I can't believe you're gonna do this," Sonny murmured to Louise as she stood at the sink washing dishes. He'd been trying to reason with her over the course of two days, but for some reason, to his mind, she was being awfully stubborn.

Louise glanced his way, her resolve weakening a tiny bit even as she once again recited her reasons. "If it'll help out the family…then it won't be for nothing, Sonny. T.J.'s father promised to…"

"But what about *Vic*?" Sonny interrupted, raising his voice a tad. "I thought you loved him…you went through all of that plottin' and schemin' this summer just so you could…"

Lilly happened to walk in the room at that moment and heard Sonny's outburst.

"Vic Matthews is gone. Mr. Blankenbaker made some inquiries," she informed the siblings, glancing over at their surprised expressions. "It seems that he left town, presumably to go to Indiana and stay with a brother." This was the first news Louise had had regarding Vic since the moment he had stalked away from her in anger.

"He didn't even have the courtesy to say goodbye to you, Louise. That should tell you a little something about what he felt for you. All he wanted was one thing, like *all* men," Lilly added derisively. "He proved that by refusing to come here and ask your father and I if he could court you…" she paused as Louise interrupted emotively, "I *told* you, Mama – he *wanted* to, but I wouldn't let him!"

Lilly pursed her lips, purposely ignoring the sadness and pain in her daughter's eyes. "Well – be that as it may, he doesn't have a job, a place of his own, or even a car. He's *gone* and I say *good riddance*!"

"But that don't mean that Louise should go off and *marry* some guy she don't even *know*!" Sonny came to her defense, moving to stand between his mother and sister. Neither of the women realized that Sonny was unconsciously trying to fulfill the promise he made to his father every time Willis left again for Bowling Green…to take care of the family and be the man of the house. That was nearly impossible, however, when his sisters and mother refused to listen to him…

Edna chose that moment to angle her head around the bedroom door, unable to resist getting in on the conversation. "Serves her *right* for what she did," she sneered over at her sister before retreating back to continue curling her hair.

Louise turned back to the sink, wiping tears with the back of one hand as mother and son exchanged a look. Softening slightly, Lilly moved over near her daughter, watching her wipe a dish and hold it under the rinse water. "It won't be so bad, Louise," she tried to soothe. "T.J. seems like a nice young man, and he cares about you…and believe me, there's been many a woman that had to settle for who would be *best* for them and not chase after a no-good who would only end up breaking her heart."

Louise winced at her mother's words; still unable to fully accept that Vic was one of 'those kinds of men' as her mother continued, "It'll all work out, you'll see…"

Louise swallowed the lump in her throat and wished fervently that her father were there. Perhaps he would not let her go through with it. However, she gave a quick nod, managing to whisper, "I know, Mama. And besides…if I can't have Vic…I don't really care anymore."

Sonny gazed at his mother and sister, feeling extreme aggravation. He wondered if he should go to their landlady's apartment and try to get in touch with Willis by phone, but he was torn. The fact that Vic left town without a word was puzzling and he was quite taken back. He'd been sure Vic Matthews had been crazy about his sister. If not, he would have stepped in long ago and let the cat out of the bag. It had even been kind of fun, playing along to see how far Louise could carry the ruse. Now…he wondered if he should have informed Vic on the sly…

He watched as Lilly wrapped one arm around her daughter and gave her a semblance of a hug as she murmured, "Everything will be all right."

All three fervently hoped so, but each one had a very bad feeling about the whole situation.

ꕥ

THE NEXT DAY T.J. gave Louise ten dollars, with the encouragement to, "Go buy yourself an outfit for our big day." Her mother accompanied her to a local shop where she purchased a street length dress, white with tiny green polka dots, shoes, stockings, and even a hat. Plans had been made to take a day trip out to Elizabethtown on the following Friday…to get married.

Friday morning, Louise found herself tugging at her mother's hand as she was being ushered out the door of the apartment. "But Mama…I thought sure you'd come with me to my wedding…" she whined, striving to push back a rising sense of panic.

To Louise, it seemed Lilly was somewhat nervous, fussing with the crocheted headrest on Willis' chair and avoiding her daughter's eyes.

"I'm sorry Louise, but I just can't. I promised Mrs. Cesar upstairs that I'd watch her little boy for her while she went to the doctor. I declare, I think that woman is expecting again," she added with a chuckle that sounded more like a gasp. "I'll see you tomorrow..." she pacified. In truth, she couldn't stand the thought of watching her daughter being wed to a man she didn't love. This, however, was hopelessly tangled with the fact that Lilly, herself, was a big part of the reason why Louise was going through with it.

"Come on, honey, we've got some driving to do and it looks like it might rain," T.J. encouraged, his voice sugary sweet as he picked up her overnight case and encouragingly slipped an arm around her shoulder to gently turn her toward the door.

Louise glanced up at his face, clearly hesitant, but unable to take a stand against the unstoppable flow that seemed to be relentlessly sweeping her along.

T.J. caught Lilly's eye in a silent bid for help, in truth afraid Louise was about to change her mind.

Lilly leaned forward and gave her daughter's cheek a soft kiss. "You go on now, it'll be alright," she whispered. Then, as Lilly watched T.J. usher her daughter on out the door, she reassured herself silently, *It's for the best. It's all for the best...*

At the car, Louise discovered a young man and woman she didn't know were waiting inside. T.J. opened the door for Louise and she slid onto the front seat, then turned around to greet the strangers. They introduced themselves as Geneva and Ralph Mocker, good friends of T.J., and explained that they were along as witnesses.

Mocker, Louise mused irrationally. *Mockers along to watch a mock of a wedding...* Biting her lip, she nodded to each of them, afraid to open her mouth for fear of laughing hysterically, and turned back around as her intended climbed in through the driver's door.

He looked over at her, and the blue of his eyes looked more like the stormy gunmetal gray of the sky above. A crazy thought went through her mind that all of the color seemed to be disappearing from her world, as if in response to her emotional condition. "All set?" he queried with a smile.

Louise felt a sharp slice of alarm arc through her body, like a strong surge of electricity, as if something was screaming *Don't do it!!* It took every ounce of strength she had to keep from bolting from the car and dashing back into the house, up the stairs to the bathroom, and locking the door against this unseen, encroaching menace. Could she go through with this? *Should* she? Desperately, she wondered if she should listen to this voice, this feeling. One hand on the door latch, she hesitated, searching her mind once again for the reasons she had agreed to the marriage in the first place. *Vic doesn't want me anymore, and if the family will stop hating me, then it's a good thing…it'll make up…atone for…all the wrong I did…and I can stop going to school hungry and facing everyone making fun of me everyday…*

Willing herself not to be sick to her stomach, she swallowed nervously and gave him a nod as she took her hand off the latch and entwined it with the other in her lap. As she pushed away thoughts of the few times T.J. had kissed her and she had felt nothing at all…or worse yet…repulsed, Louise set up a litany in her mind, *I'll get used to his kisses. I'll learn to love him. He'll be a good husband and provider, like Mama says. It'll be all right…*

A light misting rain began to fall, seeming to mirror Louise's emotions. All the way to Elizabethtown, the Mockers and the groom kept up a steady stream of conversation about mundane topics, despite being aware of Louise's apparent lack of enthusiasm.

As the car carried her toward the start of her future, Louise stared out the window through the gathering rivulets of rain, her thoughts of nothing but Vic. Where was he? Was he thinking of her? Did he regret leaving? What would he say if he knew…

If Louise could only have seen where he was – staring through the rain dotted window of a Greyhound bus on the way to what he thought would be the start of his plans for *their* future, it would have made all the difference in the world.

But she had no idea.

ꕥ

THAT NIGHT, IN a strange bed in T.J.'s family's home as her *husband* slept beside her, Louise lay with silent tears dripping down her temples, into her hair, and soaking the pillow beneath her head.

His four younger brothers had griped and groaned about having to bunk on pallets in the living room so their older brother could 'have some fun' in the room they normally all shared. She had looked over at the two empty full size beds situated in opposite corners of the room and swallowed miserably.

Unable to sleep, she thought back on the preceding hours. What should have been the happiest day of her life – her wedding day – had been anything *but.* It had surely not been the embodiment of her girlhood dreams…nor her dreams of a wedding with Vic…

It had rained all the way to Elizabethtown – a tiny burg forty-seven miles south of Louisville, where a couple could get married with virtually 'no questions asked'.

They had arrived at the house of a pseudo preacher who, for a nominal fee, opened his home to visiting couples who wanted a quickie marriage…with little to no emotion or romance. He asked just a few preliminary questions, such as the ages of the parties involved. Against Louise's better judgment, she had followed T.J.'s instructions and mumbled that she was 'twenty-one.'

In the dimly lit parlor of the house, with the man's wife and the Mockers as witnesses to the 'happy event', the parson had quickly read some words from a worn booklet. Later, Louise barely remembered what he had said, something about love, honor, and obeying, till *death* do you part. She fuzzily remembered whispering, "I do". Her new husband had slipped a thin, plain gold band on her finger before bending over to give her a tiny kiss, and the deed was done. In practically no time at all, they were on the road back to Louisville. She hadn't even held flowers.

There had been no reception, either. No cake to cut. No gifts to open. No photographs of the 'happy' occasion. No shower of rice to run through. No 'Just Married' on the back of the car with crazy things like shoes and cans tied to the bumper. No garter or bouquet to throw.

It had felt more like a business transaction…

And so had…the 'consummating'.

Shaking, Louise had slipped out of her wedding apparel and into the nightgown she had retrieved from her case, before climbing into the bed. She had waited quite a while for T.J. to finish talking and laughing with his family. From the snippets of conversation she could overhear, it seemed as if they were congratulating him on his conquest. The old man had said some very risqué comments that made Louise blush even in the next room.

When he had finally joined her in the bed, there had been no romancing, no sweet words or loving expressions, and very little kissing, before he had raised her gown and performed the 'deed'. Being her first time, it had hurt, much more than she had been ready for, and much more than Lilly had haltingly tried to warn her about. She had cried out and tried to push him away, but he had relentlessly continued. When he was finished, he merely rolled off of her without a word and turned on his side to go to sleep.

Hours later, she still felt an ache…and not just physically.

Sniffling quietly, she slipped out of bed and tiptoed to the door of the room. All was quiet, except for the ticking of a clock somewhere in the house.

She crept to the bathroom and with shaking fingers, shut the door and turned on the dim light. A wave of despair suddenly washed over her and she slid down the wooden surface to the floor.

Stifling the force of her cries, she whispered into the lonely space, "Oh Vic…why couldn't it have been *you?* It should have been you, my Vic!"

Clamping her hand over her mouth, she gave in to the tears,

weeping and shuddering under the load of despair. Her heart was heavy with a crushing sense of foreboding.

༄

"I'LL BE BACK in a couple of hours. Try to be ready," T.J. mumbled as he let Louise out at the curb. She nodded and closed the passenger door, watching as he drove on down the street.

With a sigh, she turned and looked up toward the front door of the place she had called home just the day before. Now, she wasn't sure where her *home* would be. T.J. was on his way to see some people he had been told had a room they might rent. She had been instructed to gather all of her things and be ready when he returned for her. However…she felt as bereft as a fish out of water. And she wondered if she…*looked* different. If she looked as different on the outside as she felt on the inside…

With another sigh, she climbed the steps and entered the building. The hallway seemed so still and quiet, it made her feel conspicuous, and the clacking from the heels of her shoes seemed to echo – or maybe it was her imagination… At the door to her family's apartment she almost knocked, feeling very much an outsider, but turned the handle and went on in.

Glancing in the bedroom, she saw Edna making up the bed they used to share. Her sister gave her a nod, but didn't say anything. Lilly was sweeping the floor near the sink. Her brothers were lounging by the radio listening to their favorite Saturday western. Eerily, everything seemed the same. *The only thing different is me*, she mused sadly.

"Hi everybody…" she murmured.

"Hey Louise," Billy greeted, barely giving her a glance. Sonny looked her way, but merely nodded without a word, his expression thoughtful. Lilly paused and met her daughter's eyes for a moment, then quickly returned to sweeping, her lips clamped, and her movements a tad more forceful than needed. In truth, Lilly herself had spent a sleepless night, racked with guilt and thinking about her daughter.

With a soft sigh, Louise turned and entered the bedroom, and stood gazing around at the familiar surroundings. It seemed unreal that this was no longer her home. She'd always pictured that it would be a happy occasion when she finally 'left the nest'. She didn't even have a hope chest to take with her…

Edna straightened up from her task and turned, the sisters silently facing one another…so many things said…and unsaid…standing between them. Obviously uncomfortable, Edna cleared her throat and seemed to cast around for something to say. Finally, she asked haltingly, "How, um…how'd it go?"

Thinking back on the multiple disappointments and pain she had endured the previous day and night, Louise grimaced for a moment, willing herself not to let loose with a barrage of complaints and whines. Swallowing, she managed, "It went."

Edna pressed her lips together, in truth fighting the guilt she felt for the way she had been treating her sister. Once the initial shock and anger had dissipated, she had wondered about Vic's feelings and intentions toward Louise…especially remembering his expression when he had found out her real age. She wondered why he had left town without even telling her sister goodbye. In a strange twist of the heart, Edna actually felt a sliver of empathy toward Louise that she had been treated in such a way…and that she had been emotionally blackmailed into marrying a man she didn't love.

From the other room, they both heard their mother's voice call over to their brother to pick up the throw rugs and take them out for a good shaking, and fussing that she had let the apartment get into 'such a shape'. Billy whined for a moment that he would miss some of the radio program, but Lilly brushed the argument aside with a sigh and a, "William!"

Edna sank down on the bed and moved her hand slightly in an invitation for Louise to join her. Louise placed her handbag on the dresser and moved closer. As she lowered herself down, she was unable to stop a twinge of discomfort from showing on her face. Edna, ever perceptive, caught it.

"So...did he..." she began, stopping as her blue eyes met her sister's hazel gaze.

Blinking and telling herself she was NOT going to start crying, especially in front of Edna, she whispered, "Yeah...he did. Twice." Then at Edna's raised eyebrow query, she added wryly, "Let's just say...I know now why Mama calls it the 'wifely duty'."

Both sisters looked away for a moment. When Louise looked back toward her sister, she absently noted how much Edna resembled their mother, with their features so similar. She felt a rush of affection for her volatile sibling. Reaching out, she touched Edna's hand and whispered, "I'm sorry...for all the lies...'borrowing' your things without asking...I guess I was just obsessed with Vic. I...lost my good sense for a while," she added, shaking her head in self-derision. "But he obviously didn't really care about me."

Edna let out a soft snort, her lip curling in her characteristic smirk. Thinking of her last boyfriend, a handsome devil-may-care rascal, she cracked, "I been there."

Just then, they heard Billy's voice murmur, "Hey...what's this?" A moment later, he appeared in the doorway. "Hey sis, I think this is yours."

The world suddenly seemed to slow down as Louise turned toward the door, her eyes falling to the envelope her brother was holding out in her direction. She felt her heart rate begin to speed up. "What is it?" she heard herself ask as she rose to go to him.

He shrugged carelessly. "I dunno. I found it there," he jerked his head behind him, "under the rug at the door."

A chill swept through Louise's entire body when she took the envelope from Billy's hand and saw the writing on the outside. *To Louise From Vic.*

Her fingers were shaking and her hands felt numb, with those peculiar pinpricks one feels as the circulation begins to return. She haltingly slid a finger under the flap and opened it. Inside were two folded pieces of paper.

Holding her breath, heart pounding with a mixture of joy and dread, she unfolded the letter. It was dated nearly three weeks previous. Staggeringly, she made her way the few steps to the bed and dropped down, finding her legs were no longer able to support her weight.

The first words brought instant tears to her eyes…

To My Sweet Mary Lou,

I'm writing this letter to beg you to forgive me for the lousy things I said to you when I found out your real age. I reacted like a jerk and I'm sorry. Please forgive me. My only excuse is I was scared and confused. I came by your place tonight to try and see you, to tell you in person, but lost my nerve. Didn't know what the reception would have been to that.

Girl, you're always on my mind. There ain't been a minute since we met that I haven't wanted to see you, be with you, hear your voice, and hold you in my arms…maybe too much and that scares me too. Since the night of the fight, I've missed you something awful.

But Louisville's a bust for me. Just can't seem to find a job here. So, I made a decision. I enlisted in the C's again, a two-year hitch this time. While I'm in, my pay will be sent to my brother in Indiana and he's going to keep it for me. When I get out, I'll come back here. By then, you'll be a few months from eighteen.

What I'm saying is – I love you, and I'm hoping you'll wait for me. I want to take care of you and give you all the things you've always wanted. I'm asking you to marry me.

I don't want nothing more in this life than for you to be my wife and for us to live, like they say, 'happily ever after.' If you'll have me…

Let Alec know what you're feeling. He'll know how to get in touch with me. I'll be waiting to hear from you. I'm leaving on the 9 AM bus in the morning if you want to come see me off.

All my love forever,
Vic

Barely able to read the last few words past the torrent of tears filling her eyes and spilling down her cheeks, Louise drew in a choked breath and pressed the letter against her chest, whispering, "Oh Vic, what have I done?" Her heart imploding, she burst into sobs.

Alarmed at his sister's reaction to the letter, Billy called, "Mama! Come quick!"

"Is it from *him*?" Edna murmured, reaching to pry the letter from Louise's grip. As Edna quickly scanned the words, Lilly and Sonny hurried into the room. One look at Louise's face, then the letter, and they both instantly realized what had happened. Lilly felt an instant surge of guilt; Sonny an immediate burst of anger.

"Is that from Vic Matthews?" Sonny demanded, reaching to snatch it from Edna's hand just as she finished reading the last words.

Lilly lowered herself down onto the bed next to her hysterical daughter and took her in her arms, her own eyes filled with tears. Sonny read the words of the letter out loud, over the sounds of Louise's mournful wails as Lilly rocked her back and forth and murmured gently, "Ssshh, there now."

"Well, don't this beat all," Edna groused. "Why'd he go and stick this under the door? That was a stupid thing to do!"

"If only we would have seen it sooner…" Lilly commented, her first irrational thought being that it was all *her* fault…she'd been slacking on her responsibilities…if she would have remembered to shake the rugs sooner…how had things gotten so far out of hand?

"But…" Billy mumbled, not totally understanding the full extent of the problem. In a child's way of thinking, the solution was simple. "Mr. Vic says he loves you, Louise. Can't you just write to 'im and tell him you love him, too?"

Lilly closed her eyes, shaking her head sadly as she cradled her weeping daughter. "It's not that simple, Billy. Louise is…she's legally *married* to T.J. now. She belongs to him. I'm afraid there's no going back…unless…" she paused, her eyes meeting Edna's as

Louise let out another wail. Edna knew immediately what their mother was thinking, so she shook her head. Louise had just told her the marriage had been consummated. There was no backing out now.

Sonny was angrier with his mother than he had ever been in his life. "Why'd you make her do it?" he exploded.

Lilly immediately reacted, "Don't you raise your voice to me, young man!"

Sonny ignored her warning and surged on, "You *knew* she was crazy about Vic, but you made her feel so guilty, and like the only way you'd love her again was if she'd marry this other guy, just 'cause he's got a job and a car and his daddy promised to…" he paused as Louise, unable to take anymore, tore herself out of her mother's arms and ran out of the apartment, ignoring her family's calls to come back.

Clawing her way up the stairs, stumbling and crying, she reached the second floor bathroom, slammed the door and locked it. Then sinking down in the far corner, she pulled her knees up to her chest, wrapping her arms around her legs and pressing her forehead to her knees, determined to stay there for the rest of her life.

She sobbed until she had no more tears left.

ഗ്ര

TOGETHER, EDNA AND Lilly carefully packed up all of Louise's belongings in preparation for the girl to join her husband when he returned to collect her and her things. Edna even put into the worn old suitcase her own newest outfit; one that Louise had admired so much. They pulled Louise's box of mementos out from under the bed and made sure the string that held it shut was tied tightly.

When all was ready to go, Lilly climbed the stairs to the bathroom, glad that none of the other tenants seemed to be around, and spent many long minutes coaxing her devastated daughter to come out. Finally Louise opened the door, her face tear stained, her eyes and nose red and swollen.

Looking into her mother's understanding eyes, Louise gasped haltingly, "H…how…how'm I g…gonna…do this? Why did this happen? Why didn't we find the letter before… I…I can't stand the thought of…stayin' married to *him.* Oh Mama…I want *Vic*!"

Lilly clamped her lips together, sympathetic, but realistic. "Honey, you'll just have to grit your teeth and bare it. Lots of women have married men they weren't in love with, especially in the old days of arranged marriages. You just…" she paused, thinking about moments in her own past. "You just make the best of things."

Louise pressed the back of her hand against her mouth and turned her head, a fresh surge of tears threatening to surface. Lilly went on, striving to give what comfort she could as she lovingly smoothed strands of her daughter's hair back from her tear-dampened face. "It won't be all bad…T.J. has a job, and a car…you won't have to go to school with no lunch money anymore…"

School… The thought of it made Louise shiver. She opened her eyes and met the concerned gaze of her mother.

"I'm not going back to school."

For a moment, Lilly wondered what Willis was going to say to all of this when he finally came home. She hadn't tried to get in touch with him about it, and now, knowing how much he wanted all of his children to get an education, she dreaded the inevitable row when he found out – not to mention how he would react when he found out she had allowed Louise to marry at fifteen…

Nodding silently, she put her arm around her daughter, and together the two descended the stairs.

Louise was sure she would never know a happy moment again for the rest of her life.

ജ്ഞ

CHAPTER 24

Vic…Happy, Until the Bottom Drops Out

PULLING THE OLD truck to a stop in the cleared area near where his crew was busy working on their latest project, Vic moved the gearshift into park and turned off the key.

He had traveled into town on an errand and to retrieve the mail from the post office, which he had quickly looked through and discovered to his dismay that there was nothing for him from the one person with whom he longed to connect. He did, however, receive a letter from Miss Irene and one from Alec. Opening the one from Alec first, he found it was merely a short missive informing him that he would be paying him a visit in a few weeks. That made Vic smile and nod. It would be good to see his best friend again. Besides missing Louise, he had missed the gang, and Louisville…

"Good lettah?" a friendly voice queried, and Vic looked down from the window of the truck to see his new friend Floyd standing with one foot up on the running board, and his customary jovial grin illuminating his face underneath the bill of his cap.

Vic grinned back and nodded. "Yep, from my best pal back in Louisville. Says he's comin' here to see me in a few weeks."

"Now, 'at's real nice, Chief," the young man returned with a nod, using the nickname the guys in their crew had adopted for their manager. "I know's you'll have a good visit. Ain't nothin' like a visit from a friend."

"You got that right," Vic agreed with a happy smile.

"De way you was smilin', I figured yuh girl done wrote yah a lettah like you been wantin'," Floyd added guilelessly.

Vic's smile dimmed a bit, but he gave a shrug. "Nah, not yet. She must be busy with school or…maybe she's gonna be in another play, who knows," he added optimistically.

That illusive, and much hoped for letter was a sore subject. It was on Vic's mind constantly, wondering why Louise hadn't written, if she was still upset with him, and there was the possibility her folks wouldn't let her write to him… However, if that were the case, he was sure Fleet would have found a way to help her sneak a message to him. He gave a soft snort as he thought of how Fleet had helped Louise sneak around and do so many things since he had known the two of them – he couldn't imagine it being any different now. But, that always brought him around again to wondering why no letter. So many probabilities…her mother found his letter and threw it away without letting her see it…her father forbade her to write…she was mad at him…or maybe even something good, perhaps she was planning a surprise for him, or even playing hard to get.

Whatever the case may be, now that Alec was coming for a visit, he knew his time of being totally in the dark was about to come to an end – and he couldn't wait. Vic had even written Louise another letter and had it stashed with his stuff in his footlocker, just waiting for the go-ahead to send it.

The wattage of his smile brightened again as he dwelt on encouraging thoughts. Knowing the young men were on the other side, he gestured toward the forest the crew had yet to clear on this, their current project.

"Hey, go tell the guys for me that it's chow time and I'll give 'em a lift back to camp."

"Sho' thing, boss," Floyd answered, turning toward an opening in the trees and taking off in a loping run.

Vic watched him go with a fond half grin and small chuckle. As he waited for his crew to emerge, he looked back down at his friend's short letter. He read Alec's words again of how he'd already bought his bus ticket and would arrive in two weeks, that he would spend one night, and head back to Louisville for his job on Monday morning.

Resting his head back on the worn cloth of the driver's seat, Vic thought back over the weeks that he had been at the camp. Working harder than he ever had in his life – felling trees, driving the large army trucks, digging ditches and postholes for fences, and anything else that needed to be done – he had quickly proven not only his determination and strength, but his skills and knowledge as well. True to his word, Major Connors had promoted Vic to Crew Manager after the first week.

He happened to be one of the three oldest enrollees in his barracks, including Floyd, who was also twenty-one, and a bespectacled, rather thin young man named Scottie, who helped out with clerical work in the camp headquarters' office. The rest were mere youngsters of seventeen or eighteen. Upon finding out his age, the other enlistees quickly began teasingly calling him 'old man'. As the weeks passed, however, the goad had turned into a way of showing their affection and respect.

When Vic wasn't working hard at his tasks, the other fellows would often see him gazing at the picture he kept taped to the headboard of his bunk. Each of them had snuck peeks at it, and all agreed that the girl was truly a looker – and their 'Chief' was surely smitten. Vic had shared a bit about her with them, specifically, her name, her features, and her many talents, although her age he kept as a secret.

None of the guys had seen the second picture Vic kept squirreled away in his wallet. That one was for his eyes only, and it had jumpstarted many a session of daydreams for the young man.

Floyd had quickly become a confidant with whom Vic could

discuss his plans and ambitions. The happy-go-lucky young black man had even expressed an interest in making Louisville his home when his two-year hitch was up. He shared that he had been raised by his elderly grandmother in Alabama, had spent three long years knocking around the country once he had graduated high school, and had become tired of rambling and joined the CCC – to stay put for awhile and make something of himself. Hearing Vic talk about the town on the Ohio River had warmed his heart and he felt as if Louisville might be a place he could call home.

Vic had assured him he would be more than welcome, and would definitely be invited to the wedding – provided the girl did, indeed, say yes. Sometimes, though, it seemed the two years of his enlistment stretched out before him as an eternity.

Coming out of his musings a few minutes later, Vic watched as the tired, muddy crew of 17-year-old boys trudged to the truck, playfully shoving one another as they climbed up into the cloth-covered backend.

"Thought you'd never get back, old man!" one of the young men hollered up toward the cab. "I'm about to die 'a starvation!"

"Aww I think you got enough insulation to hold you at least a day, Wolf. You ain't gonna starve," Vic called back.

Everyone laughed, including the speaker, whose nickname was 'Wolf' because he had the habit of wolfing down his food – and anything left on anyone else's plate.

Vic turned the key and started up the old rattletrap truck, casting an amused glance at Floyd as he climbed up into the passenger seat, his customary chuckle reverberating from his chest. Floyd tilted his head back and began to croon, "You get a line and I'll get a pole, honey, honey. You get a line and I'll get a pole, babe. You get a line and I'll get a pole, we'll go down to that crawdad hole…" to which all the guys in the back, and Vic as well, joined, "Honey, baby mine!"

In this way, they passed the time traveling back to the camp.

ꟻ൬

THE FOLLOWING SATURDAY, Vic looked up from checking the oil in the truck he had begun to think of as *his* vehicle, and a broad smile instantly suffused his face. He watched as his best friend made his way toward him from the vicinity of the Major's car that had just pulled up to the door of headquarters.

Quickly wiping his hands on the rag he kept perpetually in his back pocket, Vic came around the front of the cab. "Alec," he called, grabbing his friend in a firm man-hug. "You old seven times a son of a gun, it's good ta see ya!"

Alec returned the friendly embrace as they clapped one another on the back. "Good to see you too, man."

"I was just gettin' ready to head out to go pick you up in Dana…"

Alec grinned at his friend, noticing the healthy glow to his cheeks, and the joyful confidence in his expression. He could see that life at the camp had been good for Vic. There was a spring in his step, and purpose in his stride. He no longer gave the appearance of a man treading water in the center of the river, but rather a man that had 'made it' to the shore. Inwardly Alec cringed, hating more than ever the reason for his trip – and what he knew it would do to that joy and confidence.

"Aww well, the bus got in a little early, and your boss happened to be in town. I saw the logo on the car, and, well…he offered to give me a ride."

Vic nodded with a dimpled grin, thinking that was something Major Connors would do.

"How is everybody?" Vic asked, starving for information.

"Everybody's fine. Just fine," Alec returned with a nod as he glanced around at his surroundings.

"Well…come on man, tell me. You know I'm dyin' here…" Vic prompted, but his friend cleared his throat and sidestepped the request.

"Why don't you show me around this place. What'dyall do here, anyway? Besides play in the dirt," he added with a teasing shove.

Seeing nothing he could put his finger on in his friend's eyes, and knowing Alec's penchant for teasing and prolonging suspense, Vic shrugged obligingly and chuckled, "Okay, okay. I'll take ya around."

For the next thirty minutes, Vic showed Alec 'his' truck, and they made the rounds of the camp, visited the mess hall, recreation hall, infirmary, and garage, as well as some of the outbuildings.

Finally, with a grin, Vic murmured, "C'mon, I saved the best for last," as he motioned for his friend to follow him down a path that led deep into the untouched portion of the forest. Over his shoulder, he remarked, "I found this spot by accident. None 'a the other guys know about it."

After several minutes of uphill climbing, traversing bushes and boulders, they finally came to the cusp of a 130-foot sandstone bluff that overlooked a river below.

"Down there's the Illinois River," Vic murmured as he sat down. Buttoning his jacket against the brisk winter breeze, he stuffed his hands into his pockets as he allowed his feet to dangle off the rock ledge. The view was spectacular. Below them, across the expanse of the swiftly flowing river, were rolling hills and valleys, picturesque canyons, and waterfalls. Being winter, the sky was a light gray with just a hint of blue. The trees were bare of leaves, but somehow starkly beautiful.

Alec for once was rendered speechless by nature's beauty as he secured the zipper on his own jacket and silently lowered himself down beside his friend. The world, from that vantage point, seemed serene, calm, and quiet. It made them both feel like they should whisper.

Suddenly, from somewhere off to their right, an eagle left its nest high in a tree and took to flight, soaring high above, its majestic wings barely fluttering to keep it aloft.

After several silent, reverent minutes, Vic mumbled, "This is where I come when the waitin' gets too much. Lookin' around at all this…kind of puts things into perspective…you know? Like…it took a lot of years for nature to make all of this. It's like Doc and Irene tell me…good things come to those who wait…and believe."

Alec swallowed and for a moment closed his eyes, the secret burning in his gut truly squeezing his heart for what he knew he had to do to his longtime friend. At that moment, in spite of knowing and even understanding the circumstances, he felt a momentary hatred rise up inside of him toward the girl that his best friend loved. He wished he had taken the easy way out and simply written or called… But, how do you write something like that in a letter?

Vic went on, "You shoulda seen this place when I first found it. It was still autumn, and the leaves were so many different shades of oranges and reds, browns and yellows…kinda like a patchwork quilt…"

Alec mumbled something unintelligible as he continued to stare out at the view, his mind only half seeing the vista as he scrambled for a way to start the inevitable conversation.

Finally, Vic couldn't take the waiting anymore and murmured, "Is she still mad at me?"

Alec's brow furrowed and he turned his head toward his friend. "Mad?" The situation had marched on so far from the original fight, Alec had forgotten about it.

Vic shrugged, continuing to watch the eagle's lazy drift. "For the things I yelled at her when I found out. I was just…off my nut out about Ger' gettin' arrested and I…well, I wasn't very nice."

"Oh…" Alec paused, wondering if that was part of the reason…

"Did ya talk to her?" Vic asked softly, thinking it was going to take more work than he had thought to get her to come around. She sure could be a stubborn little thing…

Alec clamped his lips together for a moment, took a deep breath, and murmured, "Man, I been goin' over it and over it in my mind, tryin' to come up with a way to…but there just ain't no easy way but to just come out and say it…"

An overwhelming surge of dread and fear rushed through Vic's entire being as he turned his head and then his body toward his pal, staring at his profile. "Say *what…*" When Alec still hesitated, he added, "*What*, man?! C'mon!"

Alec turned and met his friend's eyes. "She…Louise…she got married, man."

Vic sucked in a breath and his eyes widened. He looked and felt as if he'd been sucker-punched. His mouth dropped open as he staggered up from his perch and backed up a couple of steps. Gasping for air, he rasped, "What?? B…but…*when*? *Who*? If this is some kinda joke, Alder, I'll wring your neck!"

Now that it was finally out, Alec braced himself to just spill the rest and get it over with, the way one would rip off a bandage. The sooner done, the sooner the healing could start. Standing, he faced his friend and jammed his hands deep in his coat pockets. "I went by there, like you asked, but it was a couple 'a weeks because I came down with the flu. Had a bad case of it – and then Mom and the sisters got it and…" he paused, knowing that sounded like an excuse. He had wondered from the moment he'd found out what happened, if it would have made a difference if he had gone over to see her right away. But he'd put it off, and felt positive that what had occurred was to some extent his fault.

"Anyway," Alec continued, "I knocked on the door and a guy answered, I think it was her brother…"

"Sonny…" Vic numbly supplied, hoping against hope that he had misunderstood the bombshell Alec had dropped on him.

Alec nodded. "Yeah, and when I asked for Louise, he asked who I was. I told him my name and that I was a friend of yours and he acted like he'd heard about me…then he told me she got married, like a *week* before I went over there. I'm sorry, man…if I'd gone the day you left…" he stopped as Vic shook his head with a grimace and held up a hand.

Married? She went from being just a kid to…she got married?? Nearly hyperventilating, his eyes burning with shocked tears, Vic tried to gulp in the cold air surrounding his head, but his lungs couldn't take it in. There was a pain deep in his gut, so sharp it was causing him to double over, making his whole body feel as if it had suddenly turned to lead, all the while his universe seemed to be crumbling like dry toast under his feet.

"*NO!!*" he suddenly bellowed, clamping his eyes shut and gripping his head with his hands as he sank slowly to his knees. *Didn't she love me at all? Was the whole summer one great big lie? Her kisses…so sweet…so full of fire…* The pain of *this* betrayal was worse than any hurt he'd ever felt in his life. It was over the top – way more than he could survive, he was sure. Right then and there, he wished he could just die…just be put out of his misery. In five minutes, he had gone from hopes and plans for a bright and happy future to the pit of hell, and he could see no way out.

"I…I'm sorry, pallie," Alec stuttered, swearing silently that he was the worst scum bucket on earth for botching this…*maybe I shoulda wrote it in a letter…* Drawing near, Alec dropped to his knees beside his distraught friend and reached out to lay a tentative hand on Vic's trembling shoulder in an attempt to comfort. "Man, I'd give my right arm to not 'a been the one to come and tell you that…" he mumbled softly.

However, Vic couldn't hear his friend's consoling words, above the pounding of his own heart and the buzzing in his ears.

The world had ceased to exist.

He wondered what he had done to deserve this…his sweet Mary Lou…*married*…another man *taking* what should have been his…

ꝏ

THE NEXT AFTERNOON, the two long time friends stood together at the tiny bus depot in Dana, each one with his hands stuffed in his pockets, staring at the hard packed dirt beneath their feet.

"I'm sorry, man," Alec mumbled, apologizing for what seemed the hundredth time. He still felt guilty that he'd been the one to deliver the devastating news, but the four of them – Earl, Ruth, he and Fleet, had discussed the situation at length and determined it would be easier coming from him rather than Vic reading it in a letter. Alec had truly been worried for quite a while up there on that cliff, not knowing what his friend would do, and had kicked himself for choosing that location to administer the 'blow'. For a few moments, he had even been afraid Vic might literally jump off the edge. Alec had talked to, reasoned with, and comforted his pal until his voice literally gave out before Vic finally began to come out of the shock. Then he'd been full of questions, morbidly wanting to know all the details. Although Alec hadn't planned on divulging the last tidbit of information, Vic had pried it out of him, namely who the low down scum was that had taken his girl.

White-hot anger had blazed through Vic then. He had yelled about it being that *creep* that had swept Louise right out of his arms, the one that kept calling him 'Mac.' It seemed the fact that *he* was the one made it that much worse. Alec thought the whole thing was pretty rotten, and that the guy was no better than a fox that creeps into the hen house when no one is looking. Vic had admitted that it felt like a personal slight, a punch to the jaw, as if he were being mocked and laughed at behind his back. Alec thought, privately, however, that the anger had seemed to help Vic cope, at least better than the crushing heartache.

For Vic, it had added fuel to the fire when Alec had related the 'rest' of the story Sonny had been more than willing to reveal of the emotional blackmail Louise had suffered, and he wished ardently that he had been there to whisk her away from her torturers.

Remembering that night he had gone to talk to her, but had chickened out at the door and slunk away, made him feel sick to his stomach. He should have spirited her away for a private talk – and not have left such an all-important task to a letter slipped under the door! Why hadn't he realized that it was sliding under a throw rug? Once again, it was like someone or something had it in for him.

As a result, he had spent a fitful night on his bunk, tossing and turning, and suffering disturbing dreams. He imagined Louise in a white gown, arm in arm with her new 'husband' as they laughed at him, or Louise the helpless victim as the interloper forced her to comply. That was even worse, and he longed to go to her and 'save' her, as in his dreams she was crying and whispering his name…

Meeting his friend's eyes as they stood together, and seeing Alec's obvious guilt and angst over the whole situation, made Vic attempt a tiny smile. *It ain't his fault. Like they say – don't shoot the messenger.*

Slowly offering his hand, Vic mumbled, "I 'preciate you comin' all the way here to tell me in person…"

Alec let out a soft snort as he shook Vic's hand. "Man, it was about the hardest thing I've ever had to do."

Vic nodded. There was nothing else left to say. They'd talked it all to death up on the cliff.

The two long time friends felt quite awkward together, each with their hands shoved in their pockets, staring at the trees in the distance. Suddenly remembering a happy tidbit he had wanted to impart, however, Alec smiled and cast a glance over at his friend.

"Oh, by the way…wanted to let you know, Ger's off the hook."

Vic met his eyes, a tiny spark of joy kindled. "He is?"

Alec pursed his lips and nodded. "Yep. Somethin' about they

didn't have enough evidence or whatnot. They let him go six weeks ago. I saw him last week, and he told me he and the girl are gonna get married when she turns sixt…" he stopped, grimacing as he watched the cloud come back into Vic's eyes. Looking away, Alec muttered a few choice words, cursing himself for his stupidity.

Minutes later the bus arrived. Still slightly worried, Alec met his friend's eyes again.

"Man…don't do nothin' stupid…" was all he could think of to say before climbing aboard.

Vic managed a lame half-smile and mumbled, "Aw man, you know me better than that."

He stayed long enough to see his friend off for his journey back home. Then, with a heavy heart, his mind in turmoil, Vic climbed into the cab of his truck and began the drive back to the camp.

As he drove the narrow tree lined logging road, for the first time totally alone since he'd been struck dumb with the devastating news, he allowed himself to face the truth of the matter.

She was married to another man.

Tears filled his eyes and spilled unhindered down his cheeks. During his life, he had lost nearly every person he loved, and now he had lost *the one* who had meant the most to him. His Mary Louise. He would never know what it would be like to join with her, to make love to her, have a family together, and build a life together.

He wondered if he would ever know a happy moment again…

ꕥ

CHAPTER 25

Life in the Trenches

February 1939…

A SOOTHING SONG emanated from the small Zenith radio sitting on the bureau next to the door. Ironically, it was Benny Goodman's version of *Once in A While,* with Martha Tilton's smooth soprano voice crooning the lyrics.

Louise had been running an iron over the same section of shirtsleeve for the past five minutes. The wrinkles were long since gone, but she wasn't paying attention.

Staring unseeing out the window of the one room they were renting, she sang along as she went through the motions of ironing one of *his* shirts – the man she was *married* to, yet for whom she felt no more than slight affection…or more truthfully, something more akin to dislike – while wondering if *Vic* ever thought about her, like in the familiar lyrics of the song. Memories floated through of being up on stage singing that tune, as the beloved twinkling eyes of the man she adored watched her, his head nodding approvingly. The image of the mile-wide smile that had lit up his face in pride sent waves of both pleasure and pain through her heart.

That morning she had donned the lavender flowered dress she had worn on two dates with Vic, on the strength of a vague promise that T.J. had made to her the week before. Now as her daydreams deepened and sweetened, her hand unconsciously released its grip on the iron and reached up to touch the amethyst necklace lying nestled in the V-neck of the garment.

No, she wasn't really there in the confines of their room, passing another boring day by trying to keep busy; she was where her mind usually strayed – The tunnel of love with Vic at Fontaine Ferry... Or with the gang riding in that silly old hearse... Or strolling along Fourth Street hand in hand with Vic... Or cuddling with Vic in the corner booth of the malt shop... Or on the Idlewild, swaying to the music, in Vic's arms...

With the final bars of the song playing, Louise could almost hear that masculine timbre in his voice, murmuring sweet nothings in her ear as they swayed together to the music. Closing her eyes, she could see him, as plain as if he were right there with her...his dark wavy hair fluffing in the evening breeze...his warm brown eyes twinkling down at her with intense admiration as she pulled back to gaze up at him...and his gorgeous smile, with those perfect white teeth... She could almost smell the heady scents of that night, a delightful combination of his aftershave and the wild musky essence from the river. Louise imagined she could feel the warmth of his hand as it gently pressed against her back, urging her to cuddle closer, and then moving in slow caressing circles. Her eyes drifted closed and she could see his face as it came closer and he began to lean down for a kiss...

Suddenly, she was startled from her musings as she heard the back door of the house open. Hastily glancing over at the clock on the bureau, she knew it was her husband coming home from his job as a mechanic. Shaking her head, she struggled to bring herself fully back to the present. Worried, she bit her lip; *I hope he's in a good mood...and that he remembered...*

Seconds later, the door to their room opened and he strolled in, glancing over at her before shutting it behind him. Tossing his cap on the dresser and reaching up to unzip his uniform jacket, he looked over at the tiny table and two chairs in the corner, where he could plainly see his supper had not yet been prepared.

This wasn't the first time, and T.J. sighed with aggravation. Over the months since they had married, his young wife had seemed to slip further and further into her own little world – and he had a grudging idea who it was that 'occupied' that world with her.

T.J. paused and gazed at her. Once again, he mused at how she seemed so different from the girl he had seen from afar aboard the steamboat, and then again at the K.C. dance. He had fallen under her spell and was captivated by her beauty and her singing voice. It was during their second dance that he had determined he would pursue and conquer. He'd decided she would be *his*, no ifs, ands, or buts. The reality of the other man, whom he thought of as, *'That jerk named Vic something or other'*, made him grit his teeth each time his image popped into his mind. Especially the image of how he and Louise had looked at one another. But – *Vic* was gone and *he* was here – and *he* had married the girl. She belonged to him. Period. She was now *his* possession. To his way of thinking, the other dumb cluck was just, as they say, **it out of luck. He shouldn't have left town – as that had left the field wide open.

However, Louise's lack of enthusiasm was a fly in the ointment and stung his manly pride. He knew she pined after that Vic character, and it made him want to chew nails, or punch something. It also made him angry and frustrated that she wasn't…responsive…to his overtures. Before *her*, he had prided himself on being a 'lady's man', and figured she should realize how lucky she was that *T.J. Blankenbaker*, the Louisville Stud, had picked her out of all the 'fillies'.

Tired, frustrated, and hungry, T.J. therefore was in no mood to be polite.

"Haven't you fixed supper yet?" he groused. Then looking around at their room, which didn't look much different than it had that morning, neither messy nor spotless, he added, "What do you *do* all day, anyway?"

Disappointed and hurt, Louise looked away from his piercing gaze. Unplugging the iron with a careless yank on the cord, she laid the well-pressed shirt on the bed and snapped, "Sorry, I guess I lost track of time. Supper'll be ready in a few minutes."

He watched her edge past him, the thought not even occurring to either of them that they might give one another a kiss in greeting after being apart all day. The simmering undercurrent that persisted between them was like an ever-present housemate hovering over their shoulders.

He forgot. I knew he'd forget! Louise silently fumed as she trudged into the kitchen.

Dejected and angry, she retrieved some leftover ham from the icebox and their loaf of bread from the cupboard. She was glad that the kitchen was empty, and that the couple they were renting from, Shelby and Anna Richardson, weren't around. Anna liked to stick her nose in everyone else's business, and Louise didn't relish her knowing more than she had to about her and T.J.'s testy relationship.

Louise stood at the counter, her hands busy, her mind even more so. *I guess this is what my life'll be like from now on. But…I guess it's no more than I deserve. Probably gonna be punished forever…I wish I could just go back…if I could go back and redo everything, I'd change so many things, I'd tell Vic right away how old I was…I'd…*

T.J. emerged from the bedroom then, still wearing his grimy uniform, and was headed toward the bathroom when he glanced over at Louise as she arranged the fixings for sandwiches. His eyes flicked down over her dress and he belatedly noticed she was wearing a bit of makeup and had styled her hair. Totally oblivious, he momentarily wondered why, since she usually didn't bother to fix herself up for him. Then he realized what she was doing.

"*Sandwiches* again? That's what we had *last* night," he complained. "I was hoping for a hot meal!" Swearing, he added, "Had to work on a rush job outside in the cold all day, since all the stupid bays were full."

"*Sorry*," Louise muttered with a petulant shrug. Then looking over at him, she decided to take the plunge and answered softly, "I thought you were going to take me out to eat. You know…for my *birthday*… We talked about it last week, remember?"

Shifting the clothing and bathing items in his hands, he sighed with renewed aggravation as he recalled promising to take her out for her birthday. But, with the way she'd been acting toward him lately, he wasn't feeling too generous. "I *gave* you a *card* this morning," he reminded her defensively. "Besides, I don't have money for eating out tonight. Maybe some other time."

"Like for Valentines?" Louise persisted, "We could go dancing…they're having another dance at the K.C…"

"*Maybe.* We'll see." He responded, being purposely vague. Then he ran a hand back through his hair and mumbled, "Hurry up with that food, will ya? I'm starving. I'm gonna go take a *bath*," he added.

Sharp blue eyes met a resentful hazel gaze with an unspoken message. She clamped her mouth shut and swallowed, but refused to respond as he went on into the washroom and shut the door with a definitive click.

Closing her eyes for a moment, Louise pressed her lips tightly together, knowing all too well what that look meant. Her *husband* would demand that she allow him his *rights* later when they went to bed. Since she had turned him down so many times with the complaint that he was too dirty and smelly from working in the auto repair shop all day, he had begun bathing more regularly so she couldn't use that excuse.

The truth was Louise could barely tolerate her husband's use of her body. When they had first married – after their wedding night, that is – T.J. had used his practiced 'moves' on her, expecting her to swoon in his arms; but they had had little effect. As a result, he had long since given up trying to be romantic, and in Louise's opinion, she wouldn't call what they did together 'making love.' It was more like a master using his slave. And that's what she felt like – a slave. She knew, however, that to T.J.'s way of thinking, her constant spurning stung his pride and she didn't deserve to be 'romanced'. It had become a Mexican standoff, and neither had any intentions of changing their behavior, nor for that matter trying to make amends.

She shook her head with a disgusted sigh as thoughts roiled in her brain. So far, being married was nothing like she had imagined it would be. One of the main reasons she had agreed to the marriage was because she had been sick and tired of the day-to-day struggle of living in poverty. Growing up, there had never been any money for anything – at least, not since the Depression had taken root after the crash of '29. She could barely remember the years before that, when her father had a good paying job and they had lived in a nice house. T.J. had a job and a car, and he had practically spoiled her when they were 'courting', taking her to the movies, and out to eat. So she had expected things would be better with him…but all he ever seemed to tell her was that he had no money for whatever she was requesting.

The kicker was, she didn't even know how much money he *made*. Every time she asked, he'd tell her not to worry about it, that he was taking care of it, and of *her*. All she had to do were her womanly duties, like cooking and cleaning – and keeping him satisfied. She shouldn't 'worry her pretty little head about it'.

However, the thing that had tipped the scales in her mind was what he had begun to do a few months after their marriage. One night after she had grudgingly allowed him conjugal rights, he had 'jokingly' told her that she was behind on holding up her end of the bargain, because she wasn't yet in the 'family way'. Then he had uttered the phrase that made her grit her teeth every time he said it – and he had repeated it often since then, probably because he saw that it got under her skin. That it was his 'job' to 'keep her barefoot and pregnant', and she had better get with it, as she was making him look bad. She knew it was a saying he had picked up from his father, Mr. Blankenbaker, who Louise thought of as a 'lecher' and a 'low down womanizer', and who had even indicated to Louise on several occasions that he found her quite 'fetching'. The thought made her want to retch.

Lately the Blankenbaker family had been suggesting that she go to see a doctor and find out if she was 'normal'.

However, getting pregnant and having a child with T.J. was the *last* thing Louise wanted to do, and she had managed to put off seeing a doctor about it. Thoughts of the distant future were something she avoided at all costs.

She fretted silently, using a little more force than necessary as she smeared mustard on the bread for his sandwich. *Normal. Heck yeah, I'm normal. But I'm a girl in love with one man and married to another…*

Knowing it did no good to dwell on that fact, as it would only end with her crying and T.J. getting angrily frustrated, which would turn into belligerence, she sighed dramatically as she finished making his supper. She, however, had lost her appetite.

Realizing he wasn't planning on doing anything to celebrate her birthday, she swiped at an errant bit of moisture attempting to leak out of the corner of one eye. Despite the fact that it was her birthday, she didn't hold out much hope that he would let her go to see her family that night, because he was always so 'tired' when he came home from work. The fact was he had virtually cut her off from seeing any of her old friends since their marriage – as their 'home' was too far away for her to walk. Therefore, she felt isolated and alone most of the time.

With a pout, she resigned herself to another night of listening to programs on the radio…until the inevitable moment of 'reckoning' when it was time for bed.

Pouring her husband a glass of soda, she silently fumed. *What fun my sixteenth birthday has turned out to be.*

Ꟊ

THE NEXT MORNING, T.J. obligingly dropped Louise off at her mother's on his way to work. After much badgering and begging on her part, he had agreed to allow her to spend the day there. Louise figured he felt guilty about doing practically nothing for her birthday the night before.

He'd only paused the car long enough for her to exit and shut the door completely, before giving it gas and moving on down the street. He hadn't even said goodbye.

Feeling like a petulant little girl, Louise stuck her tongue out at the retreating back end of the Phaeton as it turned the next corner. She knew he was angry – she had made excuses again the night before, and had somehow managed to escape her 'duty'. The result had been a string of heated, angry remarks exchanged in the darkness of their room, before they had rolled to the farthest sides of their bed and spent a fitful night trying to get to sleep. She grudgingly supposed she should be grateful that he never used force to get what he wanted, but at that moment, she wasn't in the mood to be benevolent.

A mean streak rose up as she fumed silently, *Let him be mad. I don't care!*

Wrapping her coat closer around herself against the cold February breeze, she climbed the steps to her previous home and hurried down the hall. That time she knocked on the door and waited for her mother's voice to call, "Come in," before entering to find Lilly at the sink washing dishes.

"Hi Mama," Louise greeted, glancing around the room. "Oh shoot, I was hoping Billy and Sonny would still be here…"

Lilly turned and smiled lovingly at her daughter. "I'm sorry honey, you just missed them."

Louise nodded and made her way over, gliding gladly into her mother's open arms. For a moment, it felt so good to pretend to be a little girl again, her problems no worse than a skinned knee or one of her many sore throats.

After a few moments, Lilly loosened her grip and stepped

back, gazing into her daughter's eyes. "How *are* you?" she asked softly.

Louise stifled the pout that wanted to take over her mouth and instead turned to shrug off her coat and lay it on the back of a kitchen chair. "I'm okay."

"He treating you good?" Lilly persisted, seeing the unhappiness lurking in Louise's expressive hazel eyes.

Louise shrugged again, thinking if she began complaining to her mother, the floodgates would burst open and she might never stop. Plus, she knew her mother felt responsible and right then she didn't have the stomach for causing further upset. "He…he treats me okay. He don't hit me or anything," she admitted.

Lilly's brow furrowed as she interjected, "And he'd *better not*!"

Louise smiled softly at that, picturing her short, stout little mama chasing T.J. around the kitchen with a rolling pin, shouting, *'You lay a hand on my daughter again, and I'll crack your skull!'*

"No, he's just…stingy…"

Lilly searched Louise's eyes again, nodding sagely. "He forget your birthday?"

"He gave me a card," Louise admitted with a roll of her eyes.

"Mmm hmm," Lilly nodded. Once again, she berated herself for her part in her daughter's unhappiness. Reflecting on the fact that none of Mr. Blankenbaker's promises had proven true, she mumbled, "I'm not surprised. Seems all those Blankenbakers do is promise and lie."

Lilly turned back to the sink with a disgusted huff as Louise leaned against the side of big old fashioned sink and built in drainboard. "What'd they lie about now?"

"Oh, all that business about it being no problem to help your father to secure a job in that factory where Mr. Blankenbaker works. So far, that hasn't happened – and Willis has been back from Bowling Green for over three months. Thank goodness for odd jobs," she added with a tired sigh.

"I miss Daddy," Louise mused, glancing around as she realized he wasn't in the apartment. "Where *is* he?" she wondered aloud as she automatically reached for a dishtowel and began drying the freshly washed dishes.

"He went early down to Harrison's," Lilly explained over her shoulder, referring to a company for whom Willis had worked ten years' previous. "Somebody told him yesterday they might be hiring."

"I hope so…" Louise murmured, glancing over at Willis's chair. "Daddy's a good worker. They ought to take him back."

For a few moments, the girl thought back on the last few times she'd seen her father. All of the ill feelings he had harbored after the debacle regarding Vic had been smoothed over, and he had gone back to his gentle, loving self. The only drawback was that T.J. seemed to always have some excuse why he couldn't bring her over to her parents' place – although they went to *his* parents' home all the time. As a result, she had very few chances to be with her daddy. One time had been when he had returned from Bowling Green shortly after her marriage. He had secured from his son the address where she was living, and came to see her, to make sure she was truly all right. During that visit he had met T.J. and informed him, in no uncertain terms, that he had better not cause Louise any pain, or he would truly regret it. Smiling fondly at the memory, Louise knew the moment was one she would remember and cherish for the rest of her life. It also gave her a chuckle to remember T.J.'s reaction, quite cowed and respectful in her father's presence.

At the sink, Lilly stood absently washing the breakfast dishes and staring out the window, also thinking about Willis. More specifically, the horrific argument they'd had when he had come back from Bowling Green after their daughter's marriage. Lilly had never seen her normally passive husband so angry as he had yelled at her, "How could you…*why* did you…marry off our Louise like that? To a man her father hasn't even met!"

Fretting and wringing her hands nervously, Lilly had stammered, "I didn't exactly *marry her off*... I didn't sign a paper or anything giving her permission... But Will, I was *frightened*...and I...I didn't want to lose everything again, like the last time..."

"That is *no excuse*, woman," he had immediately countered, a palm raised toward her as if he could stop more words from coming forth and causing more upset. "No excuse at all! To force your daughter to marry and spend the rest of her life with a man that she doesn't love, while..."

"You just don't understand!" Lilly had screeched in reaction. "You don't know what it's like to have to make ends meet on the little bit of money you'd send each month!"

Now three months later as she lowered a dish into the sink, Lilly closed her eyes and winced as she remembered that moment. She had regretted the statement the instant it was out of her mouth, as well as the sight of Willis reeling back as if she'd struck him.

Embarrassed and on edge, she had sent Sonny and Billy outside then, as quite a long verbal battle had ensued. Finally, Willis had slammed the door on the way out of the apartment and gone for a very long walk. It was late evening before he had returned.

Shaking herself from her oppressive thoughts, Lilly strove to think of something for conversation.

"So, tell me again about these people you're renting that room from..."

Louise pursed her lips for a minute, thinking back to the bits and pieces she had learned over the months. All she knew really about the Richardsons, who were friends of the Mockers, was that they had needed the money, and had moved their belongings down to a room in the basement and rented out the master bedroom to T.J. and Louise. Of necessity, the foursome had to share the kitchen and the one bathroom, with an arrangement that had worked well for the most part, as they had worked out a schedule for the shared rooms and alternated their times of occupancy.

Filling her mother in on the particulars, she added, "It makes me mad when Anna's upstairs, straining to eavesdrop on our conversations through the bedroom door."

Lilly gasped, then shook her head incredulously. "You think she does that?"

"I *caught* her at it one night." Louise shrugged and picked up another towel. "Ah, I guess I ought to feel sorry for the old biddy. I guess she's got nothing better to do."

Lilly looked over at her daughter and smiled fondly as she watched her placing the clean dishes on the shelf above the sink.

"Do you think T.J. would like to stay for supper when he comes for you? I was thinking about making a big pot of my vegetable soup, and maybe some corn bread."

Louise smiled with a tiny snort and then actually gave out a small giggle, the first laughter she had enjoyed in quite some time. "He probably would...since he hasn't exactly been getting much food at home lately," she added with a mischievous grin.

"Oh? You aren't cooking for your husband?" Lilly questioned, her sharp eyes missing none of the nuances in Louise's expression.

"Yeah sure, I've just been...kinda distracted lately," Louise explained softly. Something in her eyes before she hastily looked away clued her mother in and Lilly nodded wisely.

"Are you pregnant?"

Louise's eyes flared for a moment, embarrassed to speak about the subject with her mother. Shaking her head, she mumbled, "No."

Pursing her lips, Lilly turned back to finish the dishes. After a few minutes, she murmured softly, "I'll tell you something, Mary Louise...living in your dreams may help you get through the day, or the night, but there will come a point when you'll find you either have to give them up...or act upon them. If you let it go on too long, neither choice will be easy."

Louise turned and stared at her mother's profile, her hair

pinned up in its customary tightly rolled bun, with not a strand out of place. She wondered if her mother was speaking from experience…

Deciding she didn't want to know the answer to that question, she chose not to ask.

The two women continued on with their chores in silence.

ꕥ

"HELLO, MR. HUDSON," Louise greeted the kindly storekeeper an hour later, having been sent to the market for items Lilly needed for supper. It felt good to be out and about, and she almost skipped down the street as she had traversed the familiar route. It felt like old times, and for a little while, she could pretend her life was carefree and happy again.

The jovial old gentleman's eyes lit up when he saw her, and he motioned for her to come closer to the checkout counter. "Well, hello there, sweet girl. How've you been? I haven't seen you come in for quite a while," he crooned as he reached into his large glass 'penny candy' jar next to the register. Louise smiled as she thought about how it had been their habit since she was a child and sent to the little market for something, that Old Mr. Hudson would always look both ways, reach into the jar, and hand her a piece or two of candy with a chuckle. Then he would bring one finger up to his lips with a 'shhh' to complete their game. The sweet, familiar gesture almost brought tears to her eyes.

She cleared her throat as she reached for the candy. "Oh um…I'm not living around here anymore, so…"

"Oh that's right! Your brother, Billy, told me you'd gone and got yourself married. Got a ring through your young man's nose, eh?" he joked with a chuckle.

"My young man?" she asked, popping the piece of hard candy into her mouth and relishing the sweet butterscotch taste.

"Yes…the one I saw you talking with that time…" At her

confused expression, he continued as he gestured with one hand, "Right out there…a few days after your family came back from being evacuated during the flood." He reached for his customary dust rag to wipe down the countertop.

Louise remembered that wonderful moment when Earl and Vic had stopped to talk, and Vic had asked her out on their first date. Tears instantly sprang to her eyes. Quickly breathing in through her nose, she looked away as she tried to control her emotions, and answered softly, "Oh…no…I didn't marry him…I married T.J. Blankenbaker…"

The old man stopped for a moment, blinking as he focused on her face. He knew the Blankenbakers, of course, and truthfully, he wouldn't have given a plug nickel for the whole lot. He wondered why in the world sweet Louise would have married into that clan. Opening his mouth to comment, he thought better of it and shut it again, deciding to hold his peace. It was, after all, none of his business. He could see that Louise didn't appear to be happy with the situation, and his old heart went out to her.

Giving her a moment to collect herself, he asked, "So, what'd Miss Lilly send you down here for today?"

"Um…some tomatoes, and a couple of onions. And some powdered sugar…she's gonna make me a birthday cake," she managed to add with a touch of impishness.

"Oh, it's your birthday!" he predictably reacted, his eyes twinkling behind his wire rim glasses. "Well, happy birthday, honey. So, how old are you now?"

"Sixteen," she grinned, enjoying the fact that someone was actually friendly and excited about her special day.

"Sixteen, my my. Why, I was just sayin' to the missus the other day how time is just flying by…" he commented as she turned, nodding, and crossed the room to the onion bin, the old floor creaking as she walked. Her mind then slid into its usual mode of daydreaming and his voice was relegated to the background.

My birthday she mused, thinking back to a year before. Her fifteenth birthday had been so carefree, so happy… It had started with a wonderful family dinner and gifts, followed by laughter and fun with the gang, and a whole evening of Vic's attention.

Staring at the wall, with two white onions in her hands, she remembered the kiss Vic had given her at the end of the night. How he had leaned down, drawing her close as his lips touched hers, and how those familiar sparks had zipped through her from head to toe. They had both emitted tiny gasps as they had simultaneously leaned closer and melted into one another's embrace. After several moments, Vic had finally pulled back. Smiling as his thumb had brushed the edge of her mouth, he had whispered, "Happy Birthday, sweet Mary Lou."

"Thank you," she had smiled back, never having felt such sweet euphoric happiness in her life. "Tonight's been the best birthday I've ever had," she had confessed softly.

Turning back toward the checkout counter with the onions, it seemed like a hundred years had passed since that night.

CHAPTER 26

Life in the CCC

"WATCH OUT THERE, Matthews, or you'll be losing another finger," warned Arch Benson, the head of the camp's motor pool. The stout, balding older man glared at Vic as he stood nearby, his hands on his hips.

Vic pulled his hands back from the wheel of the truck he was working on and glanced up at the other man, casting him a half smile. "I ain't gonna let *that* happen again, believe me," he mumbled, before glancing down at the middle finger on his left hand. He had lost the tip of it in a freak accident a few weeks after Alec's visit, as he had been in the act of inspecting the bottom of a truck for oil leaks. A crewmate had hopped up in the cab and accidentally hit the gearshift. Before Vic knew what was happening, the truck had rolled backwards onto his fingers.

In reaction, Vic had tried to jerk his hand out, and in the process lost his balance. His friend Floyd had seen what had happened and leapt to his assistance, yelling, "Look out dere, Chief!" He had grabbed Vic from behind and tackled him out of the way just as Vic began to tumble forward, which would most certainly have resulted in him being crushed by the wheel. Although all four fingers were scraped and bleeding, the longer middle finger had received the most injury. The camp doctor had no choice but to amputate it at the first knuckle.

In the process, Floyd had landed wrong and fractured his

collarbone.

Since then, any time Floyd wanted a favor, he would rub his shoulder, reminding Vic that he 'owed' him. It was all in good fun, however, as the two friends had become inseparable in the months since their arrival at the camp.

"Well, all the same – keep your mind on what you're doing. I don't feel like cleaning up a bunch of blood today," the man grumbled in his morbid way of jesting as he turned back to the vehicle he was working on.

Vic nodded and pushed back the stool he was crouching on, far enough for him to stand up. "Think I'll take five," he mumbled, receiving a terse 'okay' from Mr. Benson as the man moodily turned his head to spit out a bit of juice from the ever-present wad of tobacco nestled in one cheek.

Reaching for the rag hanging from his back pocket, Vic wiped his hands. As he headed toward the office of the garage, a very familiar Benny Goodman song happened to be playing on the radio that was situated on the workbench...*Once In A While.* The moment the music had begun, it had instantly transported Vic from concentrating on replacing the worn brake drums on his truck straight into the world of memories.

He poured himself a cup of steaming hot coffee as the familiar words floated through the air in the big open space of the garage, and he wondered if it would always hurt as much as it did that moment. Would that song always bring back images of Louise...singing up on stage wearing that dress that made her look years older than she was, and even more beautiful than she usually looked? Would the words always make his heart kick start like a motorcycle, with an electric current shooting through every nerve ending in his body as his mind registered what he was hearing? Would he ever truly forget her?

He wandered over to the window, looking outside at the bleak February day, but not really seeing the view. His mind was too full of images of *her.* That lovely smooth dark hair, the creamy skin, those twinkling eyes and rosy lips… *Why does the memory of her still twist my guts so bad?*

The few fellows at the camp that knew what had happened, namely Floyd, Major Connors, and Mr. Benson, all continued to tell him the same thing. *He would get over her.* He would move on, and some day it would be as if he had never even met her. That seemed unlikely, as it didn't take much to bring it all rushing back; in spite of the fact that it had already been six months since the last time they had seen one another. Like just now – hearing a song. He hadn't even been thinking about her, but had been completely entrenched in his work. Yet the opening bars of the tune had knocked him for a loop and made him feel paralyzed, forgetting to keep his fingers out of the way as he maneuvered the drum back onto the hub of the wheel.

Listening to the final chorus, with Martha Tilton's voice sounding so very much like *her*, he wondered if *she* ever heard the song… Had she found occasion to get up and sing it before an audience again? And if she had, did it make her think of him?

Just then, the motor pool's manager decided to take a break, and to warm up next to the one small wood burning stove that vainly tried to heat up the entire garage. Coming to stand next to Vic at the window a few minutes later and taking a sip of his coffee, the older man stared out at the gloomy gray, heavily overcast sky and mumbled, "Looks like it's fixing to blow in a big snow out there."

Vic shrugged and took another sip. "Guess so."

"Lousy cold weather. Don't do much for these old bones of mine," Benson growled as he reached down to rub an aching knee.

That time Vic didn't answer, but merely stood contemplating the bare tree branches swaying in the cold wind outside of the frosty windowpane.

The other man cast a sideways glance at him. "What's on your mind, boy? You look like you done lost your best friend." Then as he watched Vic lower his eyes down to the cup in his hands and emit a soft sigh, the other man snorted in disgust. "You're thinking of that little filly again, ain't yah," he stated rather than questioned. Without waiting for an answer, he went right on, "Son, you gotta put that thing to rest and move on now, I'm telling you. Women! Pah!" he snarled, turning to the side to spit out another bit of tobacco juice. "Ain't none of 'em worth a plugged nickel. You can't trust even the best of 'em! Take it from me – I been married and divorced three times."

Vic nodded, rolling his eyes as the man continued to drone on. Vic had heard the stories of Benson's three failed marriages so many times he'd lost count. Of course, to hear Arch tell it, it was all completely the faults of the women and none of his own. All three wives had been unfaithful. As a result, Arch Benson was now a man who firmly believed there were absolutely no good women to be found – anywhere. It rankled Vic to hear the stories, but he did have to admit, it helped to take the edge off of the pain of pining for Louise.

He was, however, quite tired of being on the receiving end of a nonstop barrage of 'advice'.

Trying not to be too rude, he finished off his coffee and mumbled, "Well, guess I'll get back to work. That wheel ain't gonna fix itself."

"Sure won't," Arch agreed, walking back to the messy sink and tossing the last of his coffee down the drain before turning to follow Vic back into the colder part of the building.

"You just keep your mind on what you're doin'," he aimed at Vic's jacket-covered back, to which the younger man nodded and sent a wave of acknowledgement back over his shoulder.

Grumbling a few choice words, Benson mumbled, "Lousy no-good females."

ഇര

VIC LEANED DOWN close to the felt surface of the pool table in the camp's recreation hall as he closed one eye to line up his shot. The radio in the corner blared with an announcer's voice giving an animated blow by blow of a boxing match.

Huffing an impatient sigh, he mumbled, "Man, I wish they'd turn that thing down."

Floyd leaned against the table, his fingers nimbly twirling his cue as he watched his friend calculating his last shot. "Yeah man, who cares 'bout some college fight," he agreed as he cast a glance in the direction of the distraction. Five of their crewmates were sprawled out in chairs and on the floor, all staring at the radio as if they could see the action – which of course is what everyone did when listening to a program of interest.

Deciding on the perfect combination, Vic smoothly pulled back on his pool stick and sent it carefully forward. The cue ball bumped the eight ball and the round black object sailed without a swish, straight into the corner pocket.

Vic looked over at his friend and wriggled his eyebrows with a grin. "That's game. Five bucks. Pay up," he added as he held out his hand, palm up, and waggled his fingers.

"Aw man, gimme jus' one mo' chance," Floyd begged, in spite of the fact that it was their second game and Vic had beaten him twice, thereby winning the wager of their monthly five-dollar stipend.

"I done beat ya two to zip, man," Vic argued, although he knew Floyd would talk him into another round. He shook his head, thinking about his friend's decided lack of talent when it came to the game of pool. However, he more than made up for it in other sports, like wrestling and baseball. As expected, Floyd gave him the 'sad eye' before purposely reaching up to rub his collarbone.

Vic's lips turned up in a crooked half smile and he chuckled softly. "Okay, you bum. One more and that's it. Rack 'em up," he griped, though the twinkle in his eyes put the lie to his tone.

Floyd snickered and lazily went around the table retrieving the brightly colored balls and sending them down to one end as Vic reached underneath for the triangle.

"You wanna break?" Vic asked, handing Floyd his cue.

"Naw man, it's yours."

Vic nodded and leaned to set the cue ball, took aim, and sent the stick forward with just the right amount of punch to execute a perfect scattering of the balls for the opening of their game.

The crew in the corner cheered in response to the announcer's description of a particularly effective pummel and Floyd grinned his gleaming white smile as he leaned back against the side of the table, resuming their earlier conversation. Angling his head toward the corner, he quipped, "Now, iffen' it was Louis and dat German fella on that radio ova dere, that'd be different."

"Got *that* right," Vic agreed under his breath, thinking that the promised rematch of Joe Louis and Max Schmeling, scheduled for the following June, was something to look forward to.

Floyd shook his head as he remembered the last time he had caught a Joe Louis fight. "Man, that Joe, he can sho' land a punch," he mused, laying his cue against his shoulder and bringing his hands up in the traditional fight stance, pretending to 'jab' at an opponent.

"Yep, they don't call 'im the *Brown Bomber* for nothin'," Vic agreed as he finished chalking up the tip of his own cue and laying the well used one inch square of blue chalk to the side.

For the next few minutes, they traded shots, with Vic missing more than connecting. He was working hard to concentrate on the game over the distractions across the room. Finally, Floyd ended up winning by one point, resulting in a loud groan from Vic and a joyous whoop from Floyd.

Laughing, Vic lay his cue down on the table and reached good-naturedly for his wallet. "Okay, you win. I'm out a five spot," he grumbled, opening the billfold and taking out the money he had received from the paymaster only hours before.

"Ya win some, ya lose some," he chuckled. "Good game, man."

As he moved to close the wallet and return it to his pocket, somehow it flipped out of his hand and landed on the floor, spilling its contents in the process. Both young men reflexively squatted down to retrieve it, with Floyd mumbling, "Here, I hep' yah..."

Just then, as Vic reached to turn the worn leather item over, both men saw the two pictures that had dislodged from the interior. Vic sucked in a breath, as the sight brought memories back in full force like the blow of a sledgehammer. This time, he resented the surge of emotion he still felt whenever he came face to face with a specific reminder of *her*. Of course...it didn't occur to him to take the pictures out and throw them away...

Floyd flashed a glance at his friend's face and caught the pained expression before Vic could successfully smother it. The young black man reached for the photos and carefully picked them up, perusing the one of Louise alone, which he had seen many times, and then switching his gaze to the second image.

He remembered back to when Vic had returned from taking his friend Alec to the bus. Never had Floyd seen anyone so broken up, and it had taken him quite a while to get Vic to confide even a few of the details to him. Floyd had been truly saddened for his friend, and had made it his personal mission to help Vic recover from the unexpected, and to his way of thinking *undeserved,* heartache. Although he knew his friend was still nursing his wounds, over the months he had been relieved to see Vic regain much of his equilibrium and begin to move on with his life.

Still, gazing at the photo of Vic and the girl locked in a passionate kiss, Floyd knew that whenever his friend was reminded of what he had lost, it would always pack a 'Joe Louis' punch.

"Hee' yah go, Chief," Floyd mumbled, watching his friend take the pictures, gaze at them for a few seconds, and then with a sigh stow them away again in their customary hiding place. "Man, that was lousy," Floyd added quietly, meaning that they had been enjoying themselves until the mishap with the pictures.

"Ahh, forget it," Vic murmured with an attempt at a smile. "Been feelin' it anyway…" he paused, shrugging a bit sheepishly. "Today's her birthday." Pressing his lips together for a minute, he added, "I just hope he…" but he couldn't complete the thought that he hoped the guy who had married her was treating her well. He wondered if she was thinking about him then. Somehow, he felt as if she was…and had been all day. Puzzled, he wondered at the significance of that.

After a few moments, Floyd leaned to give Vic a friendly clap on the back. "Well, c'mon, Chief. What 'say we go shoot some hoops, huh?"

Vic gazed at his pal for a moment, truly thankful for their friendship. As they stood to their feet, he mumbled, "Might as well. Can't do much else with a foot 'a snow on the ground outside." After shoving the wallet back into his pocket, with a playful grin, he gave his friend a gentle punch on the shoulder. "Five dollars, best two outta three."

"You on, man," Floyd laughed as they made their way past their crewmates, who were whooping and cussing over the match on the radio.

ഇഗ

FOLLOWING MAIL CALL that afternoon, Vic retreated to the barracks. Thankful for the stone fireplace at one end of the large, open-raftered room, he beefed up the fire good and hot before lying down on his bunk to read his mail. Another letter had come from Miss Irene, one from his sister-in-law Goldie, and one from Alec. Irene's letters always made him feel better, so he opened hers first.

Dear Vic,

I hope this letter finds you well, and that the injury to your hand is totally healed. I prayed that it wouldn't cause you trouble and would heal quickly.

Things here are fine. The weather has been much more accommodating than last January, praise God. We certainly don't need a repeat of that, do we? Doc is fine, and said to say hello and how are you. He said to tell you he has heard many a fine report from his friend, your commander, and he couldn't be more proud.

Vic, I did as you requested in your last letter. I went by the Hoskins' apartment and had a nice visit with Louise's mother and father. They said to tell you they aren't angry with you, and that they wish you much success and happiness. I tried to get them to tell me Louise's address, but they indicated they didn't want to, and I had to respect their wishes. They assured me she is well.

Vic, I know this was a bitter pill to swallow, and I can't speak to the reason such a thing happened. But, sometimes people make bad choices, uninformed choices, or they do things on the spur of the moment that they later regret. I can only urge you to seek out happiness in your life and try not to dwell on the negative. Know that people love you and care very much about your future.

And...one never knows what the future holds. It may surprise you. Work hard and behave yourself, and God will reward you for your diligence...

Reward. Vic looked away from the words written on the page, lost in thought about what that might mean. The only 'reward' Vic would want from God would be to somehow have Louise as his wife. But that was impossible now...wasn't it? Unless, of course, her 'husband' was out of the way... The thought of the usurper was enough to make Vic's blood begin to boil, but he held back from actually wishing the man dead.

And another fact to ponder was... How would he feel if he saw Louise again...knowing she had been with another man? Vic shook his head, as those thoughts and images made him grit his teeth with a grimace.

Returning his gaze to the letter, he finished reading the last few lines Irene had written telling him about things happening in her own life, her invitation for him to write back and let her know how he's doing, and her promise to write again soon. Refolding the letter, he stuffed it back in the envelope and picked up his sister-in-law's missive. Finding it merely a friendly hello, and a gentle reiteration of the promise that they were, indeed, depositing each monthly check from the CCC into a special bank account, he gave a tiny grin and returned the page to its envelope.

Finally, he opened Alec's letter. He had only heard from Alec once since his visit, and that had been to once again apologize for having had to deliver such devastating news. This letter was light hearted and optimistic; sharing funny things that happened at work, or something Earl had done or said. It actually brought Vic a chuckle or two.

However, when he turned to the second page of the letter where his friend informed him that he and Fleet had decided to go ahead and tie the knot, he felt his stomach tighten.

Can you believe it, man? Me? Married? Who woulda ever thought? But no, really, man, Fleet's a great gal and I figure I better snatch her up before some other sneaky wolf comes along and sweeps her away.

Vic pursed his lips, knowing that Alec couldn't have known his words would pour salt into an already raw wound. He finished reading the rest quickly, which was simply a few details about when and where the wedding would take place, and his friend's regrets that one of his two best friends would not be there, as he had rightly figured Vic wouldn't be able to obtain a furlough.

With a heavy sigh, Vic sat up on his bunk as he returned his friend's letter back into its envelope. Standing, he quickly stowed the correspondence in his footlocker as he acknowledged with a nod a few of the other guys tramping in the door, stomping snow from their boots and laughing.

Wandering over to the window that looked out on the forest beyond the cleared area of the camp, he leaned against the frame with his hands shoved into the back pockets of his uniform pants, and allowed his gaze to roam over the snow-covered trees. For a long while, he simply stood there, blocking out the sounds of his barrack mates, as he imagined various scenes happening back home, including Alec and Fleet's upcoming wedding. The faces in the images slowly changed into his and Louise's as he imagined a happy wedding day…

All day he had been fighting off the memories of that night a year before, when the gang had ridden around all evening in Earl's dad's big old black hearse. But finally he allowed the images to come back in full force…the laughter and fun… and Louise perched on his lap. Closing his eyes, he could still almost smell the fresh scent of her hair…feel the warmth of her body pressed against him, hear her soft giggles, and see the sparkle in those hazel eyes whenever she would turn her head to meet his gaze.

Then finally, he remembered the kiss they had shared when he had dropped her off at Fleet's house. It still amazed him that every time they had kissed he had felt a spark pass between them that would always cause them to lean in closer and melt into one another's embrace. When finally he had pulled back, he had smiled as his thumb brushed the edge of her mouth.

Now leaning his head against the cold glass of the windowpane, he whispered with a soft sigh, "Happy Birthday, Mary Lou. I…I wish you was missin' me as much as I'm missin' you…"

It would have given him a tiny bit of perverse pleasure if he had known just how much she actually was…

ꟹ

CHAPTER 27

Bittersweet Joy in the Midst of Misery

THE DAYS PASSED slowly by, and for the embittered couple, life seemed to be stuck in a revolving door. Gone was the girl who had once made it a habit to look for joy in simple things – who knew how to take pleasure in small favors and snippets of happiness. Now, there never seemed to be any of those to enjoy! For Louise, the frequent sore throats she had suffered all her life came back with a vengeance – an occurrence that Lilly was convinced had been made worse by Louise's constant emotional turmoil.

About a month after the disappointment over Louise's birthday, things seemed to brighten up some when T.J. came home one day and announced that they were moving to a two room apartment on Oak Street, which wasn't far from the neighborhood Louise grew up in. Immediately, thoughts of being able to see her family more often, and perhaps renew acquaintances with her friends, brightened Louise's spirits.

The move had been accomplished without much fanfare – with the Richardsons practically shoving them out the door while ushering in their replacement tenants. Louise set up housekeeping in the new space, which amounted to the front two rooms on the second floor of a large old Victorian home that had been turned into apartments. Although it had seen better days, with the outside in need of a coat of paint, the rooms inside were clean and in fairly good shape. They had their own kitchen space on one side of the larger room. However, they still had to share the bathroom with the occupants of the other apartment on the second floor. But at least – the first floor tenants had their own bath downstairs.

Her joy was short-lived, however, when she began to once again experience frequent attacks of tonsillitis. The ailment was very hard on the young woman's constitution, and had caused her family much concern. Her husband handled each occurrence with his usual impatience. He was worried about their mounting medical bills, and to be truthful, they added to his increasing frustration over their marital relations.

One morning in early May, Louise once again woke up with the familiar symptoms of a scratchy throat and fever, followed quickly by her staggering down the hall to the bathroom feeling sick to her stomach. Each time this had happened, T.J. had hoped that his wife was finally pregnant, which only added to his angst when he realized it was another bout of illness.

"You sick again?" he growled when Louise dragged herself back to bed, not bothering to stay up and fix his breakfast.

"Yeah," she croaked miserably, shivering with the sudden high fever.

He sat up and glanced over at her, striving to curb his peevish state. After a few moments fighting against his ongoing resentment from yet another night with no sexual satisfaction, he growled testily, "Well, get up then and get dressed. Guess I'll have to drop you off at your folks' again." Then as he swore angrily, he swung his feet out of bed and padded over to his dresser, yanked open the top drawer, and removed a pair of socks. Tersely he informed her that he would be working late every night that week and wouldn't feel like taking care of her when he got home. "So pack some clothes. Your mama can take care of you."

Reaching for the handkerchief lying on her nightstand and smothering a coughing fit, Louise nodded wretchedly before dragging herself out of bed and around the room, gathering the items she would need. Her head felt so fuzzy she could hardly concentrate.

Thirty minutes later, T.J. dropped her off at the curb and drove on down the street without so much as a backward glance as she shakily made it up the steps of the apartment house.

Upon opening the door at Louise's timid knock, Lilly took one look at her daughter and gasped, "Oh Louise. You've got another one of your sore throats, don't you," before ushering her inside and folding her in her arms.

Louise nodded miserably as she burrowed her face into her mother's neck.

"Well, come on. I'll put you in Edna's bed and then I'll ask Mrs. Higgins to call the doctor."

Louise was so thankful to have her mother there to care for her, as she snuggled down into the familiar covers on the bed she had shared with her sister for so many years.

With a weak smile, she watched her mother fussing and flitting around the room as she brought Louise items to help her feel better while they waited for the doctor to make a house call. They knew they were very lucky that the doctor would accept payments, adding his fee onto T.J.'s bill.

The thought of that gave Louise a tiny bit of pleasure in the midst of her misery.

ꙮ

SATURDAY AFTERNOON TWO weeks after coming down with her latest episode of illness, Louise ventured outside to attend to some errands. Spring had arrived, along with warmer temperatures, of which she was especially glad. It meant being able to go outside and get some fresh air now and then without having to be afraid of coming down with a relapse – something she very much did not want to do.

Walking slowly along, window-shopping and daydreaming, she glanced forward and was pleasantly surprised to see two friendly faces walking toward her from the opposite direction.

"Fleet! Alec!" she squealed, rushing forward and colliding into Fleet's arms as her friend met her halfway. Alec laughed at Fleet's exuberance and reached the pair just as they separated. Overjoyed to see Vic's best friend again, Louise flung herself against him and wrapped her arms around his neck in greeting.

"Wow girl, long time no see," Fleet crooned when Louise stepped back.

"Oh I know! I was beginning to think I'd never see you again!" Louise gushed, a happy grin plastered across her face. A hundred questions filled her mind and she felt close to bursting with curiosity. Both Fleet and Alec looked wonderful, and very happy. Alec was well dressed, with creased pants and a nice dress shirt – he seemed...calmer, less boyish somehow. Fleet looked radiant. Louise noticed she had fixed her hair a bit differently...pulled back on one side with a pearl comb, and she was wearing the smart red and white outfit she had worn the day they had all gone to Fontaine Ferry.

Reaching out to take her friends by the hands, Louise glanced down and immediately noticed a gold band nestled next to a diamond crowned ring, adorning fleet's finger.

"Oh my gosh! Did you guys get married?" she gasped, looking wide-eyed from one to the other as they exchanged amused glances.

"Sure did. Would you believe this crazy gal talked me into marryin' her on Valentine's Day?" Alec confessed with his trademarked laugh. The two exchanged a meaningful gaze that seemed full of private history. Alec grinned and winked at his wife.

"Valentine's? Oh goodness...I wish I'd have known...I wish I could have come..." Louise murmured, the joy in seeing them again dimming just a bit as she realized how much she had missed. "Who was your maid of honor? Where was the wedding? Who was your best ma…" she queried, stopping short on the last question and meeting Alec's eyes.

"Ruth and Earl stood up with us, and we got married in that chapel over in Jeffersonville," Fleet answered carefully, feeling the pinch of the unspoken questions everyone was trying to hold back.

Louise nodded, unconsciously lifting a hand to her chest attempting to still her suddenly racing heart. *Should she ask? Would they tell her?*

"Ruth and Earl? That's good… How are they?" she asked instead, beginning to feel a bit woozy, as it was the first time she had ventured out after her most recent case of tonsillitis. Her thundering heart seemed to zap her small store of energy. Stepping sideways a few paces in order to avoid the direct rays of the sun, she wiped her forehead with the back of her hand.

"Hey…you alright?" Alec asked, instantly concerned at the sight of her suddenly pale countenance.

Fleet drew near, obviously worried. "You don't look so good…you been sick?"

Louise nodded as she reached inside her pocketbook and took out her handkerchief to wipe her perspiring face. "Been having a lot of sore throats again."

"Oh man, that's lousy," Fleet hummed, exchanging glances with her husband. They both wondered if what they were witnessing was more than just physical weakness.

Suddenly tears threatened, and Louise looked up into her friend's eyes. "I'm sorry I've been so out of touch…at first, Mama and Daddy wouldn't let me go anywhere but school…then T.J. wouldn't bring me over to the old neighborhood…I…" she paused, clamping her lips shut and turning her face away.

"Aw honey…we understood…" Fleet began, as her husband soothed, "Your brother told me what happened…" Louise looked back up, tears overflowing past her lashes as she met

Alec's eyes. She couldn't wait a second more. She had to know...

"How is he?" she asked softly. More than once, she had wondered how Vic had taken the news of her marriage. Knowing how many times in his life he had been hurt and disappointed by those who had professed to love him, it tore at her soul that she had unintentionally joined those ranks.

Alec exchanged another glance with his wife, wondering what to tell Louise. Truthfully, Alec had been quite miffed toward the girl who had broken his best friend's heart...but now that he had seen her again, he could tell immediately that her life wasn't the least bit happy. His heart softened and he smiled gently.

"He's okay. He's doin' pretty good in the C's this time. They made him a crew boss and he gets to order a bunch of seventeen-year-olds around," he tried to joke.

Louise strived to giggle through her tears, but it came out in more of a strangled gasp. Then after a struggling moment, the dam seemed to burst and she cried out, "Oh Alec! I made such a mess of things! If only I'd seen his letter! If only I'd waited...or tried to get word to one of you...or hadn't felt so sorry for myself! I...I miss him so much..." she cried as both of her friends wrapped her in their arms. Fleet's eyes filled with tears as she laid her cheek against Louise's hair and tried to whisper words that she thought might calm her. Alec closed his eyes, fighting the same malady as he remembered his best friend's melt down when he had broken the news to him.

Against Alec's now dampened shirt front, Louise mumbled, "I've never stopped loving him, Alec...never. And I never will!"

It was quite some time before Louise was able to get hold of her emotions long enough to pull back and wipe the tears from her face. For the next few minutes, the threesome shared details of one another's lives since the last time they had all been together and happy. That night of the K.C. dance seemed so long ago.

Then with the promise to keep in touch, and with the assurance that they would let Vic know that she had asked after him, the friends went their separate ways.

ꙮ

SUMMER ARRIVED AND seemed to drag on, hot and muggy. It was miserable for everyone, as it seemed that life in the city had been reduced to just trying to survive the long days and even longer nights. Sleeping with the windows open didn't help much at all, as it only let in uncomfortably warm air and mosquitoes, unless you were lucky enough to have screens on your windows.

The situation did not improve between T.J. and Louise. In fact, after the unexpected meeting with Fleet and Alec, Louise seemed to retreat more and more into a moody shell. T.J. found other places to go after work – and Louise wondered if those places included dins of 'iniquity'. Truthfully, however, she didn't much care.

Edna had become involved with a young Filipino man by the name of Gene that she had met when he had come into the delicatessen where she was working. On the spur of the moment and against her parents' wishes, they had gotten married in a quickie ceremony at the courthouse downtown. Willis and Lilly refused to attend the wedding, leaving it to the groom's brother and sister-in-law to be their witnesses. However, Lilly did consent to give them a small reception afterwards, though she fussed the whole time that now two of her daughters had married, but neither in a church wedding.

T.J. grudgingly agreed to attend the reception, although he made excuses and insisted that they leave early. That had resulted in their most ferocious fight to date, after which he had slammed out of the apartment and headed off to who knows where, and not returning until nearly dawn.

Louise was glad to see him go. Alone in their apartment, she switched on their radio for some company, and decided to indulge in her secret pastime – reminiscing.

Opening the drawer in her bureau where she kept her under clothes, she removed the treasured jewelry box she had won that magical night of the K.C. dance. Retrieving the key from another drawer, she carefully unlocked the box and lay down on the bed. The mirror inside the cover reflected the soft light in the room as she slowly opened the lid and carefully lowered it back onto the hobnail bedspread. For Louise, this was like stepping inside of a dream world, where she could shut out her miserable existence for a little while as she transported herself back in time, holding the cherished objects.

One by one, she removed the items from her 'treasure chest'…ticket stubs from the amusement park and the two dances she had gone to with Vic…the clipping of the story with Vic's photo from the newspaper during the flood, which read, "Hometown Heroes Save Six Lives."…her copy of the picture of her and Vic engaged in a passionate kiss…a blue velvet bow she had worn in her hair during the play…a Derby pin Vic had given her from the day he worked at the track…one of the 1801 quarters that Vic had given her from his treasure stash… the white knight figurine he had won her at Fontaine Ferry… the velvet box in which her beloved amethyst necklace had been housed… and finally the letter Vic had written where he had told her of his plans, proposed, and asked her to wait for him to return.

She picked up the last item and stared at the envelope, where *To Louise, From Vic,* was written in Vic's distinctive left-handed script, and then reverently brought it to her lips. Pressing a soft kiss to its surface, she imagined she could still detect a bit of his scent on the paper.

With tears welling in her eyes, she oh-so-carefully removed the two pieces of treasured paper and read each word, slowly and lovingly as she held the amethyst pendant to her lips… His sweet apology for 'reacting like a jerk', his admission that she was always on his mind, his revelation that he was going away to join the C's again, the treasured three words *I love you* that she had dreamed of hearing, along with his proposal of marriage. And finally, his salutation – All my love forever…

At that moment, as if by cosmic design, the radio announcer's nasally voice began to introduce the next song he would play. Louise's heart sped up and somehow she knew what it would be before he had even said the words, and the familiar strains of *Once in A While* began to softly fill the room…

Lifting the newspaper clipping with the picture of Vic smiling proudly with his crew, she stared at it, wishing she could make him come alive and step into her universe.

Oh Vic…I miss you so much…do you think of me…do you miss me as much as I miss you? Are we destined to spend the rest of our lives like this, because of my stupid choice? Wherever you are right now, tonight, I wish you could hear me tell you how much I love you. I pray that somehow, some way, things could be different. If God is merciful…

Pressing the letter and picture to her chest, a miserable Louise curled herself into a ball on her bed and once again cried herself to sleep. Then waking in the wee hours of the morning to the sounds of T.J. cursing loudly as he struggled to get his key to work in the outside door downstairs, she scrambled to place the items back in the box and hide it away again before he stumbled drunkenly up the steps and into the apartment. Managing to feign sleep, she was ever so grateful when he began snoring almost immediately after falling into bed.

Not for the first time, she lay there wondering if this was how the rest of her life was going to be…or if God would punish her very badly if she should somehow find a way to escape. She began to make plans…

However, as fall's cooler temperatures began to turn the leaves into the breathtaking shades of red, gold, and orange, Louise once again came down with the dreaded infection in her tonsils. For her husband, it was the last straw on the camel's back, as he had been undergoing more and more stress and aggravation in his work and his life. When she hesitantly informed him of her news upon his return from work that evening, he erupted in anger.

"Great! Just what we need! More bills – and more time of you staying over at your parents' place!"

Louise had dissolved in tears. "I'm *sorry!*" I don't get sick on purpose, you know!"

"Well, why DO you, then?" he bellowed, running a hand through his hair in aggravation.

"I don't know! But you getting mad at me doesn't help anything," she fired back, resulting in a round of coughing and a dash to the bathroom.

When she returned to their rooms, he was staring into the open refrigerator, looking vainly for something he could make himself for supper, since his wife hadn't felt like cooking or cleaning all day. He cast an angry look at her as she slipped, shaking with fever, into the bed and pulled the covers up to her chin.

"Might as well tell you now…we got too many bills and I ain't making enough money. The rent's past due and the landlady wants us out." He neglected to mention the many and various ways he had been wasting money of late.

"What?" Louise had choked, levering herself up on one elbow. "Why didn't you tell me we were having trouble?" she demanded, hating that he always seem to spring bad news on her like this.

"Because I'm the *man* and I take care of the *business*," he snapped. Angrily taking a container of leftover soup from the icebox, he unceremoniously dumped the contents into a pot and flipped on the stove's burner.

She stared at him, her eyes clearly showing her hurt and anger. "So what are we gonna do then?"

"Mom and Dad said we could stay with them until we get

back on our feet," he grumbled, hating the feeling of 'crawling back home with his tail between his legs'. Louise sighed miserably, and lowered herself back down under the covers, her high fever causing her to shiver in spite of the warmth of the steam-heated room. She hated the thought of moving in with T.J.'s family, in the big home they had rented for them and their six kids – including the snotty and hateful Helen and the aggravating Rory. Louise knew she would never have another minute to herself, and that T.J.'s mother would be forever sticking her nose in their business.

A few minutes went by while T.J. retrieved a bowl and a glass as he made preparations for eating his supper. Glancing her way and seeing tears of misery silently trailing from his wife's closed eyes, and softening just a bit, he mumbled, "You want anything?"

She shook her head. The mere thought of food made her feel sicker.

He nodded and went about his actions. Then after a few minutes, he mumbled, "I'll take you over to your mom's in the morning, and this weekend I'll get our stuff moved to Mom and Dad's place."

With a despondent moan, Louise rolled over and covered her head, wondering if things could get any worse.

ꕥ

"OH HONEY, COME here," Lilly crooned as she opened the door to T.J.'s knock. He had actually parked the car and walked Louise to the door for once, perhaps feeling guilty over how he had griped at her the previous evening.

Lilly opened her arms as she had done so many times before, allowing Louise to shuffle into them as T.J. placed her bag of necessities on the floor just inside the threshold.

"Gotta run. Hope you get better soon," he added. Reaching out to lay a hand awkwardly against Louise's back for a second before nodding to Lilly in what amounted to thanking her for caring for his wife, he then disappeared out the door and down the hall.

"I'm sorry, Mama," Louise whispered. "I wish I didn't get sick so much…and I don't know what I'd do without *you*!" she added, dissolving into miserable tears.

"There, there, I know, child," Lilly soothed, leading her stricken daughter into the bedroom and helping her to take off her sweater and shoes and get settled in the bed. "Good thing we decided to keep the extra bed in here," she mumbled as she fussed with the covers, drawing them up to Louise's chin. "Edna and that husband of hers didn't need it, since they mostly stay in hotels or boarding houses. I still can't believe she married a traveling salesman!" she added with a sniff of disapproval.

"How are they doing?" Louise croaked tiredly.

"I suppose they're fine. I don't exactly hear from her much, except when she needs a few dollars."

"How's Sonny doing?" Louise whispered as she scooted over and made room for her mother to sit.

For a moment, Lilly's countenance brightened as she thought of her wonderful son.

"He's well. He likes the camp, and his new friends there, and says their commanding officer is fair. And oh my, I don't have to tell you how much the regular money coming in has helped around here," she added, leaning to get a feel of Louise's hot forehead. "My lands, child, you're burning up."

Getting up, she made her way out to the kitchen and soon returned with a wet cloth, which felt wonderful against Louise's fevered skin and helped to ease the tonsillitis headache she'd been plagued with since she woke up.

Louise relaxed a tad, enjoying the bit of comfort. "I'm still surprised you really let him join the CCC's…I know you must worry about him and miss him."

Lilly pursed her lips thoughtfully. "Yes, I do…but as your

father always reminds me, Sonny's a man now. He's eighteen and he can take care of himself. I guess he proved that back during the crisis," she admitted as Louise nodded. "And he writes us regularly, so that helps."

Louise smiled, thinking of the letters she had also received from her brother. He wrote such wonderful letters; always full of interesting and funny things that were happening at the camp they had sent him to in Virginia.

Suddenly, Louise was hit with a coughing fit, and her mother fretted and hovered until her daughter could finally settle back against the pillows.

"No more talking now, you just lay there and try to rest. I'll get the doctor," Lilly murmured as she headed toward the door. "Surely something can be done to stop these attacks."

While Lilly was downstairs, Louise lay there on her childhood bed in her old room, allowing her eyes to wander over familiar pieces of furniture and pictures on the wall. Her fever quite high, everything seemed to be tinged with a red hue, although she knew that was just an effect of her condition. *Oh I wish I could turn back the clock and still be living here, with people who care about me,* she lamented, wondering if sickness, misery, and unhappiness would always be her lot in life. *I won't think about that right now, I've got to concentrate on getting over this sore throat,* she determined as her eyes slowly closed in fatigue. The next thing she knew, the doctor was bending over her and examining her throat.

Lilly had been right, something certainly needed to be done. Once that current bout of infection subsided, the doctor insisted that Louise have the offending organs removed, assuring her that she would feel much better once they were gone. He even hinted that the poison from her often-infected tonsils could be the reason she had not become pregnant. Upon hearing that, T.J.'s father insisted that she have them removed and graciously agreed to pay for the procedure. Privately, however, Louise figured that was less about wanting to care for her and more about helping to begin the production of grandchildren.

The surgery was a horrible experience for Louise. The doctor insisted it would amount to 'nothing' and performed the job in his office. However, as he had begun to clamp the diseased organs for removal, they had practically disintegrated and he had been forced to give Louise round after round of ether to keep her sedated.

By the time it was over, her throat was extremely raw and T.J. once again insisted that she recuperate at her parents' apartment. Her mother took special care of her throughout the ordeal, even purchasing special malted shakes to feed her daughter – the only thing Louise could swallow while her throat healed.

The time spent during her convalescence was a happy interlude in an otherwise bleak existence for the young woman.

ꙮ

THREE MONTHS LATER, in the converted attic room she shared with her husband, Louise lay on the bed listening to him scream obscenities from the room on the first floor. In frustration, she clamped her hands over her ears, trying to block out the sounds.

Her husband's behavior had degenerated into a disturbing pendulum. One moment he was verbally lashing out at her over the smallest things. Then the next, he was attempting to be 'romantic' as he tried his best to seduce her into submission so that he could assuage his manly needs. She avoided both extremes at all costs, but of necessity at times found herself with no other recourse than to submit to his overtures. During those times, she would lay motionless beneath him as he had his way, with her eyes closed, waiting until he was finished. T.J. never failed to tell her that she was the most unexciting 'lay' he had ever had, which hurt, but at the same time, she wasn't about to try and change his opinion. Over the months of their marriage, she had drifted farther and farther toward active dislike and even hatred of the man to whom she was married.

His bizarre behavior of late had not changed her opinion. She had overheard his parents discussing their son one night and thereby learned that T.J. had been fired from his job, and they were worried that he was exhibiting 'symptoms' of some unnamed mental malady. There was no doubt about the concern in their voices. Obviously a family secret, it didn't make Louise feel secure, or warm and loving toward her husband. On the contrary, it generated an uneasy fear.

Days before, he had had a sort of mental breakdown and Mr. Blankenbaker had confined him to bed – thankfully downstairs in the master bedroom. The father, himself, was tending to his son. Louise wondered if that was due to T.J.'s wild outbursts, which perhaps rendered his mother unable to control him. Louise was staying as far away from him as she possibly could and had begun to make plans to escape the house and seek refuge with her parents, even if only temporarily.

Now her heart skipped a beat as she heard footsteps on the stairs coming up to her room. They wanted her for something. Swallowing nervously, she looked toward the door as she heard a brisk knock.

"Come in," she called softly.

The door opened and Mr. Blankenbaker stuck his head inside.

"Young lady, you need to come downstairs and tend to your husband," the old man announced without preamble.

Louise's eyes opened wide, her brow furrowing. "*Tend* to him? What do you mean?"

The man allowed his eyes to rake over her form as she reclined on the bed, causing her to unconsciously shift positions and sit up, crossing her arms over her middle.

"I mean – my son has confided to me that you have been…rather lax in your conjugal duties toward him. I'm convinced that is a large part of the reason for his current breakdown…"

Shocked that he had blamed her, it took Louise a moment to register his words. Clamping her mouth for a moment and staring at him, she murmured, "*Current* breakdown? Are you saying he's done this before?"

The man scowled at his mistake and came further into the room. Reaching the bed, he leaned down and grasped Louise roughly by the wrist, pulling her to her feet. "Never mind that, missy. Your place is downstairs, with your husband, not up here mooning over another man and committing mental adultery."

Louise yanked her wrist from his hold. "NO! I'm *not* going down there. The last time I got near T.J., he reached out and grabbed me, and bit my arm! He's acting crazy! And I don't want to be anywhere near him."

"I say you *will*," the old man insisted, trying to grab her arm again, but she twisted away and scooted over to put a chair between them.

"No I won't! Because…because I'm not taking any chances on anything happening to my baby!"

The old man's eyes nearly bugged out of his head as he gasped, "Your *baby*? You're pregnant?"

Louise clamped her lips for a moment, standing up straight and proud. Looking him directly in the eye, she declared. "Yes."

"Well, this is the first I've heard of it. When did you find out?" he demanded, turning his head slightly toward the door, as if calculating how the news would affect things with the other members of the family.

"Mama took me to the doctor yesterday. I'm six weeks along. And I'm NOT going anywhere near T.J. – until he gets over whatever this is and starts acting normal again!"

The two stared at one another, and the old man could tell Louise meant every word she said. But…he felt sure the news would help his son's current problem.

Finally he nodded and relaxed his stance. "Very well. I'll inform the family."

With that, he turned and went out, shutting the door after him.

Left to her thoughts, Louise realized that the thing that she had hoped would never happen had occurred, but she wasn't as upset about it as she thought she'd be. Once she had confirmed her suspicions as to why she had been sick every morning for two weeks in a row, she had begun to think about the baby she was carrying inside her. It was *her* baby, as well as his, and a love was already growing within her heart for the tiny person.

Her only regret was that it wasn't Vic's child. But…that couldn't be helped.

ജ❧ജ

CHAPTER 28

For Vic, Life Must Go On

"WELL, VIC, I'LL say it again, I hate to see you go," Major Connors remarked as Vic sat across from him in the chair he had occupied many times over the previous two years. Only once or twice for some slight infraction; most of the time, it was for Major Connors to tell Vic what a good job he was doing.

The major thought back over the months, picturing how Vic, one of his top men, seemed to naturally take charge of a situation and keep the younger enlistees in line. He had stopped fights before they raged out of hand, and comforted young men, boys really, who found themselves homesick for family in New York, or Florida, the West Coast, or wherever they had come from. He had watched Vic and the camp's only enlistee of color, Floyd Grimes, become close friends, and had witnessed several instances of Vic taking up for his friend or setting things straight. The younger enlistees had soon learned the ropes and it hadn't taken long before those things were in the past and Floyd was considered as what he was, a decent hardworking young man and valuable part of the team.

Sitting across the desk, Major Connors noticed how Vic unconsciously rubbed the scarred end of the finger that had been damaged in the accident, and he wondered if the digit still caused him pain. That had been a traumatic incident for them all, and one of the worst accidents anyone in his camp had suffered, as the major prided himself on running a camp with safety as its top priority.

The subject of suffering brought his mind back to how he had tried to comfort and advise Vic after the incident regarding the news from back home about his girl. The major truly cared for his 'boys' and strove to make sure their time in his camp was a good experience in every way. Seeing how the young man had grieved so brokenheartedly at the loss of his girl had weighed heavy on the major's kind heart.

"I'll miss it here," Vic admitted with a sad smile. He had grown close to his commanding officer and felt about him much the same as he did about Doc; the men were very similar in age and temperament. *That's probably why we got on so well,* he mused. Vic had a great amount of respect for the major, and the way he ran Beaver Ridge with a firm, but caring hand. For those, and many more reasons, Vic knew he would benefit the rest of his life from his experiences during those two years of his enlistment.

He was also thinking back on all of the times he had watched with admiration and respect as the major had dealt with one problem or another, such as early on when a seemingly inevitable argument had ensued regarding race and heritage.

"There'll be none of that kind of talk in my camp," the major had sternly ordered when he happened to overhear rather rude comments being banded about in the barracks. Vic happened to catch the incident as he was returning from the showers.

"But Major…sir…we shouldn't have to share space with the likes of…" Gary, the enlistee that Vic had had trouble with on his first night, sneered.

The major had quickly raised a hand to silence the young man's outburst, and then uttered quietly, "Enders, I have found over the years that when a person feels the way you seem to, it is because either he has been taught to think that way, or he is just ignorant of the fact that we are all human and all equal." He then proceeded to assign teams for the following week, pairing Gary with Floyd and two other young men, who happened to be of Italian and Polish descent. He then dropped the teams off on survival missions to the far reaches of the camp's acreage, with instructions to help each other survive. Taking no provisions, they had to rely on one another and make it as a unit. Each young man brought to the team his own expertise in various fields, and by the end of the week they had developed a respect for one another.

Although Beaver Ridge had been relatively free of trouble or dissention after that, the few times incidents had occurred, the Major had handled himself and the situation with the utmost professionalism and wisdom. All of the enlistees knew they were lucky to serve under such a man.

"What are your plans once you get to Evansville?" the major asked as he relaxed into his high-backed leather desk chair.

Vic pressed his lips together as he fought the heavy feeling he'd had for the last several weeks. To think…he had once envisioned going home to Louisville…seeing Louise again…picturing her running to him and throwing herself into his arms as he stepped off the bus. Now, he merely shrugged and emitted a soft sigh. "I don't know yet, sir. Take one day at a time, I guess. Maybe see what jobs are there…maybe head out west…" He shrugged again and murmured, "I dunno."

Major Connors nodded, pursing his lips thoughtfully, as he seemed to weigh his words. Finally, he offered gently, "Vic…I know that the plans you had when you first signed up have…fallen through. And…I know it seems like the future has practically no meaning…" he paused, holding back the words, '*Without a certain young lady*'. "However, none of us know why certain things happen in our lives…only the Good Lord knows. But…things have a way of working themselves out. Each of our lives is made up of a succession of seasons…seasons of happiness, seasons of trouble…seasons of plenty, and seasons of need. What makes or breaks a person is how they roll with the punches and go on, keeping a positive attitude through the bad times, looking for the silver lining in every cloud, and seeking out happiness where they find it. You never know…something good can be right around the corner."

Vic's lips moved into his customary half smile as he nodded, thinking that at this point in his life, his season of happiness seemed like it was always just out of his reach – and the ever illusive 'corner' was actually a revolving door with no end.

Nevertheless, he murmured respectfully, "Thank you, sir. I'll remember that."

The major gave a quick nod, satisfied that he had done his best to encourage his young friend, as he reached to open a file. From it, he extracted a piece of paper and leaned across the desk, handing it to Vic.

"I've taken the liberty of writing you a recommendation letter. Feel free to give my name and contact information to any prospective employers. I'll be sure and sing your praises," he added with a grin.

Vic smiled as he reached out to take the letter, quickly scanning the neatly typed missive. His grin grew larger as he read the glowing accolades the major had poured out. With a soft snicker, he switched his eyes back up to connect with his superior. "Thank you, sir. I hope I can live up to this."

"I have confidence that you will," the Major laughed as he rose to his feet, extending his hand across the desk as Vic also stood. Passing the letter to his left hand, Vic stuck out his right and the two men grasped hands, eyes locked for a moment.

"You're a good man, Victor Matthews. You've got skill, and talent, and the drive to make something of yourself. I wish you all the best," the major murmured sincerely. "Drop me a line now and then and let me know how you're doing."

"I will, sir," Vic replied, wishing at that moment that he could stay at the camp forever. He had felt needed and accepted there, and an important part of the team. Now, he was very much heading out into unknown territory. That was never a pleasant feeling, and one Vic particularly hated, as it always took him back to the many times in his past when he had been forced into a sudden and traumatic shift of circumstances.

On his way back to the barracks for the last time, to pick up his belongings and await his transport into town, he gazed around at the large encampment that had been his home for twenty-four months.

There stood the new mess hall they had built when the first one burned down – that had been a frightening night, and a miracle that the other structures had not burned as well. Images rose in his mind of being awakened in the middle of the night by yells of, "The mess hall's on fire! Somebody man the pump! Get a bucket brigade going! You there, wet down that building there so it don't catch fire too!" Within moments, every man in the camp had vaulted from their bunks and joined the fight to prevent a major catastrophe. Vic smirked with a soft snort as he remembered hearing later that the cause was found to have been a faulty strip of lights on the mess hall's Christmas tree, which someone had carelessly left on. What a Christmas it would have been had the whole camp burned down – but thankfully they had received a Christmas miracle in the form of a heavy few minutes of snow and sleet, which helped to extinguish the fire.

As Vic passed the new fire tower…he thought about the day that past winter when a black dog had wandered into the camp and had immediately become his shadow. One of the fellows had even taken a picture of him with the animal, crouching together at the base of the tower with piles of snow all around. In a way, the dog, which Vic had named 'Sparky', had helped to fill at least a part of the void in his heart, and had helped him to emotionally survive the long snowy winter. Sparky had stayed until spring, and then just as he had appeared, one day he was gone, never to return.

The buildings, hills, trees, and surroundings were now so familiar to Vic. He had hiked nearly every inch of the acreage, and had spent quite a bit of his free time up at 'his' place. Thinking of it then, he ducked into the barracks to carefully stow the recommendation letter, and then headed off into the woods one last time.

As he came through the trees and the familiar vista spread out before him, he breathed in the cool, fresh air, filling his lungs one more time with the serenity the place emitted. Over the months, several of the other young men had stumbled upon the lookout, but between them, they had worked out sort of an unspoken agreement to share it and not encroach on one another's space.

Lowering himself down, he allowed his legs to swing free over the side of the cliff, his eyes slowly panning across the landscape as he unconsciously committed every detail to memory…the hundreds of trees and bushes, just beginning to turn over into their fall colors…the sounds, a soothing combination of profound silence, and the soft musical sounds of nature with the gentle flow of the water 130 feet below…the clean, fresh scent of the rocks, trees, and open sky…the white fluffy clouds overhead, seeming as if they were barely moving…as if time itself slowed down to a relaxed pace up there on his cliff.

Thinking over the months, a funny thought came to mind as he allowed a soft chuckle, remembering the time he had deemed to take Floyd up to his special place – and his friend had balked and stepped back away from the edge, his eyes as big as saucers.

"No suh! I ain't gettin' neah that!" he had blustered from ten feet away.

Vic had laughed, motioning for him to come closer, but Floyd had steadfastly shaken his head, backing up another step. Vic had realized then that his friend suffered from a fear of heights. No big shame, lots of men felt the same way.

Floyd, who had assigned himself the job of watchdog and encourager after Vic had confided in him about his devastation over Louise, had never again tried to follow his pal when he would go off by himself to brood and think.

Floyd…Vic smiled fondly, missing his companion. Floyd's two years had been up a week before, and they had said their goodbyes. In some ways, Floyd had become an even closer friend than Alec, and it had been a difficult parting. Exchanging addresses so they could keep in touch, Floyd had boarded the transport to town to catch a bus back to Alabama, leaving Vic to wonder if they would ever see one another again…

And then, thoughts of his lost love crept into his consciousness. Once again, he wished he could show her this magical place. He wondered what she was doing at that moment, and if she thought of him…*once in a while*… He wondered if she had found happiness with her…*husband*… That word was still enough to make him grit his teeth…

From the letters he had received from Alec and even from Irene, he was under the strong impression that Louise was decidedly *unhappy*, and not for the first time, he entertained thoughts of slipping into town and whisking her away. But, he knew that wouldn't be right. Still…Alec and Fleet had hinted that even Louise, herself, was leaning toward the possibility that she wouldn't stay married to *him* 'till death do them part'. Vic felt like a tethered racehorse and had to fight the urge to take the bus to Louisville instead of Evansville. Perhaps he could go with the pretense of visiting the gang…

Finally, knowing that he needed to get back so that he wouldn't miss his bus, Vic sighed deeply as he climbed to his feet and took one last long look. He hoped he could one day come back…or at least find another place that would provide him with as much solace.

Turning, he began the trek down through the woods for the last time.

ഗ്ര

WHEN THE BUS pulled into the terminal on Sycamore Street in Evansville, Vic gazed for a moment at the shiny new building.

Built by the bus line in 1939, its pleasant blue color and Art Modern style, with the company's image – racing greyhound dogs – gracing the top, gave the whole area a fresh, prosperous feel.

Smiling, Vic spotted his brother and sister-in-law standing off to one side. They waved when they saw him. Goldie had even made a sign that read, "Welcome Home Vic!"

Reaching up to grab his duffle bag – a newer, larger one issued by the C's – he made his way off the bus.

"Hey there, stranger!" Al greeted as Vic reached them. Vic dropped his bag on the ground and shook his brother's hand, and then hugged Goldie.

"Hey. Whew, I'm glad to get off and stretch my legs."

"I bet," Goldie responded, reaching up to smooth his close-cropped hair – regulation length for the CCC. "Where's all your wavy locks, hmm?"

Vic chuckled and ran a hand back through his recent haircut. "On the barber floor," he quipped with a dimpled grin.

"Well, you look healthy and fit…and like the C's were good for you…" Al commented, noticing a decidedly more mature appearance to his youngest brother.

"Yeah, it was alright," Vic nodded, looking around at the other passengers disembarking and heading off to their destinations.

"Well, come on, let's go home. I've fixed a big pot of stew and a chocolate cake for your coming home meal," Goldie crooned, turning to hook one arm in her husband's and one in Vic's.

He leaned down to grab his duffle. "Sounds good to me. Ridin' for miles like that always make me hungry."

"Seems I remember you're *always* hungry," his brother teased.

All three laughed comfortably as they began the walk back to the apartment.

ꕥ

"HERE YOU GO, Vic," Goldie said with a grin as she handed him a small brown bank deposit booklet first thing upon walking in the door.

He took it and smiled broadly, feeling as if he had hit the jackpot – or won the Derby. The front read, The Old National Bank, Evansville, IN. A line beneath that had been filled in by hand with his name – Victor Herbert Matthews. Carefully, he opened the cover and read the date in October of 1938 when the first deposit of thirty-five dollars had been noted in ink. Subsequent forty-dollar deposits were added each month, and Vic quickly flipped the pages to see the balance written at the last entry – including interest, it was over a thousand dollars. Speechless, he was now thinking he knew what millionaires must feel like when they survey their wealth. He had never had so much money in his life. And to think – it was his to do with as he wished!

He glanced up, his eyes twinkling as they met Goldie's shining blue eyes.

"Every cent accounted for," she assured softly.

"You guys coulda took some out for expenses…" he began, but Al interrupted.

"Nope. After all that crap happened with Jack and Liz, we were determined you were not going to be cheated out of your rightful pay this time. They really dealt you a raw deal last time and I want you to know, I let him have it over that. I don't care he's the oldest in the family, what they did wasn't right. Nope, it's all yours, brother."

Goldie giggled softly as she watched Vic in rapt concentration as he ran his finger down the pages over each entry in the little book as if he were feeling the very money itself.

"What are you going to do with it? Have you made any plans?" she asked gently.

For a moment, his countenance dimmed just a bit as he thought again of his plans that had fallen through. He pursed his lips in a tiny pout and shrugged.

"Don't know. Been thinkin' and thinkin' and tryin' to make plans, but…I keep comin' up with nothin'. Maybe…maybe buy myself a car…or take a vacation," he added, half joking.

"That's an idea," his brother agreed as they moved on into the apartment. "You always said you wanted to see Florida and the ocean. Be a good time to go, before winter sets in."

"Aww, ain't no fun travelin' alone," Vic responded with a shrug.

Al chuckled. "Oh, I think we might be persuaded to join you, if you were in a mind for some company. I always wanted to see Florida myself," he added with a grin.

Vic opened his duffle bag then and rummaged around a bit. Finally drawing out two clumsily wrapped packages, he handed one to his brother and the other to his sister-in-law.

"What's this?" Goldie asked as she took the item. "You didn't have to…"

"I know I didn't," he interrupted. "But, I want you guys to know how much I appreciate what you did…and standin' by me all this time. It…it means a lot," he added sincerely.

Al opened the paper wrapping on his gift to find a hand crafted pipe, the bowl of which was carved into the shape of an Indian chief's headdress. The workmanship was quite detailed.

"Wow, this is something! Where'd you find such a thing?" Al exclaimed as he closely examined the piece.

Vic smiled, pleased at his brother's reaction. "There's an old man who makes these in that little town near the camp. Kind of a hobby, I guess. But he sells one now and then, mostly to people traveling through. Figured you might like it…that is if you can stand to give up the cigs," he teased, knowing his older brother's three-pack-a-day cigarette habit.

Al laughed at that. "We'll see." Then flashing a grateful smile at his brother for having thought to buy him a gift, he added, "Thanks."

Vic nodded and turned to Goldie as she finished unwrapping her gift, a beautiful, enamel decorated compact, with a gold tone metal mesh base. The lid was dark green with a central cartouche featuring a romantic couple in old-fashioned dress. She gasped at the beauty of the object, carefully opening the push up catch on the front edge to reveal a circular mirror on the lid's inside. The case was empty, and ready to be filled with her favorite powder foundation.

She raised joyous eyes to his. "Oh Vic…thank you. I love it!"

Vic grinned and nodded, bending to give her a kiss on the cheek. "Glad ya like it," he murmured softly as he pulled back and watched her run her fingers gently over the decoration on the lid.

"Oh I do! I'll treasure this always. You're such a sweetheart," she added fondly, leaning over to show her husband her new treasure.

"I asked the lady that runs the little mercantile in Dana if she knew somethin' I could get for ya, and she had some catalogs…so I ordered it – all the way from New York," he added proudly, glad that he apparently had chosen right. "I knew green was your favorite color…right?" he added, watching as she nodded and brought the item up to her cheek.

"It's lovely. I almost don't want to use it and get it dirty," she added with a laugh.

A few minutes later, they sat down at the table as Goldie began serving up steaming bowls of fragrant beef stew, and Al mentioned casually, "I thought you might want to make a trip to Louisville…" he paused as Vic's eyes quickly met his. "I mean, you know…visit your pals…and that Doc fella…and that Miss Irene…"

"Oh that reminds me, a letter came for you last week. We didn't forward it on since you were getting out so soon," Goldie shared, walking into another room and retrieving the envelope.

She handed it to Vic and he saw at once it was from Irene. His heart sped up, as he had hinted to her in his last letter a hope that she would try to check on Louise for him, and to see if she could determine the state of 'things'. Quickly he tore open the envelope and read the words she had written, his feeling of hope slowly turning to one of resignation.

After a few moments, he sighed deeply and carefully stuffed the letter back in the envelope, sitting for a moment just staring straight ahead.

"What is it, Vic?" Goldie quietly murmured.

Vic shook his head, a soft whispered snort escaping as he silently chastised himself.

Pursing his lips in a disgusted pout, he admitted, "Well…I might as well tell ya. I'd been thinkin' about goin' back to Louisville…cause I'd heard that Louise…well, she ain't exactly happy with that jerk she married…"

"Oh Vic!" Goldie gasped softly. "It wouldn't be right to come between a husband and wife like that…"

"And man…didn't she dump you…?" Al pointed out softly.

Vic shrugged, "That's a long story…she didn't get my letter 'till it was too late…" Then taking a deep breath, he went on, his voice gaining a certain edge, "But it don't matter now anyway. I say, let's take that trip to Florida. Might as well get some fun outta life, right? Maybe I'll buy me a car with what's left."

Goldie exchanged glances with her husband. Reaching out, she laid a hand gently on her brother-in-law's arm.

"What's happened, Vic? What did the letter say?"

Clamping his lips together, still reeling from the news Irene had imparted, as gently as she could, in her letter, Vic softly sneered, "Louise is stayin' with her husband now for sure. Seems she had a baby a few months back."

The words left a bitter taste in Vic's mouth.

At that moment, he would have given his right arm if Louise's baby could have been his.

PART IV
THE TURNING POINT

ℵ

CHAPTER 29

The Devastating Surprise

March 1941

NINETEEN-YEAR-OLD LOUISE STARED out the window of the bus, contemplating that the miles seemed to be rolling slowly by like the days, weeks and months of her life. Endless fields still brown from the long winter seemed to stretch on and on. Houses scattered along the route only made her wonder about the people living there. Were they as unhappy as she? Or did they have love, laughter, and fun as part of their daily routine…

The child in her arms stirred in his sleep and she glanced down at him, adjusting her position and his to make him more comfortable. Her little boy, Thomas Joseph Blankenbaker, Jr., was the one breath of fresh air in Louise's life.

Slightly flushed from sleep, his sweet face was turned toward hers. *He's such an angel…* She smiled softly, lifting a hand to ever so gently smooth a few strands of light brown hair on his forehead.

Louise studied his features. Nearly two years old now, he greatly resembled his father, having inherited his blue eyes and light brown hair. However, she knew little Tommy favored her in other ways – his gentleness, the way he warmed up to people quickly, the cowlick in his hairline…

That brought to mind another cowlick…on a head of dark brown wavy hair…above the most beautiful set of warm brown eyes…

With a sigh, Louise determinedly turned her gaze back out the window and purposely set her thoughts on other things.

She reflected about her parents and younger brother moving to Bowling Green when Willis received the surprise invitation of a job as Machine Shop foreman at the company that had laid him off. She smiled softly as she remembered his twinkling eyes behind his wire rim glasses as he chuckled that the college boy they had hired must not have worked out. It was like a dream come true and it meant more money than he had been making before. After much consideration – and since Edna, Sonny and Louise were married and starting families of their own – they decided that Lilly and fifteen-year-old Billy would go with him.

That had been a sad day for Louise, watching her parents and younger brother pack their things and move away. It had made her loneliness all the more acute.

But, at least it's not so far that I can't go to see them, like Edna living in New York, Louise mused, thinking over the enjoyable two weeks she was just returning from with her family.

She had arrived at the Bowling Green terminal and eagerly lugged her suitcase and child into the waiting arms of her grinning father. Willis had relieved her of both burdens after a warm hug and kiss, before ushering her quickly toward his surprise – he had purchased his first automobile. Although it was only a 1931 Ford Model A Tudor, with slightly dented fenders, several rusted areas, and quite dull paint, he was proud of it, as well as relieved that there was one less aggravation for his wife to stew about.

It had been so good to see her parents and brother living their lives happily content, although her mother did fuss quite a bit about having to live in Bowling Green. Over those two weeks, Louise never found out the exact reasons for Lilly's displeasure, but at least the majority of the time had been spent in getting reacquainted with her family, and for them getting to know their grandson and nephew. The two weeks had flown by with family dinners, a trip to the movies, and hours of relaxation, which was a break from the norm. She had truly not wanted to return to her life back home.

Although she wasn't totally devoid of family in Louisville, as Sonny was still there, that situation wasn't ideal as far as Louise was concerned. Owing to his expert salesmanship, Sonny had settled into a job selling advertising space for the newspaper, and married a girl he had met through a friend. They were expecting their first child soon. Louise unconsciously made a face when she thought about Sonny's wife, Sarah. Though she was lovely, with honey blonde hair and soft blue eyes, there was a hard edge to her personality that was difficult to pinpoint. Privately, Louise thought of her as the 'Ice Queen', as she was a cold, uppity person – at least to the rest of the family – but she doted on Sonny. Indeed, she had succeeded, in the short time they'd been married, to successfully keep Sonny from regular contact with the others. Louise resented how Sarah seemed to regard their family as 'trash'.

Shaking her head to clear those thoughts out, Louise focused on a more pleasant subject, her friends from the old gang. She occasionally saw Ruth and Earl at the local grocer, which was always a happy meeting. When she had last seen Fleet, she had stopped by the apartment to tell Louise the joyful news that she was going to have a baby. Since Louise hadn't seen her since then, as T.J. still complained loudly and rudely if her friends visited, she now wondered how Fleet was doing, and if she'd had the baby yet. Surely they would let her know...

Thinking of T.J.'s contrary ways, Louise sighed again. Closing her eyes, she laid her head back against the seat and her cheek against the crown of little Tommy's head. She pictured their apartment, and the furniture her husband had insisted on buying – on credit – when they moved in. He'd been so excited to get it 'for her,' or so he said. Although that was fine, as they had never until that point had much in the way of furniture and nice things, the fact that they owed a large payment each month meant that he could use that as another excuse to keep from giving Louise any money. It also provided him with yet another reason not to take her out dancing, or out to eat, or to buy new clothes for her and Tommy. Resentment bubbled in her chest and she pressed her lips together in an unconscious show of displeasure.

"He's been so good on this trip," a voice crooned softly, bringing Louise out of her brooding thoughts.

Louise opened her eyes and smiled at the older woman in the next seat. "Yes…but he's always good. I'm very lucky," she whispered back.

The woman smiled and lowered her gaze to Tommy's head, and then to the necklace around Louise's neck.

"That's a lovely amethyst you have there," she murmured, still keeping her voice soft so they wouldn't awaken the sleeping child.

Louise smiled again, reaching her free hand up to lovingly touch the treasured piece of jewelry, as she had thousands of times before. She rarely took the cherished memento off. Truly, the only time had been when she'd been in the hospital after having Tommy. "Thank you…it was a gift," she added.

"From your husband?" the woman asked innocently, noting that Louise was wearing a wedding band.

Louise's eyes darkened at that and she shook her head. "No…from someone I used to know," she answered, stopping herself from saying the words she longed to say…*from the man I love.*

The lady nodded, her attention returning to the reading material in her hands, which happened to be a well worn, leather bound Bible.

As usual, it didn't take much to sway Louise's thoughts to Vic, and now images of him swam before her eyes. She saw him as he had smiled and handed her the velvet box the necklace had been in – and the expression in his eyes, as if he were holding his breath until he found out if she liked his choice of a gift. She allowed herself to relive when he leaned in and touched his lips to hers, and felt a tiny bit of the sparks that always occurred between them.

Fighting the oppressing feeling that her life resembled a prison sentence, she glanced over at her seatmate, noticing how she seemed to be quite engrossed in her reading. Louise could see there were notes in the margins, bookmarks in several places, and the tip of a small writing pad protruded out at the back. *This lady must really know the Bible…and God…* Without preamble, Louise spoke what she was thinking.

"How long do you think God punishes a person…when they do wrong? Years? Or are you punished for the rest of your life?"

The woman's lips parted and she turned her head, seeing the seriousness of the question in the younger woman's eyes. She also saw a load of hurt and despair.

Placing a bookmark between the pages, the woman closed the Bible and sat for a moment, thinking how to formulate an answer. Finally, she said softly, "Well, honey…I think that depends on many things, like on our asking for, and receiving His forgiveness *within ourselves.* I think people make rash decisions, which have consequences, and then blame God for those consequences…"

Pausing a moment when she noticed Louise's eyes react, the woman smiled gently, reaching over to pat her seatmate's hand in a motherly fashion. "Honey…my name is Irene. May I know yours?"

Louise smiled, feeling oddly at ease around the older lady. "I'm Louise. And…and this is my little boy, Tommy."

Irene nodded, striving not to show her surprise at meeting up with the girl that her young friend Vic had loved…and still did. She knew it was the same girl…by a picture he had once shown her, and by the necklace Vic had told her about… Irene knew that this must be what some called a 'divine appointment', and she offered a quick silent prayer that she would use wisdom and care in answering the young woman's questions.

Irene smiled and patted her hand again. "I'm very pleased to meet you, Louise. Now, to finish answering your question… I believe that once we have asked God's forgiveness, like the Bible says, 'He is faithful and just to forgive us of our sins, and to cleanse us from all unrighteousness'. Then, as we begin to live as close to His ways as we can, He can begin to bless us in many ways, even amidst circumstances that we created…even if it was by our own poor choices."

Louise pondered that for a few minutes. Lately, things in her life did seem to be looking up. She thought back to the time immediately after Tommy's birth, which had been a grueling two-day affair that had left her wondering several times if she would even live through it. She had spent some time praying and thanking God for giving her such a precious little son, and she had even, in a roundabout way, asked Him to forgive her for all of the things she had done wrong. But…was that enough? She asked Irene as much.

The wise lady smiled understandingly, knowing far more about Louise's life than the girl knew…but the older woman held back on telling her that she was familiar with her history. "The key is to choose to believe what the Bible teaches. It is our roadmap for life. It contains the story of God's love for us, and His rules for healthy living. He has rules, but He doesn't *make* us follow them. He wants us to obey Him out of our love for Him. We make wrong choices and mistakes, but, He's always there, ready to step in when we ask for His help."

Louise thought about this for a moment. No one had ever told her anything about God *loving* her – it was always about Him being up there ready to mete out punishment for the slightest infraction.

They continued on with their discussion, still talking in soft tones so as not to wake the slumbering child. In this way, the rest of the two-hour bus ride flew by quicker than either of them wished.

✽

WHEN THE BUS pulled into the Louisville terminal, Louise turned to Irene.

"Thank you for talking with me. I do feel better now. And…I think I'm going to try that little church up the street on Sunday," she added with a shy smile.

Irene grinned and leaned to take the young girl in her arms for a moment, encompassing little Tommy, who had awakened and charmed the kind new friend with his shy smile and adorable giggle – and his big blue eyes. When Irene pulled back, she paused for only a second, feeling impressed to open her Bible to the small notebook inside the back cover and jot down a few words. Tearing off the end, she pressed the slip of paper into Louise's hand. "Here's my address. If you ever need a friend…"

Louise nodded and slipped the note into her purse. Bidding Irene goodbye, she reached up to retrieve her luggage from the compartment overhead.

Making her way down the steps of the bus, carefully holding onto Tommy, she looked around for T.J., but he was nowhere in sight. *Hmm, that's odd. He said he'd pick me up…I hope he got my telegram of when my bus would arrive…* Louise mused as she glanced around. Threading her way through the throngs of people, she found a comfortable place to sit and wait.

Trying to pass the time, she thought back to how surprisingly sweet T.J.'s mother, Beatrice, had been to her the day she had left for her trip, and how T.J. had obligingly offered to allow her to go for a visit to see her mom and dad. He had even gone so far as to pay for the tickets. *Maybe things are getting better…I just need to look for the good, I guess.*

However, after thirty minutes, Tommy was beginning to get fussy and Louise was starting to feel a twinge of apprehension, leading her to approach a taxi and ask the driver if he would take her to the apartment and let her pay him there. He agreed.

Louise did her best to comfort her now fretting child during the trip. She couldn't wait to get home, take off her traveling outfit, and relax. Sam, the taxi driver, was a kindly older gentleman with wisps of gray hair visible beneath the shiny bill of his cap. He reminded Louise a tiny bit of her father, and he kept up a friendly conversation as they rode along, politely asking about her trip, and regaling her with funny stories.

Finally, they turned onto her street. She asked the driver to wait, left her suitcase in the cab, and walked to the door. Trying the doorknob, she found it was locked, so she maneuvered Tommy to one hip and knocked on the door. Expecting T.J. to come out, pay the driver, and retrieve her suitcase, she was already planning on the earful she would give him for forgetting to pick her up. However, after several minutes, no one came. Louise's uneasiness was worsening by the second.

Holding onto a squirming Tommy, Louise clumsily dug through her purse for her key. When she put it into the lock, she was flabbergasted when it did not fit! *What is going on here?* She felt like she was living a bad dream. A strong feeling of foreboding began to creep up her spine.

"What's the matter, missy? Can't get in?" the driver called from the cab.

She turned and shook her head, panicked tears beginning to fill her eyes. Tommy began to wail as he felt the fear in his mother. *Where is T.J.?* Stepping aside to a front window, she shaded her eyes and tried to see inside, quickly making the shocking discovery that the room appeared to be completely devoid of furniture!

In desperation, she hurried to the taxi and asked the driver if he would take her several streets over to her in-law's house. Nodding, he climbed out and hurried to assist her into the car with her now wailing, wriggling child.

"Sshh, honey. It's okay, sweetheart," Louise whispered, rocking and trying to comfort him when she, herself, also needed comfort. Her heart was hammering, and her stomach was a coil of nerves.

At the Blankenbaker's home, Louise climbed out and again asked the driver to wait. He nodded again, although now concerned. Something didn't feel right, even to him.

Louise mounted the steps and knocked on the door, balancing Tommy on one hip. Breathing in deeply to try and calm her nerves, she was glad that his wailing had been reduced to shuddering sniffles.

In a few moments, the door opened a crack and Beatrice glared out at her daughter-in-law. "What do *you* want?" the woman snapped.

Taken totally aback, Louise stammered, "I…I just got home, but…my key doesn't work…T.J. isn't home. Do you know where he is?"

Her mother-in-law raked her eyes down Louise's body and back up, as if looking at a tramp, and not her own daughter-in-law whom she had so sweetly helped pack and get ready for her trip just a mere two weeks before. The woman barely even looked at Tommy, her own grandson. Puffing herself up to her full height, she declared in a haughty voice, "T.J.'s not here, and I don't know where he is. The best thing for you to do is to go on down to your brother's."

"But…" Louise started to argue, but the woman shut the door in her face.

In shock, Louise turned slowly, tears spilling from her eyes. *This can't be happening. I must be having a nightmare. Why can't I wake up? Where is my husband???*

Sam the cabbie had turned off the meter when they pulled up. He had watched the frosty reception the young mother had received from a woman she had confided was her mother-in-law, so he opened his door and got out of the car. Walking up to Louise, he asked gently, "Is there somewhere else I can take you, Miss?"

Shuddering and holding on to her emotions by a thread, Louise swallowed and brought up a hand to swipe at the moisture on her face. Hugging Tommy to her tighter, she remembered Beatrice had mentioned the word 'brother', and so answered, "I'm sorry, but can you take me over to First Street to my brother's apartment?"

Without a word, the man inclined his head affirmatively and escorted the distraught young woman with her child back to his cab. As he moved to shut the door after they were settled in, he happened to glance up at the house to see the hateful expression on the face of the woman glaring out at them. She immediately dropped the curtain when she saw him looking. Old Sam wondered what kind of people this sweet young lady was mixed up with.

Shaking his head, he made his way around to his door.

*

"I DON'T UNDERSTAND, where would T.J. have gone?" Sarah, Sonny's wife, sighed as she stood stirring a pot of bean soup at the stove. Pressing one hand against the small of her back, she watched as her sister-in-law positioned pillows securely around an exhausted Tommy, whom she had placed on the couch for a nap. "And you said it looked as if all of your furniture was gone? Do you think…could somebody have stolen it?"

Louise turned and made her way back to the table, sinking wearily into a chair next to her concerned brother. "I just don't know," she murmured, shaking her head. "The lock had been changed. But, I can't figure out why Beatrice acted like she was mad at me…she'd been so nice the day she helped me pack to go see Mama and Daddy…and where is T.J.? The last time I heard from him, he said he would pick me up at the station. I hope nothing has happened to him. But…if that were the case, his mother would know… Oh, I just don't know!" she fumed, smoothing her hair back and rubbing a hand over the back of her neck. Her entire body felt wound as tight as a drum from the emotional pressure.

Sonny, thoroughly disgusted with the entire business, pushed back from the table and muttered, "All of this stinks to high heaven. I'm goin' over there and see what I can find out."

Louise caught his hand and looked up at him. "Thanks, Sonny. I hope you have better luck than I did."

Smiling fondly, he leaned down and gave her a kiss on the cheek. "Be back in a while." Then, he circled the table and gave his wife a kiss as well.

"Be careful…those people seem crazy," Sarah warned with a touch of derision.

The young women watched him go, and then Louise stood up and made her way to the stove. "Is there anything I can help you do?" she asked softly.

"No, I got it. Thanks," Sarah replied. The two women felt slightly uncomfortable together without Sonny's presence as a buffer.

Louise nodded mutely, scrambling for something to say. "Sarah…I'm sorry to bring all this here…I just didn't know where else to go… I appreciate you letting me stay until I find out…" she stumbled to a halt. *Find out what? Where my husband is? If I still have a home? What the heck is happening?*

Sarah gave her sister-in-law a tiny smile. "That's okay, Louise. Um…here you can set the table. Hopefully Sonny'll be back while the soup is still hot," she added with just a slight edge to her voice.

Sighing, Louise meekly began placing bowls on the table, at once hoping Sonny would come back with answers…but also afraid of what he might find out.

ജ്ഞ

"I CAN'T BELIEVE it!" Louise gasped when Sonny had finished relating the incredible tale he had managed to glean from one of T.J.'s younger brothers, whom he had happened to catch walking down the street near the Blankenbaker's house.

"Me neither. I never heard of such a thing, but I don't think his brother would make it all up, do you?" He queried, glancing up at his wife as she placed a bowl of soup in the center of the placemat where he was sitting.

"No…Keith has usually been pretty nice to me…" Louise murmured as she stared straight ahead, mouth agape. "And his brother said T.J. sold everything to buy some woman *what*?"

"A diamond ring and a fur coat," Sonny reiterated, shaking his head in disgust.

Suddenly, a thought occurred to Louise and her eyes opened wide, "But…if the landlord has already changed the locks…what about my clothes…my things…Tommy's things?"

Sonny drew in a breath, hating to unload more onto his sister, *but it can't be helped, thanks to her no-good husband.* "I'm not sure about the rest of your things, but…Keith said Tommy's baby bed is…right inside the front door in their living room."

Louise's mouth dropped open in realization, anger now superseding her earlier bewilderment. "Do you mean to tell me…that woman talked to me *that* hateful, glaring at me like she hated me – me standing there holding her only grandchild – and his baby bed was right there behind the *door*?" she ground out incredulously.

"That's about the size of it," Sonny acknowledged. Then with a sneer, he added, "Some nice family you hooked up with, Louise."

"Well…it wasn't *my* idea! I…" Louise reacted animatedly, but Sonny quickly interrupted, laying a calming hand on her arm. "I know, I know. Relax, don't get your feathers ruffled."

"Hey," Louise suddenly sobered as another thought occurred. "Isn't what he did illegal? I mean, he was making payments on the furniture…"

Sonny nodded, swallowing a bite of his dinner and reaching to take a sip of iced tea. "Yep, sure is. Maybe the law'll get after him."

Louise narrowed eyes that contained twinkles of mischief. "I hope they *do.* It'll serve him right." Again she shook her head in amazement, thinking about all that had transpired in only two short weeks. She remembered again how sweet he had been in the weeks preceding her departing for her trip. They had even…gotten *friendly* several times and she had begun to feel a small amount of affection for him. After all, he could be quite charming when he tried – the trouble was, with *her,* he never seemed to care to try. And his mother…coming over to the apartment on the pretext of helping her get ready for her trip, saying she would miss Louise and Tommy. What was *that* all about? Had T.J. been planning this – and had she known about it? *Does she hate me that much? But…why?*

Louise pondered long and hard, but the only thing that made any amount of sense was the fact that T.J. had always been a 'Mama's boy' and he could do no wrong in Beatrice's eyes. He could always talk her into anything. *I wonder what he told her to get her to go along with this? I guess he made me out to be the villain. I'm a terrible wife, yada yada. But, that still doesn't excuse her treating her grandson like that!*

Thinking about the entire fiasco was starting to give Louise a raging headache and she reached up to rub her temples, mumbling, "If it's okay…I think I'll lay down on the couch awhile. I'm not feeling too good."

The couple exchanged glances, with the wife's expression revealing her dissatisfaction with the whole situation. However, for the time being, there wasn't much they could do to change it.

Louise noticed the quick look exchanged between her brother and his wife and she added quietly, "I'll…I'll try to find some place for Tommy and me to go, don't worry."

Sarah touched her husband's arm, as if to remind him of something, and he cleared his throat and spoke up, "Um, sis…if you want I can give you the money for bus fare to go back down to Bowling Green…"

Louise sighed wearily. Although it wasn't an ideal solution, as her mother and father only had a small apartment, it was better than nothing…*if*, that is, they would allow her to stay there for an extended period. Suddenly overcome with the sad turn her life had taken, she raised her hands to cover her face and dissolved into tears, mumbling through her fingers, "Oh, what a lousy, stinking mess!"

Indeed, all three mused, as the old saying went – *When it rains, it pours.*

ജ്ഞ

CHAPTER 30

The Last Straw

LOUISE BENT DOWN to retrieve the last diaper from the basket and with a tired sigh, pinned it to the line. Swiping the back of her hand across her forehead, she briefly wondered why she felt so hot, and even a bit nauseous, since there was a nice breeze blowing.

Making her way over to the two chairs near the back door of the apartment house, in which she was temporarily staying with her parents and brother in Bowling Green, she sank down into one, grateful for a few minutes respite. Tommy had gone down for a nap a little while before.

Slouching down in the old heavy metal lawn chair, she laid her head back and closed her eyes against the mid-day sun. Letting out a heavy sigh, she wondered, for what must have been the hundredth time in the last month, what she was going to do.

As if reciting the details once again would make things clearer, she allowed her thoughts to wander back. With Sonny's help, she had managed to retrieve most of hers and Tommy's personal items from her former landlord, which she had squeezed into several old suitcases her brother had purchased for her down at Larry's Pawn Shop. *Thank God for Sonny!* Louise reflected, as her older brother had surely been her knight in shining armor throughout the whole ordeal.

The bus ride back to Bowling Green had been uneventful.

However, her parents' odd reactions when they picked her and the baby up at the terminal had caused her some pause. Although her father had welcomed her with sympathetic arms, her mother seemed distant, avoiding the offer of a hug. Picturing that moment, Louise snorted softly, thinking that Edna would have said, "Mama sure had her nose out of joint," but Louise didn't know why.

Willis had proceeded to let her know in no uncertain terms what he thought of T.J. for treating his sweet daughter in such a way; furthermore revealing that he had never held much store in any of those Blanketyblanks. That had given Louise a chuckle, and took a bit of the sting out of Lilly's frostiness. *At least Billy and Daddy were glad to see me,* she mused.

T.J. had not tried to contact her, other than a one sentence note with three dollars inside, for Tommy's 'support'. *Wow, Generous George,* Louise had grumbled upon receiving the tiny offering. Her mother had begun hounding her to start proceedings in order to make him pay child support…but all Louise could think was *where will I get the money for a lawyer?* Everything appeared to be so complicated and everywhere she turned, doors just seemed to be slammed in her face.

Over the weeks, Lilly seized every chance she could to make Louise feel as if it was *her* fault, and that she should do everything possible to salvage her marriage. "But Mama, he left me for somebody else!" Louise would argue, but Lilly would brush it aside with a flick of her hand and a crisp, "Nevertheless." As a result, Louise spent most of her time feeling miserable and confused. She did wonder at one point where God was in the whole ball of wax, and like that nice lady, Irene, had encouraged, she had tried to pray for help.

So far, it didn't seem as if the Big Guy in the Sky was listening.

Suddenly, the squeak of the screen door interrupted her brooding thoughts. Louise turned her head and opened her eyes a slit to see her mother step out the door with a dust mop in her hands, proceeding to give it an overly vigorous shaking.

Training her eyes on her daughter, Lilly sneered, "Are you going to just sit there on your behind all day, or are you going to do some work? Children don't take care of themselves, you know. They take *work*, and lots of it!"

Hurt at yet another unprovoked attack, Louise's cup instantaneously overflowed. Sitting up, she replied heatedly, "Why are you treating me like this, Mama? You act like its all my fault, but…"

Her mother cut her off immediately, stepping near and accusing, "You told me yourself that you hadn't been a good wife to T.J. A man expects a good meal when he gets home from work, and his wife is expected to perform her duty to him any time he needs…"

"I DID Mama!" Louise countered, her voice raised louder than she had ever spoken to her mother. "I *was* doing those things, in spite of T' giving me hardly any money to buy the food with or run the house with! He only started being generous right before he shipped me off to here so he could run around with that floozy! He never bought *me* a fur coat or a diamond ring!" she added for good measure. "Why are you on his side against me?!"

The emotions of both mother and daughter had risen exponentially. Lilly clamped her mouth shut as she glared at her daughter, but Louise glared right back, tired of feeling like the villain in a ten cent novel.

"Tell me, Mama! Tell me why you hate me so much!" the daughter demanded of the mother.

Lilly's mouth opened and closed like a beached fish for a moment, then she stuttered, "I…I…that's ridiculous! I don't hate you…" Then moments later, Louise saw a tiny crack begin in the mask Lilly always wore for the public. As she watched, her mother seemed to wilt before she wobbled the few steps to the other chair, dropping down as if in defeat. With tears forming in her eyes, she whispered, "Oh child…there are so many things you don't know…so many things I've never told you, never told *anyone.*"

Louise's brow furrowed, confused at this unexpected change of attitude from her normally stoic parent. Still breathing fast, her adrenaline pumping furiously, Louise strove to calm herself down.

Finally, she asked gingerly, "What…what things, Mama?" She wondered if this had anything to do with the vague hints Lilly had given her on numerous occasions that there had been some kind of secret in her mother's past.

Lilly was staring at her hands, which were fidgeting in her lap, before she reached to bring up an edge of her apron to dab at her eyes. She knew it was long overdue that she should confide in her daughter, although just the thought of revealing her secret past gave her great pain and stung her pride. As she and Louise were alone in the house, she convinced herself that the occasion had presented itself. The other tenants were at work and Billy was at school, eliminating any further excuses.

Venturing to meet her daughter's eyes, she saw the yearning for answers within and she realized she had, indeed, been treating Louise terribly of late. It wasn't easy to admit that years of heartache had twisted her personality and caused her to lash out at those she loved. With a shuddering breath, she whispered, "I…I was…married before, to a man before your father. He was…the youngest son of the family that owned the Distillery in Bardstown where my father worked. His…his name was Archie," she admitted haltingly. "He…he was lazy and good for nothing…we had two children together…your half brother and sister…Jake and Maribel…"

Louise's eyes grew large and she murmured, "I have another sister and brother?" She was dumbfounded, and wondered why she had never met these two siblings…*Why had Mama and Daddy never even mentioned them?*

Lilly went on, numbly, "You must understand…I was raised

in a strict Catholic home, and divorce was expressly forbidden – for any reason. But…my husband drank, and when he drank, he became hateful and mean, and he would beat me and the children. I would take the brunt to spare them, but…one day I grew quite tired of that and decided he had beaten me for the last time. My…my mother and father refused to help me, afraid of the wrath of God, so I…I stole some money from Archie's wallet, packed some things, and persuaded a man I knew in the town to take me and the children all the way to Lexington." She stopped and met Louise's shocked gaze. "I didn't think it through. It was a foolish thing to do – I knew no one there and had no plans, and no skills other than keeping house…"

Louise flopped back in her chair, her heart pounding now with sympathetic emotion as she listened to this tale coming from her straight-laced mother. She had never had a clue such secrets had been lurking underneath Lilly's always perfectly coifed hair.

"When I arrived, what little money I had was used up quickly, and after many days of going without food in the boarding house where I had rented a room…I was desperate. So I…I bundled the children up and…asked the neighbor to take me in his wagon out to the county orphanage, where I…left them," Lilly admitted agonizingly. Shaking, her eyes spilling over with tears as she remembered that painful day, she dabbed at their corners and sniffled.

"You left them there?" Louise asked softly, striving to take in such monumental disclosures.

"Yes," Lilly defended sharply. "It was the only thing I could *do*…I couldn't even feed *myself*." She paused as if trying to decide how much of the story to impart. "Then I began to ask around for a housekeeping position, or perhaps that of a nanny, and I happened to meet someone who directed me…to your father."

Again, Louise's eyes widened. "Daddy?"

Lilly nodded, remembering back to those long ago and very difficult days. "Yes, Willis had an invalid wife. Her name was

Phoebe. She was bed ridden from some sort of accident many years before, when she was just a young woman, and they had never had any children. Willis…he had taken good care of her, hiring women to stay with her during the day while he worked. He had a well-paid job as a machinist. I…I moved in as his live-in housekeeper, and I took care of Phoebe. My plan was to eventually ask Willis if I could get the children out of the orphanage and bring them to live with me…but…somehow that never happened," she paused to dab the tears from her eyes.

Louise leaned forward, placing her hand over her mother's, which lay on the arm of the chair. "Why, Mama?" she whispered.

Lilly paused, murmuring, "I'm ashamed to say, I was afraid to tell him that I had been married. Father Phillip, the priest of the parish where I had been raised…he had drilled into our heads that divorce is such a terrible thing, he called it the unpardonable sin…" She stopped, thinking of the oft-repeated threat that if a person divorced, they would go to hell. Shaking her head as a chill ran down her spine, she continued on, "I was afraid Willis would turn me out if he knew…so I just kept putting it off…and somehow the years went by…"

"Then…" Lilly wavered again as the memory she was about to share brought a stab of pain so shameful and fiercely deep, it nearly took her breath away. Louise suddenly had a bad feeling that the information she was about to hear would be quite shocking. "Then…one day as I was walking back to the house from the market…a man…he…he forced me into an open doorway…I had foolishly taken a short cut through an alley…and he…" she winced, unable to make herself say the words, but the look of pain and mortification with which she met her daughter's eyes explained everything so succinctly.

"Oh Mama! He…he forced you…?" Louise spoke in hushed horror.

Lilly looked away and nodded, ashamed to her core. She had never shared that information with another living soul, except her gentle and understanding Willis…

"What happened then? Did you report him? Was he arrested?" Louise fired the questions, both angered at the terrible man and aching for the pain her mother had endured.

Lilly forced herself to glance back at Louise, and haltingly recited, "Nine months later…I had your sister…Edna Marie…" She waited a few moments for the unveiling to register, and when it did, Louise squealed, "Mama! Edna…Daddy isn't Edna's father?" *Good heavens!* "Does Edna know?"

Her mother inclined her head solemnly. "Yes…when she was about ten, she unfortunately overheard a private conversation between Willis and I and…and she reacted quite harshly. She ran away, and Willis had to search for her for hours before he found her, down by the river, sitting under a tree, crying. He brought her back home…but she seemed to harbor a seething anger toward us, toward all of us, from that point on…"

Louise thought about that, and remembered back to when she, herself, was only six years old and Edna had run away.

Lilly went on, "Phoebe died several months before Edna was born, and by that time, Willis had fallen in love with me. He very gallantly asked me to marry him…down on one knee, in fact…and, I accepted. And he has never treated Edna like she was anything but his own child," she added softly, truly grateful for her wise and loyal husband. "When we married, he moved us to Louisville, to take me away from the source of disgrace and the whispers of the neighbors. They assumed that Willis and I had…well…"

Louise bowed her head, asking gently. "But…what happened to Jake and Maribel?"

"I…they stayed in the orphanage. I had been housekeeper for Willis for twelve years, and by that time, both of the children were grown." Faltering for a moment as the familiar feelings of loss and sadness threatened, she added, "Sundays were my day off. Willis would be home watching over Phoebe and so I had my day free. He assumed I was indulging in a hobby or going to the library, but I would take the trolley out to spend the day with the children…"

Louise moved from the chair then to kneel by her mother's, laying her head in her lap like she used to do as a child. "Oh Mama…I'm sorry that happened to you. You went through so much…compared to this, my problems are small," she murmured tenderly.

Lilly closed her eyes, lovingly stroking Louise's hair back from her tear-stained face. Although the retelling of the facts of her past had been quite difficult, she did feel a bit better for having shared the burden…she just hoped she had done the right thing.

For Louise, it had been quite an eye-opener…and only enforced her unspoken belief that perhaps she was destined to never know true happiness…much, it seemed, as her mother.

That afternoon marked a turning point in the relationship between mother and daughter, forged by the sharing of a tragic past.

ꕥ

A WEEK AFTER her heart to heart conversation with Lilly, Louise was sitting on the front stoop of the apartment building, holding Tommy as they enjoyed a little bit of afternoon sunshine. Hearing a car turn the corner, she glanced over and recognized the Phaeton! Her heart speeding up with cautious dread, she watched as it pulled up to the curb. T.J. was behind the wheel…and he was alone.

Unsure about this development, Louise could only stare as he opened the door and got out, walking the short distance to her position. He looked neither glad to see her, nor adverse to it. It was as if he were devoid of feeling. Although he was dressed nicely, wearing a new, crisp shirt and creased pants she had never seen before, she noticed his eyes seemed bloodshot as if he hadn't been sleeping well. As she watched, his gaze darted around as if he were afraid of attack.

"Hey," he said as he drew near.

Tommy, recognizing his father, cooed happily and leaned forward, reaching out his little hands as he called, "Dada!" T.J. took him in his arms.

"Hey," Louise answered, wondering how she should react to this visit. She truly didn't know what she was feeling, except hurt and angry, although some of that had receded as the weeks had gone by.

The conversation between them, however, was forced and stilted.

"How you been?"

"Fine."

"That's good."

An awkward lull ensued as they both concentrated on Tommy for a moment.

"You get my note? And the cash?"

"Yes, I got it."

They wavered again, looking away uncomfortably.

"Look, uh, can we talk?" T.J. finally asked as he bounced his son in his arms before reaching into his pocket for his keys, which were something little Tommy always loved to play with and jingle. Glancing up at the doorway and spotting Lilly eavesdropping, he added, "Will you take a walk with me?"

Against her better judgment, Louise agreed, and rising from the stoop she brushed off the back of her dress. They strolled together down the street and across another to a small park where she had taken Tommy on occasion. Talking pleasantly as they went along, T.J. said all the right things and was generally the epitome of charm. He told her how he had missed her, how he would never again be untrue to her, that he wanted another chance, and how he couldn't stand to not be in little Tommy's life. He promised they would begin doing all of the things she had always wanted, things that were fun. Butter wouldn't have melted in his mouth he was so smooth and *sincere*. It reminded her of how he had been toward her in those early days of courting, and it all made Louise's head spin.

With the combination of his charisma and the fact that Louise had no where else to go, plus an added reason she hadn't even told her mother, she hesitantly agreed to go back with him to Louisville to attempt to put their marriage back together.

Upon returning to the apartment, however, he began hurrying Louise to pack both hers and Tommy's possessions, making the excuse that he needed to get back to Louisville quickly. As he stowed their things in the backseat and trunk of the car, Louise was forced to say a quick goodbye to her mother. It saddened her that her father was still at work and she wouldn't have a chance to bid him or her brother a proper goodbye.

Lilly hugged her daughter tightly, whispering in her ear, "If you're sure about this…it's probably for the best…"

Louise nodded stoically, fighting back tears as she allowed her mother to kiss and hug her grandson before turning to respond to T.J.'s urging that they needed to hurry. He barely met his mother-in-law's eyes as he mumbled a goodbye.

Curiously, once they were on the road T.J. seemed to retreat into himself and refused to engage in conversation. Louise didn't know what to make of that. Looking out the window, she contented herself with pointing out interesting things to Tommy, until, as toddlers do, he became bored and hungry and started to fuss.

"Can't you keep him quiet?" T.J. griped harshly, running a hand back through his hair in sudden agitation.

"He's hungry. And he's probably wet, too. You've gotta pull over…"

"I *ain't* pulling over. I told you, I gotta get back to town. Just shut him up," he ordered.

Staring at her husband's sulking profile, Louise asked incredulously, "What's *wrong* with you? You come all the way to Bowling Green to ask me to go back with you, and now you start acting like this! If this is the way..."

"I'm sorry," he cut her short. "I just got a lot on my mind."

Resentment came bubbling up full force and Louise turned fully toward her husband. They hadn't yet touched on the subject of what he had done, having merely danced around it. Now, unable to hold back, she blurted, "*Why'd* you do it, T'? You got any idea what you put me through? What you put *Tommy* through?"

T.J. had the grace to look ashamed, and he swallowed uncomfortably. "I'm *sorry.* I just...lost my head, I guess." He glanced at her and gripped the steering wheel in frustration. "I...I met this dame, she lived down in one of those mansions near the river...she was divorced...one thing led to another..." his story stalled as he met his wife's angry hazel eyes.

The pieces of the puzzle were starting to fall into place. "A *rich* lady...so you bought her a diamond and a fur, trying to impress her? What'd she do? Dump you once she found out you're not *rich*?"

By the look on his face, she knew she had scored.

"That's it, isn't it!" she shouted, causing Tommy to begin to cry. That only made T.J.'s annoyance worse.

"So, you come crawling back to me...why? So you won't have to pay child support? So you'll have somebody to cook and sew and wash for you? Lay down for you? Bear more kids for you? So you can keep me 'barefoot and pregnant'?!"

He looked over at her, seething, all pretense dropped. "People keep telling me to do the 'right thing'."

She nodded. "I *see,*" she commented over Tommy's cries.

"Shut him up, will ya?" T.J. barked harshly.

"I told you! Pull over so I can change him!"

Angrily, he pulled the car to the side of the two-lane road and waited while she took care of their son's needs and settled him in the back seat with several of his toys. In the interim, they both calmed down a bit, and as the trip resumed they tried to speak amicably with each other. Amicably, that is, until he mentioned that they would have to go back to living in the attic of his parent's rented house since he had given up the apartment and had gotten in trouble over the furniture loan. Louise immediately balked at that idea, not wishing to live under the same roof ever again with the horrible woman who was her mother-in-law.

Ten minutes outside of Louisville, the argument escalated again, with both of them this time screaming insults and accusations at the other, over the frightened squeals of their son.

"Well, you've never been much of a husband, always being so stingy with me, *and* with Tommy! Never taking me dancing or to the movies or anything!" she yelled at T.J., ragingly angry.

He bellowed right back, "*Me*?! You've never been a wife to me, always giving me excuses why you won't give me what's rightfully *mine!*"

"By all rights, I never should have been *yours*! I was *Vic's* girl, and you knew it!" she shrieked recklessly, beyond caring about diplomacy and the fact that in all of their time together, she had never uttered Vic's name in T.J.'s presence.

"*Vic*," he practically spat the name. "What a loser that guy was," he grunted, which was exactly the wrong thing to say.

Something inside of Louise rose up like a mother bear and her tiny bit of restraint snapped as she screamed in pure frustration. "Vic has more *character*, better looks, and more strength in his *pinky* finger than…than you have in your whole *body*!"

With that, T.J. quickly drew back his right hand as if he would backhand Louise across the mouth. She screeched and turned her face away, raising her arms to protect herself.

Barely stopping in time, he instead reached to grasp hold of the amethyst necklace that was always around his wife's neck – even in bed. She never took it off, and that fact had mocked him for years.

"Let go!" Louise cried out, clamping onto his hand with both of hers, terrified that he would succeed in breaking the chain and possibly tossing the whole thing out the window of the car.

"I ought to rip it off you – you think I don't know *he* gave it to you?"

"So what if he did!" she sneered rashly.

"You think I don't know about your 'treasure box' and all the junk you keep in there? That you take it out and drool over it every time I leave the apartment?" he snarled back. "Do you think I don't know you've *mooned* over him all the time you've been married to *me*? I ain't stupid!"

"So what if I do!" she erupted right back at him, bending her head and biting his hand, causing him to let go of the necklace with a shout of pain. "In my heart…in my heart I'm married to *him!* And I always will be!"

T.J. took his hands off the wheel and grabbed her arms to give her a good shaking, and she let out a piercing scream of terror as they nearly collided with a car going in the opposite direction, its panicked driver laying on the horn.

"That's it! I've had it up to *here* with you!" he exploded once he got the car back in line, both of them quivering in reaction to the close call and the terrible argument. Louise wiped away tears and rubbed her bruised arms as he raised his hands to heaven and growled, "What was I *thinking*? Who could live with a shrew like you?"

Stung and shaken, Louise reached into the back where she had secured Tommy and hauled him forward over the seat, pressing him against her chest and pounding heart as he continued to scream and cry in fear and confusion.

Just up ahead, T.J. saw a cabbie waiting for a fare, and to his way of thinking, the timing couldn't have been better. Making a quick decision, he hastily pulled over to the curb behind the cab.

Jumping out of the car, T.J. approached the driver and showed him a five-dollar bill. "Hey Mac, I'll give you this five spot if you help me with the lady's luggage and take her anywhere she wants to go, alright?" The man mumbled assent and climbed out, helping to transfer the items. In this way, T.J. made short work of ridding himself of Louise and the baby. Within a minute, he gunned the Phaeton's motor and roared away.

Once again, Louise was left with a baby and nowhere to go.

In the back of the taxi, feeling déjà vu, she sat shaking with residual emotion and swiping at her tears with nervous fingers. The driver stared at her expectantly, waiting for instructions and wondering about the volatile couple's story. Rummaging through her purse for a handkerchief, Louise came upon the note Irene had given to her on the bus weeks before.

Barely able to see through the torrent of tears, she opened it and read the hastily scrawled words:

What time I am afraid, I will trust in thee, Psalms 56:3.

Irene Waller, 513 S. 6th, Apt 1

Deciding quickly, she handed the paper to the driver and sat back in the seat to rock her still trembling and crying son – hoping this time she would receive a sincere welcome when she arrived as an unexpected guest.

She was hanging on to the tiny bit of fringe at the end of her rope.

ഇന്ദ

CHAPTER 31

Pushing Away the Memories

VIC HAD SETTLED in Evansville after he had finished his hitch in the CCC, staying for a while with his brother and sister-in-law until he had lucked into a good paying job driving a delivery van for Diamond Dry Cleaners, the largest dry cleaning service in town. Several months later, he had taken a room at Graham's Rooms for Let, idly passing the days and weeks in a comfortable routine of work and relaxation.

Comfortable yes, albeit a tad lonely. He missed the camaraderie he'd had with the guys in the C's – especially, of course, Floyd – and often wondered how his friend was getting along. He had tried writing several letters to the address Floyd had given him the day he boarded the bus for Alabama, but had never heard back. So, apart from an occasional date, or a night out shooting pool or maybe knocking down a few pins at the bowling alley with the guys he worked with at the plant, he spent most evenings whiling away the time listening to the radio in his room. He knew, however, that he needed to just move on with his life and try to find someone with whom he could share it.

One Friday night in May 1941, he found himself on a date at the Alhambra Theater with a lovely blue-eyed blonde by the name of Julie.

The small theater on Adams Avenue was packed with patrons giggling and erupting in guffaws over the antics of Bing Crosby,

Bob Hope, and Dorothy Lamour, the popular trio in the movie *Road to Singapore.* Vic and his date had barely found seats near the back when they had arrived with mere minutes to spare before show time.

He reached over to grab another handful of popcorn from the bag she was holding, as yet another song began; this time a solo by Lamour.

Something about the actress, probably the dark eyes and dark hair, reminded Vic of Louise. Although Lamour's singing voice was deeper, Vic wondered for a moment what the song would sound like if it were Louise singing…

Swearing under his breath, Vic impatiently upbraided himself as he realized his lost love had once again wormed her way into his thoughts. *I'll be glad when I'm finally free of her for good*, he silently grumbled.

Just then, Vic's date wrapped one hand around the generous bulk of his bicep and gave it a squeeze as she snuggled closer to him. He purposely turned his mind to concentrate on *her* and the film.

"I'm having such a good time," Julie whispered near his ear. "I love the movie."

"Yeah. It's great," he agreed, allowing his eyes to glide down from her neck to her chest, unable to help noticing the low-cut dress she had worn on their date. He had to admit, the girl was a looker, and she had made sure he knew she was keen on him. The pleasing fragrance of her perfume wafted up as she cuddled closer still. Crossing one leg over the other just then, she surreptitiously took his right hand and positioned it on her knee in a silent invitation for him to do whatever came to mind.

He thought about it. Julie was a good kisser and was known to be quite free with her favors. He had even come close to indulging on several of their dates, but something always stopped him. Something he couldn't quite put his finger on…it just didn't seem right. Thinking of the occasional ribbing he took from the other fellows at work when the 'guy talk' turned risqué and he purposefully didn't contribute, he gave a soft snort and short shake of his head. *Maybe I should just take what she's offerin'. A guy could do worse…*

Once again, Dorothy Lamour's image lit up the screen, and her dark beauty and sweet innocence immediately sidetracked his mind back to his long lost love. Louise, singing so beautifully as she lit up the stage… He unconsciously sighed in frustration. *Why won't she leave me alone?* Silently he wondered why he felt so restless, and had been feeling like that for weeks, like some big, ominous unknown, unseen *something* was hanging over his head.

"Don't you like the movie?" Julie asked, aware of her date's obvious preoccupation and silently acknowledging the fact that when they were out together, Vic was often distracted and quiet. Many times he just stared into space, the quintessential 'strong and silent type'.

Julie was a popular girl, and knew she was pretty – all the young men told her so. But she had set her sights on Vic Matthews from the moment he had first come to work, driving a truck for Diamond Dry Cleaners, where she was employed as one of the steam pressers. All the girls thought Vic was just the 'bee's knees' and vied for his attention. Yet, it was Julie who had finagled a date with him by pretending to be stranded at work one day and had appealed to the gentleman in him to take her home in his car. That had led to them going on a date…several, in fact. So far though, she hadn't been able to start his engines. Among themselves, the gals at Diamond's figured he was carrying a torch for some girl who broke his heart. None of them, however, had had the nerve to come right out and ask him.

"Yeah, it's fine," he murmured, striving to focus on the action.

"We can go see something else if you want…" she offered.

"No, really, it's fine…" he replied back, prompting their fellow moviegoers nearby to react with a chorus of, "Ssshhh!"

Embarrassed, they glanced around before settling down again to finish watching the film. It truly was funny, and Vic enjoyed himself. Then, he was the perfect gentleman to Julie on the way to take her home. He opened doors for her, made sure he was on the outside nearest traffic as they walked to the car, and made polite conversation all along the way.

Evansville wasn't a very large town, and it didn't take all that long to traverse the darkened streets to her apartment. Julie didn't want the night to be over, but she had a feeling this date would end like the others, chaste and sweet. This time, she decided to take the bull by the horns. When they reached her door, she turned, throwing herself into his arms. As guys would say, she 'really laid one on him.'

Encouraged that he was participating in the kiss, when she finally pulled back, she murmured languidly, "My roommates are both away for the weekend...you want to come in for some coffee...or a sandwich?"

This threw Vic into a quandary. In the soft glow of her porch light, he gazed down at her, contemplating how truly gorgeous she was. He knew any red-blooded male with even a spark of fire still left in the furnace would jump at the chance to take her up on her offer. Oh yes, he knew *what* she was really offering – and it was a heck of a lot more than coffee and a sandwich. He opened his mouth to agree, but at the last second, he stopped and closed his lips again, unable to take that final step. *I'm just...not ready. I'll know when it's the right time,* he assured himself, inwardly resenting the ever-present 'presence' of the girl back in Louisville.

Smiling softly, he reached up, gently grasping Julie's hands from either side of his head, and brought them down to cradle against his chest. "Not tonight, I'm...kinda tired. Been a long week," he murmured. "Thanks, anyway."

Searching his shadowed eyes for a long minute, weighing her options, Julie finally shrugged as she strove to hide her disappointment, and then whispered, "Sure."

"Goodnight," he mumbled with a relieved smile as he leaned in to give her one last, slow kiss before he turned to walk back to his car.

"She really hurt you…didn't she," Julie softly called to his back. He stopped, and then turned around slowly, meeting her eyes. His heart was suddenly thumping as if he had been caught with his hand in the till.

"Who?"

They stared at one another for a moment. Vic was uncomfortable, and felt as if he had suddenly been forced under the beam of a microscope.

"Whoever it was that ripped part of your heart out and left you bleeding."

He visibly winced, her words coming too close to the truth. Swallowing, he answered just above a whisper, "I guess you could say that. But it was a long time ago."

Julie took a step toward him, holding out her hand, palm up. "I've got bandages inside…and iodine…I'm a good nurse…I could fix what ails you, if you just give me a chance…"

Vic clamped his lips together in a pout, wishing it were that simple. If it were, he would have surgically removed Louise from his heart years before. In answer, he shook his head slowly from side to side.

"Thanks," he mumbled. "But… if its okay…I'd like to have a rain check…"

She smiled gently, thinking he really was a sweetheart – and the girl that broke his heart must not have a brain in her head. "Sure Vic. The offer'll always be open."

Then, inclining his head with a tiny smile, he turned to make his way back to the car, wondering if he needed to have his head examined.

༄༅

THE NEXT EVENING, Vic lay on his bed listening to a baseball game on the radio. The announcer's rich baritone voice expertly described a line drive straight down center field, allowing his listeners to truly picture the players running at top speed around the bases. Vic shut his eyes for a moment as he 'watched' in his mind.

It was a warm evening, the kind that leant to being lazy. With one hand behind his head, and the other holding a cigarette to his lips, Vic took a long draw and then opened his mouth in the form of an O to allow the smoke to escape. Moderately pleased with his 'skill', he watched as lazy circles floated smoothly forward.

Just as he was wondering if his landlady had finished preparing supper for her boarders yet, a knock suddenly sounded at his door.

Turning his head, he blew the rest of the smoke from his mouth. "Yeah?" he called through the closed portal.

"Matthews, you have a long distance call downstairs," the proprietor's voice informed him through the wooden panel.

Long distance? Vic pondered, wondering who would be telephoning him, and hoping it didn't spell some kind of trouble.

"Be right there," he called, turning to snuff the cigarette out in the ashtray on the nightstand. Swinging his legs over the side of the bed, he located his shoes and quickly stamped into them. Then pulling the door shut behind him, he made his way down the steps to the foyer where the telephone was situated on a table. The landlady, Althea Graham – a middle-aged widow who reminded him of an older version of Liz, his sister-in-law – stood holding the receiver, her face wearing her customary 'been sucking on a dill pickle' expression.

"They called *collect*," she announced without preamble, and without covering the mouthpiece. "I'm not running free long distance telephone service for my tenants…" she began, but he stopped her with a hand upraised. "I'll pay, Ms. Graham."

"Just see that you do," she grumbled as she handed him the

weighty black handset.

He waited for her to go on about her business, before he put the receiver up to his ear. "Hello?"

"Victor Matthews?" an operator's nasally voice answered.

"Yeah, that's me."

"I have a collect call from a Mr. Alec Alder. Will you accept the charges?"

"Yeah sure. Alec?" Vic spoke a bit louder into the phone, unconsciously making up for the distance between he and his friend on the other end of the line.

"Hey old man, how you been?" Alec crooned, emitting his trademark snicker.

Vic smiled at hearing the friendly, familiar voice and eased himself down in the chair next to the table. "Aw, fair to middlin'. Can't complain, you know. How 'bout you?"

"Same."

"Fleet okay? She popped that baby out yet?" Vic asked, figuring that was what the price of a phone call would be about.

"No, she's got a few weeks to go, yet," Alec informed, then laughed again, adding, "But she wishes it was out. Man, you should see her, she's big as the backend of the Idlewild."

Vic laughed. "Man, she hears you she'll skin you alive, you better watch out."

"Don't I know it!"

The long time friends laughed together and then paused, causing Vic to suddenly get the feeling that there was something else…some other reason for Alec to call; something that couldn't wait for the delay of a letter. His pulse started to speed up.

After another few moments, he heard Alec clear his throat. "Uh, Pal? I, uh…that is Fleet's been badgering me to…what I mean is…aaaah," Vic heard his friend swear under his breath and then come out with, "There's somethin' you might wanna know…"

Vic's heart jumped like a racehorse and he *knew* the subject was about to turn to Louise. He swallowed and moistened suddenly dry lips, managing to croak out, "What's that?"

"It's Louise. She…well her and her old man split up and believe it or not, she's staying with your friend Irene."

Vic drew in a deep breath, his brow furrowing as he thought about this development. *Irene?* He hadn't been aware that Miss Irene and Louise had ever actually met and he wondered what could have happened to orchestrate such an event. Clearing his throat, he murmured, "What brought this on?"

"I don't know for sure, man, but…that guy Lou's married to…word has it that he stepped out on her, and even bought some other dame a diamond ring with a stone big enough to choke a horse, and mink to boot. Fleet said Lou told her the jerk kicked her out of the car down on Main – with her little boy in her arms – and she had to take a cab." Swearing again, he added, "Always knew that joker was a no-good son of a…"

"Kicked her outta the car? Is she *all right*? And the baby?" Vic interrupted, instantly sitting forward on the chair and picturing the worst, that the guy opened the door and booted her out.

"Yeah, they're fine. But she's sayin'…she's not goin' back to him anymore…"

Vic lapsed into silence, realizing what Alec was saying. Louise was planning on getting a divorce…she would be free… However, he knew that she and her husband had broken up before and gotten back together again. Through Fleet and Alec, he had kept tabs on her over the months and years. Now, the wheels of his mind were spinning a hundred miles an hour.

Is this for real? Does this mean… Could it mean… Would she want to see me? Remembering the heavy feeling he had been experiencing of late, a cold chill passed through him as he realized he must have been tapping into her emotions over the last few weeks. The thought made him shake his head in awe. *How is that possible?*

"You *there*, Chief?" Alec murmured, knowing this information had probably just twisted his best friend up in knots.

"Yeah…I, uh…" he paused again, tossing ideas around in his head. Finally he asked, "Ya think you could put up with a border for a few days?"

"I figured you'd say that," Alec answered. "Couch is plenty big. Comfy, too. I oughta know, slept on it more than a few nights when Fleet kicked me outta the bed," he added with a chuckle.

Vic nodded, his mind made up. "See ya in a few days…soon as I can make arrangements."

"Okay, man."

"And Alec…don't tell her I'm comin'… I mean…you know…just in case…"

"Gotcha. And hey…if we ain't home when you get here, the key's under the mat."

Vic smiled. It felt like old times.

"Thanks, Pal. See ya."

With that, the two friends rang off and Vic sat in the chair a few minutes longer, mentally calculating if he had enough money for gas and expenses, since he hadn't exactly been saving his pennies for an emergency. Briefly, he wondered what excuse he was going to give his boss in order to take off a few days.

Standing quickly, he reached into his pocket and tossed a quarter on the table to cover the cost of the call. Then he turned and bounded up the stairs two at a time.

He had preparations to make.

ꕤ

SEVERAL DAYS LATER, Vic passed through Boonville on Route 40, about a half hour into his trip back to Louisville. His car, a dark blue '31 Buick Coupe – the kind skirted with running boards and a rumble seat in the back – had been his big purchase after he had finished his hitch in the C's. He reached back just then to raise the shade and gave the rear window a crank for some air. Straightening up again as the refreshing breeze began to flow through, he reached over and gave the dashboard a pat, musing how good the little car ran, even if it did need a little sprucing up on the paint job. However, he had never taken it on a road trip, so he hoped the tires held out.

It being a Wednesday afternoon, there was very little traffic on the two-lane road. That left him with few distractions to occupy his mind. He tried to focus on Doc and Irene's encouraging letters, reflecting that he kind of considered those two as surrogate parents and he unconsciously wanted to make them proud of him.

The three-hour trip to Louisville was something he had thought about doing for a long time…but now that it was happening, he found himself plagued with doubts and fears.

What will she say when she sees me? What should I *say to her? And what about her little boy… I wonder what he's like…if he's a brat, or if he behaves…wonder what kind of a mother Louise is…*

With every mile that drew him closer, the coil of nerves in his gut wound tighter and tighter…and tighter. Rolling down the driver's side window, he allowed the air to flow over his face as he tried to clear the thoughts from his head, but they just wouldn't cease.

Will she want to see me? What if I go to the door and she refuses to talk to me? Will she look different? She's got to…she's four years older…lots of things have happened to her, just like to me…she's a woman now, not a little girl anymore… I wonder if she still thinks of me… I know she told Alec she did, but still…she had a life with him.

"Aaah," he groused, swearing under his breath at himself. Reaching into his shirt pocket, he drew a cigarette out of the pack, and his lighter out of his pants pocket. Lighting up, he sucked in several deep drags, hoping the nicotine would help to uncoil the knot in his stomach.

But no such luck. Alone in the car with miles to go, his mind kept up its relentless torture.

*But how do **I** feel about **her** now? She's been with another man…she gave herself to him…she's had a baby for him…she's not the same girl that I knew four years ago.*

Swearing again, he admitted to himself that it gnawed at his guts that he had not been her first. It tore at him, slicing him with vicious claws every time he thought about it. *She'd been MY girl, but he had swept her away, the no good son of a…* Many times over the years, Vic had pictured himself coming face to face with *'T.J.'* and letting loose with all of the pent up jealousy and anger he had harbored since the moment he had found out. He'd imagined thrashing the other man bloody until somebody intervened. And now, to find out the jerk had been mistreating Louise – even been unfaithful to her! It was almost more than he could stand.

Yet…the thought that his Mary Louise had *been* with that guy still stuck in his craw like a rock in his shoe. He could still see the smirk on the jerk's face as he had swept Louise out of his arms and onto the dance floor, making Vic feel like a clumsy twit. It was all one big ball of confusion in his head…*and* his heart.

Determinedly, he turned his mind away from his conflicting feelings and back to that morning, when he had approached his boss and asked for a few days off.

"I don't know, Vic," Ralph Harford, the shop manager for Diamond Dry Cleaners and Vic's immediate supervisor, had answered as he rolled the ever-present cigar around in his mouth. He tipped his cap toward the back of his head and scratched the front edge of his hairline. It was the man's unconscious habit each time he was faced with an unexpected problem.

"It should only be for a few days…" Vic had offered, although in reality, he had no idea how long he would need to be gone. Besides that, he knew he was essentially rushing into the unknown, with absolutely no idea as to the state of mind of the other party… After all, she might possibly change her mind again and go back to her husband… Mainly for that reason, he had taken care not to leave his bridges totally torched and beyond repair.

"That means Charlie'll have to cover your stops if you aren't back..."

"I know, sir. I wouldn't ask if it wasn't important..."

Harford studied the young man for a few moments. Vic Matthews had been the best delivery driver he'd ever had – hard working, conscientious, reliable, and had never missed a day of work. He got along with everyone and caused no trouble. However, something about this situation didn't sit right. Somehow, he felt that if Matthews went to Louisville for whatever this emergency was...he might not come back. The thought of that put the man in a bad mood. It would mean finding a replacement and training him to do the job – more work added to his already full schedule. Yet, he couldn't think of a good reason to deny the request.

"Alright, you haven't taken off any days since you've been here, I guess you're entitled. You just be sure to be back here first thing Monday morning," he added, pulling the wet cigar stub from his mouth and pointing it at Vic. "If not, I'll have to find a replacement driver – and you know how many young bucks are out there wishing they had your spot!"

Vic nodded, thinking he knew that well, as *he* had been one of those bucks for too long. "I know, sir."

Satisfied that he'd instilled fear into the young man, Harford dismissed him with a flick of his cigar.

"Go on then, get going. I got work to do," he grumbled before shoving the unlit stub back in his mouth. He had watched as Vic inclined his head in the affirmative, placed his hat back on his head, and turned to go.

Vic had paused to glance over at the presser area, his eyes meeting Julie's inquisitive gaze. At that moment, a strong wave of relief swept through him that he had listened to his gut and not taken her up on her offer. He could tell by the look in her eyes that she was probably wondering why he had shown up to work out of uniform and seemed to be having a very intense conversation with the boss. However, he had no time to explain things, as he needed to get on the road. Now that he had made the decision to go, he couldn't help feeling that time was of necessity. Something kept urging him to hurry.

With a brief lift of one hand aimed her way, and a nod to several other co-workers, he had turned and exited out the side door.

He hadn't looked back.

Now, glancing down at the dials on his dashboard, Vic realized he was on the verge of running out of fuel. "Man, I wish this coupe had a bigger tank…" he grumbled aloud. Figuring he was about half way, he saw a sign for the tiny town of St. Meinrad, and running on not much more than fumes, he managed to make it to a small gas station.

In ten minutes, he was back on the road again, his mind unfortunately also back in the groove of going round and round the same old turf.

An hour later, he passed a sign that read, "Corydon 25 miles." With an agitated sigh, he pulled another cigarette out of the pack in his pocket and lit up, feeling as if he were about to explode from the tension.

Twenty-five miles. Thirty minutes.

But…what will happen once I get there…

ꕤ

"BEEN A LONG time, but I'd say you're still the handsome devil you always were," Fleet teased as she pulled back from giving Vic a hug.

Vic grinned at the compliment, his eyes deliberately dropping to her considerable baby-belly filling the space between them. "I'd say you haven't changed, Mrs. Alder, but…"

Fleet laughed and play-smacked his arm. "If you're getting

ready to say that I look like I've swallowed a basketball…"

Alec chimed in with a chuckle, both hands raised in warning, "Oh no, man, don't do it. She can still move pretty quick, and she swings a mean rolling pin."

The three laughed together in comfortable friendship, with each one asking the polite questions of how've you been, what've you been up to, and filling one another in on the particulars in their lives.

Eventually however, the mirth left Vic's eyes, to be replaced by the shadows under the mountain of concern and turmoil roiling around in his head.

Unable to side step the reason for his visit any longer, they glanced at one another.

Fleet cleared her throat and placed a hand at the small of her back as she turned to waddle the few steps over to the couch, accepting her husband's assistance to sit.

"Have you seen her yet?" she queried with any further preamble.

Vic shook his head and flopped down in an adjacent chair. "No…I came straight here. Just…not sure what I'm gonna say to her, or…" he paused and shrugged with a sigh, truly at a loss to explain his jumbled thoughts and emotions.

Husband and wife exchanged glances. This was an unexpected development. Fleet had envisioned something like a scene from a movie, where the 'hero' would come rushing to the door, the heroine would fling the portal open, and they would sail into one another's arms. She watched Vic for a moment, sitting forward with his elbows on his knees, his hands rifling through his hair as if unconsciously trying to dislodge his thoughts, or at least comb them into order. For the first time, she was afraid that perhaps he had changed. Could it be that Vic no longer had the deep feelings for Louise he once had?

Fleet opened her mouth to question him, but at the last second caught her husband's eye and slight shake of his head. Alec knew his friend, and he knew Vic had more than likely worried himself into a frazzle on the long, lonely trip back to Louisville.

Emitting his trademark snicker, Alec leaned over to give his friend's shoulder a playful shove.

"Tell you what, Chief. The company's got me on third shift right now so I've got some free time…how 'bout you and me head on over to Vernon's, bowl a few games, kinda hang out for awhile, hmm? Stretch your legs after all that drivin'."

Vic contemplated that for a moment. Truth was, he despised himself for being double minded now that he was actually back in Louisville. He was ashamed to even admit to his ambivalent feelings.

With a tired sigh, he shrugged. "Sure, why not."

Standing, he headed toward the door as Alec leaned down to give his wife a quick kiss.

"Be back in a little while, babe. You know where I'll be if you need me."

When he pulled back, their gazes met. No words needed to be said. It looked like their friends were going to need a bit of help – and this time, both Fleet and Alec were determined no stone would be left unturned.

Fleet watched the men leave the apartment, and closing the door behind them, she leaned against it for a moment. Pondering her best course of action, she chewed on her lips for a minute.

Then finally, she nodded to herself, grabbed her purse, and prepared to walk the three blocks to where her friend was staying.

CHAPTER 32

The Emotional Reunion

"IS HE ASLEEP?" Louise asked as she reclined on the couch in Irene's apartment.

"Yes. Your little Tommy is such an angel," Irene murmured as she stepped out of her roommate, Betty's, bedroom. Betty, who was away on an extended visit with her married daughter in Seattle, had given Irene permission to offer her room as temporary lodging for Louise and her son.

Glancing over at her young friend, Irene smiled as she thought back to the afternoon the two had arrived. Having just come back from the market, she had been putting groceries away when she heard a tentative knock on the door. Crossing to answer it, her mouth dropped open when she came face to face with the mother and child she had met on the bus those weeks ago – both of whom were red faced and sniffling.

"Goodness, child, what has happened? Come in, come in!" Irene had blustered, stepping back to usher in her two distraught visitors.

Little Tommy had hidden his face against his mother's neck as Louise lowered herself down on the couch, quivering with residual nerves as she dried her tears with an already damp handkerchief.

"Miss Irene…I'm…I'm sorry to drop in on you like this, but…" Louise had begun, pausing to fight back another wave of tears. Confused and upset, Tommy had continued his huddling, clinging to Louise's neck and whining softly.

"There, there, honey," Irene had soothed. "Tell me what's going on…"

Louise shook her head slowly from side to side, her life's situation looking more hopeless than ever, and she was kicking herself for leaving Bowling Green with her despicable husband.

"Oh ma'am, so much has happened since we met on the bus…and just now I found the note you had written…I didn't know where else to go…"

Reaching over to lay a gentle hand on Louise's back, and to softly pat Tommy's arm, Irene murmured, "Why don't you start at the beginning…"

So, that's what Louise did. Taking up the narrative from when the three had parted that day from the bus, she told the kind woman everything that had transpired, and the telling of it had brought back all of the hurt and heartache she had been dealt over the intervening weeks. By the time she finished, Irene was shaking her head in sympathetic amazement. Of course, she had immediately offered for Louise and Little Tommy to stay with her until Louise could get her life sorted out. Since then the three had grown quite close.

During that time, the two had discussed at length the fact that Louise had some very tough choices to make concerning her and her little boy's future. Irene had given her some suggestions that might work, but the future had seemed so totally uncertain to the young mother.

Although Louise had *not* been looking forward to seeing her husband again after that nightmarish trip from Bowling Green, she had sent word to him that they had things to discuss. That encounter had occurred a week after the terrible fight. He had shown up at the door with yet another woman on his arm – a rather plain woman, a bit shorter than Louise, with dark hair and sad looking brown eyes. T.J. had introduced her as Alice, and had proceeded to tell Louise that he had made his final decision. He wanted a divorce.

The whole thing had been quite hurtful, embarrassing, and upsetting. Yet at the same time, it had given Louise an unexpected sense of freedom. She had been willing to reconcile, for little Tommy's sake, but T.J. had taken the decision right out of her hands.

However, the problem of what she would do and how she would provide for herself and her son loomed large. T.J. had made a point of saying that he would 'try' to give her money for Tommy's support…when he *could.*

Now, as Irene gazed down at her guest, a look of concern crossed her face. Watching as Louise gingerly sat up and removed the damp cloth from her forehead, the older woman thought she still looked pale and a bit fatigued.

"Are you feeling better, dear?"

Louise nodded. "Yes, much better. I don't feel sick to my stomach anymore…and the pain went away. Maybe it was something I ate after all."

The kind woman stepped close and gently pressed a soothingly cool hand against Louise's head and cheeks. "No fever. I suppose it could have been, although we ate the same things…"

Louise shrugged. "I've been feeling funny for a couple of days…" she paused, knowing the probable cause of her distress.

Irene nodded, seeming to read her mind. "It could be that, too."

Just then, they both heard a knock. When Irene opened the door Fleet bustled in and, without preamble, hurried over to Louise and reached out to grasp her hands. However, on second thought, she lowered herself down onto the couch next to her friend, as she was quite winded from her walk.

"Fleet, what in the world are you doing?"

Unable to contain her excitement, Fleet expounded between deep breaths, "Right now…my husband is… over at Vernon's, bowling a few... friendly games and shooting the breeze. I'll give you three guesses...who he's with, and the first two don't count," she puffed teasingly.

Louise's heart immediately began to race as she stared into her friend's eyes. *Could it be true...?*

"Oh my God...Fleetwood Alder, if you're teasing me..." she gasped. Then pressing a hand to her lips, she turned to meet Irene's twinkling gaze.

Irene chuckled fondly, thinking privately, *It's about* **time** *the hero on the white horse came riding back into the picture!*

Having begun to think of herself as a mother figure to Vic since meeting him during the Flood, Irene felt deeply invested in the life of the man she thought of as her surrogate son, giving him the best advice she knew how, praying, and worrying about him. Then meeting Louise and little Tommy, and having already known about the misunderstanding and Louise's ill-advised decision that had torn the couple asunder four years prior, she and the young woman had become quite close as well.

Now it seemed that circumstances had finally come full circle and these two were to be given a second chance at happiness. Irene said a silent prayer that nothing would happen to stand in their way.

ꕥ

HER HANDS SHAKING, Louise tried for the third time to apply mascara to her lashes.

"Oh dear, I'm making a mess of things," she mumbled, leaning back as Fleet bent down to help.

"Here, let me."

Louise managed a smile, in spite of her nervous jitters.

"This feels a lot like getting ready for that dance at the K.C."

"Yeah, except now..." Fleet began, but hesitated.

Louise knew what she meant. Except now there was a lot

more riding on the outcome.

Sitting on the vanity stool in Irene's bedroom and staring at her reflection in the mirror, Louise wondered how she would even make it through the next few hours. She had rummaged through her things and located the purple dress, and while Irene pressed and freshened it, Fleet was styling her hair the same way she had for the dance four years before.

But Louise was a bundle of nerves. She reached for the small glass of water with a dash of bicarbonate Irene had prepared for her, and took another sip, allowing the salty, alkaline taste to slowly descend into her jittery stomach. *I can't believe it's been four years…will he think I've changed too much?* ***Have*** *I changed a lot? What has he been through in the years since I saw him last? Does he still feel the same way that he did when he wrote me that beautiful letter?*

Fleet had clued her in on the subtle changes she had noticed in Vic, and now, along with Irene, she'd had had a tough time convincing Louise that she needed to be bold and take a step of faith.

In her customary, non-nonsense way, Fleet had fussed at her, "Girl, you need to go down there to Vernon's and *get your man*!"

After much primping and fixing, and Irene calling a taxi for Louise's ten-block trip to the pool hall, the three ladies stood together in the doorway after they heard the toot of the cab's horn.

"We'll take care of Tommy. You take all the time you need. Don't worry about anything," Irene encouraged, smiling at the girl she had taken under her wing as she pressed the money for the cab into Louise's quivering hand and shooed her out the door.

"Remember, tell the truth and don't keep secrets. Things will work out better all around," Fleet advised, her eyes locking with Louise's as they shared unspoken thoughts.

Irene took her young friend's hands in hers and whispered, "Go to him, honey. Talk to him. Don't hold anything back."

With a nervous swallow and exchanging quick hugs with both

women, Louise drew in a deep breath, clutched her pocketbook close, and turned to go down the hall – on the way to what she hoped would be her first step toward the happiness that had been ripped away by a savage twist of fate four years before.

A sentimentally tearful Irene, and a widely grinning Fleet, watched together from the doorway.

ꙮ

SINCE IT WAS early afternoon, Vernon Lanes only had a few regular customers, and most of them were bellied up to the bar at the far end of the billiard room. Cigarette smoke and the pungent scent of beer permeated the atmosphere.

Alec had offered to buy Vic a brew, but it sat on the corner of the table only minus a few sips, as he wasn't much of a drinker. Alec, however, had tossed his own down rather quickly.

The two friends had bowled a few games, but Vic, normally a good bowler, was not surprisingly off his game, considering the circumstances. They had been talking for hours…or rather…shooting the breeze. Not much actual discussion had taken place once they had arrived, beyond the 'what ifs' and 'yeah, but's' Vic had mumbled in the car. Eventually growing tired of knocking down pins, they had moved on in to the pool tables.

Alec figured that when his friend felt like unloading things off his chest, he would. Until then, they would just rack up another game. Thinking practically, however, he realized they didn't have all night. He did need to go to work later.

Watching as Vic leaned over to line up for a game-opening break, Alec asked casually, "You stewed enough yet?"

Vic shot him a glance. "You got somethin' on your mind?"

"Me?" he grinned, shrugging and leaning nonchalantly against the side of the table. "Just figured you might need some help figuring things out, is all."

Vic heaved a sigh. "I been doin' nothing *but* figurin'. It don't get me nowhere, 'cept round and round the maypole."

Alec studied his friend, weighing his options. Finally, he decided to let him have it, both barrels, and see if he could force a reaction.

"So…you figure she's just a no-good tramp and in the morning you'll head back to your job and your life in Evansville, right? Easy as pie," he added with a snap of his fingers.

Vic's head jerked up and he glared at his friend. "I didn't say that!"

"Well, you didn't say you were staying, neither. So, what's it gonna be? You gonna go over and see her? Talk to her? Hear her side of things? Or are ya gonna stay here in this smoky joint and brood all night?"

Vic swore under his breath. "I don't know, man," he fumed, drawing the pool stick back and sending it forward with way more force than needed. With loud, crashing tings, the balls shot all around the table, a few nearly leaving it. Sizing up for his first shot, he had just leaned down and grasped the cue again when he heard Alec clear his throat. Vic glanced up, ready to tell his friend to lay off, when the look on his face – and the fact that Alec was staring past his head toward the door – made the fine hairs at the back of his neck begin to tingle.

Vic sucked in a deep breath and slowly turned his head, peeking back over his shoulder. He wasn't prepared for his reaction – it was if he had stuck his finger in a light socket.

Louise.

There she stood, looking just like she had the night he had taken her dancing on the Idlewild, just like she had thousands of times in his memories and dreams. Only…he wouldn't have thought it possible, but she was even more beautiful now than she had been then.

Releasing the pool stick, it clattered to the table as he turned to face her.

Louise stood stock still, hugging her pocketbook to her chest.

Gazing back at Vic, she was so nervous she could barely breathe, and her heart was pounding so fast she thought she might faint.

All the way there in the back of the taxi, she had tried to allow Irene's words, and Fleet's encouragement to buoy her confidence. Irene had reiterated that God didn't punish a person endlessly for making a wrong choice, as both she and Fleet had encouraged her that Vic coming back was a sign that things were about to turn in her favor.

When the cab pulled up at the bowling alley, however, she had given the driver an extra twenty-five cents and asked him to wait around for ten minutes before moving on…just in case the worst happened and she found out Vic had ultimately changed his mind…

Using every ounce of courage she possessed, she had checked her hair, smoothed her dress, took in a deep fortifying breath, and opened the door, expecting to see him right away at one of the bowling lanes. When he wasn't, she had almost panicked. Then suddenly, from the room to her left, she had heard the distinctive sound of a cue ball striking its targets and something had told her…

Now, staring at the man who had never left her mind or her heart since the last time she had seen his face – or for that matter – since the *first* time she had seen his face, she felt tied up in knots and none of her carefully planned words would come to mind. Having pictured herself running up to him and jumping into his arms, she now held back as she had unfortunately overheard the exchange he had just had with Alec and she wasn't sure at all what to do next. The worst thing in the world for her would be if she threw herself at him and he spurned her advance.

Gazing at him, she thought he looked wonderful, even more handsome and virile than he had four years before. He looked healthy and fit…his muscles seeming more pronounced through the thin material of his shirt. And the potent way his darkening eyes were boring right into hers made the short hairs on the back of her neck prickle.

It was as if electricity was charging the very air. Neither of them could seem to move.

Then suddenly, the spell was broken as one of the patrons at the bar let out a loud wolf whistle.

"Hey, hey! What do we have here?" the man called, beginning to saunter in Louise's direction in the doorway.

That instantly spurred Vic into action and he began to move toward Louise. The other man got there first.

"Never seen you around here before, cutie. What's your name?" the unknown man asked as he stopped close to Louise. She dragged her eyes from Vic to glance at the man, about to tell him to get lost, but in the next instant, Vic was there. He reached out and smoothly maneuvered an arm between them as Louise took a step back out of the way.

"She's with me," he murmured to the man. The no-nonsense warning in his eyes spoke volumes. The man didn't argue, merely inclined his head, flinging an arm out in a mock bow as he turned to saunter back over to the bar and rejoin his chuckling drinking buddies.

Now close together, the two long lost sweethearts turned to face one another. For a few moments, time seemed to hesitate, and then start up anew. It was like their first and last encounters all over again and rolled into one, as they became acutely aware of one another's close proximity. Vic hazily registered Louise's perfume and the nervous energy she seemed to be projecting, while she luxuriated in his familiar natural scent that she remembered and adored.

One of them had to say something to break the ice, and figuring it probably should be her, Louise moistened her lips and murmured, "Hello, Vic."

Unconsciously, his eyes twinkled at the impact of hearing her voice utter his name.

"Hey," he whispered.

Both of them were holding back, longing to launch themselves into the other's arms, but each was so painfully unsure…

Alec, still over by the pool table, once again cleared his throat, amused at the star struck expressions on both of his friends' faces.

Louise tore her eyes from Vic's to glance at their mutual friend, and managed to murmur, "Hey Double A."

Immediately, her eyes reconnected with Vic's and he smiled softly, mumbling, "How'd you know where I was?"

At that, her eyes sparkled and she smiled back, her gaze caressing his lips and face as she hummed, "Fleet came to see me." Then remembering the message her friend had sent, she leaned her head a bit and addressed Alec again, though not breaking eye contact with Vic. "By the way, your wife says to come get her, she don't feel like walking back home."

Alec laughed, placing both his and Vic's cues in the rack on the wall, quipping, "I best get to it, then!"

Just then, several patrons appeared at the doorway. Attempting to push their way in, they unintentionally jostled the two obstructing the entrance. Vic reflexively reached out to grasp Louise's arms to steady her as she touched his chest. Together they gasped at the intense sensations from the unexpected contact.

"Let's uh…let's get outta here…go somewhere and talk…okay?" Vic murmured to Louise, then he called over his shoulder to Alec, "You want us ta drop you off?" although he was hoping Alec would turn him down.

Vic tried to suppress his smile of relief when Alec waved them on with, "Naw, man, I'll catch a ride."

ꙮ

THEY REACHED THE parking lot and Vic steered Louise over to his car. When he put his hand on the door handle, she stopped and surveyed the vehicle. Admiring its cute design, Louise found she liked the running board and rumble seat, as well as the color. At that moment, she realized she had always hated T.J.'s car, thinking perhaps it was its color, dark green like heavy moss, or the convertible top that always leaked…*or maybe just because of all the bad times…*

Refocusing on the present, she glanced up at him. "This is yours?"

Vic smiled proudly and gave a nod. "Yep. Bought it with some 'a the money I earned in the C's."

Louise smiled at that and met his warmly familiar mahogany gaze. "I'm glad…that things worked out good with that." He nodded again, understanding what she meant – that he had benefited from the money from his second hitch.

Opening the door for her, he watched as she slipped quickly inside, and then he jogged around and slid into the driver's side. For a moment, both wondered if they should pinch themselves, as the thing each had hoped, dreamed, longed, and prayed for was finally happening.

Vic looked over at Louise and she at him. He raised one eyebrow as she nervously drew her lip a tiny bit between her teeth.

"Where ya wanna go?"

She shook her head with a small shrug. "I don't care." And it was true. She didn't care at all, as long as she was with Vic.

Pressing his lips together, he bowed his head knowingly and reached to start the car, turning the wheel to head north.

They couldn't have been more aware of one another, sitting quite closely on the bench seat – especially when he would accidentally bump against her arm when working the gearshift in the floorboard.

Louise watched him, hungry for anything her eyes could feast upon – his arms, his hands…his trouser-covered legs and even his shoes as his feet manipulated the pedals with ease. She realized that in all the time she had known him, she had never before been in a car with Vic at the wheel. She felt safe with him, and found herself proud of his driving prowess and wondered if his time in the C's and his job in Evansville driving a truck had taught him such expertise with the manual gears, or if he was just a natural at it – and she suspected the latter. The thought that she might try to drive such a thing, with the complicated pedals, gearshift, and trying to remember when to press the clutch and when to let off, fairly boggled her mind.

In much the same way, Vic was intensely aware of Louise…of every move she made… if she raised a hand to brush back a strand of hair blown by the breeze from the open window… His eyes strayed time and again to her shapely legs and high heel shoes. Though her dress was somewhat modest, and she was sitting primly with her legs to one side, they still attracted his gaze like a moth to a flame. He was also aware of the fact that *she* was perusing *him*, and that knowledge gave him a strong feeling of masculine pride.

Ten minutes later, at a wide patch on the side of River Road, Vic slowed the car and pulled over. Hopping out, he rounded the rumble seat, where he reached inside to grab an old quilt he kept in there for emergencies, before he opened the passenger door for Louise.

Gracefully swinging her legs out and accepting his offer of help, she reveled in the sweet familiarity of the simple act, remembering the many times he had held her hand on their dates during their idyllic summer. Conscious of the warm, smooth, firm strength of his hand, she closed her eyes briefly to cherish the moment, and then opened them again and looked around at her surroundings. "Where are we?"

Vic smiled as he gently squeezed her hand and led her down through the undergrowth to his favorite spot, under a tree overlooking the river. Looking around, he noticed a few changes from the last time he had been there – the tree was larger…the foliage thicker. "It's my special place. It's not as pretty as the one I found when I was in the C's, but… I never showed this to anyone." Louise admired the private spot, bordered by trees and bushes. She smiled at his admission that he had never shown it to anyone else, that knowledge causing a warm, satisfied glow to permeate her being. Vic went on to explain that in all of the times he had come there, no one had ever intruded upon his privacy.

The Ohio River stretched out on both sides, with Indiana on the far shore. Gentle waves lapped against the pebble-covered edge of the bank as he guided Louise over, and he paused to quickly spread out the quilt for them to sit on. He watched as she sat down, carefully tucking her legs to one side and arranging her skirt becomingly. It touched his heart when she looked up at him and he connected again with those breathtaking hazel eyes, admitting to himself that he had always loved their color.

Clearing his throat, he gestured at their surroundings. "I used to come here a lot…to fish…stare at the river…think. I…I came here the night we had that big fight," he added softly as he gazed down at her. She visibly winced and he added, "Sorry…I didn't mean to bring that up, I…"

"No, that's alright," she interrupted. "We…we need to talk about it," she added as he sank down beside her on the quilt.

For a moment, they were uneasy with one another again, each wondering what the other was thinking.

Then they spoke simultaneously, "Oh Vic, I'm so sor…" "I was such a jer…"

She put up a hand to interrupt; actually glad the time had come that she could say things to him she had yearned to be able to do, for so very long.

"No, Vic…you had every right to be mad. What I did was stupid and immature. Lying to you, keeping the truth from you, playing silly games. It…it became a challenge to see how long I could get away with it. Then…when everything hit the fan…I got in more trouble than I had even dreamed…" she admitted with a doleful expression. Unable to look him in the eye then, she dropped her line of sight down to her lap.

Vic smiled gently and reached for one of her hands, cradling it between his larger one and the strong barrel of his chest. "I overreacted," he murmured. "See, I'd just been told about the trouble Ger' was in... That threw me for such a loop I kinda lost my head. But...that night after I stayed here for awhile, I went to see Doc and Miss Irene at the church, and they set me straight." He paused, remembering his very dear friends and the positive influence they'd had on his life. "They helped me make a good plan..."

At that, she gasped as her eyes snapped to his and began to fill with tears. "And I ruined it! Oh Vic...I thought you were so angry, that you would never forgive me for lying to you. I felt like my life was over, that nothing would ever mean anything again," she wavered, fighting for control. "It was like I was in a fog and couldn't see or think straight. All I knew was I had to do *something* to get some relief...Mama was so mad at me...Edna harped at me constantly...Daddy wouldn't speak to me...even Billy was disappointed in me...so I..." she stopped, unwilling to say the dreaded words. "Then...when we found your letter...it was the next morning after..." she gestured helplessly with one hand.

Vic's eyes grew large as he realized what she was saying. *The morning after...after she married that no good son of a...* He swore silently, not knowing what to say, it was all so unfair, and so unnecessary.

The hated, oft-imagined picture of Louise on her wedding night, once again began to worm its way under his craw. He clamped his lips together and looked away, fighting against the surge in his emotions. However, Louise saw it, lurking in his eyes, and her eyes filled even more.

"Vic...I hated it every time he touched me," she softly confessed, watching him wince as he heard the words. "I...the day I...married him...I felt like I was making a mistake...but I didn't listen to my own conscience. Now…now I know God was trying to tell me not to do it…"

Desperate to make him understand how repulsed she was with the whole situation, Louise reached up with her free hand and grasped the amethyst necklace around her neck, drawing it forward so he could see. "I never take it off, Vic. I've worn it every moment of every day since you walked out of my life. It was my way of keeping you with me."

Vic observed the purple stone sparkling in the late afternoon sun and he remembered the joyous day he had placed it around her neck. He knew he had to get past this, to reconcile with it, get over it, but…it was so hard…

"Oh Vic…if you only knew what I went through…how much I missed you, wanted you…how much I…wish it had been *you*," she squeaked.

He met her eyes then, seeing the depths of her anguish. Knowing everything needed to be on the table for them to move forward, he sucked in a breath, mumbling brokenly, "When I found out you'd been with that bas…" he stopped himself from uttering the explicit word, "I felt like my guts had been kicked in. It 'bout killed me."

Tears spilled down Louise's cheeks as she raised their joined hands to her lips, her tears wetting Vic's fingers, as she sobbed, "Please forgive me, Vic. I've cried a million tears for you… If…if there were some way to go back…to undo all of it…I'd wait for you for the rest of my life if I knew you would really return!"

Overcome, Vic finally pulled her into his arms with a groan. Crushing her against his chest, his hand cradled the back of her head as her arms wound tightly around his back. They stayed that way for quite a while, rocking back and forth; weeping together for all the lost time, and unnecessary circumstances that had kept them apart. Each begged the other's forgiveness for their shortcomings that had led to such misunderstandings and tragic decisions. They whispered their confessions to one another until all had been talked out and resolved. Finally, Vic felt as if he could move on; the knives that had tormented his soul his whole life dissolving in the warm glow of Louise's love.

When at last they pulled back, Louise reached for her purse with a shaky hand to retrieve a handkerchief. She dabbed his eyes, and he in turn lovingly wiped her tears away.

Rays of the setting sun dappling through the leaves on the tree warmed their skin as they sat for a time drinking in one another's features, each feeling as if they were living a scene in a movie. Everything seemed alive, and beautiful…seemingly for the first time in longer than either could remember. Each one became acutely aware of sensations, the mesmerizing sounds of the water lapping at the river's edge nearby, and the earthy aroma of the moss at the bank.

She reached up and ran a hand gently through the tousled waves of his hair. Gently, he touched a finger to the amethyst pendant around her neck, truly moved that she had confided that she wore it all the time.

Smiling softly, she murmured without thinking, "He hated that I wore it…'cause he knew you gave it to me. During our last big fight, he nearly tore it off me…"

Vic's eyes flared with anger at that and he shook his head, gritting his teeth. "If I ever come face to face with that guy…I'm liable to beat him to within an inch of his life," he fumed. Then with a wry smile, he added, "I used to dream about doin' that."

Louise chuckled softly as he lifted a hand to gently caress her soft cheek. She nuzzled his warm palm, totally content. Totally, that is, except for one more detail that she was trying to get up the nerve to tell him. Then she saw the look in his eyes change from anger to something else, and her pulse began to speed up.

He slowly leaned in, giving her time to stop him, before softly pressing his lips to hers. She immediately felt herself responding, as she had every time he had kissed her during their enchanted summer. The effect instantly became akin to complete and total intoxication.

"I love you, Louise," Vic whispered against her mouth.

"I love you, too," she managed between kisses. Then remembering again her promise to herself, to God, and to Irene to keep no secrets and tell no untruths, she began, "But Vic, there's something I need to tell you. I…" but his lips suddenly opened to surround hers, inhibiting her words. With a shuddering sigh, she surrendered to him, helpless to pull back and deny him. Within moments, he had turned her in his arms and gently laid her down onto the quilt, his lips never leaving hers as their kiss dramatically deepened. Never had they shared such intimate loving. Vic found himself tossing caution to the winds, his hands caressing her cheek and neck, and then roaming further down her anatomy as she curled into his embrace. Her hands stroked his cheeks, finding their way into his hair and trailing toward the back of his neck as she gloried in the invigorating sensation of their tongues dancing in familiar rhythm.

They kissed hungrily, as if each one wished to become immersed in the very essence of the other. Tongues fondled, breaths mingled. The taste of her mouth and the delightful scent of her hair and skin drew Vic with such irresistible force that he mindlessly pushed aside his earlier determination to exercise prudent restraint. He was like a man possessed, and wholly focused on the fact that the love of his life was finally, willingly, in his arms – and responding with a fervor he had only experienced with her in his wildest dreams.

Louise was also overcome by the myriad of sensations bombarding her consciousness. Never had T.J. ignited her passions as did Vic's touch, taste, and scent. She was thoroughly caught up in *him* and in sharing this moment with the man she loved…

Then in the blink of an eye, everything changed.

Vic both felt and heard Louise gasp and then tense up, as if she were in pain.

Breathless, he pulled back enough to see her face, and became instantly alarmed that her expression reflected that she was, indeed, experiencing discomfort.

"What's wrong, babe?" he whispered, his concern growing as he watched her hand find its way to her abdomen, where it pressed in firmly.

"I…I don't know…" she gasped as she tried to rub the puzzling pain away. "All of a sudden…I…aaahh!" she wailed as it increased as if a knife was stabbing her insides.

Then her eyes flew open and stared into his in a panic as she whispered, "Oh Vic…something's wrong…"

Vic started to sit up, becoming more alarmed by the second. "Babe, you're scarin' me…what's goin' on?"

She drew her knees up higher and lay on the quilt, dropping one hand over her eyes as the pain mercifully began to slowly subside. Hot tears began to pool and drip down her temples as she shuddered uncontrollably.

"Babe…hey…don't cry, honey…it'll be alright," Vic soothed, reaching to gently wipe away a tear with one finger.

Ashamed and guilt ridden, Louise took a deep breath, confessing softly, "I didn't tell you everything, Vic…I was afraid…that you wouldn't want me…" she hesitated, more afraid than she had been from the start, but she knew she had to be honest and not wait a minute longer.

"I…I'm pregnant, Vic…"

He had gently laid his hand over hers on her abdomen, but at her words, his eyes widened and he pulled back a bit. Stunned at her revelation, he whispered incredulously, "*What?*"

She went on, "I started to tell you earlier." Moving her hand from her eyes, she chanced a look at his face, but his expression was blank, as if he were in shock. "I…I got so caught up…in being with you…"

He stared at her, battling truly conflicting emotions. Anger threatened to rise in his heart as he thought about her keeping secrets from him yet again.

But before that thought could take a firm hold, she gasped again, "Oh Vic…I've been feeling…odd…for days…but now…aaahh!" she suddenly screamed as a white hot searing pain ripped through her lower belly, accompanied by a rush of hot, thick liquid between her legs.

"Vic! Help me!" she wailed.

In further shock at this completely unexpected occurrence, Vic turned his head and looked down at the quilt beneath them – and the frightening red stain that had begun to appear.

"Oh my God!" he whispered. She was bleeding! His Louise! He had to DO something!

"Hold on, honey!" he ground out as he quickly maneuvered to his knees. He had never been so scared. "I'm takin' you to the hospital!"

Securing the quilt around her, he scooped her up and pulled her tight against his chest. Staggering to his feet, he shouldered through the thick underbrush and immediately took off at a run for the car. A glance at her face frightened him even further – she was already appearing quite pale, her eyes shut as if she were starting to lose consciousness.

"Stay with me, honey… *Mary Louise*…don't leave me…just hang on…please don't leave me now!"

ഇഗ

CHAPTER 33

God Please Don't Take her From Me Now

VIC REACHED UP to rub his chin, turning for the hundredth time as he paced back and forth in the waiting area at the hospital emergency room.

Louisville City Hospital – he hadn't been inside its doors since he had helped rescue that family during the flood. Truly, he hoped this visit would have as happy of a result. He gazed around at the other people gathered in pockets around the room, and then at the stark white walls and gleaming white tile floors of the waiting room. Its cleanliness should have instilled a feeling of confidence within his heart, but the reason for his visit overshadowed every other thought.

What's takin' so long? Why won't anybody tell me anything? Did I get her here in time? Vic wondered. *Oh God, don't take her from me now…that'd be the last straw…*

Unbidden, the graphic images came rushing back in living color as he relived running to the car, managing to get the door open and placing her carefully inside…driving at breakneck speed down River Road on the way to the hospital as he kept glancing over at Louise and her deathly pale face. The pool of blood had expanded steadily on the seat beneath her…her eyes, so woozy they hardly focused the few times she had opened them in response to his impassioned pleas. And then the mad dash through the swinging doors of the emergency room with him screaming like a banshee for someone to help them…the flurry of orderlies and doctors as they came running with a gurney and whisked her away from him. Then finally, she was gone, through the doors and down the hall to emergency surgery, leaving him standing there…with her blood on the front of his clothing as the only thing left to prove she had even been with him at all…

He glanced down at it now, the sight turning his stomach. *Why had she bled like that?* He'd never heard of such a thing happening – just from being pregnant? He assumed she was losing the baby…the baby she had told him about only seconds before. Of that detail, he was not entirely certain *how* he felt.

"Vic!" a familiar voice brought him out of his troubled thoughts and he turned, relieved to see his friend and mentor, Doc Latham, striding toward him.

"Doc. Thanks for comin'," Vic murmured as he took a few steps to meet his friend and they shook hands warmly.

Immediately, Doc's eyes widened as he took in his young friend's appearance. "Are you injured?" he asked, concerned, as he tried to remember the details of the frantic phone call he had received from Vic.

"No, I'm alright…this is…hers…" Vic mumbled, gesturing to the dried blood on his clothing.

Nodding in relief, the kind pastor inquired, "Tell me what happened."

Vic recounted what details he knew, although he left out the part about he and Louise engaging in some passionate kissing just before the attack. He did speak to the fact that the staff had taken him back and allowed him to donate blood, upon his offer to do so, in case it might help the woman he loved. After that, he shared his frustration that since then he couldn't seem to find out anything about Louise's progress, even though he had been waiting for two hours.

At this, Doc laid a hand upon Vic's shoulder and pressed his lips together in determination before turning to approach the reception desk to try and use his influence as a man of the clergy to receive information about Louise.

However, after only a few minutes, he turned away from the attendants, and shook his head in response to Vic's hopeful expression. "They said she's still in surgery, but the doctor will come out to speak with us when he is finished."

Vic closed his eyes; the worry was nearly driving him insane.

"Vic…let's send up a prayer for her…okay?" Doc murmured softly. Vic nodded as Doc joined hands with him, delivering a heartfelt prayer that Louise would survive whatever had happened to her, that the doctors would know exactly what to do, and that she would make a full recovery. Vic drew in a deep fortifying breath of gratitude when the clergyman also asked for God to strengthen Vic and let him know that he wasn't alone.

Feeling a bit better after the prayer, Vic managed a half smile for his friend and they moved over to some seats near the door.

"Did you let her family know?" Doc asked, clarifying when he saw the flash in Vic's eyes and knowing he thought he meant her husband, "I mean…her brother, or her parents."

"I called Sonny and left a message with his wife. She said she'd let him know," Vic acknowledged, privately wondering about the tone in the woman's voice. "I didn't know how to get hold of her parents."

"Do you know what might have brought this on?" Doc wondered. Having been privy to similar occurrences in the past, the reverend had a feeling he knew what had happened. However, he chose to keep his speculations to himself so as not to unnecessarily worry his young friend. Vic shrugged helplessly and shook his head.

"One minute she seemed fine, and the next…she started gettin' these real bad pains…and then…" he moved his shoulders in speechless confusion.

A few minutes later, Vic looked past the clergyman and

smiled. Although it had been four years, he recognized Louise's brother coming through the swinging doors with a woman clinging to his arm. The pair were nicely dressed and seemed quite anxious and worried, Sonny especially, as if he were expecting the worst. The woman looked to be with child, and Vic figured instantly that she must be the one he had spoken with on the phone. Sonny went right to the desk and inquired, but received the same information Doc had only a few minutes before. They seemed both relieved and a bit disheartened, but when they turned to find seats to wait, Sonny caught Vic's eye and headed in their direction.

"Hey Vic. Good to see you again," he greeted, shaking hands with first him and then with Doc as introductions were made. "This is my wife, Sarah," he added, and the men acknowledged her respectfully.

Looking at Vic, Sonny asked in concern, "I just heard and we came right over. What happened?" In truth, his wife had exaggerated and embellished Vic's message, prompting Sonny to imagine that Louise had been in some horrible auto accident and was not expected to live.

Not that he wished to recount it again, Vic complied, filling Louise's brother in on everything he knew, hesitating only briefly before saying that Louise had confided to him that she had been pregnant. Although he was quite certain that she wasn't anymore, he felt her brother had a right to know.

Sonny's eyes widened and he exchanged a deliberate look with his wife. "I kind of wondered if she was…she'd been saying she was sick to her stomach and things…"

No one wanted to say the words out loud that they were all positive, from Vic's description of how much blood she had lost…that the baby would have had no chance of survival. But the question on everyone's mind…did Louise?

ꕥ

A DOCTOR, WITH traces of dark red blood on the white material of his physician's coat, came through the doors and looked around at the different clusters of people in the large waiting room. Everyone had been quietly talking among themselves, but when the swinging door opened and he came in, they all went silent and stared wide-eyed at him, wondering if it were their loved one's blood they could see staining his coat.

"The family of Louise Blankenbaker?"

Vic immediately jumped to his feet and hurried over to him. "Is she all right?"

The physician took in Vic's appearance as he offered a handshake. "Mr. Blankenbaker?" he asked innocently.

Vic blanched and shook his head. "No…Vic Matthews…I'm…I'm her…" he stopped, unsure of his current role. Was he her boyfriend? The man who loved her? "I…I brought her in when it happened."

"Is her husband here?" the surgeon asked, leaning his head past Vic's to look at the others who were drawing near.

Sonny stepped around Vic then and shook the doctor's hand. "I'm Joseph Hoskins, Louise's brother. She's uh…she's separated from her husband. I don't know where he is."

"Ahh, well then…" the doctor hesitated. Glancing at Vic, he wondered if *he* had been the father of the child. However, he reminded himself that was none of his business, and continued with the task at hand.

"I'm Chief Surgeon John Hamilton. Mrs. Blankenbaker has suffered an ectopic pregnancy…" he paused as he met the puzzled expressions of the three younger people, although he could see in the eyes of the clergyman that he understood and maybe even had expected as much.

"What's that?" Vic asked, feeling decidedly in the dark.

The family had no way of knowing, but Louise couldn't have been in better hands. Dr. Hamilton had recently been recognized by the American College of surgeons for developing an implement that greatly helped in complicated abdominal cases. A tall man, with short-cropped black hair, dark eyes, and bushy black eyebrows, he would have been quite imposing if not for his practiced gentle manner when speaking with the family members of his patients. He smiled understandingly at Vic's question. "In layman's terms, it means that at fertilization, the baby becomes implanted in the wrong location, where it cannot continue to full term. At some point, it becomes impossible for it to remain viable and it separates, causing massive hemorrhage."

Vic, visibly shaken, ran a hand through his hair as he tried to wrap his mind around the doctor's words. "Is…is she gonna be okay?"

The doctor hesitated, but seeing the obvious depth of emotion in the young man, he continued as if Vic were, indeed, the young lady's husband.

"She made it through surgery, and she's stable now, but the next forty-eight hours will be critical. She lost a lot of blood before we could get the hemorrhaging stopped and for a few minutes…" he gave pause, picturing the panic in the operating room when they had realized the hospital's stock of Louise's blood type was quite low. "Well, the fact that you were here and happen to possess the same blood type…" Then laying a hand on Vic's arm, he added in an attempt to encourage him, "She's a lucky young woman. If you hadn't saved us the time to search for a donor with the correct type, and gotten her here when you did…if she had been alone when it ruptured, there is a good chance she would not have survived."

Dry mouthed, Vic could only nod, hoping his actions had truly been enough.

With that, the doctor turned to go back inside, with the assurance that Louise would be well cared for, and they could see her in the morning.

Once he was gone, the four concerned people stood together for a minute, trying to absorb the enormity of the situation. None, except the reverend, had ever been involved in such a serious occurrence.

"Where's Tommy?" Sarah suddenly asked. Vic's eyes widened, as up to that point, he had totally forgotten about the existence of Louise's son.

Doc offered, "Louise has been staying with one of my parishioners, Irene Waller. She's taking care of the child. I telephoned her and let her know what happened." Again Vic reacted, his brow furrowed as he recalled the information about Louise staying with his dear friend and surrogate mother.

Glancing at his wife, Sonny spoke up, "Well…we can't do anything more here tonight. Might as well go home and come back in the morning, like the doctor said."

Sarah slipped her hand into the crook of his elbow. "You might want to send your parents a telegram and let them know what has happened…" Sonny acknowledged that was probably a good idea.

Vic glanced over at the closed doors that led to the rest of the hospital, wishing he could crash through them and find Louise. He desperately wanted to stay with her and make sure she was soundly recuperating. However, knowing that was impossible, he only sighed softly.

"Think I'll…go let Miss Irene know."

ꟹ

IN RESPONSE TO a soft knock, Irene glanced at the clock on the wall, noting the time as 9:45 pm. Dreadfully worried and wondering what was going on with Louise, and with Vic, she had been in the act of turning off the lamp in the living room in preparation for retiring for the night. Now, she reached down to securely fasten the tie on her robe and crossed to the door.

When she opened it, she found a worried but otherwise fine Vic occupying the hallway. He had changed out of his stained clothes in order not to frighten her.

"Vic! Come in!" she greeted. Reaching out for his hand and drawing him inside, she noticed there appeared to be traces of bloodstains on his skin where he had only given them a cursory washing. Thoroughly concerned, she shut the door and then gave him a quick hug before gesturing for him to have a seat on the couch.

He gratefully sank down onto its smooth, slip-covered surface, thinking it had been a long and emotionally taxing day since he had risen that morning in his room in Evansville. When he had set out on his journey to Louisville, he could not have had an inkling of the things that would transpire before the sun went down. And it was certainly not the circumstances with which he had pictured his reunion with this woman for which he cared so deeply. Gazing at her now, he noticed in these four years her hair had acquired quite a bit more silver than before, but like he remembered, a certain glow…a gentle goodness, still radiated from her countenance. Her green eyes, just then, appeared quite concerned and he realized, belatedly, that she seemed to have been on the verge of going to bed. It made him feel bad that he hadn't looked at the clock before heading over to see her.

Closing his eyes for a moment, his tired brain seemed to make his thoughts more muddled by the second.

"How is Louise?" the kind, dear woman asked as she studied the face of the young man before her. She could plainly see he was still quite distraught. She had been thinking, as well, about the fact that this was not the way she had envisioned their reunion. The quiet young man she had seen at their parting was now a confident, mature man of twenty-five.

"The doctor said she's stable, but she lost a lot of blood…they wouldn't let us see her until tomorrow." His despair pulled at his face as he said the words.

"When Reverend Latham called and told me she had collapsed, I…" she paused, unsure if Louise had told Vic about the baby as she had encouraged.

Vic met her eyes. "She told me about the baby…just before it happened. The doctor said she had a…eckt…" he hesitated, trying to remember the exact term.

"Ectopic?"

Vic nodded, bringing one hand up to rub the heel of his palm against his forehead, trying to stave off a stabbing tension headache. "Yeah…she…she almost bled to death," he added softly, the memory of the words the surgeon had confided making him shiver.

"Oh Vic," Irene crooned with sympathy, reaching out to once again touch his arm. They spent the next few minutes discussing the situation, with Vic sharing what a horrible experience it was, and how frightened he had been that he wouldn't get her to the hospital in time.

Just as Irene was about to say what a shame it was that such a thing happened just hours upon his arrival back in town, they both heard a soft voice from the doorway.

"Mama?"

Vic looked over and saw a small boy of about two, with light brown, wavy hair that was mussed from sleep. The child, still heavy lidded, was wiping his eyes with one hand and holding a small blanket with the other – a corner of it pressed to his face as the rest trailed behind him.

"Tommy, what are you doing out of bed, young man?" Irene asked the child, albeit gently. Holding out one hand, she encouraged, "Come here."

The little boy shuffled barefoot over to her, sailing straight into her arms before turning his head to look over at the unknown man. He stared at Vic, his big blue eyes seeming to search his features as if there was something familiar about him.

Vic smiled in greeting as he perused the child, looking for some feature that resembled Louise. Realizing the young boy looked like his father, he held his emotions in check. He was striving hard not to let it show that he was thinking that perhaps if things had been different, this might have been his son. With a heroic effort, he pushed back the familiar thoughts of whether or not he could accept this and take it all on.

Suddenly, recognition dawned in the child's eyes and he smiled shyly. Turning to meet Irene's eyes, Tommy pointed with one finger toward Vic as he said to her proudly, "Vic!"

Surprised, the adults stared at him for a moment, then Irene asked for clarity, "Tommy, sweetheart…you know Mr. Vic?"

The bright child vigorously bobbed his head.

"But…" she lingered, meeting Vic's astonished gaze. "How do you know Vic?"

"Mama's tweasure box," he explained, quite seriously. Then, he mimicked someone holding a photo and 'hugged' it to his chest as he mumbled, "Mmmm. Pitchur of Mama's fwend, Vic!"

Irene's eyes widened as she hugged him close, feeling utterly amazed. Obviously, Louise had shown the little boy Vic's picture, no doubt many times, and had told him the man's name – and he remembered. He'd even recognized him from the photo. She and Vic shared a smile as he felt his heart at once begin to warm toward the toddler.

Vic did have some practice with children when he lived with Jack and Liz and had interacted with his niece and nephew. Knowing he was a stranger to Louise's little boy, nevertheless, he took a chance and leaned near, keeping his smile friendly. Holding out his hands, eyebrows raised, he silently asked Tommy if he could hold him.

Tommy seemed to consider that for a moment, and then from Irene's arms, he reached out with both hands toward the newcomer as he tilted toward him.

Vic took him in his arms and gently set him on his lap, marveling at the handsome little man. He felt drawn to him because he was a part of Louise as he realized the boy had inherited his mother's sweetness.

Tommy stared up at him with his wide, angelic blue eyes for a moment. Then realizing he hadn't seen his mother, he looked around the room and back at Vic.

"Where Mama?" he asked softly.

Vic clamped his lips together in a small pout and gave one negative shake of his head.

"Your Mama's not here…but she's gonna be alright…I promise," Vic murmured. It was as if Tommy knew that Vic was a good man and one that could be trusted. Children always know – they can sense a person's character. Totally at ease, the child leaned toward Vic, cuddling into his arms as they closed around him.

"Your Mama's gonna be just fine, Tommy," Vic reiterated, meeting Irene's misty eyes. "She's gotta be."

Vic then closed his eyes, sending up a silent prayer.

ꕥ

THE FIRST SENSATION of awareness she experienced was the feeling of smooth, cool fingers touching her wrist.

Gradually, Louise broke through to consciousness, becoming aware that she was lying in a bed with sunshine streaming in through a window nearby. Her eyes opened slowly, and she found herself gazing up at the nurse who was in the act of taking her pulse. The dark haired woman glanced over and saw that her patient was reviving, and she responded with a friendly smile.

"Good morning, honey. How do you feel? Are you in much pain?"

Louise tried to focus, swallowing dryly. Her mouth felt like it was lined with cardboard.

The nurse noticed and promptly stepped to the bedside table, pouring some water into a glass from a pitcher and helping Louise to take a few sips.

Louise gave her a groggy smile of thanks and relaxed against the pillow.

"W…what happened?" she asked, confused.

"You were rushed here to the hospital yesterday…and you've had surgery…" the nurse paused, determining if the patient was stable enough for details. "But you're going to be fine. I'm Nurse Nancy. You just let me know if there is anything you need."

Louise had latched on to the words hospital and surgery as she forced her mind to reach back into memories of the day before. Suddenly, as if switching on a light bulb, she remembered…Fleet coming over…getting dressed…the taxi ride to the bowling alley…Vic!

She gasped involuntarily and tried to lift her head, croaking, "Vic…Vic?"

Nurse Nancy smiled understandingly. "Is that your husband? He and your family are right outside waiting to see you."

Louise's eyes clouded for a moment; her brow furrowed. "Husband? But…did Vic leave? Oh NO!" Tears began to pool in her eyes, and the nurse immediately became concerned. "Ssshh, honey. You're all right. Everything is just fine," she soothed, reaching out a gentle hand and smoothing back a lock of Louise's hair from her forehead. "You mustn't upset yourself. You need your strength to recover from your surgery," she added caringly.

"Vic…I want…Vic…" Louise whispered, her lip quivering like a little girl, which is what she felt like at that moment – totally powerless, confused and weak. The frantic pounding of her heart made her feel dizzy due to the tremendous strain her body had endured, and she feebly raised a hand to her forehead. Hazy images swam across her mind as she tried hard to remember…the terrible searing pain…the concern on Vic's face as he gazed down at her…then the sensation of being in his arms as he ran with her to the car. There were bits and pieces of the harrowing ride to the hospital, and Vic's voice seemingly from far away, begging her to stay with him…then the last few dregs of memory – Vic's voice screaming for help…bright lights above her as she felt herself being wheeled down a corridor…and then…nothing.

And now…her *husband* was here? Did T.J. make Vic leave? Louise moaned miserably as she tried to make sense of everything and she wondered frantically what had happened while she was unconscious. Was there a fight? Did Vic get disgusted and leave? And the baby…she was sure, with the amount of pain she had experienced, that she had probably lost it. That thought caused a confusing combination of relief and guilt.

The nurse patted Louise's arm consolingly and quickly crossed to the door, opening it slightly. Louise could hear only muffled words exchanged in the hallway.

Five people were milling nearby and Nancy gazed at them – three men and two women, one of which was very pregnant.

"Which one of you is Vic?"

Vic stepped forward instantly, cutting short his pep talk from Alec as the others gathered behind him.

"I'm Vic…"

The pretty brunette nurse smiled, thinking that the young woman inside was quite lucky – she had a very handsome husband and he seemed quite worried about her.

"She's asking for you."

ꙮ

LOUISE HAD CLOSED her eyes in exhaustion, when the next thing she knew, Vic's voice was murmuring, "Louise? Honey? Its me…"

Opening her eyes, she was half afraid that her memories of yesterday had been a huge, elaborate dream. But he was real, and he was right there with her. She hadn't been dreaming!

"Vic," she whispered in immense relief, forcing her eyes to focus on his beloved face. With much effort, she raised a hand and caressed the dark morning stubble on his cheeks and chin where he hadn't taken the time to shave after he had crashed on the couch at Alec and Fleet's.

"Are you really here?" she whispered.

He smiled that smile she adored and had dreamed of and fantasized about for so long. His dimples were so pronounced, and stars were in his eyes as he gazed at her.

"I'm here…I'm right here," he spoke softly, covering her hand with his own and moving it to his mouth, he kissed her fingers before cradling it against his chest. She seemed so small and pale lying there in that hospital bed. He'd been so afraid he would never see her looking back at him again. However, his heart squeezed overwhelmingly at the look of love he now saw shining in her eyes as he watched them fill with tears that slowly spilled down her temples.

"Don't leave me…Vic…I need you…so much…"

Vic teared up as well and he sniffled as he shook his head. "Don't you worry, my Mary Lou, I ain't *ever* leaving you again. *Ever.* Racehorses couldn't drag me away. Heck, the muddy Ohio couldn't sweep me away!" he joked, trying to get her to smile.

He reached up and gently brushed her tears away. "We're finally together again…and everything is gonna be just fine. From now on it'll be smooth sailin', like the Idlewild cruisin' down the river at sunset." Smiling tenderly, he watched as her eyes closed and her body relaxed; a sweet, contented smile adorned her face as she slipped into a restful sleep, trusting that he would be there to take care of every detail.

Just before she dropped off, a wispy smile crossed her features as she mused, *Thank You, God. My Vic came back to me…we'll finally…be…happy…*

ജ്ഝ

EPILOGUE

"WHAT HAPPENED THEN?" David asked from his position on the floor next to the couch.

We had long ago drifted into the living room where we could be more comfortable, as the oft-told story had been shared. This time, however, Mom had added a good many details none of us had ever heard before, the keenness of her memory astounding her listeners.

Mom raised an ever-present hanky up to her face and dabbed at her eyes. Chuckling a bit, she looked over at David, once again marveling at how the young man had inherited the Matthews' traits, especially his Grandfather's breathtaking brown eyes.

"Why, we got married, of course," she teased with a wink, the hazel eyes still just as sharp as they twinkled with mischief. Although her sable brown hair had long ago turned more salt than pepper, and her creamy skin had slowly developed lines of age and worry, she was still a pretty woman. All her life, people had always told her she didn't look her age – and that still applied. At eighty-nine she could, most of the time, pass for a woman in her seventies. Except on bad days when the arthritis flared up, or tiredness overtook her energy. But none of that had ever dampened the spark behind those eyes…the eyes her Vic had loved so dearly…

"You got married right away?" my husband chimed in then from his lounging place across the room, which was sitting on the floor in the circle of my arms and legs as I reclined in a chair.

"What about the divorce from T.J.?" Jim piped up.

"What about Vic's job in Evansville? Where did you guys live once you got married?" Bud added.

"I've never heard the details of that myself," Tom – who had long ago insisted that he be relieved of his moniker of 'Tommy' – interjected with an indulgent smile. Being the oldest, he had heard the tale more times than any of us, but he never tired of hearing the stories about the man who had raised him with patience and love, and whom he had always affectionately called, 'Chief'. Indeed, Vic had been the Chief in all of our lives, and Tommy, or rather, *Tom*, had always known that Vic adored our mother.

Mom laughed and shook her head, her voice tired from talking so many hours. "My, my," she chuckled with a flip of her hanky. "You're right, we couldn't marry right away. Too many incidentals to take care of. But that would be Part Two of the saga and will have to wait for another time. I'm afraid this old filly needs to bed down for the night." Gazing around the room at us, her family, she smiled delightedly and asked, "Aren't you young folks tired? It's been an awfully long day."

Tom let out a chuckle as the rest of us groaned in the affirmative.

Us 'young folks' who were now middle-aged and senior citizens, rose rather stiffly to gather our things in preparation to go home and leave Mom in her new, much smaller house on her own. Actually, on her own for the first time, ever. We had done everything we could to make her comfortable on her first night.

"But I want to hear more," David complained, laughing when his father laid a hand on his shoulder and quipped, "Next time, son. Your old man's tired!" Our son, a confident man with an important job as a computer network administrator, sent his father a look of slight contrition.

We helped Mom get up off the couch and she walked us to the door to say goodnight as we all filed out into the cool spring evening air.

Stretching up to give David a kiss on the cheek, Mom queried enthusiastically, eyebrows raised in eagerness, "You come over tomorrow to help me unpack boxes?"

"Sure I will," he nodded and leaned down to give her a hug.

"Good, and we'll have more pizza – and I'll tell you all about when my Vic finally got the break he deserved… he got his *Bold Venture.*"

The End

Coming soon – The Bold Venture!

The Real Vic and Louise, shortly after their Reunion.

DEDICATIONS

- First of all, thank you, Mom, the real Louise, for sharing with me the details of your extraordinary and colorful life. Your ability to remember facts, songs, names, and places from seventy-five plus years ago continues to astound me. Without you, there would be no story! Love you Mom.
- Thanks go to God, who put the idea to write it in my mind, and helped me in thousands of ways along the long road to completion.
- To my faithful and hardworking editor/beta, Venessa Vargas – you are one in a million, and without your keen eye and expertise, constant support, encouragement (Sully pompoms!) and belief in me and in the story, this book would still be a jumble of haphazard notes in three separate word files.
- Thank you to my pre-readers, Mom, Steve, and Belinda Ross, for your excitement and interest in the story and always wanting to know when you could read more chapters!
- A big thanks goes out to the readers and fans of my Fan Fiction (Linda4him59). Your encouragement and enthusiasm for my stories were the catalyst that made me believe I could write a 'real' novel. And, with my story *Michaela's Choice,* you gave me the amazing distinction and honor of receiving the most reviews, by far, of any Dr. Quinn story on the DQ pages of fanfiction.net. Thanks all of you!
- Thank you, also, to my friends, Indie authors H.D'Agostino and Kristine Raymond, for your encouragement, advice, and invaluable help.
- And last, but not least – thank you to my sweet husband, Steve. You've been so patient and helpful all through this arduous process. Thank you for being my number one fan, my helpmate, my adviser, my confidant, and my sounding board. I couldn't have finished it without you! I love you sweetheart!

ABOUT THE AUTHOR

Linda Ellen lives in Louisville, Kentucky with her husband and youngest son. A lifelong avid reader, after encouragement from her family and friends, she tried her hand at writing in 2009 and never looked back. Prior to the release of her debut novel *Once in a While* (fashioned from the real-life story of her parents' romance), she has written 30 well-received Fan Fiction works, including short stories, missing scenes, novellas, and four full length novels, based on the TV show Dr. Quinn Medicine Woman. Linda keeps very busy with her work in her church's prison ministry and writing every spare moment she gets. Under production are two more books in the Cherished Memories series. To keep up with the latest news on her books, including trailers, cover reveals, release dates, and book signings, visit and 'like' her Facebook page, *Linda Ellen – Author*. For a special treat, go to her Pinterest page to see many pictures related to this story:

www.pinterest.com/linda4him59/my-novel-once-in-a-while/

Made in the USA
Charleston, SC
15 February 2015